Trunk Wax II

Trunk Wax II

Bill's Bonheur

Howard Lentzner

To order additional copies of this book, contact:
Xlibris
1-888-795-4274
www.Xlibris.com
Orders@Xlibris.com
540089

Contents

It ain't always easy to predict success;
sometimes it's just a lucky loop

—Fess Dempster, Byron, California, 2013

CHAPTER 1

Roger Jones

"Get in the pickup, Tigger," Bill said in a voice that wasn't exactly a shout but packed more authority than conversational speech. The sleek black dog took a couple of steps and shot into the air, arced gracefully in his ascent, and landed in the middle of the bed of the pickup truck. Bill smiled, took a long spit, and kicked dust onto the dark spot on the ground. He looked back at the corral and the fifty-some head of commercial Black Baldy steers he had just gathered off the old Martin place, a ranch which was a little north of Jim Delahunt's spread. It had been a good morning's work. He'd let the steers drink for a day before he loaded them up the next morning for the trip to the Galt Livestock Market. Jesus, he hoped he'd get enough money to at least pay Gene Martin the rent he owed him. He'd been coming up short for the last couple of years and was running out of places to lease. It wasn't just him. The cattle business had been in decline ever since the drought of '77. It seemed like a good year was always followed by ten bad ones. Deep down, he knew he was a good cattleman. His old man had taught him right, but lately, the training didn't seem like it was helping him make any money.

He was about to get back in the truck when he remembered that Tigger was probably thirsty. He pulled a plastic bowl out from under the truck seat and walked over to the spigot in the barn and filled it with fresh water. Tigger was only a dog, so most likely, he never thought too far into the future, but the notion that Bill would ever forget his water never crossed his mind. He stood up straight, wagged his tail, and stared with concern at his master. The old guy was looking a little ragged, he thought: a bit of a limp in his stride, carrying a few too many pounds, and in real need of a professional haircut. When they got home, he'd do his best to cheer him up some: grab an old plastic milk carton out of the garbage and shake and bite holes in it, wiggle his backside a couple of times, and let loose with a couple of barks and farts. That was all it usually took.

Over the years, Bill had had a lot of dogs, big and little, usually thin and short-haired, all kinds of breeds and mixtures, but always with a good sense of the cow in them. Tigger had to be one of his favorites, and that was no surprise because Tigger was the great-grandson of his first working dog, Roger Jones. Bill was still in high school when he got Roger Jones from his uncle Ralph in Hollister. Most years, all the way through high school, he had gone down there to work in the feedlot during the busy season. One spring vacation, when he was a junior in high school, he took a fancy to a particularly talented cow dog, a mixed-breed bitch with an easy disposition, smooth movements, and the knack for always being in the right spot. He asked Uncle Ralph if he could have one of her pups the next time she had a litter. Six months later, Uncle Ralph telephoned him to let him know that his favorite dog had had pups.

The next morning, he was in the pickup and heading south even though he should have been in school. Picking a puppy wasn't difficult. He chose the first one in the kennel that walked toward him and looked him straight in the face. Bill named the pup Roger Jones, after a school friend. After growing for a few months, Roger Jones didn't look much like a typical cow dog, more like a black and tan greyhound, leaner than a border collie, and narrower through the shoulders. Bill didn't mind; Roger Jones followed him wherever he went and kept looking up at him.

While Tigger lapped up his water, Bill thought some and came up with the idea that although he had had a bunch of good dogs after Roger Jones, Tigger had to be his favorite.

CHAPTER 2

Cowboys

One evening, when Jim Delahunt's wife, Terciley O'Malley, was back in Massachusetts visiting a sister, he brought a bottle of Scotch and a couple of steaks over to Bill's place in Briones Valley and swapped them for a long story. He brought along a small recorder and placed it on the table between the meat and the potato salad.

"How did the Robeiros get started in the cattle business?" he asked Bill as he flipped on the recorder switch.

"The way my old man liked to tell it, when we started running cattle in the East County, Feudeer Valley especially, most people were named Evans or Robeiro. The Evanses came with the bunch of other coal miners from Wales and Cornwall to open the Black Diamond Mines. A fella named Stephens, a Yankee ship jumper, had discovered a coal seam while he was diggin' for gold and figured he might be able to make some money sellin' black diamonds. Coal, even the low-grade stuff in the Antioch Hills, was just good enough to ship down the Sacramento River. Stephens had a friend back home in Cornwall post some notices around the British Isles, sayin' that there were good jobs in California for experienced miners. 'Course, it was a damn lie because the seam was no thicker than four feet, and most of it could only be mined by miners lyin' on their backs. The old graveyard in Nortonville is proof of how dangerous that work was. Ain't many tombstones over there that have more'n forty-five years between the birth and death dates. And there's also plenty of children buried in that cemetery too, kids who probably died from the dust and bad air in them mines.

"The next to come were the Italians, mostly from around Genoa. Why Genoa? Nobody seems to know. Weren't any coal mines there as far my old man knew. Anyway, it seems like they got out of the mines as soon as they could. The smart ones bought land in the flat parts close to water and planted orchards: olives, figs, and nuts mostly. According to my old man, Grandpa came to California as a sixteen-year-old. He landed in San Francisco on a boat from Genoa a few years after the Gold Rush, got a job carrying vegetables at the old Colombo produce market down by where the Ferry Building stands now, and started pitching pennies and shooting dice in the alleys after work. He had a talent for it, and it wasn't too long before he started playin' cards for bigger stakes in the Gold Coast bars. He wasn't a big kid, but bigger guys learned quick not to cheat or rob him. He would fight for a nickel and kill for a quarter. One night heading up Chestnut Street for his room in Gloria's Guest House, a bigger kid who had lost a couple of dollars put a knife against his throat and took his money back along with a couple of dollars that had never been his.

"The big kid only had a couple of weeks to enjoy the loot. He made the mistake of having a couple of beers too many and sitting down on the curb while his head cleared. Grandpa, he was called Gino in them days, saw him sitting, picked up a convenient brick, and beat his brains in. He took everything off the body—money, clothes, and watch—and dragged it out onto a dark street where a milk wagon was sure to run over it in the early morning. The guys around the produce market noticed the big kid was missing, and none of them ever tried to cheat or rob the kid from Genoa.

"Grandpa had his rules. He never cheated, worked hard, and banked his wages and winnings. It took him four years, but when he had a couple of hundred dollars, he started looking around for a place to settle. He found it in the hills around Antioch, where the miners were pulling coal out of them narrow seams I was tellin' you about. While he walked the hills sizing up the grass and water, he noticed that the miners were mostly single men, lonesome for a good meal and a clean place to sleep, among other things. He figured he could build a small hotel in Sommersville with his money and serve cheap old-country-style meals to miners. He had grown up in a big family in hills like these ones out here and with people like the ones he saw. His mother back in Italy knew how to feed a family on a shoestring, and he was pretty sure he knew how she did it. But first, before he could start, he needed to find a woman just like her to be his partner.

"So he went back to San Francisco to look for one. He parked himself on a bench in Washington Park in front of Saint Francis Church and watched the girls go in and out. Every now and then, he followed a pretty one who was coming out of church. He was looking for a girl who was on her way to work in an Italian family restaurant. It took him a while, but he finally found one who went straight from church to a small restaurant on Green Street. He followed her right in and sat down at a small table topped with a green-and-white checkered tablecloth and waited to be served. In a way, he had messed up because she was serving another group of tables. In another way, it was good because he got to watch her from a distance. The next time he came in, he sat at one of her tables. She approached his table, pretty as the girl on the Rainbow Bread wrapper, he used to say, but wearing a white apron and carrying a menu in one hand and a pencil and pad of paper in the other. The closer she got, the prettier the picture: light hair, a little on the curly side, full lips, ample hips and bosom, and a quick step. She gave him a bright smile and asked if he wanted red or white wine. He was embarrassed to answer because his English was still poor.

"'White,' he said, trying to hide his accent. She came back with a small decanter and a bowl of soup. Minestrone, they called it in America. It was good, but not at all like his mother's. She pulled out her notepad and waited for him to order his entrée. Sensing that he might not be able to read, she ran down the choices: rib steak, lamb chop, roast chicken, and fried fish. 'Steak,' he said, still trying to hide his accent. The soup came with a small crusty loaf of homemade bread, which he used to wipe down the bowl when the spoon couldn't scrape up anymore. The pasta came next, simple rigatoni, homemade also, with a small tin pitcher of olive oil and a bowl of Parmesan cheese. He always told my dad that it was so good it made him homesick."

"You know," Delahunt said, "I think I was in that restaurant when I was in the Merchant Marines. "We were bringing Italian olive oil from Marseilles. I think the dinner was probably five or six dollars by then, but it sure was good."

"Grandpa was real particular about his food, even in them days, and the old man always said that whenever Grandpa told the story of their early days, he never forgot to mention that he thought the steak was a bit overcooked. Of course, he only said it when Grandma wasn't close by. Overall, though, Grandpa was sure it was the kind of meal they could sell to miners for less than a buck and still make money. Dessert was a pudding and a cup of strong coffee.

"Grandpa went back every Thursday for three months and was never disappointed. Just to be sure, he tried a place in Oakland, another one in Daly City, but the restaurant on Green Street, the Po Valley, was the best. He found out that the girl he had followed from church was called Joanna Lunari, and the restaurant where she worked was owned by her uncle, who was also her guardian. She was seventeen years old, single, without a boyfriend.

"All Grandpa needed was the courage to ask her uncle for her hand. He always said it took a lot of nerve for a twenty-year-old porter in the produce market to ask a tough old restaurant owner for the hand of his niece. And the first time he asked, the uncle, I think he was called Danny or Dante, told him to get lost. But Grandpa was as stubborn as they come. He kept coming every Thursday to eat and always pretended he couldn't read the menu so Joanna had to help him. It took a while because she was a little shy, in sort of a flirty way, but eventually, they warmed up to each other. One afternoon, after Joanna had cleared the table, her uncle walked out from behind the bar, put a big hand on Grandpa's shoulder, and asked him to come over to the bar and have a drink with him. 'Why don't you take Joanna to a movie some night, buy her dinner and a cup of coffee afterwards?' he asked Grandpa. 'She comes home every night and cries. She is seventeen, works all day, and is in a strange country with no friends.'

"So you can probably imagine what happened after that: a couple of movies, walks in the park, Easter dinner, a talk with Uncle Danny, and a proposal. Grandpa bought an old house in Sommersville and fixed it up into a small hotel with five bedrooms, a big kitchen, three tables that could seat five customers each, and a long bar with twelve stools. They got married in San Francisco, moved out to Sommersville, and started selling beds, breakfasts, and booze. Grandpa worked in the mines every now and then and used the money he earned to buy a dozen ewes and a ram. Raising sheep was something he knew about from the old country."

"It must have been a lot wetter in those days," Delahunt said. "I can't imagine keeping sheep on this land now. And all the coyotes."

"I don't think there were that many coyotes in them days. Anyway, Grandma and Grandpa produced four hefty sons, enough manpower to buy more land and switch from sheep to cattle. One of those sons, who they called Joe, was my dad. For a while, they had ranches in Nevada, oil wells right here in East Contra Costa County, and a big feedlot for more than three thousand head of cattle. That's sorta where I came in. Everything was goin' like gangbusters until the drought of '70s and the collapse of the cattle market. There was some bad loans thrown in to boot, and the government chased us off our main ranch at the end of Oil Canyon so's they could have a park there.

"The truth is that me and my brothers didn't help things. I was never what you'd call a model citizen. I was big and rough for my age, and the family pulled a lot of weight in the area, so I got away with a lot of shit I never should have. So to make a long story short, after me and my brothers went through the old man's money, we were always broke, a half step away from a jail cell, and a nuisance to women. It wasn't so much that we were bad kids. It was more that we grew up with an idea of right and wrong that had been out of style for fifty years. Look at it this way: When ranchers in this county ran cattle on 98 percent of the land, the towns were small, and most folks could ignore and be ignored by the courts and sheriffs. In them days, if cattle came on your property and stayed too long, you could rebrand 'em and keep 'em. If the brand couldn't be altered, they got barbecued at the next roundup. I got to be an expert at it. If I used a couple of irons and a wet burlap bag, I could change the Lucky J brand of Howard Jones to our Rocking R brand so's it could pass the brand inspection and only be suspicious to an expert. It was just another piece of cowboy artwork."

Delahunt slid the bottle toward Bill.

"One time, a big Bar M Simmental bull decided he liked the Robeiro cows and groceries better than those at home. When my dad spotted that Bar M bull on his property for the fourth time, his instructions to us boys were short and loud. Cut off his balls and give them to Wayne Evans. 'Course, the huge bull had a set of cojones to match, and they got bigger every time my dad told the story. We boys knew that the Bar M's owner, Wayne Evans, spent most days in the Jam Inn in Oakley, whiling away the hours with John Barleycorn, so we decided to return Wayne's goods to him in person. When we got to the Jam Inn, Old Wayne was sitting in his usual place. Me and my brother Frank pulled up stools at the opposite end of the bar, but Wayne never even looked up at us. After we downed our drinks, Frank put the sack with the cojones on a plate and slid it down the bar where it came to rest in front of a groggy Wayne Evans, who stared at the sack for a while before he opened it and looked in. He peered at the contents like someone inspecting a bag of groceries for a while and then reached into his pocket and pulled out an old Smith and Wesson 45 revolver, which he slowly and quietly placed on the bar in front of him."

"Congratulations," he said slowly. "Looks like you finally found the guy that was screwing your sister."

"I was of a mind to call the old fart's bluff, but my brother held me back.

"I think I said, 'I'll pretend I didn't hear what you just said, but next time you say something like that, it'll be your nuts in the paper bag.'

"That's pretty much the way things used to be around here."

CHAPTER 3

The Silo

Bill hooked Tigger's collar onto the short chain in the pickup bed and headed down the dirt road toward Highway 4, kind of lost in thoughts about his money problems. The needle on the gas gauge was bouncing on the empty pin when he got to Byron Corners. *Shit.* He only had twenty bucks to his name, and he was about to put it all in the gas tank. Those days, twenty bucks only bought him enough gas to get fifty miles or so. As he coasted to a stop in front of the closest pump, he spotted Karen Clements. She was coming out of the Four Pedro's, the latest in a long line of Mexican highway restaurants destined to go broke after a couple of months. Even though the Pedro's were serving up very high-end Mexican fusion cooking, proudly eschewing the standard tamales and burritos, the odds were against them. Byron Corners had been bypassed by a newer highway years ago, and the local folks preferred their tamales with red sauce, not mango reductions.

Bill slid out of the seat and hit the ground with a hop and a stumble. His knee was killing him. He waved at Karen, but she didn't see him at first.

"Karen!" he shouted.

She stopped, smiled, and tilted her head and raised her eyebrows in a way he recognized as sympathetic.

"Hey," she said. "Been up the silo lately?"

"No reason to!" he shouted back and shrugged.

Bill's memory was that Karen had asked him to take her up to the top of the silo at the feedlot. They were seniors in high school, and he was game for almost anything: big, mature for his age, confident, and strong from the hard ranch work he had been doing most of his life. He had pitched a no-hitter his senior year and anchored the line on the Panther's football team his sophomore year, the only year he played football. Girls followed him around, just hoping for the chance to be seen talking to him. The only thing that wasn't big about him in those days was his grade point average, and that didn't bother him any. He was more than proud to tell people he was never going to be a doctor or a college professor.

It was August, the summer of their graduation. They agreed to meet at the base of the big concrete silo at the feedlot, she after feeding and bedding down her horses, he after stacking hay at the DeSousa place in Knightsen. Karen, her last name was McGregor in those days, was a local girl whose parents had come down from North Dakota to train horses. She was a quiet, comely lass: outdoor skin, slender, with sad gray eyes and straight hair. When they got to the silo, he fetched her up onto his shoulders, much as one would a child, without saying a word. She was taller than average but wasn't that heavy, and she pulled up her skirt as he lifted her. Her tan legs hung easily over his shoulders and down on his chest as he began climbing up the narrow steel ladder. He could feel her curly hair, damp against the nape of his neck as he climbed.

Karen hadn't said a word as he lifted her off his back and gently set her feet down on the steel plate that sat like an oversized manhole cover on the top of the silo. The silo was probably the tallest building in the area, a good fifty-feet high, but it seemed much higher once they were on top. There weren't many lights in those days, but the ones that did shine were down in Pylewood's center a couple of miles away. They could see streetlights on Second Street, the blinking seventy-six at Dutro's gas station, the A&W drive-in, and the marquee on the Delta Cinema, but the view in the sky was the real attraction. The moon highlighted the hills and fields, and the stars, glittering in the thousands, stood out like diamonds on a velvet tray in a Union Square jewelry shop.

Bill put his arm around her and stood silent for a long time. Karen never really said much in those days. After about five minutes, they sat down on an old plaid blanket someone, probably one that one of his brothers, had stashed up there. After a while, they both stretched out together and snuggled up close enough that he could feel the curves of her body. She kissed him gently on the cheek and then on the mouth. She wasn't the first girl he had taken to the top of the silo, and almost all of them were eager for sex. But that night, the two of them sat for a long while, wrapped tightly in the blanket, kissed and shivered, and then climbed back down the ladder and headed for home. That was the last time he ever climbed up on top of the silo. Once when his dad asked him to get up there and fix a clogged valve, he refused, something he almost never did.

Usually, when he thought about that night, he was overcome with a kind of emptiness. He'd been roping around Central California, winning a little prize money here and there, and hoping to go to college on a baseball scholarship. He'd been kidding himself. Really, his grades weren't even good enough to get him into one of the sports factories in Southern California or Arizona. It was a time, though, when he expected everything to turn out good. Maybe they'd get the wrong transcript or Mr. Boone, the social studies teacher, would change his F in American history to a C. He even managed to get an F in auto shop, even though he had been fixing trucks and tractors since he was thirteen.

After graduation, they both joined the local rodeo circuit. He was roping, and she was barrel racing. It was natural that they started hanging around together, never saying too much, just happy to stand next to each other between events. One night, when they both had won a little prize money at Oakdale, they went to Reno and got married. The marriage didn't last all that long between his hard drinking and her moody spells.

That night, on top of the silo, he had felt incredible sweetness. It was hard to explain exactly what it was, but it had been real: a feeling he never had again. She had bounced around those parts of the country where there were open spaces and horses, remarried, got divorced again, and eventually came back to Pylewood. It had been nearly a year since she had returned. He kept bumping into her at the Byron Corners gas station and taco shack or at Bailey's hardware store. It was as if fate was trying to push them back together. They always exchanged a few pleasant words, but that day at the gas station, her eyes said more than her words. They told him she might like another climb back up on the silo.

"I'm thinkin' I wouldn't mind goin' back up there on top the silo," he said.

"For old time's sake," Karen said. "What's it been, fifteen years?"

"Long time ago," he said. "I bet the view ain't nearly as pretty as it used to be. Don't know if I could even make it anymore. But you know what? I'd sure like to try. It'd be a little riskier this time. There's two-hundred-eighty pounds of me now and a bum knee. You know, sometimes I can't hardly get out of my truck."

"I'd risk it," she said, turning away and walking quickly to her car.

CHAPTER 4

Dog Bites

Jim Delahunt's dog, Hardley, had waited around most of Saturday morning for his master to show up so they could take their daily walk down to the pond. The walk wasn't all that exciting, but he felt he owed it to Delahunt. Without the walks, the old man would only get fatter and more cantankerous. After all, he owed Delahunt plenty. He and Terciley O'Malley, the resident female, had rescued him at a time when he had been sleeping under trees and on the verge of eating marmots or stealing chickens.

He finally gave up waiting and trotted down to the barn to check out the food situation. Usually, he didn't get fed until evening, but he could pretty much tell what would be in his dish by what the cats and chickens got that morning. If the chickens got slabs of fat, he was probably in line for the meaty leftovers. If the cats got the carcass of the Thanksgiving turkey, he would probably get the skin and stuffing.

That morning, it was obvious that Terciley had fed the animals: extra small portions of grain for the chickens, cat favoritism, and failure to sort the paper and plastic out of the scraps. He felt sorry for the chickens; they were the only ones paying their way: a couple of dozen eggs a day during the summer, and even though production fell off some during the fall and went almost to nothing in January and February, they still worked hard. The rooster crowed in the morning like he was supposed to do, the hens crawled into their beds at sundown, and they all scratched around for food even when there wasn't much left in the feeder or on the cold ground. For their trouble, Terciley fed them banana peels and cheese rinds.

The cats, on the other hand, who did absolutely nothing except kill a ground squirrel every now and then, got all the best stuff: fresh ground beef, bacon rinds, and the organ meat whenever they butchered a cow. The cats, all eight of them, really only worked in the summer when it was easy to catch mice and ground squirrels. Two or three could have done the job, but their numbers kept increasing until there were at least eight, maybe ten, of them, wasting time pulling on string, digging little holes for their turds, fighting for food, and lolling in the sun. When Terciley wasn't around, Delahunt locked up the cats up so they couldn't squeeze into the chicken coop and rob the poor birds of the little bits of meat and fat that had made their way into their share of the garbage.

And what did he, the loyal family dog, get for his trouble and constant exposure to danger—chasing the coyotes and raccoons away from the chickens, keeping the family safe from prowlers, and guarding the property when they were gone—old soup bones, leftover Italian and Chinese food, and the occasional steak that had been left in the refrigerator too long. Judging from the paucity of what the chickens got that morning, he was pretty sure he was destined to get some cheap, discount Farmer's Lumps and some mossy old yogurt for his evening meal. How she ever got the idea that dogs liked yogurt was beyond his ken.

On the positive side, as long as Delahunt was busy somewhere else, the guy couldn't drag his prickly brush through his tangled coat. Sure his hair was full of snags, mud, and burrs and stickers from the weeds, but it hurt like hell when Delahunt used that implement of medieval torture on him. Where he got the damn thing, Hardley could only guess. At least Delahunt didn't try to give him a bath. It wasn't as if he didn't like water; he loved to swim in the pond any time of the year and jump into the water trough when it was summer. But did his keepers ever smell the shampoo they dumped on him? The thing about humans was that their noses were absolutely useless, as outdated as their toes and tonsils. When he first got established there, he used to be able to roll in the cow shit to get the soap smell off him. Now since they had started collecting the stuff in buckets for Hrubel Kwasnik, there wasn't any just lying around on the ground.

Hrubel Kwasnik, now there was a piece of work. He hardly ever got to visit with Kwasnik's dog, Lamanon; but when he did, did she ever have the tales to tell about her master (she eschewed the term "owner"). Her favorite story was about the time he almost got thrown in the clink for leaving her in the pickup cab outside of Don Gusto's Bar. Lamanon had made it as clear as she could that she hated being taken places and then just left to languish in the car, so that evening, she had moaned and put on her most hangdog expression for the Pylewood cops to see when they took a stroll through the parking lot looking for expired license plates. She stuck out her tongue and panted as hard and fast as she could when they looked in the window. She said the result was hilarious. The cops stormed into the bar, kicked over some barstools, dragged Kwasnik out, and stood him, legs spread apart, against the wall at Don Gusto's so that everyone driving between Stockton and Knightsen could see him.

The whole day spent looking for Delahunt had tired him out so much that when he finally went back into the house, he pulled Delahunt's coat off the bed where Terciley had thrown it and dragged it out to the spot in the shade where he slept on it. When he woke up, the porch was bathed in sunshine.

CHAPTER 5

Kwasnik's Formula

Bill ambled over to the whiskey bottle on the table and loaded up another double-shot-sized charge. He was taking his medicine in larger aliquots than usual, partly to ease the pain in his knee and partly to fill vacant spaces in his heart and head. Vicodin, Tylenol, Red Bull, and Uncle Meyer's Elixir: none of them seemed to help. The only potent medicine was the potion cooked up from peat-filtered water and malted barley kernels by red-faced, bearded magicians on small cold islands in the North Atlantic. He stared deep into his whiskey glass and saw a likeness of Karen Clements shivering under one of the ice cubes. Her image was popping up everywhere these days: on the top of silos, in crowds of strangers, and now in his whiskey glass. He put the glass down as gently as a momma cat moving one of her babies. In another hour, he was going over to Hrubel Kwasnik's place to talk about a crazy scheme the three of them had hatched a week earlier. Their plan was to mix up some new kind of fertilizer that you sprayed on trees, sell it, and make some money. Shoot, money. He didn't need a lot, just enough to buy a spread in Oregon or Idaho, get some new teeth, and spend some time with the flesh-and-blood version of Karen Clements.

Jim Delahunt had set off the whole thing a week earlier when he staggered wet and muddy into Bill's yard, spouting some lame-brained tale that his wife, Terciley O'Malley, had tried to drown him the day before. Since it wasn't normal for Delahunt to go off half-cocked, he offered his neighbor a shower and a meal. After Delahunt showered—he had come in muddier than a wild hog in February—they had a few drinks and a meal. The two of them had been occasional friends over the last fifteen or sixteen years. They had partnered up every now and then to run rental cattle or share a load of hay. When Delahunt kept carrying on about how Terciley had tried to drown him in their old pickle barrel and how hell-bent he was on revenge, Bill figured he needed to get a second opinion before he took any action. He telephoned Hrubel Kwasnik, who farmed a few acres over on the flat land on the other side of Feudeer Valley Road and invited him to come over to hear Delahunt's story and maybe help calm him down. Maybe because he had run for the irrigation district board once, Rudy, the moniker Kwasnik had brought back with him after a stint in Vietnam, had become the de facto leader, facilitator, and ombudsman for that segment of the East County's undereducated agricultural misfits and over-educated alternative farmers who couldn't afford lawyers or psychologists.

Even though Kwasnik wasn't sure what the argument was about, he fired up his vintage Toyota pickup and drove over to Briones Valley to hear Delahunt's story. The three of them ate some polenta, drank some whiskey, and bullshitted for the next day and a half, finally deciding that rather than call the cops on Terciley or have Delahunt committed, they'd try to get rich. They'd cash in their assets, which weren't too many, and try a secret scheme that had been bouncing about in Hrubel Kwasnik's brain box for a couple of decades. According to Kwasnik, he had figured out a secret formula for a biodynamic tree paint that made apricots and figs shinier, tastier, and healthier and would most likely do the same thing for peaches, pears, plums, apples, kumquats, and mangoes. It didn't bother Bill or Delahunt any that they weren't sure what a biodynamic tree paint was once they had picked up and processed the get rich signal.

Kwasnik was quick to point out that while the biodynamic concept wasn't original, their implementation would have to be. The trick that would make them rich was that besides having the best chemical formulation, they would design, build, and sell a sexy applicator that the customer had to buy along with their tree paint. Once the buyer had the applicator, he or she would be obliged to stay loyal to their liquid product. Kwasnik emphasized, though, that they still had a bunch of work to do. Besides perfecting the chemical formula, they would have to come up with a novel applicator that would uniformly spread a slurry of Kwasnik's concoction on a tree trunk. Delahunt, suddenly homeless, and Bill, broke as usual, didn't wait long to agree to follow Kwasnik into the tree-painting business.

A week and two days later, Bill and Delahunt found themselves seated around the big table in Kwasnik's living room staring at the long-haired orchardist.

"Your nickel, Rudy," Bill said. "Never done no project planning before. Out on the ranch, we just saddle up. Everybody already pretty much knows what to do or they wouldn't be ridin' with us in the first place."

"I think we ought to start with a goal-setting exercise," Kwasnik said. "I want to start by having you guys visualize being rich and successful."

"That's a wet dream," the usually stoic Delahunt blurted out.

"Well then, why don't you lead off, Bill," Kwasnik suggested. "What do you see?"

After he finished gagging on his mouthful of zinfandel, Bill said from the top of his mouth, "I see three ugly old farts sittin' around a beat-up old table in some ex-hippies' house drinking cheap wine."

"No, that's not what I mean. It's not what you see right now. It's what you see in the future. Imagine that our product has been a big success, and we're all richer than Gordon Gecko. Now what do you see?"

"Three . . . ugly . . . old . . . *rich* . . . farts sittin' around an old table, drinking wine from a bottle with a screw top."

"OK, if you're gonna be that way," Kwasnik said, "what do we look like?"

"Pretty much the same as now, except for Delahunt, who looks like he just had his hair styled at the Pink Poodle in Concord, and you, who got a big diamond stud in your earlobe instead of that old piece of corncob that's usually there."

"What about yourself?" Kwasnik asked.

"Got something I can spit in?" Bill asked.

"Why do you chew that stuff? Don't you know it's bad for your teeth? Anyway, I think the previous owner threw away all the spittoons."

"A jam jar will do, pardner," Bill answered.

When Kwasnik got back from the kitchen with a wide-mouthed Ball jar, Bill took a long spit, leaned his chair back, and closed his eyes.

"First off, I see some new chompers in my mouth: big, white, and sharp. Lost my last ones years ago when a horse they were breaking down at the place they called the Sheep Ranch kicked up a dirt-clod missile that hit me in the face. Oddest thing folks had ever seen, or so they said. I was walking over to a pony they had just tripped, rope in hand, when the horse jumped up, bolted, and kicked a bunch of dirt darts in my face. When I spit out the dirt, I realized all my front teeth and some side ones were in the spit."

"Could you try to stay on target, Bill?" Kwasnik suggested.

"Well, Rudy, if I get rich from this idea of yours, I can see me chewin' up calf fries at the next roundup. Most times, I end up just cookin' 'em for other folks."

"Anything else?"

"Yep. I see myself waltzing around the dance floor at the Veteran's Hall in Clayton on two rebuilt titanium knees with a special lady.

Maybe they couldn't fix the old ones, and I had to get them totally replaced like my old man did."

"He'd ride all around on these hills when Terciley and I first got here," Delahunt chimed in.

"He even team roped with the second set: replacements he got free from Stanford University in Palo Alto when he plumb wore out the first ones," Bill continued. "Once I got my fill of fries and dancin', I'm see myself buyin' a small ranch in Idaho or Oregon. One that'd hold fifty head of Angus-cross cows. I could make a livin' on a ranch like that, especially if I owned it outright. Then I'd buy me a new pickup with an extra-large cab so's I could get in and out more easy, some ostrich-skin boots, and a—"

"Whoa. That's plenty for now," Kwasnik interrupted. "That's a lot of stuff. Try and keep your expectations realistic."

But Bill wasn't finished. "Just one more thing, Rudy. I'd like to take a certain lady with me up to that ranch in Oregon or Idaho, but I ain't tellin' you guys who I have in mind."

"Your turn, Delahunt," Kwasnik said, pointing a long beat-up index finger at the former engineer-machinist. "How do you see yourself when our enterprise makes you rich?"

"Like I told you guys earlier, I'm still suffering from the shock of my wife trying to drown me," Delahunt answered.

"Try to forget about the events of the last couple of weeks," Kwasnik said. "Put them out of your mind for now. Try to imagine how you'd look if you had got rich a week ago?"

"I think I'd have changed my hairstyle. Dyed it jet black and got it curly. Terciley always said she thought my green eyes didn't match my hair, even when it got white. She always said she wished I looked more like Robert Taylor."

"With dark, curly hair, you'd probably look more like Elizabeth Taylor, except for the jugs," Bill interrupted. "Yours are bigger."

"Come on, Bill, try and stick to positive comments. They're way more valuable."

Delahunt closed his eyes until his face worked itself into a slight grin. "I see myself looking like Marlon Brando in the *Wild One*: smirk, leather jacket, pack of smokes in my T-shirt sleeve, big boots, and a tilted aviator's cap."

"What about your goals, Jim?"

"Right now all I can think of is revenge: sweet, simple, and swift, like Edmond Dantes, the count of Monte Cristo. Maybe I'll think of something more original next year when I have my share of the money."

"What about you, Rudy?" Bill asked, staring at Kwasnik. "You ain't gettin' out of this without tellin' us what you're gonna look like when you get rich. I already got a picture in my mind, and it's pretty dang funny."

"I'm more interested in revolutionizing agriculture than making money or getting even with somebody. My formula, which is a natural product, could make chemical fertilizers and pesticides obsolete. I'm sick and tired of seeing farmers poison the water and soil."

"Yeah, but how do you see yourself?" Bill asked.

"I don't know. I'm not good at visualizing, that's why I'm the facilitator, and you guys are the facilitees."

Kwasnik got up from the table, grabbed three wine glasses, uncapped another bottle of ancient-vine zinfandel, poured out three robust measures, and offered up a toast.

"Here's to new teeth, curly black hair, and a world without chemical sprays and soil amendments. Now let's divide up the project tasks between us. Here's my suggestions: Delahunt, you're the engineer. Why don't you design and build the applicator? Bill, could you take care of the animal angle, which is basically getting cows that produce microbe-rich poop and don't eat too much. I'm the dirt farmer, so I should be in charge of procuring the ingredients that aren't poop: dirt and a sensational beeswax-based binder."

"What are we gonna call the stuff?" Bill asked. "I don't think we should keep calling it *the product* or *the formula*, and no way should the words shit, poop, or excrement be in the official name. *Sure as Shit, FormulaEx,* and *PooPooPaint* are all catchy titles, but I think it'll be hard to charge a lot of money for something that's named after waste."

"TrunkWax," Kwasnik half bellowed. "The only thing I'm not sure of is whether to put a space between the k and the W."

"Sounds like some kind of beauty treatment or something you shine your suitcases with," Delahunt said. "I like Tree Balm better. It has a soothing sound."

Kwasnik squirmed and made a sour face. Anyway, it didn't take any hard thinking for Bill and Delahunt to figure out they were in the game regardless of what they ended up calling the stuff.

Next, Kwasnik doled out the marching orders: Delahunt to China to build a prototype tree waxer and find a source of loess—the clay thickener of choice; Bill to France to get the bulls that would sire the animals that would produce the world's finest excrement; and himself to Bohemia to get the best wax-making bees.

"Before I go flyin' off to France, Rudy," Bill announced, "there's somethin' I gotta get off my chest. You're saddlin' me with a damn tall order. It'll take me years, not months, to build the right herd if we have to start by importing bulls. I don't have that much time left. In another ten years, I'll be as old as Delahunt is now and probably even more wore out. Besides, odds are the French cattle association won't want to sell us the kind of bulls you want."

"So what's the answer then, Bill?" Kwasnik asked, head out in front, lip curled.

"Semen or embryos," Bill answered. "Semen's got its advantages. So do embryos. In case you don't know, semen are tiny little swimmers you can't see without a microscope. You can pack lots of them in straws, skinny containers that are easy to transport, or hide if you need to. Embryos are lots bigger but still a lot smaller than a live bull."

Kwasnik started shaking his head from side to side. "What makes you think the French will sell us embryos or semen if they won't sell us bulls?"

"Like my cousin Donnie keeps tellin' me, size matters. It might be a lot easier to buy semen or embryos on the black market or under-the-table from a breeder than to buy a full-size, fully loaded bull. With semen or embryos, we could get the job done without anyone noticing. And for what we're doin', we won't need certificates or paperwork. Security-wise, stealin' a thousand of them microscopic buggers might turn out to be our best option."

"Hold on, Bill," Kwasnik interrupted. "I hope you're not suggesting we do something dishonest. I don't even want to think about building the TrunkWax brand, an undertaking aimed at bettering the world, on an unethical foundation. It would taint the whole enterprise."

"Consider the end result," Bill said with a wink in Delahunt's direction. "I think the theory is called utilitarianism. I'm very fuckin' surprised you ain't never heard of it, a highly educated scientist like yourself."

"Let me mull it over for a day or two," Kwasnik mumbled.

"What's there to mull about, Rudy? There won't be no super TrunkWax if we can't get the premium poop. No supergood figs and apricots for rich and poor alike and no end to chemical fertilizers and bug spray. The good outweighs the bad. It ain't like stealin' a guy's tires or stash. Think of it as kinda a Robin Hood deal. We'll share the semen with people who couldn't otherwise afford them. And we'd be takin' semen from a bull or embryos from a cow that no normal cattle breeder wanted anyways. It would be a fine example of combining utilitarianism with local, sustainable agriculture."

"OK, I guess I never looked at it that way," Kwasnik said with a nervous double wiggle of his head.

"Sounds ridiculous to me," Delahunt said. "You gonna parachute into some French farmers field like D-Day, only with a sperm collector strapped to your back instead of an M1? An overweight guy like yourself and then paddle back out to a submarine."

"All right," Bill said. "You guys think about it for a day or two."

Kwasnik looked at his watch and decided it was time for lunch. He and Bill went outside to roast some sausages, while Delahunt seemingly lost in thought ignored Kwasnik's invitation. When the sausages puffed up and took on a nice mahogany tinge, Kwasnik refilled his glass and went inside to try to talk Delahunt into coming out.

"Can't get Delahunt to come out," Kwasnik whispered to Bill when he got back outside. "Keeps mumbling about his kids and how he's lost touch with them these last few years. Hope he isn't going Alzheimer's on us. It seems kind of risky to send him to China in this condition, don't you think?"

"Don't worry, Rudy. He'll be fine. He gets this way every now and then. You know he worked at that atomic laboratory in Liveryville for twenty years. No telling what kind of strange, subatomic particles he's got colliding around in his head."

"Of course I know. I worked there too," Kwasnik said. "I don't have any strange particles bouncing around in my head, do I?"

"Of course not," Bill roared. "You just signed up the two of us to paint cow shit on tree trunks. Sure you're OK?"

Just then, Delahunt wandered out into the sun. "Hey, guys I been thinking, how's Bill gonna tell the good poop from the bad. We gotta give him some parameters, don't we? And up the road, sampling is going to be another problem. You got a PhD in chemistry, Rudy, and think you know about everything. How are we gonna avoid sampling errors when we collect the poop."

"I'll just hire a guy in the parking lot at SelluWood to follow the cow around with a shovel and a bunch of Mason jars," Bill interrupted.

"You're going to France, not Stockton," Delahunt interjected. "The way they do it at my health provider is to send you a sampling packet with a big piece of wax paper, a small plastic dauber, and a little bottle with some preservative solution in it. You spread the paper at the bottom of the toilet bowl prior to your dump, stick the dauber in your product when you're finished, drop the dauber in the bottle, and send it off to the laboratory in Visalia. I've been doing it every year since I turned sixty-five."

"That's very fuckin' interesting, Delahunt, but as far as I know, the cow toilet ain't been invented yet."

"Maybe we should do that first," Delahunt answered. Kwasnik poured another round of zinfandel, and they clanked their wine glasses together again. Each of them agreed to put up ten thousand dollars for the capital needed to get the project off the ground.

CHAPTER 6

Planning for Paris

The next time Bill saw Karen Clements, he asked her to help him buy a plane ticket to Paris, France. It was sad, but the fact was he didn't know how to do it himself. Delta Travel, who had made all the family reservations when the ranch was going good, had shut its doors ten years earlier when Expedia came online.

"Paris, France," Karen Clements repeated with raised eyebrows. "Sure you don't mean Paris, Texas."

"Nope," he said. "I'm hookin' up with Rudy Kwasnik to try and make some money in the fertilizer business. He's got people goin' every which way. First stop for me, Paris, France."

"What are you going to do in Paris, France? They got ranches there?"

"Don't know about ranches, but Rudy has this idea that they got plenty of the right kind of cattle. I'm supposed to find some for importation back here. Sorry, but that's as much as I can tell you now. The rest is all secret."

Anyway, she figured that was all she really needed to know. Only, she did worry that he might be getting himself into some sort of trouble. They were more than old friends; they had even been married once upon a time. He never told her all that much even when they were married. Now when there was a chance they might get back together, she was helping him buy him a plane ticket so he could leave town. Things just never seemed to work out between

them. Besides buying him the FlyUwhere? Airlines ticket, direct
flight to Paris, Karen had arranged for Claudine Fortet, the secretary
of the French Cattle Society, to meet him at the Paris Airport. She
hoped Claudine would be there. She could tell Bill was already
feeling nervous about landing solo in a country where most folks
didn't speak English.

***

Back home in Briones Valley, Bill spread out on the sofa, puffed
up the pillow behind his neck, and tried to rearrange himself so
he could straighten out his leg. *Damnedest thing,* he thought, *Rudy
putting cow shit on trees to invigorize 'em.* The truth was Kwasnik's trees
did grow faster, greener, and healthier; he had seen it for himself.
And the fruit—he had eaten lots of it the last few years—really was
bigger, sweeter, and tastier. His apricots were as big as peaches,
orange as the setting sun in the summer, sweet as sugarcane, and
tasty as mangoes; and his figs—yellow, purple, and green—subtle
as truffles, soft as a baby's rump, and refreshing as the clear, cold
water in Briones Creek.

At first mention, his part of the TrunkWax job had seemed the
easiest. He'd put up the sides on his flatbed trailer, pull it over to
Machado Island, and load a ton or two of Braydon Silva's cow shit
into it. He'd haul the load back to Rudy's place in Bryon, where
he'd dump it all next to his former hot tub. Then he'd go home and
visualize himself in Idaho with new knees, strong teeth, and that
special gal in his lap, looking at a bunch of proud white-faced black
cows, each one with a calf at her side. But as it turned out, first, he
had to go to Paris, fuckin' France. Why? There were already plenty
of good cows in California and even more just across the borders in
Canada and Mexico. *Why Paris, France, then?* According to Rudy, who

had some sort of advanced degree, all excretia wasn't equal: spring poop was better than fall; fresh better than stale; calf better than bull; French better than English; and red-haired cows better than black ones. The best cows for microbe production, in Rudy's view, also had black hooves and gray tongues. French cows—Salers, Limousin, and Aubrac—fit the bill. English breeds like Herefords and Angus didn't. For some reason, they had inferior biota: smaller, less-diverse, microbe populations; inconsistent microbe yields; and low microbe feed efficiency. Other continental breeds like Chianinis, Gelbviehs, Hapsburgs, and Hollenzollerns were only marginally better than American stock.

And to make it worse, you couldn't just pull up to a pier in France and load up a boat full of biodynamic excretia like it was Chilean seagull guano. It had to be fresh when it was processed. According to Kwasnik, who read the weirdest magazines, research at the Chennai Technical College in India had shown that the distribution of microbes in bovine excretia was changing all the time. A day later, it was different than when it first hit the ground. Kwasnik insisted that the source of the poop had to be near the processing plant. That meant that if they were gonna produce TrunkWax in Pylewood, the cows had to reside in the East County. And that was why his plane ticket was to Paris, France, and not Butte, Montana; Wighair, England; or Wienstampfen, Germany. When he raised his hand and protested that he had seen a sale ad in the *Western Livestock Reporter* for Roan Pollanks, a French breed already established in the county, Kwasnik ignored him and kept on talking about French breeds in France.

While he was waiting for Karen to get the tickets, he had a chance to do some thinking on his own. Like Delahunt had said, before they started collecting semen or embryos, they'd have to figure out how to choose the best donors and receivers for traits that nobody else had ever wanted. Even though Kwasnik claimed he already knew that the best cows for the job were red French cattle from the center of France, Bill knew that they'd have to do better than that if they were to succeed. He knew of at least four breeds of red cattle in France. They ate different grasses, drank different water, and lived in different climates. After all, Rudy was only a fruit farmer, and a new one at that. You didn't have to know too much or be too smart to buy a little tree, stick it in the ground, and give it a few drops of water every now and then. On the other hand, in the cattle business, a potential buyer was expected to check experimental progeny data (EPDs) before even considering buying a breeding animal. Small birth weights, high rates of gain, and large scrotal circumferences were the traits that buyers generally looked for. When you got right down to it, his problem was how to figure out the relationship of visual and measurable traits to poop quality and productivity. As far as he knew, there were no EPDs for bacteria, fungi, and viruses, no list of desirable microbes, and no measures of microbe production efficiency. Established procedures for testing dairy-cow manure existed, but they didn't seem relevant. Nitrogen content, minerals, and microbe characterization were directed toward figuring out the fertilizer value of the manure for soil, not for tree-trunk applications.

He swung his legs off the bed and headed for the bathroom. He needed to brush what was left of his teeth before he fell asleep. *So many problems, so many questions.* He really needed a lot more information and education, but he was out of time. He figured that he'd have to get help in France from a French scientist, preferably a female like Madame Curie or Katherine Deneuve, without giving away any secrets. And even when he got that all figured out, he'd have to solve the problem of getting the goods back to Pylewood. Live animals were pretty much out of the question. That left semen and embryos. Both had to be kept real cold to guard against heat-induced changes, ruptures, additions, and rearrangements. Then there were the airline security regulations that prohibited the carry-on of pastes, liquids, and gels, which more than likely applied to the transport of semen or embryos on any commercial flight. It would also be risky to subject expensive semen to X-ray exposure. Security rules weren't nearly so strict for rail and boat travel. Unfortunately, there weren't any trains that crossed the ocean, and it took the fastest commercial ocean liner four days to cross the Atlantic.

He hobbled over to the refrigerator, weary of all this thinking about bulls, semen, and breeding. It only reminded him that he could use a refreshing bout of sex himself; it seemed like a long time since something soft and curvy had pumped up his ejector. Maybe the trip to France would turn out good. All of the sudden, the pain left his knee, and sleep turned off his lights.

CHAPTER 7

Foreign Travel

Yep, it was really happening. He was about to drag his aching knee and oversize ass off to Paris, France: part of a crazy scheme he, Jim Delahunt, and Rudy Kwasnik had cooked up one night in his trailer in Briones Valley. He had no notion of just how he was going to get off an airplane in a foreign country where he didn't speak the language and start searching for some exotic cattle. Kwasnik had promised to set up the contacts, but in the end, all he had given him was a scrap of paper that said *Societe de Agricole au Vache* with an address on one side and the name Claudine Fortet scribbled on the other. He had asked Karen to send a letter to the address notifying Ms. Fortet when he was arriving and asking her to please meet him at the airport, but they hadn't heard anything back.

Truth was he was getting cold feet. In the last twenty years, he hadn't gone anywhere but to the sale yard in Galt, and the last time he went, he had even missed the turnoff. Now he was going to Paris, fuckin' France, a place he didn't know much about, except that they didn't speak English. Artie Jones, his old neighbor in Pittsburg, was the only person he knew who had ever been to France. He had been there when he was in the service just after the war and always said he didn't much care for the people; they pushed and shoved a lot and never smiled. Couldn't be that bad, Bill reckoned. People told him he'd hate Great Falls the first time he went to Montana, but he ended up liking the place. Paris, France, would probably turn out to be the same way.

He did have a valid US passport, though, something left over from time he thought he might go to Costa Rica to pick up some cattle for the guy that ran the auction yard in Escalon. And come to think of it, he and his second wife had taken a Caribbean cruise twenty years earlier. They had visited Jamaica, Haiti, and a few more places he'd lost track of. It had been OK: cheap drinks, good food, and lots of dreadlocks. She loved it, but the cruise really wasn't his cup of tea: a boat with no fishing poles, snooty waiters, and a tiny bed.

He pulled his ticket out of the envelop Karen had given him and stared at it. It looked more like the time card he used to punch when he worked at the Reno stockyards than a ticket to anything. She said he had to be in Pittsburg in the morning if he expected to be in the San Francisco airport by noon. It seemed like plenty of time. His plane didn't leave until 2:00 PM. When Tigger started barking, he knew Karen was coming up the road. She always drove real slow up the dirt road, trying hard not to kick up a lot of dust. Most folks drove as fast as they could, with no regard for the dust, ruts, or anything else. She pulled her big blue pickup right up to the front of his door. Her Ford was a vintage set of wheels: big tires, souped-up engine, and customized flatbed with a grated chrome shield behind the back window. She sat tall in the driver's seat, close to six feet tall, broad-shouldered for a woman but slender everywhere else.

She rolled down the window. "Get in. You got a plane to catch," she half shouted at him through a big grin.

His knee started hurting as soon as he put his foot on the running board and tried to push up. It got even worse when he pulled himself up into the Ford's high cab.

"When you gonna get a new truck? This one's high enough to ford the Mokelumne River in spring?"

"When I win the lottery."

"Don't waste your money on them lottery tickets anymore. I'm figuring on coming back from Paris, France, rich. I'll buy you a little ladder with the money. That is if anybody understands me when I get there. You know I never took no foreign languages in school, not even junior high school Spanish, even though my aptitude tests showed I'd be good at foreign languages."

"Don't worry about not speaking French. Just smile and talk in English. Somebody'll understand you."

That was Karen, always looking on the bright side of things. What'd she know about France anyway?

"But just in case, take this," she said, pushing a small yellow French/English dictionary into his jacket pocket.

When he saw the last bit of her and her blue pickup disappear from the Pittsburg BART station, he realized he'd miss her a bunch. He should have asked her to come with him to Paris, France. If he had only asked, she might even have done it. It was the story of his whole fuckin' life, shitty timing. Well, he was on his own now.

Karen had given him a BART ticket and told him to just push the thing in the green slot in front and then pull it out the top to make the gate open. Just like she said, the gate slid open when it swallowed his ticket, but the space didn't get any bigger when his ticket came back. For a big guy like him toting a suitcase, squeezing through the small opening was harder than getting around a big horse in a small stall. People must have got smaller since the last time he had gone anywhere. An attendant, who was surveying the area, finally rescued him, shouting and motioning for him to come over to the booth where there was a wider gate.

The BART train jangled its way from Pittsburg to Concord, over the pass and down to the flat where he could see the old Port Chicago naval yard and golf course. He had been in most all of the places he could see from the train, some a long time ago, mostly on horseback chasing cattle. He watched the passengers get on and off: every age, shape, and color, every language too. He recognized Spanish from paling around with Jeff Rodriguez and Chinese from the year he delivered meat to Chinatown in San Francisco. "See the world," people said. Shee'it, you could see a good bit of it from a seat on the Pittsburg BART train.

When he got off the train at the San Francisco airport, he headed straight for the International Terminal, where FlyUwhere? had their checkout counter. After a short wait in line, the attendant, an attractive girl with an attention-demanding lip piercing, found him on her computer terminal, took his bag, punched up a boarding pass, and sent him on his way to airport security, where he joined a long queue that wove back and forth around a bunch of ropes and posts. *Just like the alleys in the big sale yards in Reno,* he thought, *only without the HotShots.*

The first big snarl came when he finally got through the alley and up to the first gate, where he was supposed to take off his boots. Big unwelcome surprise. Nobody told him he'd have to pull his boots off. Taking his boots off to make sure he didn't have weapons or bombs in them was a joke; there was hardly enough room in them boots for his feet. Even without the confusion and noise of an airport line, he needed a stretch of time and some help to get them off. And he sure couldn't do it standing up. When he tried to get out of line to find a place to sit, he bumped into a tall guy with a shaved head wearing a red Jeepers Creepers Memorial Concert T-shirt. He apologized but heard the guy mutter a cuss word under his breath. Even when he found a seat and started tugging, he still couldn't get the dang things off.

Help finally came in the person of a good-natured guy wearing an Australian bushwhacker's hat who sat down next him.

"Need a hand, mate?" the fellow said. "Guess you haven't traveled in a while. Damned nuisance, isn't it. Let me pull 'em off for you."

"Thanks," Bill said. "I'd probably be here for days. My feet sure ain't gonna get any smaller sittin' here." He looked down at his Aussie rescuer's feet and saw he was wearing flip-flops.

"I'll be danged," Bill said. "I got a pair of them things at home, but I left 'em in the shower."

First time Bill waddled barefoot through the metal detector, the top of his hat hit the metal detector hoop, and his butt banged the side, errors that earned him an immediate scowl from the uniformed lady facing him from the other side of the alley.

"Sir, go back and put your hat in a tub along with all your money and metal items." The next time, though, his belt buckle, invisible under his stomach, set off the alarm.

"Sorry," he said. "Won this here buckle years ago at a roping in Oakdale." Meanwhile, the line behind him was growing longer, and the already-uptight passengers, some who were probably already late for their planes, were getting increasingly restive. He wasn't finished, though, setting off the alarm on his next trip through the metal detector. His interrogator pulled him aside for another time and waved her wand over him and then had him spread his legs while she rubbed the flashlight-shaped thing up his legs, around his crotch and crack, and then finally around his neck and jaw until she got a beep.

"Sir, you don't have a metal plate in your head do you? Why didn't you tell us?"

"No metal plates, ma'am, just a knife, fork, and spoon."

The security officer flipped on her emergency radio and asked for more help.

"Dumb shit," the tall Jeepers Creepers fan with a shaved head and red T-shirt muttered loud enough for Bill to hear. "Dumb mutherfucker."

Bill turned around to see who the talker was. "Yeah, you," he said.

"Sorry," Bill said apologetically. "I don't fly much. All this is new to me. If you want, you can get ahead of me."

"What good would it do? I'd still have to wait for you to drag your fat ass onto the airplane."

It took him another couple of passes, but Bill finally got through the security check. Halfway down the boarding ramp, he remembered he had left his wristwatch in the gray plastic tub that he had put through the X-ray machine. He hurried back to the security checkpoint, back past the girl checking boarding passes, the waiting area, and the concourse. One of the attendants was waiting with the watch.

"You got here just in time, sir. I was on my way to lost and found."

He retraced his steps back to the boarding ramp, his knee now throbbing with pain. He felt the ramp dip and sway as he hurried toward the plane's door. Getting into his seat was almost as hard as getting through the BART gate. The seat was half as big as it needed to be for someone his size, and when he sat down, his knees touched the seat ahead. Delahunt and Kwasnik had talked about getting him into first class and a bigger seat, but in the end, they figured they just didn't have the money. He could fly first-class when they got rich.

Then there was no place for his hat. The overhead compartment was jammed tight by the time he got on the airplane. Del Hopper, the steer wrestler from Oxnard, who was six-foot-five, had told him a few years back to be sure to take a hatbox if he ever did any traveling, but he hadn't out of vanity. He thought he'd look ridiculous carrying a hatbox around Paris, France. The only place for his sombrero was on his head, but it touched the ceiling, and it blocked the fresh air vent, light, and almost touched the red flight-attendant summons button.

Once they were in the air, he tried to tip back his chair to get a little more leg room, but it wouldn't go. His knee was sorer than ever, the pain downright crippling, and he doubted that he'd be able to sit in the chair for twelve hours. No way in hell. He finally figured out that the guy behind him was trying just as hard as he was to push forward while he pushed backward. In fact, everyone in the cheapskate section of the FlyUwhere? Airlines Airbus303 was pushing in one direction or the other. Just as he found a tolerable resting position, the passenger in front of him reclined his seat as far back as it would go, putting his shaved head almost in Bill's lap and banging his sore knee. As bad luck would have it, the head belonged to the rude guy with the red Jeepers Creepers shirt that had cussed him out in the security line.

All right, that didn't really matter. Everyone in the security line had been in a hurry, and the ball-headed guy was just voicing his frustration. Lately, Bill had been listening to the old Zen Buddhist tapes of Alan Watts on KPFA when he couldn't sleep, and they had provided a calming counterweight to his normally uncontrollable temper.

"Suppose you could lift up a bit, pardner," he said. "Yer seat back is resting on my knee, and yer head's just about in my lap."

"Nope, don't think so, buddy" was the answer he got. "It's my right to tip back to the max. Bought my ticket same as you. If they didn't want you to tip back, they wouldn't have put that feature in the seat." Then he paused and looked back. "You're the dumb cowboy with the steel tooth, aren't you? Kept everyone waiting in the security line. Fuck you."

Temper or not, Bill wasn't one for arguing. He wasn't good at it, and it always ended up seeming like a waste of time and energy.

What he did feel like was a chew, so he pulled his tin of Copenhagen out of his shirt pocket, put a dip in his mouth, and worked it up with a goodly bit of saliva. Unfortunately, just as he raised up a bit and leaned forward over the shaved head that was attached to the red Jeepers Creepers T-shirt, a couple of dark rivulets of tobacco juice escaped from the corners of his mouth, ran down his chin, and dripped right into the eyes of the head that was almost in his lap. Then a whole bunch more dripped down on the Jeepers Creepers T-shirt and even more on the shaved head.

The head pitched forward and made loud noises that kinda sounded like "Oh my god. Something's in my eye," and "I can't see no more." With all the squirming about and hollering, the poor guy even sucked a dollop of the viscous black stuff up his nose.

Bill leaned back and pulled out a handkerchief that Karen had washed and ironed for him the day before and offered it to the stricken passenger. "Always help the stranger in distress," Alan Watts preached. "When you help others unselfishly, you really help yourself." But this stricken passenger refused all offers of unselfish help. Bill wiped his own chin with the handkerchief and rubbed it on the bald head before he put it back in his pocket. Bill raised up a bit so his Stetson touched the help button and set off a loud ring. The FlyUwhere? flight attendants, busy preparing the first-class mid-flight snack of croissants and camembert-flavored chartreuse cheese, signaled back that they were unable to help the sobbing blinded passenger until after they had moved their carts out of the aisles and collected the plastic trays. Bill helped them out by pushing the bald-headed guy's chair back into the upright position, taking his pillow away, and throwing his peanuts, iPod, and sunglasses into the trash bag the flight attendant was carrying up the aisle. He finished by slamming the folding tray back into the safe-to-land position.

With a little more room now, Bill was able to close his eyes and bring up an image of Karen Clements. Even though he had seen her only a few hours earlier when she had dropped him off at the Pittsburg BART station, the mental image that came up was of an eighteen-year-old high school girl: tanned face, hazel eyes, long straight black hair, 4-H Club jacket, no smile. Funny thing was he had forgotten what she had looked like just a few hours ago. Yep, he had to admit he still had a crush on her even though he had been married a couple times more after they got divorced, or was it just once. He was sure it would come back to him in a day or two. Now on this flight to Paris, France, he wondered how his life might have been different had he stuck it out with Karen. Maybe with some dough from this TrunkWax deal, he might be able to get her back. He was sure she still carried a torch for him. With a little money, he could take better care of himself too: shed a few pounds, buy some bigger boots and a new truck, and go callin' and courtin'. Why the hell not? He'd just have to make this TrunkWax shit work if he was ever going to reclaim his life.

When he mentally rejoined the real world, he took a look at his watch and realized that he still had eleven hours left on his twelve-hour flight. His knee was killing him, his teeth hurt, and his back had started to ache. The longest he'd ever been on an airplane before was twenty years ago on the three-hour flight from Oakland to Bozeman, Montana. He didn't remember it being so cramped. He really needed to get up, walk around, stretch, and get his blood moving around. When he stood up to get out of his seat, he noticed the guy in front of him with the red T-shirt was sleeping with a couple of damp towels on his eyes. As he wiggled out into the aisle, Bill dropped a heavy elbow down hard on top of the guy's head.

"'Scuse me, pardner," he said. "Sure's cramped in here. Let me help you with your dirty laundry." He snatched the towels off the guy's face and shuffled down the aisle with them in his hand. Halfway to the back of the plane, the flight attendant met him.

"Let me take those for you, sir," she said.

"They belong to the guy in the seat in front of me who's having trouble with his eyes. He says he don't need them no more. He also wants to change his food to vegetarian for the rest of the flight."

"Oh, you must mean the jerk in seat 23A. He's been trouble ever since he boarded the plane," she said, giving Bill something a little better than a standard flight-attendant smile.

"You wouldn't have a bigger seat somewhere, would you, ma'am? I got a bum knee, and I don't think it can stand another eight hours in that tiny seat I'm in."

She looked Bill up and down, from the retreating patch of sweaty gray hair on the top of his head, past his enormous belly, down to his size thirteen, triple-cee boots.

"You certainly do look like an extra-large to me, but it's against FlyUwhere? policy to move passengers from coach to first-class just because they're uncomfortable in a standard-size seat. That is, unless it's a medical emergency, and you look like you might be on the verge of a medical emergency." This time, her smile was wide.

She led him toward the front of the plane and pointed to a gray leather seat at the back of the first-class section. The seat was about the size of the La-Z-Boy lounger in his trailer back in Briones Valley, and he flopped down in it with a sigh of gratitude.

"Bless you, darling," he said. "Look me up if you're ever in California, and I'll try to repay this kindness. Do you ride?" he asked.

"Whenever I get the chance," she answered. "Write your phone number on the napkin and leave it on the tray, and thanks for flying FlyUwhere? Airlines."

Next thing he knew, she brought him a little plate with a green cheese ball covered with pistachio nuts and a glass of white wine. He popped the cheese ball in his mouth even though it was the size of a small orange and drank the wine down in a couple of gulps. He fell right to sleep and didn't wake up until he felt the plane slow down and start going downhill.

CHAPTER 8

The Sommet de l'Elevage

Bill was hoping Claudine Fortet, the representative of the French Cattle Breeders Association, would be there to meet him at the Paris Airport. She would be able to calm any misgivings he had about being alone in a strange country where he didn't speak the language. Thanks to the kindness of Vicki, the FlyUwhere? flight attendant, who had moved him up to first class, he had slept a bit and had no trouble getting out of his seat, into the aisle, and out of the airplane. Limping along the ramp and into the huge gallery, he quickly found himself packed in the middle of what seemed like a million milling foreigners. The terminal was way bigger than the San Francisco Airport, and the white curved steel structures and massive straight ceiling beams made him dizzier than a bronc rider with a migraine. He expected to see Claudine Fortet standing in front of the exit ramp: short, dark hair, tight skirt, scarf, and wearing a name tag, or at least waving a tiny American flag. When he peered out over the churning crowd, he did see plenty of pretty women with dark hair and tight skirts, but none with a name tag he recognized or waving an American flag. He reckoned he had about as good a chance of spotting her, as he did of seeing a wild pig in clump of greasewood. Even though the posted directions along the concourse all had arrows and little picture clues like forks for food and cars for taxis, it was still confusing. Lucky for him, the word for baggage was the same in French, so he headed off in the direction of the next little

picture of a suitcase. On the way, he recognized the Australian who
had helped him with his boots and the girl with the purple hair and
toe ring who had sat across the aisle from him and followed them
to a carousel topped with a big sign with a number 12 and a big red
and purple FlyUwhere? logo.

Standing around spinning his Stetson-topped head from side
to side, looking for a little American flag, he must have looked very
lost to the big man, nearly as tall as he was, who walked straight up
to him and let out with a loud, happy "Bonjour, monsieur. Perhaps
I can help you find your way."

Bill blinked a couple of times and stared at the guy. He was
wearing a rough tweed jacket and a flat blue French cap and guessed
correctly that he was probably French. He started a search through
his mental flash cards for French words he had been trying to
memorize before he left but only drew blanks.

"Are you going to the International Livestock Show in Clermont-
Ferrand?" the man in the beret asked the man in the Stetson.

Bill looked the fellow up and down. "Yer not Claudine are ya?"

"No, no. I am Claude, not Claudine. Claude Raimbaut, from
Arles in the Camargue."

"Pleased to meet you, Claude. I'm Bill Robeiro from the
Pylewood in California, but I don't know nothin' about no livestock
show. I'm supposed to meet Claudine Fortet from the French Cattle
Association. My boss lined her up to show me some red cattle."

"Oh yes, I know her," The Frenchman said while he methodically
scanned the baggage area from one carousel to the other. "I don't see
her here. Perhaps she is waiting for you at Orly, our other airport."

"Dang, I didn't know you had mord'n one. We only told her I
was landin' at the Paris Airport."

"Don't worry, Monsieur Roberto. We will see her at the train
station; I'm sure of it. She is going to the livestock exhibition and

must have planned to take you with her. You are more than welcome to come with me."

"Thanks, but she never said nothin' about no exhibition. I thought we was just goin' to ranches. Anyway, my name is Robeiro, not Roberto, but just call me Bill. Most folks do."

"OK, Bill, and you must call me Blondie, as my friends do."

Just then, Bill caught a glimpse of a wheelchair being rolled up to the luggage carousel. It was his old friend from seat 23C, sleeping, probably sedated, with a couple of wet tissues over his eyes.

"Excuse me, Blondie, I see a fellow passenger over there that I think needs some help."

With a combination of hand gestures, some English words, and a twenty-dollar bill, Bill convinced the FlyUwhere? representative that the man in the wheel chair had been heavily sedated and needed to be taken to a connecting flight to Addis Ababa. Unfortunately, he told her, the poor guy had lost his ticket at the same time he lost his sight. A large lady, heavyset for a French woman, gave Bill a tired look as she started wheeling the Jeepers Creepers fan toward the sign that said International Connections.

"Sorry, Blondie, but I had to get that fella off to his connection. Got something in his eye the nurse said."

"Perhaps Claudine intended to surprise you. You are lucky to be in France at the time of this famous show. We call it the *Sommet de l'Elevage,* and livestock people from all over the world come to Clermont-Ferrand to attend. It's the leading show for the beef breeds of Europe."

"How do we get to this fair?"

"By train. Clermont-Ferrand is four hundred kilometers from Paris. If we catch a fast train from the airport to the *Gare Lyon* and jump on the TGV we will be in Lyon in two hours; then we must wait for another hour for our connection to Clermont-Ferrand. The last part of the journey is slow and very beautiful. I'm sure we will find Claudine Fortet somewhere along the way."

"What kinda cattle are we gonna see at this fair?" Bill asked as he grabbed his bag off the luggage carousel. "I seen Charolais and Limousin cattle before, and one of neighbors even got a few Salers, but that's it."

"As I'm sure you know, Charolais and Limousin are the big French export beef breeds, Salers less so, but you'll also see Aubrac and Gasconne beef breeds that are popular in France but are probably less well known in America. Dairy breeds like Normande, Tarentaise, Abondance, and Montbeliarde will also be on display."

"I know this sounds like a funny question, Blondie, but do you guys have a breed that stays small even if it eats a lot?"

"None that you will see at this exhibition, my friend. In most of France, we value size over all else. Huge bulls, massive horses, and rams as big as ponies. But in my region, the Camargue, we have a small rustic breed of cattle that we call Camarguise. These cattle are always black and have long pointed horns. They are small, eat a lot, and produce very little milk or meat. We keep them for bullfighting and entertaining guests. Most of what they eat goes straight to their brains. They are remarkably brave and intelligent and have a sly sense of humor."

"Don't think I ever heard of a cow with a sense of humor, although my cousin Donnie swears that he seen one in a dairy in Oklahoma that wouldn't get in the milking stall unless you gave her a Milky Way candy bar."

"We do get a little bit of milk from them, and we use it to make a special cheese we call Sachaguittre. When this cheese is aged over a year, it combines the flavors of burnt bread and hazelnuts. We think these cows produce a special enzyme that gives this cheese its unique taste."

"I think I had that cheese on a pizza in Antioch once."

"We also use these cattle to do tricks for tourists, so we breed them for their sense of humor rather than for growth."

"No kidding," Bill said.

"Perhaps if you have some extra time, you will come to visit me in Arles and see them for yourself. You might even want to take one back with you to America. They are much easier to export than the more popular French breeds."

The train to Lyon was, as Blondie said, fast, modern, and comfortable. As soon as they got to their compartment, Bill pushed out the footrest and dropped into the big comfortable seat. He covered his face with his gray Stetson and surrendered to sleep minutes after the train got up to speed. Blondie walked through the entire train looking for Claudine Fortet without success. Bill didn't stir until the train was almost to Lyon. When he pulled his hat back and looked over at Blondie, he saw the Frenchman was reading a paperback novel with a French title.

"You ain't readin' *The Count of Monte Cristo* by any chance, are you?" Bill asked.

"No, why do you ask?"

"Got a friend, Jim Delahunt, who swears by it."

"Yes, our author Alexander Dumas is famous throughout the world, but really a literary lightweight. Proust, Stendhal, Camus, and Pierre Gallimand: these are the giants of French literature according to my brother-in-law, who is a professor of French literature at the Université de Haute Rhin."

"Could you get him to recommend me a French book that ain't too hard? I figure I can learn some French while I'm on this trip."

"With pleasure," Blondie answered. "I am somewhat surprised that you are interested in learning our language."

"I gotta tell you, Blondie, that when I took the aptitude test in junior high school, I scored real high on the foreign language part, but I never had a chance to do nothin' with it. My cousin Donnie laughed at me when I told him I was gonna learn French or Spanish, and my dad was always pullin' me out of school to fix fences and move cattle."

"You should try something contemporary, like Marcel Pagnol. His novels have been made into films, which makes them good learning aids. I also have a copy of the poems of Jean Giono in my suitcase. He is a Provençal poet, a man of the earth like yourself."

When they pulled into the Lyon train station, Blondie suggested that they get something to eat. "We have an hour's wait," Blondie announced. "After we eat, we'll check the book stall for a good beginner's book. I couldn't find Claudine on the train, so I will try on the telephone again."

"How about a drink, Blondie? I usually have a whiskey about this time of day."

"Yes, of course, the station bar is not far from the arrival gate. But I think you should try a French drink, calvados or cognac."

"OK, if you try some American hooch."

Bill ordered a calvados for himself and a double shot of Kessler's for Blondie.

"It's in a big plastic bottle!" he yelled at the barman when the man cocked his head, pushed out his lower lip, and turned his left hand palms up, the French gesture for not understanding. When they couldn't find any Kessler's, they settled on Bill's second choice, the Glen Barnacle, a fourteen-month-old Highland single-malt from a little-known distillery on the Garscube Road in Glasgow.

They clinked their glasses and toasted each other. "To better days," Bill toasted as Blondie said, "A la votre."

"Don't think I ever drank whiskey made out of avocados. But it ain't too bad. How's yer scotch? Never cared too much for it myself until I started drinking it at my friend's house in Pylewood."

"Yes, it's very good," Blondie said. "It reminds me of the Clyde River. I think I had some a couple of years ago when I accompanied my wife to Glasgow for the Second Annual European Conference on Dismantling Public Housing Estates. Let's go over to the book stalls. We still have a few minutes before the train leaves."

"Do you want to start with something simple with pictures?" Blondie said, holding up a big thin book with the title *Tresor de Rackham de Rouge*.

"That's a kid's book, Blondie. I'll look like an idiot if I'm readin' that on the train." Bill pulled a book off the bargain cart. "*Madame Bovary*, that looks like it might be interesting. Sounds like it might be about a prostitute with big tits."

"Maw," Blondie said. "It's a French classic, a pivotal book in the development of the novel. Don't you want to start with something easier."

"Nope. I got a dictionary, and I don't mind goin' a word at a time if I have to. Besides, I can learn some grammar along the way. Might even help my English, which ain't none too good as you probably noticed."

The train to Clermont-Ferrand was much slower than the TGV from Paris. It crept along through beautiful valleys, stopped at Thiers for a while, and finished up by passing great bare rock outcroppings. Bill didn't see too much; he had his face stuck in his new book. He had skipped the introduction and was already halfway through the second chapter. He had understood the part about Charles Bovary being ridiculed for his hat on the first day of school. It wasn't too far from what happened to new kids in his school in Antioch. Of course he was always the biggest kid in the class, so it never happened to him personally; but every now and then, he'd rescue some poor kid from the hazing.

When they got to the Clermont-Ferrand train station, Bill followed Blondie out to a curbside stop where a big Renault touring bus was taking on passengers. Blondie flashed his association badge at the bus driver who waved them past the fare box.

"We are going to Grand Cournon, an area just on the outskirts of town. It is very close to the exhibition area. Perhaps we will find Claudine there," he explained.

After a short climb up a hill, the bus pulled up to the front of a modern hotel splayed out along the hill. Bill was the first one off the bus and started stamping his foot, trying to get it awake.

"My knee's been botherin' me the whole dang trip. Now my foot's asleep."

"I am very sorry," Claude Raimbaut said. "Perhaps after some days in the French countryside, it will feel better."

The entrance to the Hotel Gergovie was framed by two rectangular massive red pillars embossed in gold with the hotel's name. Each pillar had a large concrete statue of a horned bull at its side.

"The bull you see is Vailliant, the most famous bull of this region," Blondie said. "His semen and progeny were sent all over the world and brought much money and prestige to this area. Most of the red bulls you have in your country can probably be traced back to Vailliant."

"I seen some in California, but to tell the truth, my dad always liked Beefmasters better. Anyways, I think I'm more interested in them small bulls from your area that you talked about, the ones with the good sense of humor. I'm tired of telling jokes to dull cows."

Blondie handed Bill a piece of paper with the names and room numbers of other English-speaking guests who were staying at the Gergovie Hotel. "Pleasant dreams. I'll see you tomorrow morning."

CHAPTER 9

Dog Days

Tigger just started barking because he was upset. He missed Bill, he didn't like living in town, and he hated being on the end of a rope, even if it was long. He knew that his relatives, living and dead, would be ashamed of his outburst. He wasn't like most dogs in the East County. He came from an old family going back to Gaspar Portola's dog, Fidel Miperro. Along with having deep roots in Hollister and Monterey County, the Miperros had a long tradition of composed behavior, civic responsibility, and a reputation for being able to cope with any problem. A lot was expected of a Miperro. Now here he was wailing like some shelter giveaway. Even worse, he felt like biting someone or tearing up a blanket. Roger Jones, his revered great-grandfather, would have been ashamed of him.

But what did they expect? Bill had been gone for a couple of weeks already. He had gone to some Frankish country on some low-class project conjured up by the renowned local idiot Hrubel Kwasnik and supported by the retired half-deaf machinist Jim Delahunt. He had always worried about the kind of friends Bill attracted, and now his concern had been justified, and he was the one suffering. He had been carted off from his home in Briones Valley by Bill's girlfriend, Karen Clements, and left in the care of a Marsha Misch, a self-styled professional dog watcher who had a tract house in Pylewood, a dump of a city if there ever was one. The traffic in Pylewood was outrageous and dangerous. Dogs from

all over the city were getting killed and maimed willy-nilly, run
over by soccer moms in big SUVs, low riders with boom boxes, and
senior citizens in silent Camry hybrids. Even worse, the Pylewood
water was almost undrinkable; it tasted like it came straight from
a toilet—something he knew all about from the time when Bill left
him with his cousin Donnie, who locked him up in the bathroom
when he went out to play pinochle at the Veteran's Hall. Right now
he would gladly trade a dozen meaty beef bones for a drink of cold
water from the creek in Briones Valley.

It was only faith that kept him going. He had been flirting with
Zen Buddhism ever since he had accidently killed one of Bill's
chickens and found he couldn't overcome his remorse. In a way,
he considered himself lucky. Thousands of other dogs were deeply
interested in spiritual things, but in a human-dominated world,
they were denied the succor they craved. His lucky break had come
one evening when Delahunt, the screwy engineer, had come over
to their place in Briones Valley to help Bill install an antenna for
his new digital radio. Later that evening, for some reason, the radio
came on by itself and tuned itself onto KPFA, the left-wing Berkeley
station that was rerunning the Buddhism lectures Alan Watts had
given years ago. Turned out it was pretty interesting stuff, and he
stayed up all night listening intently. He learned a lot of things about
controlling his emotions that night. Afterward, he made it a habit to
spend a couple of minutes meditating every morning. So it wasn't
a surprise that after a couple of deep breaths and some low-pitched
growling, he realized things could be worse. Marsha Misch never
forgot to feed him, and she always made sure he had water, even if
it did taste like it came from a toilet.

On the other hand, he did have legitimate complaints. Ms. Misch
was too busy to drive him around to places during the day, she
refused to take him to work with her, and she never let him ride in
the cab of her pickup. How was he supposed to keep up with current

events? Ever since Bill had dropped their subscription to the *Contra Costa Times*, he had been forced to rely on the radio in the pickup for all his information. He missed the radio more than anything else. How were the A's doing? He hadn't a clue. Had Clint Conatser regained his stroke? Had Pedro Perez learned to hit a slider? What was the state of the economy? He needed to know. Dogs were the first to suffer in hard economic times. When food was short, they were the first to go hungry. Some were even euthanized. He had heard from one of Delahunt's former dogs who had once lived in the home of an unemployed plumber that the family actually ate the dog's food at the end of the month. There was no justice in it. Cats got fed even when their masters went hungry. Dogs, who were more loyal and often saved the lives of humans, were dragged off to dog pounds. Was there even such a thing as a cat pound? Cats refused to work, even if you gave them credit for the odd mouse they caught.

Now Bill was off in France searching for a source of special cow manure for Kwasnik's poop squirter—an idiot's pot of gold if there ever was one. At least he was in a civilized country. It would do the old cowboy a world of good to immerse himself in the culture of France. The art, the music, the architecture would help fill the massive intellectual void that was the root cause of his troubles. Learning the French language was bound to improve his English, which was usually a disaster. He howled when Bill mixed up "lay" and "lie" and messed up his pronouns, but it hadn't helped. There wasn't even a paperback dictionary in the trailer. Bill just assumed his howling meant he was hungry.

Moreover, the whole idea of spraying some biodynamic paste on tree trunks was absurd. He had urinated on plenty of tree trunks without ever noticing any improvement. He could have explained that to them if they would have taken the time to listen and understand him. Why was it that when they made noise, he listened until he understood; but when he made noise, they just told him to shut up? It was so frustrating not being able to communicate with people. Some owners even put electric belts around their dog's necks to keep them from speaking. He could understand their language. Why couldn't they understand his? He had even seen Delahunt's engineering drawing when Bill took him over to Kwasnik's place the first time they discussed the poop paste idea. When the three imbeciles took a nap break, he jumped up on the pool table where the plans were spread and studied the blueprint. Their poop squirting contraption looked like a vacuum cleaner with training wheels. Any numbskull could tell it would never work. First of all, it ran on line voltage; second, it had no braking system or recovery capacity. What if the fucking thing got stuck in some tree branch? His first impulse was to piss all over the plan like one of his cousins used to do on Bill's homework when the water dish went dry. He resisted the temptation. He had to remember his lineage and the Miperro family motto of "Honor Above All."

When he mentioned his reservations to Rudy Kwasnik's dog, a big spoiled Alsatian bitch who was conceited as hell and dumber than a Chihuahua, she just sat down and stared at him like she expected him to bow and present her with a new collar. It was something he had half expected. Her boss, the dumb ex-hippie, thought she was the greatest thing since organic figs. He routinely fed her steaks and ground round, took her to bars, and even let her sleep in bed with him. Of course none of that changed the fact that both of them were freakin' idiots. Hardley, Delahunt's low-bred Australian-style dog, had told him that one afternoon he had actually seen Kwasnik pulling up weeds and eating them like a chicken. Now the same guy had some crazy idea to build a machine to spray cow shit on trees.

Tigger stopped barking and went back into his dog house and laid down on the blanket. Back home in Briones Valley, he had slept in the trailer and came and went as he pleased. He had had the run of the valley. Now he was confined to a one-room wooden structure in a suburban back yard. Even though he considered himself a Buddhist, he prayed to Jesus like J. Willard McVay, whom he heard on the radio one time on the way to Stockton, that Bill would get home soon.

CHAPTER 10

The Purple Rope

Bill toppled on to the bed and grabbed the brochure that was laying on the nightstand. From it, he found out that the Hotel Gergovie was a three-story building strung out along the hillside in a way that afforded each of the fifty-nine rooms on the top two floors a clear view of the exhibition grounds of the Sommet de l'Elevage. He pulled off his boots and tossed his trousers in the direction of the television before he settled down to read the list of attendees Blondie had given him. The list told him that the third-floor guests included Will McNea, the president of the All Ireland Drovers and Herdsman's Group (AIDHG); Max Thomson, the secretary of the Australian Charolais Association; Trevor Dos Picos, a Limousin breeder from Argentina; and Scotty McIver, a prominent Scots Highland cattleman. Bunked on the floor below were Ivor Gryyffwwdd of the Welsh Stockman's Association and Nils Jensen of the Danish Dairyman's Cooperative.

By eleven o'clock, the hotel guests, all suffering from various stages of fatigue or jetlag, were bedded down, and most of the staff had gone home. At midnight, seconds after the automatic timer had dimmed the hotel lights, three gray Citroën vans pulled up in front of the hotel and disgorged a phalanx of wiry, athletic-looking characters clad in tight black outfits with ski masks pulled over their faces. The intruders burst through the front doors of the hotel and clubbed the night doorman and desk clerk with odd little sticks that each carried. With extraordinary precision, the intruders moved into the stairwells and corridors where they quickly found the rooms of the guests whose doors had been marked with hat-shaped paper stickers. On the third-floor, a gray Stetson sticker was stuck to Bill's door, a green facsimile of a floppy bushwhacker's hat was on Aussie Max Thomson's door, Will McNea's door was decorated with a tweedy-looking tam-o'-shanter, and Trevor Dos Picos's was marked with a flat, tasseled gaucho hat. Down below, on the second story, a black derby sticker decorated Ivor Gryyffwwdd's doorway, and a gray and maroon likeness of a knit cap was on Nils Jensen's door.

One intruder moved quietly along the third floor until he found the gaucho hat he was looking for. Using a hotel pass key to enter, he tranquilized the dozing Argentines with a fluorinated hydrocarbon aerosol. Another intruder found the floppy bushwhackers hat, slipped into Max Thomson's room, which was next to Bill's, and jabbed the sleeping Aussie with a syringe loaded with a strong animal tranquilizer. The intruder in Max's room, who was nearsighted and whose ski mask was a size too large, groped around the room, stumbled over an open suitcase on the floor, and hit his head on a light fixture but finally found the large oval hat box that he was looking for. Bill, who couldn't get back to sleep after his short sound nap, heard the noise but was so engrossed in reading *Madame Bovary* that he paid little heed to the disturbance.

"C'était une de ces coiffures," he read aloud. *Blondie was probably right*, he thought. I shoulda started with somethin' simpler. He was in the middle of "du bonnet, a poil, du chapska" when the unmistakable mechanical sound of a key being pushed into his door lock stunned him into action. He pushed *Madame Bovary* under his pillow, leapt from the bed, faced the front door in a fighting stance, and tiptoed slowly backward into the bathroom.

"I don't fuckin' believe this," he whispered to himself. "Some son of a bitch is trying to burgle me before I even finish the first chapter in my new book."

He partially shut the bathroom door, leaving a narrow crack that he could see through. As the prowler passed by, he sprang from behind the door and brought his right forearm down on the burglar's neck. He spun the staggering intruder around and drove a straight punch into his face. The masked man collapsed like a bad sponge cake and remained shivering in an unconscious heap. When Bill looked around for something he could use to tie him up, all he could find was the rigging for the heavy drapes that covered the large picture window in his room. He yanked the drapes down and pulled out the sash cord, which he used to bind the hands and feet of the intruder. Then he grabbed a pillow case off the bed and tore it in half, gagged the burglar with one piece, and ripped the other half into strips, which he stuffed into the elastic band of his shorts. It was only then that he realized that he was still wearing one sock.

"You ain't goin nowheres tonight, bad boy," he said quietly triumphant.

He picked up the soft purple braided rope that had adorned the drapes, coiled it up, and guessed he had about thirty feet. He fixed a honda in one end, pulled a loop, and stepped out into the hallway with the coiled rope cradled loosely in his left hand to see what in the hell was going on.

As soon as he stepped into the hall, he got rear-ended by another black-clad burglar. He took a wild swing at the burglar as he passed by but missed. The burglar tipped and then regained his balance and took off trotting down the hall. It took Bill a second to line up the runner. It was a tough toss what with the hallway being narrow, the ceiling fairly low, and the light dim, so he threw his purple loop underhand so it rolled out nicely down the hallway, caught up with the fugitive, and dropped over his head. Bill gave the cord a hard tug, snared the neck, and dallied the purple cord around the nearest doorknob. He followed the taught rope out to the struggling burglar, kicked the guy's feet out from under him, and quickly tied both his legs to his left arm with a piece of sash cord. He snuck a quick look at his wristwatch—twelve and a half seconds, not bad for a hotel corridor considering the conditions: lousy rope, narrow alley, bum knee, dim light, no trousers, and one sock. He pulled a couple of pillowcase strips out from the elastic band of his shorts and sat down on the black-clothed body to catch his breath.

He reckoned it was the first time this burglar had ever been bulldogged because he started to wiggle and scream. When he pulled off the ski mask to gag the guy, he found a girl's face instead. She wasn't bad-looking, he thought, but her face was so knotted up with anger he couldn't tell for sure. She was also kinda skinny: thirty-two, twenty-eight, thirty, just a heifer.

"Vive Quebec libre," she hissed.

"Same to you, honey," he said, smiling, as he stuffed pieces of pillowcase in her mouth.

He coiled up the purple rope and hung it over his shoulder as he limped down the hall until he found another door with a colorful hat symbol on it. When he pulled open the door, the sight inside made him dizzy: a man and a woman were lying bloody on their bed. They were moaning, so at least they were still alive.

He inched down the corridor until he hit the stairwell, and then he made his way carefully down the stairs to the second floor, hoping to surprise any burglars still in the building. When he got to a room where the door was ajar, he pushed it open and found a woman standing in front of him shaking. She had an ugly welt that ran down her face from her forehead to her chin.

"A man and a woman," she croaked, "they drugged Ivor and ransacked our room while they held me at gunpoint. They asked me where his derby hat was, and when I said I didn't know, the

woman hit me in the face with a funny-looking stick. She said to tell
the Canadian president that Canada was French forever. The funny
thing was that her French was very bad and heavily accented. I'm
still seeing stars," she said, "but I got the man good with the heel of
my boot. I could hear his toes break. He headed straight for the front
door." Then the injured woman started to shake uncontrollably and
wobble. Bill grabbed her before she hit the floor and gently lowered
her down and propped her up against the wall.

"Don't move, ma'am. I'll be back as quick as I can. I gotta see if
I can catch a couple more of them bastards, especially the guy with
the broken toes that messed you up. He probably ain't movin' too
fast just now."

Bill took another piece of pillow case out of his pocket and gave
it to the woman. "Hold this on your face, ma'am, and don't leave
this room. I'm gonna see if any of them guys, and, er, gals, are still
around."

He slid the glass balcony door open and stepped outside just in
time to see the black-clad intruder limp out the front door of the hotel
and head down the steps toward the last Citroën van. The moon
wasn't too bright, but there was one streetlight close to the curb. It
was a long toss, and he hoped he had enough rope. With plenty of
room this time, he spun his loop out so that it rose over the burglar
and dropped all the way to his ankles before he jerked it tight. The
intruder fell forward down the last step, cracked his head on the
base of one of the concrete Vailliant statues, and didn't move. The
last Citroën van screeched away from the sidewalk just as several
police cars skidded to the curb in front of the hotel. One of the cars
spun around, narrowly missing the stone Vailliant monument, while
another burned rubber as it took off in pursuit of the last van.

Bill hobbled down the stairs. His knee was throbbing again, and
his teeth were starting to hurt. He knelt over the motionless intruder
to retrieve his rope so he could return it to his room. When he looked

up, he noticed that a knot of people had gathered around him. When he lifted his hand to doff his hat, the onlookers started to applaud quietly. He stood up and reached down to search his pockets for his French phrasebook, intent on saying something modest. All he got though was a reminder that he was half naked. Luckily, he was in his best skivvies, no buttons missing or stretched out elastic band. He wanted to say something like "Aw, shucks, it wasn't nothing" in French, but instead he said, "Oh shit, I must've left my dictionary on the bed."

The gendarmes piled out of their cars, and their boss, who Bill judged was a captain from the patch on her shoulder, started immediately giving orders to the cops standing around. Several went into the hotel, another jumped into a big black Citroën and made several calls, while another hustled the crowd back into the hotel parking lot.

Bill hobbled up to the police captain, held out his hand, and introduced himself. "Bone jar, my dam." Embarrassed that he was in his skivvies and barefoot except for one sock and carrying a coil of purple rope in his hand, he was still able to manage a "Como tally voo."

The police captain blinked hard while she tried to process the image in front of her. She figured out everything except the single sock.

"Monsieur, I have called for some ambulances and the coroner. Others from the police force are on their way and will begin the search. We will have to interview you at length, but for now may I ask your name and your business here in France."

Bill stuck out his hand again. "I'm Bill Robeiro from Pylewood, California. I'm here for the International Livestock show, ma'am. I was gonna buy me some small cattle that eat a lot but don't grow much. I never expected to get in the middle of no hotel burglary."

"Inspector Dercanges," a voice from the side interrupted. "The man by the monument is dead. He fits the description of Vital Nordhoff."

"Mon dieu!" Madame Dercanges exclaimed. "Monsieur, you have killed a famous criminal with your purple rope."

"It was nothin', your honor," Bill said. "It was just a matter of me bein' in the right place at the right time."

Just then, another car pulled up, and Blondie Raimbaut jumped out. "Are you OK, Bill?"

"I'm fine, but I just remembered I left an injured girl up on the second floor. Come on, Blondie. Let's see if we can help her." Inspector Dercanges stood aghast as the two men in front of her bolted and dashed toward the hotel door, one half naked and hobbling and the other fully clothed but carrying a long stick that looked like a herdsman's trident.

When they got to the second floor, they found the injured woman struggling to get to her feet.

"Claudine, what happened?" Blondie gasped.

"They kidnapped Ivor, but they also wanted his derby hat. They beat me when I wouldn't tell them where it was. I think they were Canadians. Their French was so archaic. We must find Ivor. The thieves seemed desperate."

"Who's Ivor?" Bill asked. "Why does your door have a picture of a derby hat pasted on it?"

"Ivor Gryyffwwd is the president of the Welsh Stockman's Association," Blondie answered. "Claudine, come outside with us. The police are here along with an ambulance and several medics. They can treat the bruise on your cheek."

"Who are you?" Claudine asked, looking straight at Bill.

"He's Bill Robeiro," Blondie answered. "You were supposed to meet him at the airport."

"Sapristy, I was at Orly."

"And he was at Charles DeGaulle."

"Mr. Robeiro, you must excuse me for my error. Many guests have come to Orly, but of course, it is normal for transatlantic passengers, Americans and Canadians, to land at Charles DeGaulle. Luckily, though, Blondie has found you."

"We better get back downstairs," Bill said. "That Inspector Dercanges wasn't finished asking me questions. I don't want to land in the hoosegow my first day in France."

Back in the hotel lobby, Inspector Dercanges doled out the orders and asked the questions. "Madame, go immediately to the ambulance. They will tend to your wound. Blondie, what are you doing here? And you, monsieur," she said, turning to Bill. "May I see your passport? Then she realized he was almost naked, clothed only in his shorts and one sock. "How silly of me. Of course, you don't have your passport. How could you?"

"Why were them burglars all dressed up in black?" Bill asked, looking at the snarling girl and the groggy man who had been brought out of the hotel and were throwing up at the curb.

"It's their trademark. They are members of the infamous Vital Nordhoff gang. The gang is finished now that you have killed their leader with your rope. He was a scoundrel, and no one will weep for him."

"What'd he do that was so bad?"

"He stole hats. He was the founder of an international gang of hat thieves that was originally based in Canada but had spread all over the world."

"Never heard of them. Anyways, what's so bad about stealing hats? I stole my Cousin Donnie's hat once, but that was because he shot holes in one of mine with a twelve gauge."

"Because of him, there has been a worldwide shortage of hats, especially in cold climes. In Manitoba, a simple stocking cap costs nearly a hundred dollars. It's the theory of supply and demand.

It's thought that most body heat escapes from the head, you know, and so one may not go out in a Canadian winter without a hat. The same is true in Norway and Russia. Ah, it's also not well-known, Mr. Roberto, especially in America, but there is a huge and lucrative black market in stolen hats supported by collectors in the Middle East and China. Most of the stolen hats end up in the closets of wealthy sheiks, rich Chinese businessmen, and Colombian drug lords. Your hat, for example, might have fetched thirty-thousand dollars on the rare Western hat black market."

"No shit. Wisht I woulda known that last month when I didn't have enough money to put gas in my truck and that same thirty-thousand dollar hat was ridin' right on top my head."

When one of the cops handed Bill a bathrobe, he noticed that he was surrounded by reporters, photographers, and TV cameras. The photographers and reporters waved Blondie, Claudine, and Inspector Dercanges out of the way while lights popped and questions were hollered out. When Inspector Dercanges gave the signal, the gendarmes standing behind her formed a line and began moving the crowd toward the parking lot.

Bill excused himself and stumbled back up to his room, hoping to get some sleep. When he opened the door, he was stunned by the devastation in front of him: nightstand overturned, drapes on the floor, linens torn to shreds, and sofa upside down. He hadn't seen hotel chaos like that since the time he had stayed at the Nugget for the 1972 Reno Bull Sale.

CHAPTER 11

Pols and Flics

Bill pushed his things into a corner in his hotel room, piled up the sheets and blankets, and cleared off enough space on top of the bed to expose a patch of bare mattress for him to sleep on. He didn't even look for his pajamas. He'd tidy up later. Right then, he needed to sleep if he was going to be any good for the morning's Sommet de l'Elevage cattle show. Sprawled out on the sheet-less mattress, he quickly lapsed into dreams of the old feedlot in Pylewood. He was climbing up the steel ladder on the side of the silo with Karen Clements perched on his back. The ladder was cold and damp even though it was summer, and the star-filled night was warm. They were both eighteen and delighted in the notion that the heavens were eternal and the stars would forever shine down on kids like them. It was 1968, years before news that the universe was expanding at the speed of light had reached Pylewood. Pheromones were flying everywhere but not yet traveling at relativistic velocities. He was well along the way to surrendering himself to the sweet sensation of his dream when the telephone rang. He cursed at the interruption. When he couldn't find the pause button on his dream, he groped for the phone, hoping that if he found the phone cord, he could yank the damn thing out of the wall and keep his dream from fading into oblivion. His frenzied attempts to gather up the fleeting bits of the dream were ended by loud thumping noises on his door.

"Go away," he barked, but the only answer he got came in a muffled French/English pudding. "Monsieur Bill, open the door, s'il vous plait."

"Come back in a couple hours," he mumbled and then added his own, "see vu play."

"But it is I, Claudine Fortet. Please open the door."

"Go away, whoever you are. Let me sleep," he repeated.

The next thing he heard was the clicking sound of a key in the door.

Shit. Not again, not another gol darn burglary. "Come back tomorrow and I'll give you my hat. I'll even throw in a sock. Take my shirt and skivvies too."

Claudine Fortet swung the door open quietly, stepped over the pile of blankets, stumbled over the upturned nightstand, regained her balance, and cautiously moved bedside. She put her hand on his shoulder and gently shook it.

"You cannot sleep here any longer," she said. "The mayor of Clermont-Ferrand won't permit it. When he heard about the events of this evening, he insisted that I transfer you immediately to the executive suite at the Oceania Carlton Hotel in the center of town. He has already moved the Greek minister of agriculture down to a smaller suite to make room for you. He also insists that you have breakfast with him and Bernard DeLavoy, the manager of the Sommet, in the morning."

"Tell his honor I don't need no fancy hotel room or a French breakfast. I seen a restaurant downstairs. When I wake up, I'll grab me a cup of coffee and a couple of donuts and head straight to the exhibition hall to see the cattle. I think they're startin' with Aubracs, a breed I don't know much about."

"I don't think it's an invitation you can refuse. You know, of course, about the special relationship between France and the United States."

He thought a few seconds before he said no.

"France helped America win its independence from England. We gave you the Statue of Liberty and sent our Marquise de Lafayette to lead your Revolutionary army."

"I guess I missed that part in school. They musta covered it at roundup time."

"And you Americans have come to the aid of France in our last two wars with Germany. It is a grand association. Surely you don't want to jeopardize it." Claudine larded her invitation with a pouting smile and blue eyes bright enough to light up the darkened room.

"Oh, I 'spose not, if what you're sayin' is true," Bill said while he sat up and tried to straighten out his bad knee. "But you know I ain't got a lot of time to spend monkeyin' around here. I got work to do so's I can get back home and make sure that that Marsha Misch is feedin' Tigger, my dog."

"Good," she said, "I knew we could depend on you. Don't worry about your belongings. A policeman will gather them up and bring them over to the Oceania Hotel. I think that tomorrow Mayor Godard plans to accompany you and Monsieur DeLavoy to a private viewing of the livestock with the various breed presidents."

Oh great, Bill thought. *I'll just tell the breeders I'm only interested in their cow shit. Don't care about the animal's teats or jewel box, feed conversion efficiency, or fertility, just excretia or whatever they call it in French.*

Claudine went into the bathroom to straighten up the bandage on her cheek, while Bill searched for his clothes and boots. He found his shirt under the fallen drapes but couldn't find his trousers. When she found his trousers under the upturned sofa, she gave them a quick ironing. Once he had his trousers on, he found himself face-to-face with his boots, and he balked. He didn't want to put the damn things on in the first place, and now he had been hustled out of a warm dream, forced to change hotels, and was expected to

jam his swollen feet into a pair of tight boots. All this by a French
chick who had forgot to meet him at the airport. He thought about
borrowing some flip-flops from the Australians down on the second
floor but figured he couldn't just walk through the lobby of a classy
hotel like the Oceania with his bare feet exposed, especially since
his feet weren't in any condition to be representing the US of A or
even Pylewood. While it burned him up, he was still like most guys
his age, proud to be an American, even if he didn't know too much
about the Revolutionary War, the Declaration of Independence, or
the Articles of Confederation. In the end, he figured he really didn't
have a choice; it was clearly his duty to put on his boots.

***

The executive suite at the Oceania was a penthouse on the top
floor of the hotel with a commanding view of the surrounding
countryside. Even though it was nighttime, the lights below formed
a brilliant image of the city. His room was nice enough: big desk,
small kitchen, three TVs, and chocolates on the pillow. What he
really needed, though, was a swig or two of the Famous Grouse
along with something to chew on, even if it was only a piece of deer
jerky. The only bottle he could find was in the bathroom and had
a girl's name, Hazel Savon, on it. It was greasy-looking stuff, so he
poured a bit on his hand and took a sniff. Smelled like pesto, but
felt slippery like number-four ball-bearing grease. He had the idea
that it might help him slide his swollen feet out of his boots. A shot-
sized portion poured down the inside of a boots sure enough did
make his feet slippery, and he pulled his right foot out fairly easily.
The left one took a little more tugging, but it came out too. He filled
the bathtub halfway so he could wash Hazel's oil off, and he ended
up soaking his feet for the better part of an hour. When he couldn't

keep his eyes open any longer, he crawled into the Oceania bed and
fell asleep in a minute.

***

The telephone woke him up long after the sun had risen but
before he was really ready to ramble. When he threw back the
covers, the first thing he saw were his feet, and they sure looked
a lot smaller than they did the last time he saw them. Could have
been Hazel's Savon, but more than likely it was the good soaking
they had got before he bedded down. He waited for a few more rings
before he picked up the telephone. The voice at the other end was
deep and clear.

"Monsieur, this is the front desk. Mayor Godard and International
Manager Bernard DeLavoy are in the lobby and wish you to join
them for breakfast in the Platini Room. After breakfast, they are
hoping you will accompany them on a tour of the livestock pens at
the Sommet de l'Elevage."

Bill shook his head for three or four seconds before he answered,
"Sure, but tell them to start without me. No sense in them havin' to
eat cold bacon on my account. I still gotta get my boots on, shave,
and brush my teeth."

When Bill walked out of the elevator on the ground floor twenty
minutes later, he found a tall dapper middle-aged man and a shorter
slightly rumpled one waiting for him."

"I am Bernard DeLavoy," the shorter one said. "I am very happy
to make your acquaintance."

"And I also," the tall one said. "I am Don-Luc Godard, the mayor.
DeLavoy is the manager of the show."

"Pleased to meet you both," Bill said. He looked down at his
watch before he thrust out his right hand for the handshakes. "Sorry

I'm late, your honors, but I couldn't find my shorts or a sock to match the one I was wearing. A policeman brought over my clothes last night and stashed them somewhere where I couldn't find them. I hope you didn't wait for me and went ahead and ate your breakfast."

"Never, no question," the mayor said. "We would never abandon you to eat by yourself. You are a hero in France and an American guest. We French have been enthralled with America since the days of your colonization and then your inspiring war for independence from the English."

"And with your philosophers, your revolution, and the settlement of the West," DeLavoy added. "So, Monsieur Robeiro, we are privileged to have you, a true son of the American West, a scion of pioneers and cowboys, in Clermont-Ferrand. Allow you to eat alone. Never! If I could find the key to the city, you'd have it in your hand right now. Unfortunately, I think we gave it to an American cyclist when the Tour de France came through here, and alas, we never saw it again."

"To tell the truth, I never thought too much about our French connection," Bill said. "Most folks in Pylewood, where I come from, don't know too much about France. Me, I ain't nothin' special, especially a hero. Made plenty of mistakes in my life already, and I ain't even quite fifty yet. And I'm no pioneer either, but I have been somethin' of a cowboy, more or less. Pushed around cattle from Idaho to Northern California, but I wouldn't make too much of that either. Plenty of guys back home done the same things as me and maybe done 'em more and better."

"Have they ever roped a famous criminal and stopped a burglary?" Bernard DeLavoy protested. "If the Nordhoff gang had succeeded in their terrible crime, think of our embarrassment. We might have had to cancel the Sommet de l'Elevage. Even if we had been able to save our show, the crime would have been a black mark not only on Clermont-Ferrand and the Auvergne but also on all of France."

"Come, let's eat. The hotel has a breakfast buffet for the guests in the Platini Room," the mayor said, pointing. "Follow me."

"Maybe I'll try the Platini if it's already cooked."

"It's pasta on a tiny plat, a specialty of the region," DeLavoy chimed in. Then he couldn't hold back a smile. "No, it's not food but the name of a famous football player, Michel Platini. His goal against Italy in the 1970 World Cup is often called the greatest soccer goal of all time, at least in France. However, the Platini that is the namesake of this room is a Charolais bull and, like the soccer player who he's named for, the best of an entire decade, or maybe even half a century. You can see his picture over there by the coffee machine."

"What if I just stay here in the hotel for a while and sneak over to the show a little later when most of the people have gone home. I ain't much good in front of a lot of people I don't know. I can be pretty funny at a party, but that's usually after a few drinks and with friends. I'm kinda afraid I'll make a fool of myself if I go over there this morning. Besides, I don't speak no French to speak of, and even my English ain't nothin' to brag on. No, thanks, guys, I think I'd rather stay here and have some cornflakes in my room."

"Come, come, my boy, you'll be fine," DeLavoy said. "People only want to get a look at you and maybe take your picture. And to be honest, I want to be seen with you. No one will really care what you say."

"I'd like to get in a picture with you myself," the mayor said. "It might be good for my political career. Standing next to a celebrity will cause people to remember me. When they see your picture, they will see me at your side."

"I think you guys are just tryin' to make me feel good. When I pitched my no-hitter in high school, Mr. Cimini, the principal, made a big fuss about it, but it didn't help me none. I still got bad grades, and I couldn't even get a baseball scholarship."

"This is France, my boy," DeLavoy said. "Your hero status will open many doors for you. For example, after the press conference, I'm sure you will get substantial offers to appear on French television and also to promote products from tractors to groceries. A man like you, larger than life, a hero who lassoed a group of terrorists on the eve of the biggest livestock show in France, maybe Europe, will not go unnoticed. And of course, you will be paid well for your commercial appearances. Surely, this is also true in America."

***

When they finally got to exhibition hall at the Sommet, a crowd was waiting at the door for them. Dozens of questions were shouted out at Bill. Monsieur DeLavoy and Mayor Godard translated them as fast as they could:

"How do you like France? What will you do while you are here? How many hectares is your ranch? How long will you stay in France? How many criminals have you captured with your rope? Will you keep the purple rope?"

Bill said that so far he liked France but hadn't been there for very long and seen much. He pointed out that he had seen the airport and then fallen asleep on the train. He was trying to learn French, and he was already improving. He didn't think it was going to be too hard and hoped to finish reading *Madam Bovary* in the next couple of weeks. He tried to explain that he didn't own ranches and only fattened cattle that he didn't own. As far as roping criminals, he had never done it before, but he had a lot of practice roping his nieces and nephews. When he ran out of answers and DeLavoy and Godard got tired of translating, the director signaled the gendarmes to herd the reporters out of the room. After that, he took Bill over to a small private bar where a number of the event sponsors had gathered.

Representatives from France Soir, Caisse Epargna, Charolais France, Delaval, Danone, Michelin, Sersia, Fournier, Boehringer-Ingelheim, ABS Global, Lamborghini, and Landini approached Bill, introduced themselves, and proffered their business cards. The Michelin representative flat out offered Bill a chance to make a couple of large-tire commercials

"A large hombre for giant tires," he said. "It wouldn't take too much of your time. Stand on a giant excavator tire with your hat on and the purple rope in one hand and say that Michelin tires are just as good on your car as they are on the world's largest tractors."

Photographers took more pictures with Bill standing between Mayor Godard and Event Chairman DeLavoy. They mayor presented Bill with a large cloth sack imprinted with the Clermont-Ferrand coat of arms and had him dump in all the business cards and trinkets he had collected.

"Hang on to these," DeLavoy told him. "Get yourself a business agent and profit from your fame while you can."

***

Bill didn't get back to the Oceania until well after dark. He slept fitfully, fishing and groping for Karen's interrupted dream but ending up dreaming about the bald tires on his pickup truck until a knock at the door woke him up.

"Who's there?" he called out from under the Oceania's fancy green bed covers.

"I am Officer DePluson from the gendarmerie. I would like to take you to the police prefecture so you can record your statement and fill out some forms for Inspector Dercanges."

Bill thought for a second about what he ought to do. He was still exhausted from the day before: lunch with the Sommet's major sponsors, an afternoon tour of the Michelin museum and factory on the other side of town, dinner at the hotel with the region's teachers of agriculture, and, finally, drinks with the city fathers and directors of tourism. And his cloth bag was nearly full of business cards and brochures. They had kept him so busy that he hadn't had a chance to take a careful look at any cattle. He just wasn't used to talking that much.

"Would you like some breakfast before we go?" the French cop asked.

"I'd like a jelly Bismarck, raspberry if you can get it," he finally said, "and a cup of coffee, no cream or sugar, but with a shot of whiskey or calvados in it."

"Yes, I'll see if that's possible. Perhaps you wouldn't mind a croissant, café au lait, and a shot of cognac instead. It will be easier and quicker."

Bill hoped he wouldn't have to face any more reporters. Yesterday's reporters had questioned him about life in Pylewood, his youth, cattle ranching, and his impressions of France. Did he know that Michelin tires were made in the United States? Did he think Americans would use French toothpaste? Who did he think was a better president, John Kennedy or Bill Clinton? Then they had insisted on taking him out to a bar where they drank wine and ate frog legs, which the reporters called grenoolies.

When they finished breakfast, Bill had to admit to Officer DePluson that it was pretty dang good. The croissant was more like a bear claw than a donut, and the cognac, while not as tasty as his usual Kessler's, had the same amount of kick. After he brushed all the crumbs off his trousers, Officer DePluson led him out through the hotel to the curb, where a long black unmarked Citroën was waiting for them. After a brief ride, their uniformed driver pulled up in front of an imposing stone building: Doric columns, wide stairs up to the tall doors, and a pair of matched rearing stallions at the entrance. *Prefecture de Surite,* the sign on the door read.

"Kinda reminds me of the cathedral in Rouen," Bill said as he and Officer DePluson coasted across the polished marble floor.

"I've never been there," Officer DePluson said. "Isn't it true that people never see the important places in their own country?"

"Oh, I haven't been there neither. I just read about it in *Madame Bovary.*"

"Bonjour, madam, comment allez-vous," Bill said as soon as Inspector Dercanges opened her office door.

"Ah, you speak French, monsieur. That is very good, but I think for this deposition, we can speak English. First, I must apologize for the inconvenience you have suffered in our city. You came to France to see cattle, and on your first night in France, someone tried to rob you and the rest of the international guests at the Hotel Gergovie."

Bill took a long look at Inspector Dercanges. He hadn't formed much of an impression of her in the nighttime darkness of the burglary. Sitting behind her desk, she reminded him of Ms. DeGason, his seventh-grade social studies teacher: roughly the same age, red hair, and same face, only filled out a little more. Nose a little more rounded. Never had thought much about it before, but DeGason was probably a French name.

"That's OK, ma'am. Stuff like that happens all the time in Pylewood, where I'm from. Back home, it's usually about drugs or women. Tryin' to steal people's hats, though, that's a new one on me."

"Yes," Inspector Dercanges answered. "For some people, collecting becomes an obsession, a sickness that destroys any sense of danger and overrides all concerns for ethics. Traditionally, people have collected such things as postage stamps, coins, and classic cars, but the world has changed: postage stamps now come with contact glue on the back, coins are minted in base metals, and classic cars contribute to global warming. Hats, on the other hand, are not only useful but also very collectible."

"I still don't get it. Why would anybody want my old hat? What's so dang special about it?"

"The way it's been used," Inspector Dercanges answered. "It's been worn on great American cattle drives and in gunfights and saloon brawls. It has the flavor, scent, and sweat of the Wild West on it. I can almost smell it myself."

"Well, ma'am, truth is, mostly, I only wear this here hat when I go dancin' or to weddings and funerals or like now when I go to a police station. Most of the time, this ole hat hangs on a hook in my trailer."

"Whatever," Inspector Dercanges said. "In the words of our great philosopher, Blaise Pascal, 'It isn't what is that matters. It's what man thinks is.' Hats are history in felt and straw. Besides, they are practical. You can't carry around your stamp collection or drive your classic car to the MonoPrix, but you can always wear a hat to keep the rain or sun off your head, carry water or fruit, or cover up a bad hairdo. Please, monsieur, may I look at your hat."

Bill popped the gray Stetson off his head and gave the inside a quick look. "Sure," he said, "but lemme wipe off the inside first. It's probably still sweaty from last night."

He pulled out a red handkerchief from his pocket and spun it around inside the band and then passed the hat to Inspector Dercanges. Ariane Dercanges inspected the gray felt carefully, studied the writing on the inside band, and took note of the metal buckle on the outside band that had the word EDDY inscribed on it.

"You may not know it, monsieur, but you are wearing an extremely valuable hat. First, it has been designed by Chris Eddy of Dallas, Texas, who has been making hats since 1929. Second, it is lined in satin, and third, it is very large: XXX. Normally, since it is in good condition, has been properly cared for, and is unusually large, it would sell for anywhere between five and ten thousand euros. However, now that it is famous because you were wearing it when you roped Vital Nordhoff and broke up the *Chapeau Noir* ring, I think this hat of yours might fetch a hundred-thousand euros at auction. Just think how much Emir Musa ben Ali, the Abu Dhabi sheik, would enjoy wearing a hot hat such as this in his palace and to parties."

"Holy shit, er, I mean, shoot, ma'am. That's a lot more than I got for bein' the best all-around cowboy at Oakdale. I also got a dirty old Escalon Livestock Market hat at home. What do you think that's worth?"

"I think the market has dropped out of the baseball-cap racket," Inspector Dercanges said. "Cheap Chinese exports have flooded the market. Old hats from the baseball major leagues are still valuable, and any hat made in America is worth something. Whimsical hats like a Kubota tractor hat made in Orange City, Iowa, is very much sought after, even though it has a plastic strap in the back. It's the whole idea of a Japanese tractor company buying marketing hats in America that gives it its value."

"What about the gang that attacked our hotel? I'd say they had funny accents, even though I'm just now tryin' to learn French and only been here a couple of days."

"They called themselves the Black Hat Gang, Chapeau Noir, in French. They started out as a French Canadian group dedicated to furthering independence for Quebec. They wanted to encourage the wearing of the beret, so they gathered up other kinds of hats— baseball caps, brimmed felt hats, and even straw sombreros—and burned them in big bonfires in rural Quebec. When Vital Nordhoff came along—he is the man you killed—he decided it was stupid to destroy good hats when they could be sold to help finance the separatist movement. When he found that many people outside of

North America collected hats and were willing to pay high prices for them, he went international."

"Nordhoff don't sound like a French name to me."

"Nordhoff was his nom de plume, so to speak. It means north court in German. His origins are sketchy, but we think he was born at home in rural Quebec. Viktor Cornfeldt is the name on his baptismal certificate."

"What about the guy that I caught in my room and tied up? Is he a Canadian too?"

"No, monsieur, he is a Frenchman, a renegade chemistry professor from Corsica. His criminality is completely apolitical. Prolonged exposure to seven-membered heterocyclic rings in his laboratory at the Université de Corse left him feeling that the top of his head was always cold and that he needed a warmer hat. Vital Nordhoff met him at a scientific meeting and easily recruited him for the gang. We hope that a few months at our *Centre de Malaise Chemique* will put him on the road to recovery."

"What's a seven-member heterocyclic ring?" Bill asked Inspector Dercanges.

"I'm not sure," the svelte French cop answered, "but they are widely abused in Corsica."

"What about the gal I bulldogged on the second floor of the hotel? She was pretty scary," Bill said.

"She is Cecilia Citronet from Ciotat, a resort community on the Mediterranean not too far from Marseilles. She is the last in a long line of Vital Nordhoff's girlfriends, a former gymnast and professional oyster farmer. Her association with the gang was purely romantic, and as far as we can tell, she was completely uninterested in the hats she stole for Nordhoff. She is looking at a long stay in prison because she was carrying a nunchucku, which is classified as a dangerous weapon in France."

"I saw Claudine Fortet, the secretary from the Association of Livestock Breeding, last night," Bill said. "She still had that nasty welt on the side of her face."

"Oui, she is a very brave girl. We had the doctor examine her last night. There were no broken bones, and she should heal without any scars. The bad news is that we haven't been able to find Ivor Gryyffwwdd, her Welsh friend, who was kidnapped. A taxi driver claims he saw three suspicious persons, all with ski masks and clad in black, push a taller man into a van parked at the curb. That is all we have to go on. However, we did lift several sets of fingerprints from the door handle, and we think one of them belonged to a Vilma Valli, a Finnish national from Vaasa, another of Vital Nordhoff's girlfriends. We are still trying to ascertain the authenticity of the print."

Inspector Dercanges shrugged and pushed a paper toward Bill.

"If you will sign this paper, I think we will be finished, and you can resume your business here in Clermont-Ferrand. On behalf of the French government and our president, I apologize for all the inconvenience and thank you for your service to the Republic. Incidentally, there is an Interpol reward for information leading to the arrest of Vital Nordhoff and another from the European Community for the interdiction of the Black Hat gang."

She passed Bill a sealed envelope.

"No thanks," he said. "I already got my money from the Michelin girl yesterday."

"No, No. This is another reward. Interpol doubled your reward because you did more than just provide information, you also terminated the bugger, as Chief Inspector Jane Tennyson might say in *Prime Suspect*. I also have a pile of letters and contracts from people wanting you to endorse products and appear at stores throughout France."

"You mean like Tony Parker?"

"Yes, maybe for the moment, you are even more famous in France, but I must run now. This is the week I do performance appraisals. Perhaps you might use some of your newfound wealth to buy me dinner before you leave Clermont-Ferrand. Tomorrow evening would be perfect. I usually finish work about 18:30, 6:30 PM for you. Agent DePluson is waiting in front of the building with a car. I've instructed her to drive you wherever you wish to go today and to pick you up and drop you off here tomorrow evening. She speaks some English, which she can improve by having some conversation with you. A bientôt."

Just as promised, Bill found Agent DePluson sitting behind the wheel of the black Citroën at the curb reading a paperback book.

"Mind if I sit up here in the front seat with you?" Bill asked. "It looks kinda lonely back there in the rear seat."

"No, no," she said, her stern official face busting into a tilted French grin. "Usually, I am restricted to chauffeuring petty white-collar criminals who, of course, must sit in the rear, so I am welcome to have a passenger of note up front with me. I am recently new on the force, and you are the first important personality that I have driven."

"Don't worry, mamsel. I ain't all that important," Bill said while he looked embarrassed. "People are making a big fuss about me now, but it won't last too long. Next week, I'll be back to being just another beat-up old cowboy. Say, I got a dinner date with your boss tomorrow. Problem is, I didn't bring any fancy clothes with me. Never figured I was gonna get wined and dined. You know where I can buy me some nice duds? Maybe some dress pants, nice shirt, and some regular shoes. My boots have been killin' me since I left home."

"There are some shops for clothing and shoes near the Centre Jaude, which is near the Rue Blatin, not too far from your hotel. Galleries Lafayette is a large department store with a wide selection of men's suits, socks, trousers, and shoes, some from famous designers. But beware, it is also expensive. My boyfriend buys shirts at Cafe' Coton, which is nearby, and of course, there are a couple of men's stores in the area, but I know little about them. There is also a MonoPrix, where clothes are more cheap but also not so stylish. It is where the Rue Blatin makes a big curve to become Rue Desaix."

***

When he got back to his room, Bill pulled out the envelope Inspector Dercanges had given him to make sure he had enough dinero to buy the clothes he needed. The envelope was jam-packed with French bills: all five-hundred-euro notes, maybe fifty of them. He didn't bother to count it but pulled out a couple and stuffed the rest in the sock where he had put the Michelin money. He collapsed on the bed and grabbed his book. He read for a while, napped for half an hour, and then went out to buy shoes and clothes even though he didn't have a real good idea of what he was looking for. *How does a guy dress for a date with a high-ranking French cop?* And he didn't have a clue about where to take Inspector Dercanges for dinner, although he figured something special was probably in order. And he was clueless about prices. Clermont-Ferrand wasn't Paris, but he still reckoned there were some expensive restaurants in town. He wanted to take Inspector Dercanges someplace nice but didn't want to be a big showoff just because all the sudden he had come into a bunch of money. His dad had always told him that if he ever made big money, he should spread it around, but in a way so's nobody noticed.

As far as feeding cops went, Headley Richards, back in Pylewood, was the only cop Bill had ever broken bread with, and that was only the liver-and-onions Friday Special at the Pylewood Café. Headley never made much money from police work, although he did score a free donut every now and then. Even though Inspector Dercanges was some sort of boss, he figured she was probably on a tight budget too, so he should treat her to something nice. Anyway, he had a whole day to think about it.

CHAPTER 12

The Perfect Cow

Claudine Forte stared into the mirror and ran her index finger along the scarlet welt on her cheek. It was healing slowly. She thought about the American cowboy who had materialized out of nowhere and who, it now seemed, was going to be her responsibility for a while. He seemed gentle, even a bit dainty, for such a big man, funny, brave, and *tres charmant* for an American. Robert DeLavoy, the manager of the Sommet, had asked her to do her best to make the rest of Bill's stay in Clermont-Ferrand safe and pleasant. In a way, she welcomed the change and respite from the growing boredom of her daily routine.

After the burglary, she had moved from the Hotel Gergovie to another hotel that wasn't as grand as the Oceania Hotel, where Bill was staying, but within walking distance to it. Her mission this morning was to meet Bill in the lobby of the Oceania, make sure that he got some breakfast, and then shepherd him on a tour of the *Sommet de l'Elevage*. She fussed with her hair for a minute or two, grabbed a light jacket, and headed out the door for the walk over to the Oceania.

"*Bon jour,*" she called out when she saw him exit the elevator and look her way. She offered him her left cheek and then the right for the customary kiss when they met, and he held out his hand.

"Have you had breakfast yet?"

"No, ma'am, I slept in. Guess I'm finally gettin' used to the time change."

"What did you do yesterday?" she asked as she led him to the breakfast buffet.

"Went to the police station, answered a lot of questions, picked up my reward, and went shopping."

"What did you buy?"

"Got some new shoes," he said, pointing down at his feet, "A lot easier to get on and off than my ole boots and more normal for France, I reckon."

"What else?"

"A shirt, slacks, and some socks. I still need a jacket and a tie I guess. Seems like people dress up pretty formal around here."

"What are slacks?" she asked. She furrowed her brow while she thought. "You must mean trousers or pants."

Bill nodded.

"Go ahead, take a plate and load it up as if you were at a HomeTown Buffet. They have fresh eggs and a cooker, fruit, charcuterie, croissants, and bread, and of course a nice selection of cheeses. There's also a coffeemaker that you can program to make a cup of coffee just the way you like it."

"Don't know if I'm up to any kind of programming this early in the morning, Claudine. At home, the waitress at the Pylewood Café takes your order and tells Jesus, the cook, how to make the eggs and then makes the coffee herself. Takes care of it all for the guys."

"I'm happy to cook you an egg and fix the coffee. How do you want your eggs: soft or hardboiled, and your coffee: *au lait* or American style?"

"Don't matter. Whatever you pick is OK," Bill said and ambled over to the counter, where he grabbed a couple of croissants, four maroon slices that looked like some kind of bologna, and fished out a spoonful of something from a large bowl that he guessed was fruit cocktail. For a while, he trolled the serving bowl with the slotted spoon, hoping to catch a couple of maraschino cherries. When he gave up, he went back to the table where Claudine was waiting. He sat down and sliced open the croissants and placed a couple of pieces of meat in the space between the halves.

"I been eating croissants since I got to France, thinkin' they might be even better with a slice of ham or salami on them."

Claudine, enthralled with the procedure, followed his example.

"I ordered café au lait for both of us," she said. It is normal for a French breakfast."

"You didn't happen to see any mayonnaise did you?" Bill asked.

"Why?" she asked.

"Our sandwiches are gonna be kinda dry without a little mayo, don't you think?"

"Yes, you are probably correct. I will ask the attendant if they have some in the kitchen."

"Naw, it's OK. How do you know about HomeTown Buffet?"

"There's one next to the US Army base in Weinstampfen, where I did an internship. What would you like to see at the Sommet?"

"I guess I'd like to get a good look at the red cattle. Hrubel Kwasnik thinks that red cattle with black hooves will be the best for our breeding program."

"Beef or dairy?" she asked. Bill paused for a long time. "You're gonna think I'm crazy, Claudine, but really neither one. I'm not interested in milk or meat, just poop. I don't know how you say it in French."

"You must mean manure. We call it *fumier*, among other things," she said with a single-syllable laugh. "You mean to tell me that you came all the way to France to find manure. Visitors think our perfumes are magnificent, and our cheeses delicious, and they come great distances to smell them, and we hope buy them, but I've never heard of anyone coming here for our *fumier*. I guess it's a matter of taste, or maybe I should say smell."

"Yeah, I seen plenty of it in the duty-free shop when I was lookin' for you in the airport. Stunk up the place real bad even though it was sealed up in bottles."

"I'm surprised. They usually don't have it in the duty-free shop. Oh"—she laughed—"you must mean the perfume. Although, the same can probably be said of our manure. Anyway manure is worldwide, and it's all the same, n'est pas."

"That's where you're wrong, sweetheart. My friend Rudy Kwasnik can tell you what the cow had for breakfast and what she had for dinner with one sniff. Trust me for now. I'll explain the details later. But me and my friends back home in Pylewood want to get some cattle that make a lot of manure. It also has to be a certain kind that carries a bunch of special microbes. It kinda means that the cows we're after probably eat like crazy but don't gain weight or make a lot of milk."

"You mean that when we evaluate cattle, we will be looking at our data upside-down, favoring low-average weight gain, mediocre weaning weights, and meager milk production. C'est tres bizarre."

"Yep. You got the idea."

"So the less milk a cow makes, the more we shall like her? The skinnier the cow, the better?"

"Trust me, Claudine. It's all about the manure."

"Finish your coffee. The Aubrac judging will start in twenty minutes. We'll talk more about it while we walk to the car. I think maybe Salers will be the breed of choice. They are red, rustic, and reliable, and I know the breed very well. I started my career in agriculture working for the Salers breed association."

"You think I could grab another croissant before we go? They're real good. And yeah, we might end up wanting to buy genetics from what your normal ranchers think is their poorest animals. It ain't my idea, Claudine. Rudy Kwasnik is the crazy genius back home in Pylewood who thought all this up."

"Is he the man that arranged your trip?"

"Yep."

"But he knows nothing about cattle. I knew this quickly from his e-mail."

"Well, that's why I'm here, honey. I'm supposed to be the cow expert. While Kwasnik don't know nothin' about the cow herself, he knows plenty about her *fumier*."

"This may turn out to be very complicated," Claudine lamented. "In the Auvergne, the home of red cattle, no one keeps their poor-looking animals. They would be so ashamed of ugly cattle that they would dispose of them as quickly as they could and probably do it in secret."

"Same as back home in the USA, except we try to sell our poor-looking cattle to computer millionaires who want to raise organic beef. And some folks I heard of keep livestock for pets."

"Even if we find the kind of cattle you describe, you say we will have to do all our work in secret. Why?"

"'Cause this is a top-secret project, sweetheart. We don't want no one stealing our idea and getting rich on it before we get our share. Rudy calls it agspionage. It goes on all the time. The guy that invented the medicated slow-release plastic ear tag never made a nickel. It's like stealin' secrets for bombs or maps for old gold mines, except in this here case it's a secret manure paint. Don't ask me no more. I already told you way too much. I got to be super careful because France already stole a lot of American secrets like airplanes, television, and cartoons."

"For your information, Sir, the Frères Lumiere invented television, Louis Bleriot built the first the airplane, and Jim Perry drew the first comic strip."

"See, that's what I mean," Bill said. "Anyways, we'll probably want to buy semen and embryos instead of live animals."

"Embryo transfer requires skill and experience and is time-consuming even under the best conditions," Claudine responded. "Doing it in secret will just add another degree of difficulty."

"Naa, I seen it done a couple of times. Didn't look that hard. You flush a pregnant cow to get her embryos and then stick one of them in another cow through a hole you punch in her side. If you ain't ready to do the implant, you freeze the embryo and wait till you're ready. I figure I can take the embryos back with me to California and get Manual Fargas, the retired Cadillac salesman, to help me plant 'em," Bill said as he pulled out his red handkerchief and dusted the croissant flakes off his chin and moustache.

"Optimist," Claudine said. "It will take at least five time-consuming steps just to get the embryos. And what does selling Cadillacs have to do with transplanting embryos?"

"I don't know. I just know he's good at it. Maybe you have to have soft hands for both jobs."

"First, we'll have to find a proper semen donor. Then we must collect his semen and find the right cows to inseminate. In this case, we are only interested in cows that are genetic freaks." Claudine giggled and then exploded with laughter. "And having accomplished all this, we still have to flush the donor cows, collect and store the embryos, and ship them to America."

"I guess I never really thought that hard about it. That's what my second wife always complained about. I started doin' stuff before I ever thought things through."

"Let's go to the Sommet and see what we can find in the way of ugly cattle. Don't worry, though, I think it will be great fun to try something that has never been attempted before in the history of animal science. Normally, our goal would be to get eight or ten embryos of the same sex: females for a dairy or males for a beef herd.

I have no idea which is best for fumier." This time, her laugh had multiple syllables.

"Darn it, Claudine, now yer laughin' at me. I bet my two partners back home are laughing at me too. They didn't only give me the hardest job, but the funniest one too. I didn't expect to have people laughing at me in France already. I just now got here."

Claudine put her hand over her mouth as an apologetic gesture.

"What are your partners doing besides laughing?" she asked.

"One is collecting dirt and the other beeswax. Dang simple jobs compared to what I'm up against."

"Don't you already have these things in America?"

"Sure, but it's just like the fumier. Rudy is very particular about each ingredient. One guy by the name of Jim Delahunt is going to China to get special dirt called loess, I'm here in France lookin' for cow poop, and Rudy Kwasnik himself is supposed to be going to the Czech Republic to get the beeswax."

"Good, now I understand everything," Claudine said, looking upward, trying to hide her huge smile and keep from laughing by shaking her head back-and-forth. "I know we can do it, whatever it is. It will just take time. As they say in Gascony, 'Always look on the sunny side of life.' The number and variety of these tasks will give you a chance to visit different and interesting places in France. For example, the embryo laboratory is in Limoges, the red cows with black noses are in the Cantal, and I have an idea that you will find the best donor bulls for your purposes in Provence or Languedoc. I know for sure you will enjoy experiencing all these places."

"Where's Languedoc?" Bill asked.

"In the south of France, west of Provence, where Blondie Raimbaut comes from."

"Come to think of it, Blondie did say something about the black bulls they raise in the Camargue. Says they're exceedingly intelligent and even have a sense of humor."

"I don't think anyone has ever bred a smart skinny red Salers cow with a witty black Camargue bull. It will be an historical event. The product might be a red animal with black spots that sings and tells droll stories."

"If they're real smart, maybe we can train the offsprings to poop in a bucket," Bill said.

"It would save a lot of time at the other end."

"Why not? Blondie tells me that the Camargue horses do it. And cattle are supposed to be much smarter than horses. Maybe cows can even learn to milk themselves. The milking parlors keep getting more robotized. Why not teach the cows to run the milking machines themselves?"

"Are they clever enough to do it?"

"I'd bet on it. I've run across plenty of cows that are smarter than some of my friends."

"Even if you did breed supersmart cows, I don't see how they could milk themselves."

"I seen a circular milking parlor at the AgExpo in Tulare not more than five years ago where one guy sitting at a computer milked thirty cows at a time. It didn't seem all that hard. All you'd have to do to teach a cow to milk herself would be to get her to step into a stall whenever she felt like bein' milked. Once in the stall, she could push her nose against a green button that would start the robot working and a red button when she felt like stopping. Once the milk was extracted, the robot would pull the milking machine off her teats and sprinkle a little grain on the other side of the door, so she would get the idea to leave. If she were stupid or asleep, she'd get a little electric jolt to remind her to go home."

"I think we are getting ahead of ourselves," Claudine cautioned. "Let's go to the show. That's why you came here, right? Ceemensee, France's largest artificial breeding company, has an exhibit on the concourse, and their technical representatives are sure to be on the prowl. We can stop and talk to them about the specifics of artificial breeding."

"Claudine, remember not to say nothing about us bein' interested in the fumier. We got to keep it a secret for now. All we need from Ceemensee is practical info on how to artificially fertilize the embryo, flush it, and store it and a list of the equipment that we'll need."

As Claudine suspected, the Ceemensee representatives were more eager to sell them a whole embryo-transfer package (off-the-shelf semen or embryos and their technicians to inseminate and implant) than they were to share any of their expertise. They were quick to brag on the quality of their product: champion bulls with low birth weights, high growth rates, gargantuan scrotal circumferences, and colossal rib eyes—all stuff Bill wasn't interested in.

***

"How do you guys make sure you always get the semen labeled right?" Bill asked one representative, a wide flaccid fellow with thick dairyman's fingers. "What happens if I get a big-boned Charolais calf stuck in one of my thrifty Angus cows?"

"Impossible. It's never happened," the Ceemensee rep said. "All our sample numbers are triple-redundantly quality controlled. Our system is computerized, digitized, and prioritized. We've never mixed up samples in the entire history of the company, except for the time a summer student labeled a straw of Crème d'Argent as Champaigne d'Argent. It was a regrettable but understandable mistake because rabbit semen straws are so small that you can barely see the labels with the naked eye, let alone read them. An experienced technician would have used a magnifying glass."

The representative did reveal some interesting details when he tried to sell Bill and Claudine some articles of clothing from

Service Extraordinaire, the company's fall line of semen-collecting apparel. He urged them to attend the fashion show later in the day, which would feature their latest coverall styles: seven designer colors, alpaca-linen blend fabric, specially sized pockets to hold a dozen of the most popular-length semen straws, a holster that held Ceemensee's latest Penimatic semen collector, and a set of nose clamps on an elastic lanyard.

"Come and look at our semen-capturing devices," the salesman said while motioning for them to follow him. "We carry all the major capturing systems, including SnugFit's artificial vagina, Doit Industries digital manipulation, and Volts Aplenty electro-ejaculator systems."

"Excuse me," Claudine said to the salesman. "But I promised my granny in Grenoble that I'd call at precisely 11:30 AM. She hasn't been feeling well of late."

Bill said he didn't want to hear anything more about digital manipulation and passed on electro-ejaculation when the representative told him it was used mostly for lions and elephants. That left artificial vaginas or AVs, a collection technique he thought he might be able to live with. The representative was happy to show him the company's new line of AV's called the Jet Collection, named not for the speed of the operation, but rather for a bull that had sired over fifty-thousand offspring. When the rep started talking about collecting chinchilla semen, Bill felt like he had learned enough, so he excused himself so he could go find Claudine, and they could go to the Maine-Anjou show. He found her several booths up the line of vendors in the clutches of another reproduction salesman who was pressing her with the notion that detecting estrus was the critical step in all phases of semen capture, insemination, embryo flushing, and transplanting and was a technique best done by a skilled human, dozens of whom were employed by Polzonitza, his firm in Poznan. He also stressed Polzonitza's expertise in shipping frozen embryos, explaining that Polzonitza had the world's only long-life packaging material. When Claudine saw Bill, she turned and waved and then skedaddled when the Polzonitza representative relaxed his grip on her arm.

"How did it go?" she asked.

"I think I'll buy one of them AVs to take back home and lease to my friends down at Don Gusto's Bar. I guess I'll need to buy a couple: goat-sized for Delahunt and bison-sized for my cousin. How about you?"

"Polzonitza has a special Sommet de l'Elevage sale price for estrus checking. I promised them I would think about it. The salesman also enticed me into signing up for a special drawing for one of their patented, long-distance embryo shipping containers, and ten Polzonitza baseball caps."

"I wouldn't mind having the baseball caps," Bill said, "and I haven't even started to think about shipping, but I don't think we want a bunch of nosy Polish-speaking breeding technicians hangin' around our cows. They might get suspicious if they saw us spending a lot of money on skinny livestock. Speaking of which, let's go look at some."

The two of them headed for the livestock pavilion to look at cattle. They searched most of the pens but couldn't find a single animal that didn't have a huge butt, strong legs, a regal head, and a straight back. Black, white, red, and spotted, there wasn't one that came close to meeting Rudy Kwasnik's criteria of slow growth, low milk production, poor marbling, and extreme intelligence.

"I didn't see any *fumier* to evaluate in any of them pens. Not a single lump." Bill said. "I reckon that either the handlers scooped it up before it hit the ground or that French show cattle only shit once or twice a week."

Heading back along the concourse toward the parking lot, Bill spied Blondie Raimbaut in the center of a gaggle of tall light-haired people clustered around the Bouche de Rhone booth. When their tour guide finally got the group moving to the next exhibit, Bill and Claudine moved in to greet their friend.

"Whatever you're givin' away, I want some," Bill said.

"Scandinavian dairymen, mostly Danish. They're interested in our winter feed practices."

"They could probably use some of them hairy Scottish cows too. A guy I know had good luck with them in the Sierra foothills."

"I'm heading back to Arles in a couple of days, Bill. Why don't you come with me? We'll do some riding, maybe some shooting, and drink pastis."

"Can't come right now, Blondie," Bill answered. "Me and Claudine got a bunch of small jobs to do. How's about we meet up two or three weeks from now?" Bill said, nodding toward Claudine, who had joined them.

"Absolutely. Trains run all the time. Just let me know when you're coming, and I'll pick you up at one of the stations: probably Avignon or Arles or maybe even Hyeres. Good to see you, Claudine. Glad to see the two of you together. That's a nasty-looking bruise on your cheek."

"It's getting better fast, Blondie. Is there anything interesting over there in the pens?"

"Aubracs. A guy from Colorado wants to import some. He likes their feet and size. Thinks they'll do well in the Rockies."

"How's their feed conversion?" Bill asked with a wink at Claudine.

"Not all that great in the feedlot, but they'll survive a cold winter on what they can find in the snow."

"Will you be coming with Bill to the Camargue?" Blondie asked Claudine.

"I don't think so. I have very much paperwork to do in Paris. I'll put Bill on the train in Aurillac and leave the rest to you. Don't lose him out there in the marshes. We still have some work to finish."

CHAPTER 13

Dinner with the Cop

Agent DePluson buzzed Bill from the lobby at the Oceania Hotel at eighteen hours exactly. French time: it was something he would have to get used to. In a way, the French system made more sense than having twelve numbers with PM and AM. Getting himself up and down the elevator, traversing the hotel lobby, and getting into Officer DePluson's squad car turned out to be harder than he had imagined. He tripped entering the elevator, banged his elbow on a bronze statue of Nicolas Podgorny in the lobby, and bumped his head squeezing into the car.

"Attention," the young policière admonished. "If you arrive at your date all banged up, the boss will blame me. A bad report could severely damage my chances for a promotion."

His head was in a muddle. After the grueling day at the Sommet, he had fallen asleep reading *Madam Bovary*. Semen collectors, the Viscount's cigar case, skinny cows, dancing embryos, and Emma's low-cut dressing gown had all sloshed around in his brain box until Officière DePluson's buzzing had brought him back to life. The worst thing about it was that as hard as he tried, he hadn't been able to form a stable image of Emma Bovary: black curly hair, ample bosom, petulant face. They never came together in any memorable image. It was the same problem he was having trying to imagine Karen Clements, who he had actually seen in the flesh and blood more than a few times in the last year or so. When he finished tumbling into the patrol car, he felt like he had just been glued together. Twisting around to apologize to Officière DePluson, he hit his sore knee on the gearshift lever, cursed, and apologized.

Officière DePluson dropped him off at the front curb when they got to the Gendarmerie, wished him a cheery goodbye, apologized that she had a long busy day ahead of her: check in her vehicle at the Hotel Police, jump on her moto, and meet her boyfriend at some bistro in the billiards district. They would, she said dreamily, eat and drink among friends, sing, and maybe even dance. Then she sped off in the Citroën with half a sentence still in her mouth. He envied them both: their youth, their future, and the chance they'd have to make love. Sweat, smeared lipstick, the feel of nipples and ears, fingers, young buns in young hands. For him, he lamented, those pleasures had vanished forever.

***

He and Inspector Dercanges ended up at a Moroccan restaurant off the main square that she had suggested. The food was good, even though he wasn't comfortable scooping up saucy rice with his stubby fingers. The menu claimed the meat in the platter was lamb, but he was pretty dang sure it was goat. Decbie Dantzler, who raised goats in Knightsen, had fed him some when he helped had her build a fence for her potbellied pig, so his suspicion was based on experience. When the waiters took the large silver platter away and served them some strong coffee in tiny cups, Bill asked Inspector Dercanges what she thought he ought to do with all the money, letters, and annotated business cards he had collected at the Sommet de l'Elevage.

"Find a French person to help you sort it out and tell you how to turn your collection into more money," she told him.

"You got that right. The reason I came to France in the first place was to make some money so's I could afford to get my knees fixed and maybe buy me a piece of ground up in Idaho or Oregon. I never been any good at promoting myself or hanging on to money. Problem now is I only know a couple of French people. You're in the police force. Do you know someone honest who I could go to?"

Inspector Dercanges tilted her head a tad, lifted it so she could stare at the ornate ceiling for a second, and ran her hand through the hair that was along the side of her head. "How much do you have?" she finally asked.

"About twenty-five pounds. I've been stuffing the bills in a sock and the other stuff in a hotel pillowcase."

"What if I helped you? I don't expect to be a cop forever. This might be a chance to test the water, as we say in France. Earlier in my life, I traveled with a female punk-rock band called the Four Francoise's and did some of their booking and publicity. I was pretty good at it and enjoyed the experience. I think I might like to try that kind of work again."

"My sister had a job like that for a while," Bill said, "but the musicians, if you could call them that, mostly wanted her to keep them supplied with weed and booze. Did you have pink hair?"

"Blue," Inspector Dercanges said. "I'm used to handling the press, and my current job has introduced me to most of the brass of the big companies in this area, so I think I could do a good job."

Bill picked up one of the tiny cups and took a sip. He wrinkled up his face. "This coffee's pretty dang strong," he sputtered. Think I could change it in for a cup of tea or a shot of Ancient Age?"

"It's Turkish. Sorry, I shouldn't have ordered it for you."

Bill started to thrust out a big hand to Inspector Dercanges to close the deal but noticed grains of rice were stuck to his fingers and some shreds of lamb, maybe goat, were on the back of his hand. He looked around for napkin but couldn't find one so he stuck his hand in his pocket and pulled out his red handkerchief.

"Next time we have dinner, can we go someplace with silverware and American coffee."

"Sure, it's a deal," she said and leaned over to kiss him on both cheeks. "Don't you want to know how much my commission will be?"

"Naw, I got no idea of what's normal, so take whatever you need. Buy yourself a new coat or something."

When they got their hands cleaned off, Inspector Dercanges suggested that they walk down to a café a few blocks away to have a digestif. She ordered a couple of glasses of Poire Williams for them, but before their drinks arrived, the other customers in the bar started sending bottles of wine to their table.

"I think they recognize you from the television coverage of the capture of the Chapeau Noir gang," Inspector Dercanges said. "You should lead them all in a toast."

Bill stood up, raised his glass, and shouted, "Vive La France!" The same thing would happen over and over again throughout his stay in the country.

When he got back to his hotel and finally bedded down—he had a hell of a time getting his body under the covers—he opened *Madame Bovary* but fell asleep before he finished a page.

CHAPTER 14

Marcel Würtzenhaben

"Maybe I should just go visit Blondie for a couple of weeks in the Camargue and then head home," Bill groused in between swallows of a 2010 Cote de Rhone and spoonfuls of rabbit stew. "Hrubel Kwasnik will just have to do the best he can with the domestic Feudeer Valley manure he can already get for his tree paint. I already got enough money for a new start, and I'm starting to get homesick. I miss the dry brown hills of Pylewood and the guys at Don Gustos. Too much talkin' around here and not enough doin'. Just thinkin' about collecting embryos makes my head wobble."

Claudine went through a familiar sequence of expressions: sympathetic, serious, optimistic, and, finally, hopeful, all the while moving her lips and eyes without making a sound.

"How we ever gonna to do all this stuff?" Bill protested. "Our success is gonna depend on how accurate we determine estrus, which we'll have to do at least twice. I've been around cattle all my life, and I can tell when a cow's in heat, but I never had to be able to tell how much in heat. Then we got to superovulate and inseminate and be sure the cow is pregnant real quick by analyzing progesterone in the milk. Six weeks and then palpation. That's what I'm used to and good at. Getting a milk sample at twenty days and getting it to some laboratory is all new to me. That means we got to have sanitary sampling gear and get the sample to some laboratory. Then we still have to flush the embryos. And on top of that, everything has to be done in secret. And now the Polish guy got me thinkin' about transportation, which as far as I know requires liquid nitrogen and all the special pots and pans you need to handle it."

"You're right about all that," Claudine said. She put a gentle hand on his shoulder and asked, "Why did you come here in the first place?"

"Mostly, to make some money. I was down to my last tank of gas. But that ain't true no more. I got the reward money plus a bunch of public appearances that pay pretty good."

"What about your friends? They are depending on you. Do you want to let them down?"

"They screwed me, gave me the hardest job."

"But you accepted. You can't renege now. Perhaps they are thinking that they have the hardest jobs. You are correct. We can't do everything ourselves, but we can get help. While we might not have the skill or experience to produce and collect embryos by ourselves, I'm sure we can find an expert already skilled in detecting estrus, inducing superovulation, inseminating, and evaluating the flush. It would also be good if the person we get is comfortable working outside the law. It would be even better if we can find someone daring, yes, even someone with a criminal mind."

"Sounds a little like my cousin. He's pretty good at preg checking and keeping track of time but not at lab work. Once when he was supposed to mix up a batch of fly spray, he got it way too concentrated and turned sixty Charolais cows bright green."

"Zut, that's it," Claudine said. "Green cows. Just made me think of someone who might be able to help us, a renegade Alsatian geneticist named Marcel Würtzenhaben. My former boss in Normandy, Alain Gavy, was an expert witness at Würtzenhaben's trial in Paris. The judge sentenced him to ten years at Clairvaux, our maximum security prison, but he was paroled several years ago."

"What got him in jail?" Bill asked.

"He tried to splice sheep genes into bovine DNA and marked all the gene-spliced animals with green paint, something that's against French law."

"Why didn't he use orange or purple? They show up pretty good, especially on sheep."

"It was the gene splicing that was illegal," Claudine tsked.

"Why'd he want to do that?"

"He dreamt of creating a new cheese, Roquebert, which combined the creamy goodness of camembert with the blue moldiness of Roquefort."

"Can't say as I care for either one," Bill said. "But I do like the cashew brie log they carry at the Antioch SellUfood. How do we get a hold of this Marcel guy?"

"Last thing I heard was that he had a small laboratory in Brünstatt, a village just outside of Mulhouse."

"Where's that?"

"Alsace, it's in the formerly German part of France, between the Rhine and Lorraine."

"Nobody ever said anything about Germans before."

"Stop worrying. I'm going to help you find him," Claudine said, "and I guarantee it will be good fun. It will also be a good experience for me, perhaps one that will boost my career as long as no one ever finds out that we bred French cows for their fumier. So I also have a reason to keep our activities secret. Like I said before, it will give us a chance to see France. There's so much to see that isn't in Paris or Clermont-Ferrand. In the South, there's Marseilles, Arles, the Pont du Gard, and the Abbey at Montemajor. In the North, there's Mont St. Michelle and the cathedrals at Rheims, Rouen, Amiens, and Tours. In the East, there's the Route de Vin and Colmar."

"You know, I'm not big on visiting a lot of churches. I was a real poor altar boy, but I agree that we should get out of here and out into the country. You're also right about not lettin' my friends down. As it is, they'll be pulling their hair out waiting for me to deliver their excretins. And one of them, Jim Delahunt, don't have that much to spare."

"Well then, let's find Würtzenhaben and get him to help us to choose a couple of Salers cows in the Cantal. You and I can preg check them to make sure they're open, and then we can cycle them with shot of Lutalyse. Go visit Blondie while we wait for the cows to go into estrus. We'll reunite with Würtzenhaben in Aurillac when we're ready to inseminate the cows. After the flush, you'll have to figure out how to get the embryos back to the United States.

Bill pulled Claudine close to him and kissed her on both cheeks, French style. "You're a genius, girl," he said. "Why don't you come home with me? We could be partners in the cattle business."

"Who can predict the future? But I'm French, and I can't picture myself living anywhere but in France."

***

Marcel Würtzenhaben wasn't hard to find. Six hours on the expressway from Clermont-Ferrand, with a short detour to Claudine's favorite restaurant in the hamlet of St. Georges en Couzan, and they were in Mulhouse. Brünstatt was only a couple of miles away along the Rhone-Rhine Canal. An inquiry at the Merigny Café, on the outskirts of town, got them directions to a small house on the rue Jacques Schultz, several blocks up from the Avenue d'Altkirch. When nobody answered the doorbell, Bill and Claudine walked around to the back and poked around the place until they found a small man in a white lab coat hard at work in his garage. He was grating heads of cabbage on a large noisy contraption that used a hydraulic ram to jam the cabbages against an upside-down converted rotary lawn mower. Claudine walked up behind the cabbage chopper, tapped him on the shoulder, and asked, "Are you Würtzenhaben?"

The man nodded and said something that couldn't be heard above the din of slashing blades and resisting cabbages. Claudine tried to introduce herself, but the white-haired chopper turned around and wouldn't turn off his machine until his last head of cabbage had been completely shredded.

"I am Claudine Fortet, and this is my American colleague Bill Robeiro," Claudine announced when the spinning blade finally came to rest. "Are you Würtzenhaben?"

"Si, señorita," he replied. "Mucho gusto en conocerla," he said, bowing from the waist. "Yo tengo muchos amigos auf Mexico."

"What are you doing with all this chopped cabbage, amigo?" Bill asked.

"Making *choucroute*. I think you call it *chucrut* in Spanish. How are things in Mazatlan?"

"Don't know," Bill answered. "Haven't been there since me and my cousin went to a Corrientes sale outside of Ensenada."

"Beg your pardon," Würtzenhaben said, "but to tell the truth, I never cared much for Guadalajara. I prefer the artist's colony in Guanajuato. Lovely señoritas," he said with a wink.

"We have an interesting proposition for you, Monsieur Professeur," Claudine said in a bid to stifle the idle chitchat.

"It'll take you a thousand years to eat all this cabbage by yourself," Bill chimed in anyway. "Do you have a large family?"

"No," the old man answered. "It's just me and my housekeeper, Sonjia, here. I was married at one time, but my wife got romantically involved with a chemistry student who was studying the condensation of seven-membered heterocyclic rings at the Université de haut Rhin. It's just up the road from here on rue Frères Lumiere. They ended up running off together to Canada, Waterloo, I think it was."

Würtzenhaben continued to be cagey about telling Bill why he had chopped so much cabbage. Finally, enthusiasm for the project got the better of him, and he admitted that the cabbage was destined for basic *choucroute* research.

"I have genetically altered these cabbages to speed up their fermentation and increase the content of isothiocyanates in them. Isothiocyanates are highly nutritious molecules but are only present in small quantities in the choucroute made from all of the common cabbage cultivars."

"How'd you ever think of that?" Bill asked.

Würtzenhaben rubbed his head with a gloved hand until he concluded that he couldn't answer the question. So instead of answering, he snapped to attention.

"*A sous ordenes*, but, señorita, if you are from *El Diario*, I no longer give interviews to the press."

"Thanks, Professor," Claudine said. "I assure you that we are not from the press. On the contrary, we are scientists much like yourself. In fact, we have come to ask your help in a project aimed at breeding a special type of cattle. We came to you because we knew of your success in the field of embryo capture and manipulation. You were the first scientist we thought of when we realized we needed expert help in the field of embryo manipulation."

"Please call me Marcel, señorita," the professor said. "I would like to help you, but I'm on parole. Some of my genetic experiments with sheep were misunderstood, and I was unjustly arrested and sent to prison. Now I am forbidden by the French courts to leave the country or work with vertebrates in any capacity. According to the conditions of my parole, I am restricted to edible plant research. If I waver, it's straight back to Clairvaux, a notorious prison, which holds some of the republic's most dangerous prisoners. Imagine me, a scientist, a graduate of Strasburg University, a man devoted to unlocking nature's secrets, under the same roof as Carlos the

Jackal. Even if I were inclined to engage in the reckless behavior I think you are suggesting, I fear the years in prison have sapped my skills in the field of animal breeding. I am old, rusty, and no longer up-to-date in modern gene-splicing techniques. Much has changed in the field of performance genetics since I did my seminal work with sheep, and though I tried to keep up with the literature while I was in prison, the prison authorities saw it their duty to take away my library privileges."

"Why'd they do that?" Bill asked. "It wasn't like you were stealin' anything. Besides, you were already in prison."

"Too many overdue books. I like to read a book two or three times. If you return a book in prison, you don't know if you'll ever see it again. Besides the book learning, the field of practical animal genetics requires exceptional visual acuity and manual dexterity, and you probably noticed that my eyes are cloudy, and my hands are shaky. That's part of the reason I work with cabbages nowadays. If I happen to drop one, it's not the end of the world."

"C'est ne pas grave, Professeur," Claudine said. "We have confidence that you can help us. Abandon your cabbages for a few days and travel with us to the Cantal, where you can help us select some cows to cycle, inseminate, and flush."

"For you, señorita, I would do it. Beautiful women have always been my weakness, and I am honored that a lovely young lady like yourself would journey such a great distance to show her faith in an old man and jailbird like me. But who's he?" Würtzenhaben asked, pointing at Bill. "He isn't coming with us, is he?"

"Yes," Claudine said. "He's my boss."

"My fee is usually three hundred euros per day for consulting, but since this job sounds illegal, involves animals, and requires that I violate my parole, I don't think five hundred euros a day would be outrageous."

"Let us pay you by the piece instead," Claudine said, casting a glance in Bill's direction. "Four days of work, even at five hundred euros, only adds up to two thousand euros. On the other hand, thirty successful embryo transplants at three hundred euros is nine thousand euros. Do the arithmetic, Professor."

Bill had already started in on the arithmetic. He reckoned that they should probably settle for fifteen births at three hundred euros per birth for the first go-around. He nudged Claudine and flashed three fingers at her, paused for a second, and repeated the gesture five more times.

Würtzenhaben didn't need a translator. He scratched his beard for a few seconds before he thrust a hand at Bill.

"You drive a hard bargain, señor," he said with a wink. "Give me a one-thousand-euro advance and a couple of days to clean my fermentation vats, water my fuscias, and put up several jars of experimental chucrut, and it's a deal."

"We'll be staying at the Holiday Inn in the center of Mulhouse. Call us when you're ready to leave, and we'll pick you up. And thanks, Professeur."

"De nada," the old man replied, throwing his rubber gloves in the hazardous waste bin. "When we get those cows in the Cantal synchronized, you and I can take a short vacation in Cancun," the professor said, looking at Claudine. Palm trees, sandy beach, and unlimited margaritas. José over there can watch my cabbages while we're gone," the professor said, casting a sideways glance at Bill.

"The name's Bill, amigo."

"He can also choose a bull and collect the semen while we snorkel and water ski. Bring me home after a couple of weeks, and then don't bother me until we're ready to inseminate the cows, probably a week or so. That should give me enough time to test choucroute batches 11679 and 11800."

"What's so special about your cabbages?" Bill asked.

"They've been genetically modified with a gene fragment from an Armenian cucumber. It's never been tried before. After your embryos are collected, inspected, and refrigerated, I'm done amigos: *finito, terminado,* and *finishini, comprende.* You'll pay me for each good embryo in cash. No paper trail. And I'm not helping you sneak back to Mexico—although I do dream about a good plate of enchiladas suizas from time to time—or accept responsibility for the number of live births. Five hundred euros for every good embryo: that is the deal."

Bill and Claudine looked at each other and nodded their approval in unison, even though that wasn't exactly the deal.

"Have you ever been to Cancun?" Claudine asked Bill as they walked back to the car.

"I don't think he invited me, señorita."

***

When they got back to their hotel room, Claudine headed for the shower, and Bill flopped down on the bed. He pulled *Madame Bovary* from his travel bag and flipped the book open. But he didn't start reading. He was beginning to think that learning French was going to be easier than he had first thought. He was having no trouble understanding Emma and her plight. Maybe, he figured, it was because, even though he and Emma weren't the same sex, he wasn't French, and the story happened before he was born, the two of them seemed to have a lot in common. Like her, he was a helpless romantic. While she had been undone by the Romantic Movement in France, he had been undone by the US Country-and-Western Romantic Revival of the late '60s. Jimmy Rodgers, who had sung about riding his pony on the reservation had given way to Hank Williams and cheating hearts. And like Emma, he could never really break free of his longing for happiness, in his case, personified by his first love, Karen Clements. Just like Emma Bovary, his hunt for romantic passion had led to adultery in vehicles and eventually dubious business activities like changing a brand every now and then and leaving holes in fences when there was surplus feed on his neighbor's side. And like Emma Bovary, he had been having big trouble adapting to everyday life. In his case, everyday life kept changing on him. He was sure that the grass was always getting shorter, hay more expensive, and folks more interested in making money than in having a good time.

CHAPTER 15

Salers

Three days later, Bill, Claudine, and Professor Würtzenhaben were in Aurillac, the capital of the Cantal, a region renowned for its red cattle and the beef and cheese they inspire. Bill and Claudine booked themselves into the Hotel Bordeaux, which was right on the town square, and suggested to Professor Würtzenhaben that for security's sake he stay at the youth hostel in the nearby medieval walled town of Salers, where he wouldn't attract attention. He wrinkled his nose and cocked his head at the suggestion.

"Professor, we're concerned that if your name turns up along with ours on a hotel register in a major town like Aurillac, the police might start to get nosy and compromise our project security," Claudine said, trying to mollify the pouting scientist. "After all, you are very well known all over France, especially to French law enforcement because of your notoriety, the seriousness of the crime that landed you in jail, and the suspicion that, given the chance, you will violate your parole. Any connection with us would immediately arouse suspicion."

"But it's embarrassing for a man of my age and education to have to stay at a youth hostel."

"If anyone asks, Professor, tell them your name is Gaec Fonteneau and that you are a salesman from Mouries." It was a name Bill had seen on a salt shaker in Clermont-Ferrand.

Würtzenhaben stared straight ahead seemingly in another world.

"You'll enjoy Salers," Claudine said to him. "The town is on a hill, picturesque, surrounded by stone walls and turrets and spectacular scenery. Today is market day, and if you hurry, there still might be some fresh cabbages left in the stalls. Surely, your research will profit from your trip if you are able to add fresh regional-cabbage data to your cabbage spread sheet. I envy you because we, on the other hand, will be stuck flapping our gums in a stuffy office at the Salers Association headquarters in Aurillac."

Professor Würtzenhaben affected a stunned look. "Tell me again where I am and why I'm here. Something tells me I should return home immediately. I think I have nearly a hundred kilos of cabbage fermenting in my laboratory in Brünstatt."

"Don't worry, Professor, everything is all right," Claudine assured him. "We are in Aurillac, and you are going to help us with our cattle project. You should be home in three days, in plenty of time to stir your cabbage. Right now you are going to take the bus to Salers, where you'll stay the night in the Youth Hostel. We'll pick you up tomorrow morning in front of the city hall."

"That's right. Now I remember. Salers is the center of the cattle-raising region and an ideal place for us to start our research. But how can I stay in a youth hostel. I am already seventy or maybe even eighty years old?"

"Don't worry, Professor. No one will ask about your age. Your only problem in Salers may be that all the cabbage at the market will be imported from Argentina at this time of year," Claudine cautioned.

"Not a problem for me. Cabbages are cabbages. I don't care whether they are from France or Herzegovina. Who knows what interesting cultivars they might have in Argentina?"

"Remember, Professor, not a word to anyone about our mission here," Bill cautioned."

***

After they dropped the professor off at the bus stop in front of the Aurillac train station, Bill and Claudine went directly to the Salers Breeders Association office. The office staff, most of whom remembered Claudine, greeted her warmly. She introduced Bill as the American cowboy who had come to *Sommet de l'Elevage* to evaluate red cattle and ended up destroying the notorious Chapeau Noir gang. Bill shook hands with Antoine Lanob, her ex-boss, and met the rest of the staff, all of whom had questions about the burglary at the Hotel Gergovie. After Bill did a couple of tricks with the purple rope, Claudine asked her friends to help her make appointments with six Salers breeders whom she remembered from her days as a breed representative at the Aurillac office.

"Paul Gaillard, the guy that bred Jet and Luisante, retired and sold his herd just after you left for Paris," Lanob said. "He has a boat docked at Ciotat near Marseille and spends all his time fishing. Raoul Deslaut, who had that nice herd over in Rislan moved to Canada and opened a chain of waffle shops. He sold his place to a Swiss doctor who relocated from Bern and sleeps with his herd in a small trailer. Other than that, the cast of characters is pretty much the same."

"How sad," Claudine pouted. "I was looking forward to seeing both Raoul and Paul. I remember Raoul had this stone barn where he stored his cheeses and always gave us a slab of Cantal and opened a bottle of Sancerre for us when we went to test his bulls."

Claudine flashed back to the early days of her career. Fresh out of university, she had started her livestock career in Aurillac. Though

Parisian, she fit in perfectly and developed a strong affection for the area and the farmers. They, in return, enjoyed the touch of Parisian sheen she brought to their fields and pens. Besides Gaillard and Deslaut, her favorites were Paul Belloc at St. Julien aux Bois, Didier Freyssac at St. Bonnet, Pierre Galvaige at Veze, and finally Albert Garçelon at Murat. The staff agreed that she should start out with visits to the four whom she already knew. In the event that she and Bill didn't find the kind of cattle they were looking for, Antoine Lanob suggested that they could come back the next day and visit two new breeders that had joined the association since she had left.

"Let's get some lunch," Bill suggested to Claudine when they finished up with the paperwork, the toast, and the socializing. "I'm pretty dang hungry. Seems like the petit dejeuner in the hotel was plus petit for me."

"I think you mean trop petit."

"Do you think Professor Würtzenhaben is going to be OK by himself in Salers?" Bill asked as they walked along the square toward Avenue Gambetta.

"I'm sure he'll be fine as long as he remembers to change buses in Mauriac. It can be a little confusing. Once he's in Salers and sees a cabbage or two, our vieux bonhomme will be fine."

CHAPTER 16

New Friends

Bill held the door open for Claudine when they got to the bistro and pulled out a chair for her when they found a table she liked. A small smile, lips tight, eyebrows vaulted, let him know how much she appreciated the gesture. He looked around the restaurant before he sat down, a habit he had picked up in small-town cowboy bars. Fancy bar with old-fashioned tables and chairs and not too many customers. Looked to him that they were early for lunch. An old beret-crowned customer was at a corner table by himself fiddling with a glass of wine and staring at a plate of bread and melted cheese. Three big rough-looking guys were quaffing beer in another corner. The old guy didn't lift his head, but Bill had the immediate sensation that the three guys in the corner were sizing him up. He figured it was probably his gray Stetson that had got their attention. He grabbed a menu and gave it a quick look.

"What's a Croque Monsieur?" he asked Claudine. "Sounds like a dead guy on a bed of baby spinach."

"A ham sandwich with melted cheese on top: classic French bistro fare. The lonely-looking guy over there in the corner has one. You probably couldn't find one on a menu in Paris these days, but I'll bet they'd make one for you if you asked for it. I'm surprised they still serve them. So out of fashion, like Proust."

"You mean Marcel Proust, the poet."

"I don't know about poet, but he was famous novelist a hundred years ago."

"You think they might serve grenoolies at this place?" Bill asked. "I wouldn't mind having a big bowl of them with a bottle of Chablis, 2005, maybe, if they have it. Probably still needs to age some, but it's worth a try."

"You amaze me, Bill," Claudine said. "You don't know what a Croque Monsieur is, but you're up to date on vintages of French Chablis wine and French authors. How do you know so much about French culture?"

"I just started learning. Back in Clermont-Ferrand, I bought a book about French wine. I liked the pictures and figured it might be a good way to learn about France and improve my French at the same time. Blondie also took me to the book store in the train station in Lyon, where I bought *Madame Bovary*. With my little yellow dictionary, I found I could pretty much understand the sentences. Back home in the Pylewood area, we raise a lot of wine grapes, so I already knew a little somethin' about wine. I already knew that soil and climate determine the best type of grape to grow in any particular region. Chablis wine is a good example. What are you gonna eat, Claudine?"

"I think I'll stick with *biftec* and *pommes frites*."

Just then, the smallest of the large men that had been staring at them from the corner strode into view.

"Say, Jimmy, ye wouldnay happen to be the American bloke that roped the hat thief in Clermont-Ferrand, wouldye now?"

Bill looked up into the face that was riding atop the extra-wide torso in front of him. The guy reminded him of Abe Gomes, the old longshoreman who used to box out of Rio Vista: broken nose, handlebar moustache, loose flap of skin on one eyelid, diced eyebrows, and ears that looked like chanterelles.

"Er, yeah," Bill said. "Howdja know? But my name ain't Jimmy."

"Recognized ye from the telly and noticed your big hat. Come on over and join us. You can bring the lassie we'ye, if ye want. We want to stand ye dinner and some drinks."

Bill looked over at Claudine for a sign of her preference, and she obliged with a nod and a smile. The man opened his eyes wide, cast a broad grin, twisted the ends of his moustache and led the two of them over to the corner table.

"Bill, right?" he said. "I'm Andrew Craik. Call me Andy, and these are my mates Mano Sulapanni and Jules Bisoni. We all play for Stade Aurillacois, the local rugby team. We played Nîmes yesterday, and we're takin' the beer cure to relax our brains and soothe our aching muscles. What brings ye to the provinces?"

Bill looked at Claudine before he said anything, "Cattle. I'm thinking of buying a few here in the Cantal. You're English, ain't ya?"

"Ach, no, far from it. I'm Scottish. Manu, the dark one, is from Samoa, and Jules hails from Marseilles. We're here for the rugby. All three of us are trying to make it back up to a Top14 League team. I did a couple of turns for Glasgow Warriors before I came to France. Had part of a season with Toulon, but right now I'm down here rehabbing a bad knee."

"I know what that's like, and believe me, it's a hard road back," Bill said. "Once a knee's wrong, it's hell getting the thing back to workin' right. I twisted mine a few years back wrestling a crazy gray steer at Oakdale, and then a year ago, I fell off my flatbed trailer and reinjured it. Sometimes I can't hardly walk."

The waiter, also a big man but taller and lankier than the others, put a couple of large platters down in front of Claudine and Bill and went back to fetch the others their food.

"Thanks, John," Craik said. "That's John Cramer. Used to be the Aurillacois prop forward. Quit a couple of years ago to manage this restaurant."

Craik had a steak and frites like Claudine, the Samoan had a pile of pork, Jules had *pounti,* and Bill had his bowl of grenoolies.

"Frogs! Yer no gony eat them slimy creatures in front of us, are ye? Them being all nobbly and whatnot?" Craik said to Bill. "I dunnay know if I can watch. They hae the looka human crotches, if ye get ma meaning."

"Never occurred to me," Bill answered. "Had 'em in Clermont-Ferrand, and they were tasty. Since then, I been eating them every chance I get. We used to spear 'em in the San Joaquin Delta when I was a kid. Always did like 'em. But the ones here in France are especially good eating. They call 'em grenoolies, as you guys probably know. Maybe it's the local garlic, thyme, and tomatoes that make the difference."

"This time of year, the garlic's probably from Uruguay," Jules, the big French prop forward, said.

"What are you eating?" Bill asked Jules. "Looks like it ought to be dessert."

"Pounti. It's a local specialty like a pâté de campagne, only a lot better. It's lean pork, bacon, bread crumbs, lots of prunes, and some onion and garlic mixed up and baked. It's the prunes that give the dish its special flavor. They're local and have the taste of the Cantal."

After Manu had destroyed the pork pile in front of him, the steaks and frites were history, pounti was no more, and Bill was mopping up his frog sauce, Craik announced that the three rugby players usually arm wrestled for the tab.

"Big Jules hardly ever pays," Craik said. "Me and Manu usually end up with the tab, depending on who's the most banged up."

"Want to have a go, Bill?" Jules Bisoni asked. "Don't worry. We won't stick you with the ticket even if you do lose. You're our guest."

"Why don't you get us goin' by wrestling Jules," Craik suggested. You guys are about the same size. What do ye weigh Bill?"

"Last time I weighed myself, it was 275 pounds."

The two of them jiggled themselves into position and then huffed and puffed and grimaced and groaned until Jules pinned Bill. Craik beat Manu, and Jules vanquished Craik, meaning that the Samoan got stuck with the check.

"Thought you'd be a lot easier," Jules told Bill. "We play this game a lot with tourists, and even the big tough guys go down easy."

"Bill, jevver play rugby?" Andrew Craik asked.

"Nope. I seen it on TV though. Not too complicated. Ball looks like an overweight football—throw it, run with it, and kick it. I was doin' that up until my twenties. I won the punt, pass, and run contest for the whole county when I was in the fifth grade. I only got to play football for a year in high school and played some baseball, but mostly, I worked on the ranch with my dad."

"You should be good at rugby. For big guys like you, rugby's more like steer wrestling than American football," Manu chimed in. "Never could understand why you Americans put on helmets and padding when you play your football. Isn't it strange that you guys wear your armor when you bang heads with each other but take it off when you wrestle animals four times your weight, animals that are solid muscle, horns, hoofs, and have short tempers."

"You got a point there, Manu," Bill said. "Aside from a rope burn or two and a mild concussion, I never got injured much from rodeoing, but I dislocated my shoulder playing football. Shit, did my dad ever get mad, a week before roundup time and me with cast up to my neck."

"Want to run around with us tomorrow at practice?" Craik asked. "We could use a rough guy your size in our scrum, especially when we play Montpellier. They got a guy, Barry Carpenter, that's more zebu than man. Jules is our heaviest player, and Carpenter throws him around like rag doll."

"And you?" Jules said. "He heaved you into the third row one day in Montpellier."

"Jules only weighs 122 kilograms," Craik interjected. "He has to battle the guy for the whole game. I only bump into him now and then, and Manu is way too fast for him. Jules is also on the short side. You say you're 275 pounds: that's close to 140 kilograms, and you must be five or six centimeters taller than Jules, perfect for the line out."

"Sorry, boys, sounds like fun but me and Claudine are kinda busy for the next few days. Besides, with my knee being the way it is, I can barely walk. Haven't even tried to run for almost a year."

"I wear a knee brace, myself," Craik said. "High tech it is, and the club bought it for me. I'll wager we got another couple or three lying about the locker room, mostly from guys that didn't make the squad or retired. Why don't you come over and try one on first thing in the morning. We also got a good trainer, South African, Barry Smyth, who might be able to give you some exercises to smooth out that bad knee. If it feels right, you can kick the ball around with us. Whataye got te lose? If you end up playing a few minutes for the Aurillacois, they might give you a couple of hundred euros."

Bill turned to Claudine. "I guess I'd like to work out with these boys and talk to their trainer," he said. "Maybe one of their braces might shore up my knee. Could we spare a couple of hours tomorrow morning before we head for Salers?"

"Sure," Claudine said. "I have some catching up to do myself. When you finish practice, we'll still have time to check out four herds."

CHAPTER 17

Murielle

Next morning, when Claudine picked up Bill in front of the Stade Aurillacois clubhouse, he was wearing a happier face and standing a little straighter than when she had left him off.

"How do you feel? You look marvelous."

"Pretty darn good," he said as he eased into the car, slipping through the small opening in a single motion. "They gave me an exercise program and let me borrow the brace for the morning. Then I ran around with the players for forty minutes or so. At first, I was too stiff to run good; but gradually, I got loose. With a few adjustments on the knee brace, I started getting up some good speed; nothin' like when I was eighteen, but a lot better than yesterday. I drop kicked a couple of balls in the direction of the goal and even put one between the uprights. I'm still sort of weak, and I got pushed around pretty good in the scrum."

He noticed confusion and then disinterest on Claudine's face and slowed down. "The scrum is kinda like when we hike the ball in American football, and the two lines crash into each other, except in rugby you can use your hands."

Later, when Claudine looked up "hike" in her French/English dictionary, she was more confused than ever.

"The trainer said that if I came back here when we finished looking at cattle, he'd fit me for my own brace, no charge. I guess

I'd like to take him up on his offer and go to the club for a couple of workouts. Who knows, I might even get into a game."

"Good for you," Claudine said. "Once we get set up with a couple of donor cows, you can go down to Arles and join Blondie."

"What are you gonna do while I'm ridin' around in the Camargue, getting my knee brace, and learnin' how to play rugby?"

"Once we choose some Salers cows and get them cycling together, I can go back to Paris. I'll try to catch up on my correspondence and write my monthly report. Let's go to St. Julien this morning and have a look at Paul Belloc's herd. Belloc's been raising red cattle for years and is known for being able to look at any Salers cow and tell you her weight, breeding lines, pelvis dimensions, and behavioral traits. St. Julian is a beautiful spot along a road that winds through an exceptionally green valley, and it's close to Salers, the old town where we are supposed to pick up Professor Würtzenhaben."

"Good thing you got a good memory," Bill said. "I plumb forgot about the Professor."

***

Meanwhile, Würtzenhaben, who, in spite of his early reservations about staying in a youth hostel, had had no trouble falling into the spirit of youthful adventure. He pasted on the fake dark beard that he always carried in his briefcase and replaced his beret with a baseball cap, which he tilted sideways at a jaunty angle. After successfully registering at the hostel and getting his towel and cot assignment, he made friends with two Austrian girls and found three kinds of interesting cabbages—varieties he had read about, but never seen—at the town market.

Würtzenhaben dined with the Austrian girls that evening, sang folk songs until midnight, and slept soundly on his cot, even though the wind blew noisily throughout the night. He was feeling quite chipper when he saw Claudine's gray Renault approach the city hall where he was snuggled up with Heidi, the more buxom of the two Austrian girls. Although it was still early in the day, Würtzenhaben and Heidi were already snacking *choucroute* from a glass jar, pulling out the long, translucent shreds of cabbage with their fingers, and sucking them up through their lips.

"Hop in, Professor," Bill called out to him from the car.

"What about Heidi? Can she come too?"

Bill put an index finger to his lips to remind Würtzenhaben of the project's tight security. Heidi pouted and gave the professor a long sloppy kiss on the lips before she let loose of him.

"How was breakfast, Professor?" Bill asked Würtzenhaben as soon as he was in his seat and buckled up.

"They give you a baguette and oatmeal," Würtzenhaben said, wrinkling his nose. "Lucky for me, Heidi and Gretel had some Tyrolean würst, which they were happy to share with me."

"What's it like, kissing a young girl with a mouthful of sauerkraut?"

"A little sour, a little salty, but with a refreshing aftertaste. You should try it."

"No, thanks. I never eat anything pickled before lunch."

***

Paul Belloc was on the porch of his stone house at St. Julian, smoking an antique pipe, ready to greet them when they arrived. He embraced Claudine and kissed her on both cheeks. Bill kept behind Claudine, hoping that the kissing would stop with her, while Würtzenhaben, the diminutive scientist, stayed completely hidden behind the wide American.

"We can have something to drink now," Belloc suggested, "or wait until after we've seen the herd."

Claudine said something that sounded like "work before pleasure," but Bill wasn't sure.

They looked through the herd quickly—heavy-shouldered, rust-colored bulls with lyre-shaped horns and cows with huge udders—drank the wine that was offered, chatted for a few moments about the Sommet de l'Elevage, said goodbye, and shoehorned themselves back into the small gray car. It was much the same at St. Bonnet and Veze. But it was at Murat, at the farm of Albert Garçelon, where Bill found his eyes fixed on a tall thin dark cow tied up next to a hay barn in an adjoining field. He stepped away from the group and, after a minute, motioned the others to follow him.

"Monsieur Garçelon," Claudine said, "could we take a closer look at that cow standing over there by the barn."

"Of course," the kind-faced farmer answered with a puzzled look. "But why?"

"I don't know," Claudine said with a funny face. "But by now you should know that Americans have some funny ideas about cattle. Have you ever seen longhorn Texas animals?"

"Maybe in Western movies, but I don't remember anymore."

Bill, who had bought plenty of cattle in his day, was well schooled in the routine, walk slowly, and try hard not to show too much interest in the animal that interests you.

"Claudine, find out more about this cow," Bill whispered when they got closer to the animal.

"Monsieur," Garçelon said, "I must tell you that this animal we call Murielle is more a pet than an important cow in my herd. I usually hide her when visitors come. As you can see, she is skinny, but it is not for lack of eating. Sometimes I think she eats twice as much as my best cows, all of whom produce a marketable calf every year and enough extra milk for several hundred kilograms of cheese." Garçelon laughed. "The only thing Murielle produces is, how do you call it, shit? Tons of it."

"Has she ever had a calf?" Bill asked, even though he could tell she had.

"Every year without fail," Garçelon answered. "But they all look like her."

Bill looked off into space, trying to conceal his interest, while he motioned for Würtzenhaben to examine the cow. The Alsatian scientist approached Murielle and slid around her so that she stood between him and Garçelon.

"Where did that fellow come from?" Garçelon asked, staring at Würtzenhaben, while the old man pulled on his shoulder-length gloves and placed his right hand on Murielle's vulva and his left on her tail."

"Oh, he's with us," Bill said. "Sorry, I forgot to introduce him. He's just hard to see sometimes because of his bad posture. Why do you keep her?" Bill asked, pointing at Murielle.

"You won't believe it, but she saved my life."

"How'd she do that?"

"One morning, a fully loaded manure cart tipped over on a steep hill in one of my farthest fields and fell across my legs. My wife was in Paris visiting a cousin, and my son was away at college in Besançon. Murielle, this cow that we are looking at, was out in the pasture waiting to be butchered. When I yelled for help, she walked over to me. Salers cows are extremely intelligent and curious. She understood the situation immediately and stuck one of her horns under the wagon tongue and lifted it high enough for me to crawl out from under the wagon."

"Albert, I've never heard this story before, and we've known each other since the time I started working for the Association," Claudine said.

"I rarely tell this story to people I don't know well. I don't want them to think I'm crazy."

"I heard of cows chasing off mountain lions but never lifting things," Bill said.

"I know," the stocky farmer replied. "It's God's truth though. But there's more. She backed up to me and stood there until I realized she wanted me to grab her tail. Salers have long, very strong tails going back for centuries. When I had hold of her tail, she dragged me to the gate."

"You're not gonna tell me she opened the gate, are you?" Bill said.

"Yes, I am," Garçelon replied. "She jiggled the latch with her nose until she could get a horn under it and popped the thing open."

Bill rolled his eyes.

"Then she dragged me a hundred meters to the road where Eduard, the postman, found me and took me in his van to the hospital in Aurillac. So, my friend, this is why I keep her, even though she eats up my profits and her calves have crooked backs. If not for her, my bones would be in the cemetery in town."

"Would you sell her?" Bill asked. "If I bought her, I guarantee I'd take good care of her for as long as she lived."

"No, never, she belongs here. It's her home, and I could never part with her."

"Would you sell me some embryos for transplant?"

"Well, I don't know," Garçelon said, looking straight at Claudine. "The association monitors embryo and semen transfers very strictly."

While they talked, Würtzenhaben quietly and skillfully checked out Murielle's reproductive organs, sliding his arm up her cervix.

Bill looked over at Claudine. "Mademoiselle Fortet," he said with a wink, "would you let me take some of Murielle's embryos back to California?"

"I don't know. The association has rules, and it requires time and much paperwork to arrange a foreign sale. You would have to put in a formal request."

"Why do you want to do this?" Garçelon asked. "This cow is obviously useless."

Bill grinned widely. "To you, maybe, but not to me. I want to start a rodeo act with a trick cow. In France, I'm learning that fun and excitement are an important part of everyday life. It's something we don't know about in America. We always separate work and play. When I worked cattle with my dad, it was work, work, and more work: round 'em up, shoot 'em up, brand 'em up, tag 'em, and get 'em out of the corral as fast as we could. Play was afterwards: eat, drink, and kiss the girls. Seems like in France you can do all those things while you work."

Albert Garçelon grinned and rattled off a string of French words that Bill didn't understand. "What'd he say, Claudine?"

"He says he doesn't understand what you are talking about, but he will ask the association for permission to sell you semen or embryos."

"Ask him if he thinks he could train Murielle to poop on a piece of newspaper or better yet in a wheelbarrow?"

They were back in Aurillac before nightfall. Würtzenhaben had urged them to drop him off at the youth hostel in Salers and come back the next morning when they went to view more cattle. He had argued that while Murielle seemed perfect, they needed a second cow as a backup. He had claimed that in the genetic alteration business, "Something unforeseen will always go wrong."

"You just want another one of them sauerkraut *baisers* from Heidi, don't you, you old goat," Bill had answered, while Würtzenhaben smiled at the mental image of Gertyl, the less buxom of the two Austrian students, in her dirndl and low-cut blouse.

"Don't worry about me," Würtzenhaben had insisted. "Just pick me up at the city hall like you did this morning."

"Don't stay out too late, Professor," Bill had hollered as he half pushed Würtzenhaben out the door of the Renault and on to the sidewalk in front of the youth hostel.

Back at the crepe restaurant in Aurillac, Bill talked as he chewed away on his frog-leg-stuffed pancake. "I say we put all our chips on Murielle. We'll never find another cow like her. How many cows you ever heard of that saved their owner's life."

"I think maybe Marcel has a point," Claudine said. "In college, my animal husbandry teacher always said, 'never bet on a single bull.' You should always have at least two, no matter what the size of your herd."

"Just like girlfriends," Bill said.

He winked at Claudine, but she ignored him. Maybe she didn't get the joke. Maybe it wasn't a French kind of joke.

"Why don't you go do the office first thing in the morning, Claudine, and get the dope on two more breeders? I'll go to the rugby club and meet you there after I get my new knee brace."

CHAPTER 18

Rugby

The next morning, Bill was waiting at the door of the Stade Aurillacois when Andy Craik arrived. He followed the stocky center forward through the locker room, weight room, and sauna cabins until they got to the kitchen. The Scotsman opened the refrigerator and pulled out a glob of glassy, translucent material laced with heavy fibers, some going vertically and others horizontally.

"This here's the newest, sweetest, space-age, knee-brace material known to man," Craik said to Bill as he handed him a Frisbee-sized piece of the stringy mass.

"You sure this is it? Looks more like a celery pizza than a knee brace. Why don't you look in the refrigerator and see if you can fine one with anchovies."

"Give us a break, man. There's a tin tub under the table over there."

Craik pointed to a giant commercial stove on the other side of the kitchen.

"Fill it with water and put it on yon stove. Then leave this boorach in the hot water until it gets pliable," he said, handing Bill the glossy glob. "After that, we'll shape it on your knee and put it aside to let it harden a wee bit. At room temperature, it'll be just flexible enough and have plenty of support. If we've done it right, you'll feel like you have a new knee. Our team's been using this stuff for two seasons now, and it's prevented new injuries while rejuvenating old knees.

When you've finished, come on out on the practice field, and we'll teach you the rules a rugby and show you how to maneuver in the scrum."

The game was simple, but the terminology and rules complicated. There were fifteen starters and seven substitutes on a team. Just like American football, there were backs. Linemen were called forwards. Any player could run about the field, pick up a ball, run with it, or kick it, and even throw it backward. However, only forwards could be in the scrums and lineouts. The rest of it seemed like mayhem with referees, whose job it was to supervise the lineouts, rucks, and scrums and penalize "unsportsmanlike" conduct. Tackling had to be below the waist, and butting, punching, and gouging were not allowed. And whenever the ball stopped moving, the forwards had to form a scrum. In a scrum, the forwards, like Jules Bisoni, gathered in teams and tried to move the ball through their legs to the backs, usually the scrum half. Bill found he had a lot power in the scrum, especially with his new knee brace, but he lacked the balance and leverage that the more experienced forwards had. Even so, the B-Squad, which he was on, was able to push the A-Team off the ball several times. Craik pulled him aside, while the other team took a penalty kick.

"Next time I get the ball, drift back behind the line and I'll toss it at you. Catch it in the air, run off toward the right sideline, and give the ball a good kick toward the goal we're facing."

A couple of plays later, Andy tossed the ball Bill's way. He caught it, ran a few yards, and kicked it thirty yards down the field, straight between the goal posts. It was only a practice scrimmage, but the lads all stopped and looked straight at him. Five minutes later, the club secretary was out on the field with a sheaf of papers on a clipboard, urging Bill to suit up for the weekend game against Nîmes. The secretary assured him it was a strategic move, and that it was highly unlikely he'd play, but they reckoned that Bill's notoriety, size, and presence on the bench might jangle the nerves of the Nîmes players and probably bring in some extra fans eager to see the recently famous American cowboy play their game of rugby.

CHAPTER 19

Pierre Nosay

Claudine was in her car waiting for Bill when he rumbled out of the Aurillacois complex carrying a large translucent striated knee brace in one hand and trying to smooth out his tousled hair with the other.

"What are you doin' here, Claudine? I was gonna walk over to the Salers office to meet you."

"I got tired of waiting. Do you know what time it is?"

"Nope, guess I lost track. What's the matter? You're lookin' glum as a hound dog whose owner just won a Pekinese bitch in a poker game."

"It is much worse than that. The association won't let us take any Salers embryos out of France."

"Why? We're not gonna show, sell, or eat any of the offsprings. We just want their fumier."

"It doesn't matter to them. Purebred, hybrid crosses, or low-scoring cows, you can't take embryos out of France without their permission."

"Shoot. Don't worry, honey," Bill said in the calmest voice he could muster. "We'll just get them from Belgium or Ireland or some other more advanced country."

He felt sorry for Claudine. French women were more emotional than American girls, except for Devon Pugh, the waitress at the

Waggin Wrangler, who once upon a time conked his cousin on the head with a serving platter when he made a joke about her hairdo.

"They think that selling you an embryo from a cow that looks like Murielle would be very risky. Once you were back home in America, you could do anything with the calf, perhaps even use it in a circus or a movie. It would be a mockery of their years of work in perfecting the Salers breed. And what if you produced a herd of cows that looked like her?"

"Garçelon breeds her every year, doesn't he?"

"And every year they ask him to butcher her, and every year he refuses. They understand his reason, and they know and trust him. The association's answer is no, never, not under any circumstances."

"What if we did it without their permission?"

He was surprised when Claudine paused to think about the idea. He had expected a quick refusal. After all, she was a product of the French educational system and a loyal former employee of the Salers breed association.

"How could we pull it off?" Bill asked while Claudine was still in a thinking mood.

"Pull what off? What are you talking about?"

"Sorry, I mean, do it. Get our embryos without the breed association's permission."

"We would have to work at night, perhaps on a French national holiday like Transit Workers Appreciation Day. How was your workout?"

"They offered me a one-game contract to play against Nîmes this Saturday. Let's get them cows rounded up and cycled so I can be at practice on Thursday. All I have to do is show up to get three thousand euros."

"What is that thing you are carrying?"

"My knee brace. Where'd you say we were going?"

"To the outskirts of Pleaux, a small village to the northwest, to see a new Salers breeder named Pierre Nosay, and after that, we will visit his neighbor, Dr. Eduard Huppthapfell, a Swiss farmer who just bought some land and a herd of Salers cattle."

"You mean we're gonna be out of the Cantal.

"No, just to the western end."

They found Pierre Nosay's place without any trouble. A big sign on the road pointed the way to his farm, Le Petite Théière, a tidy place with a good view of the Maronne River. They were greeted effusively at the gate by Nosay, a voluble rotund man who spoke fluent English with a pronounced Oxbridge accent.

"I call this place Le Petite Théière, the little teapot. It's a joke among the locals because I drink a lot of tea. No café au lait for this Frenchman. I fired my first housekeeper because she insisted on scrubbing my tea pot with soap and water. Tea drinking: it's a habit I acquired when I taught at the London School of Economics. That was a long time ago, in the '80s, during the Thatcher era. I returned to France when Tony Blair got elected. I missed France and was tired of London. But the main reason was that my financial models had all predicted that the West's financial nexus would shift from London to Sofia, Bulgaria, a nonunion place where costs were low, and there was ample clean air and water. When the shift didn't happen, my clients lost a lot of money, and my services were no longer sought. It was a financial catastrophe but a personal parole that got me out of the city and back to the timeless French countryside."

"Parole, sounds like a French word," Bill said. "Bunch of my old friends back home are on parole, but I don't think they like it as much you do."

Pierre, who was as proud as rooster of his flock, couldn't wait to show Bill and Claudine his animals, which were uniform in confirmation, deep-red in color, and had black hooves and noses, calm dispositions, and wide mouths. They looked like they were all smiling. Talk about contented cows; Bill figured the guy had to be doing something right. Even though Nosay was relatively new to the breed and to the whole idea of livestock production, he projected an aura of certainty that he had worked a good deal of magic in his breeding program.

"Mouths," he announced, "they define a race. I breed my cattle to have large mouths. It's the only measurement that survives statistically when you apply rigorous mathematical standards to the data. Others breeders like to boast about their giant scrotums, huge pelvises, high weaning weights, and heavy milk production, but I no longer even measure those parameters. They are not significant factors in breed performance. It's not Monte Carlo or Lagrange, just simple logic. The bigger the mouth, the faster the cow can eat?"

"I don't know if I can go along with you on your big-mouth ideas," Bill said. "I haven't done much statistical research like you, but it seems to me that with people, a big mouth usually goes along with a big ass. My old football coach in Antioch could yell so loud you could hear him from one end of the field to the other, and his butt was so big they had to build a special seat for him on the team bus. What do you think, Professor Würtzenhaben? Is it the same gene that causes both traits?"

Bill turned around look for agreement from the professor.

"Where'd he go?" Bill asked, shading his eyes with his hand.

"Merde," Claudine gasped. "We forget to pick him up. He's probably still in Salers waiting in front of the city hall. We'll have to go back and get him as soon as we're finished here."

"Würtzenhaben, isn't that the name of the mad scientist that's locked up in Clairvaux? I read about him in *News of the World* when I was in England."

"Nope," Bill said, "yer thinkin' of Schwartzenhaben. Seems to me that even if cows are different, ain't it more logical that the bigger the stomach the more the cow can eat," Bill said, trying to change the subject. "What holds more wine, a gallon jug with a small neck or a pint jar with a wide mouth?"

"You forget, my friend, that we are dealing with living systems, not jugs and bottles," Pierre Nosay said as he waggled his index finger at Bill. "While the grapes are going through the narrow neck of your jug, the fermentation is already changing the first ones in. The last ones in will be way behind the first ones. The mouth and the throat will play an important role in the quality of the product. I search everywhere for cows with big mouths. And I have also developed the methodology required for standardizing the measurement. I take a ratio of several measurements of the mouth and divide it by an empirically derived constant, which I call the oral coefficient. The result is a number I call the Nosay Term, NT. Using the latest techniques in classical genetics, I have been able to increase the average NT of my herd from 5.9 to 6.7."

"Is that feet or inches?" Bill asked.

"It's dimensionless. "Haven't you been listening to what I've been saying?"

"Don't get all excited, Pierre. It was just a joke. You know, feet or inches. No cow can have a mouth that measures seven feet."

"Most cows have a Nosay number of less than five. Compare that to my average of 6.7."

"How does that translate to pounds and feed efficiency? Do your big-mouth cattle grow faster, get fatter, and fetch higher prices, or do they just get filled up faster and have more leisure time?"

"I don't have any way to measure that kind of data, but my observations, anecdotal as they may be, lead me to believe that big-mouth cattle grow faster, marble better, and produce more effective microbes in three out of four of their stomachs."

Bill's eyes lit up like firefly luciferin on a hot summer night in Baltimore when he heard the word microbe. It was, of course, what Rudy Kwasnik was always going on about. In fact, it was why they were in France. What if Nosay's cattle were the perfect microbe producers that Kwasnik had been searching for all these years?

"Why do you think that's so?" Bill asked.

"Statistical kinetics. Protein synthesis must be slower than bacterial growth. One makes great big molecules, while the other one makes tiny ones. It's Occam's razor, Aristotle's balance, Solomon's sword, and Wittgenstein's cradle. I'm just surprised no one figured it out before me."

"What do you think of cattle with big mouths?" Bill asked Claudine.

"I . . . think . . . they will . . . revolutionize . . . agriculture," she replied between biting her thumbnails, choking back laughter, and covering her face with her hands.

"Why don't you let us inseminate your cow with the biggest mouth?" Bill asked. "You can be part of a program that we think will revolutionize agriculture."

"Please. Tell me more," the economist turned herdsman said.

"We'll cycle her, come back in eighteen days, inseminate her, and flush some embryos ten days after that? We can split the embryos fifty/fifty. You implant yours in whatever cow you like. We'll take our share and implant them in commercial cows back home."

Pierre Nosay scratched his head for ten seconds before he answered.

"What kind of semen are you going to use, and where are you going to get it? The Salers Association won't allow us breeders to use just any old semen. They're entrusted with maintaining a quality herd. It's a big responsibility."

"Me and Claudine are set on using semen from a black bull from the Camargue. You know Blondie Raimbaut, don't you? He claims his bulls are smarter than jackasses and have a sense of humor, besides. What good's a cow with a big smile if she doesn't get a joke?

And we're gonna do all the genetics work on the sly. We already know the association won't go for the idea."

Pierre Nosay tipped his head back to laugh and then thrust out a big hand. "Count me in," he said. "At the LSE, we always tried to mix some fun with the drudgery of modeling failing capitalistic economies."

"What's an LSE, some kind of foreign sports car?"

"London School of Economics. I thought I told you I used to work there."

"How'd you get into the cattle business?" Bill asked.

"I already told you that my prediction that Bratislava would pass up Taiwan as a high-tech electronics center cost some important investors a lot of money and essentially ended my career in economic modeling."

"Same thing happened to me when I bought a bunch of Holsteins cheap," Bill said. "They stayed in the valleys and wouldn't walk up a short hill to graze. Before we close the deal, though, you gotta promise not to tell anybody about what we're doing. Most people won't understand, and we don't want to have to start answering a lot of questions or be ridiculed. I think we should use a code name for the project in any future conversations. How about Bonheur? It means good luck in French."

"Yes, I know, old boy. I do still speak the language, you know."

"We'll send you the data and pictures when the calves are born."

"Do you mind if I give you a NosayMeter to measure their mouth sizes at birth and at six months," Pierre said. "They retail for 1,200 euros, but since we're partners, you can have one for 750 euros, my cost."

"Can't I just use a cloth tape-measure? My cousin keeps one to measure scrotums. He usually adds an inch or two for good measure, but you can do the subtraction yourself."

Nosay banged the heel of his hand against his forehead. "I don't believe what I've just done. I usually just put my bulls in with cows, wait two months, and take them out. Everything's natural."

"Don't worry, Pierre. Claudine and me will do the technical work along with the professor that's helping us. We got lots of experience."

"I suppose it will work," Pierre said, much of his bravura gone. "Let's use Bouche de Sancerre. She has the biggest mouth in my herd, 7.06 Nosays, and most likely in the world. She hasn't stopped eating since the day she was born. If we put a flake of hay in front of her, she won't even notice or feel the needle when we synchronize her. When will you have the semen?"

"Sometime around Transit Workers Appreciation Day. I'll get it in the Camargue. It will be frozen, in the straw, and certified. We'll inseminate Bouche de Sancerre and our cow Murielle and collect the embryos after a couple of weeks. After that, the balls will be in your court."

"Where will you store the embryos?"

"Ceemensee has a big center in Limoges, so I'll probably take them there."

"Want a glass of wine?" Nosay asked them. "I have a real nice bottle of Sancerre given to me by my neighbor." When the wine was poured, Nosay tipped his head back and talked for a while with his eyes closed. "Switzerland might be a better place to bank our embryos because of that country's vast experience in the food and financial business. When I was at the LSE, I taught a course on Swiss Banking. Banking ova should be no different from banking gold or financial instruments. And something tells me it's already being done for cultivars for persimmons and pomegranates. The bank would probably assign us a drawer in a refrigerated vault, ask us to invent a unique password that required two numerals, three symbols, and at least one capital letter. You'd have to remember the last name of your dog's first vet, but that's not too hard."

"Hope your large-mouth theory is right, Pierre, and we get a bigger, better, and more intelligent cross. But me and Claudine got to skedaddle now. We forgot all about the third guy on our team, left him in front of the city hall in historic Salers. We got to find him, pronto. Then we still have to go visit that Swiss guy up the road."

"Don't bother with old Huppthapfell," Pierre Nosay said. "His cattle have an average Nosay number of less than four. Some of his cattle can barely swallow an alfalfa nugget. You'd only be wasting time. Make sure the guy that's helping you is Schwartzenhaben not Würtzenhaben."

CHAPTER 20

Where's Würtzy?

When Bill and Claudine pulled up in front of the city hall in historic Salers, Professor Würtzenhaben was nowhere to be seen. Just to the left of the main door, they found a note taped to the head of the ornamental stone cockerel.

Got tired of waiting. Gertyl and Heidi will drop me off in Brünstatt on their way back to Linz. Hope you found another cow. It is never good to conduct science on a single sample. Marcel

"Brünstatt, what does he mean Brünstatt?" Claudine sputtered. "He cannot go home. He must help us synchronize Murielle and Bouche de Sancerre on the day after tomorrow."

"He must mean Aurillac. He's probably pretty confused, a poor old guy like that, spending so much time with those Austrian teenagers, gobbling down pastries, and having all them choucroute baisers."

"What if we never see him again?" Claudine lamented.

"Don't worry, darling. We're sure to see him in a year or two. It won't take him long to get tired of them two Austrian chicks."

"Even if you are correct, Bill, we cannot wait a year or even two months for him to reappear. We will need his help in two days, and then we will need him again for the insemination in less than a month. We must find him now."

That night, the two of them searched all the pizza joints, arcades, and dance halls in Aurillac without turning up a trace of

Würtzenhaben. After a light dinner of crepes and tea in the square, they returned to their hotel room and watched *Shoot the Piano Player* on France Today TV. Claudine bedded down as soon as the movie ended, while Bill pulled a lamp over to his side of the bed and opened up his new book, *Le Etranger.*

***

Claudine rose with the sun the next morning and dressed without waking Bill. She walked over to the association office on the town square on the off chance that Professor Würtzenhaben might have stopped there or been seen around town by one of the staff. When all responses turned out to be nos, she headed back to the hotel. When she entered their room, she was surprised to see Bill wide awake with his face stuck in *Le Etranger.*

"No sign of the professor anywhere. I even checked the hospital and the jail. We will just have to cycle Murielle and Bouche de Sancerre without him. I brought back two syringes and a vial of Lutalyse. Do you think you can manage the shots?"

"Claudine, who do you think is a better writer, Camus or Flaubert?"

"Don't change the subject," she said using the diminutive Billy. "Besides, it's an impossible question. They wrote in different epochs and were different in every respect. One was a romantic and the other an existentialist. Now please, answer my question: do you think you can give the shots?"

"Sure, synchronization is the easy part. Jab and stab, rock and roll. In the neck or in the rump, it don't matter. Just push the pump. The next step will be harder, and we'll need him for the flush for sure."

"Yes, I agree. Remember, we have to inseminate within eight hours of the start of estrus, usually about eighteen days after the Lutalyse shot."

"I hope we're not gonna have to sit around in Murat for a long time watching for them cows to go into heat," Bill protested. "Maybe Mr. Garçelon can watch them for us and give us a heads-up."

"Maybe not. Don't you remember that one of the technicians at Ceemensee told us that they sell a remote estrus checker? You strap it on the cow's leg. When she goes into heat and gets restless, the instrument sends a radio signal to alert the stockman. Nevertheless, I hope we find the professor soon. It would be perfect if the cows come into heat on Ascension Day. We would have sufficient time because the men will be in Mauriac rolling boules all afternoon at the tournament. And then they will probably hang around in the cafes for the rest of the evening."

"It's already April 29, ain't it," Bill reminded her.

"If we give the shots the day after tomorrow, May first, the two cows will come into estrus on Ascension Day. We can flush them in ten days on Pentecost. That makes every operation fall on a major holiday."

"Perfect! If we get finished in early June, I'll have plenty of time to go to Hawaii."

"You haven't ever said anything about a trip to Hawaii," Claudine said, her hurt showing in the area between her nose and upper lip.

"You sure I never mentioned it? Us TrunkWax guys all agreed to meet in Hawaii on the fourth of July for a powwow. It'll be almost a year since we met at Rudy Kwasnik's house to get the Bonheur ball rolling. At the time, we figured we'd probably need to get together to hash over all the problems we didn't think of a year ago. For me it'll be a good chance to figure out how to get the embryos back to Pylewood. The other guys might have some good suggestions."

***

The first of May dawned bright and warm in Aurillac. Bill put on his workout clothes and headed down to the Stade Aurillacois to run some laps and do some stretching exercises. He was getting in shape pretty fast for someone who had been out of shape for so long. His knee felt stronger, and he was beginning to harbor the hope that he might not need knee surgery after all.

Andy Craik was already on the field doing sit-ups when Bill trotted out of the locker room.

"You got something like a sled that I can push around for a few minutes?" he asked his new teammate.

"Nope, rugby's old school, anti-machine. But come to think of it, we got that old black Panhard over there by the fence that the boys like to push around sometimes. If you want, I'll go over there and steer. Or if you'd rather pull it, there's a rope and sling in the boot. How ye bin?"

"Good. Got some things to do this afternoon, and then I'm goin' down to Arles for a few days to do some ridin' and cowboyin'. But I'll be back for the Nîmes game. Tell me again how you score points. I know you get five for a touchdown, and you can kick field goals on the run, but I forget how many points you get for that."

Craik popped up from his sit-ups and began running through the scoring rules. "A try, we don't call it a touchdown, gets you five points. Kicks are conversions worth two points and penalty and drop goals are three. It's really pretty simple."

"Let me finish my sit-ups and sprints, and I'll see you in the locker room," Craik said. "Go over there and see if you can move the Panhard with the handbrake on."

***

When Bill got back to the hotel room, Claudine was already packing up their gear: boots, overalls, disposable gloves, syringes, and the vial of Lutalyse.

"How'd it go?" Bill asked.

"I ran into Antoine Lanob, and he seemed surprised that I was still here. He said he had a package for me, but I couldn't imagine what it might be. It turned out that I had won the Polzonitza raffle prize, the ten baseball caps. Now I'm afraid he might be really suspicious, especially since we asked for permission to import Salers genetics, and he could not help to notice that I was visibly upset when he denied our request."

"Hang on to them caps, Claudine. Who knows, we might be able to use them some time. We can put one on Würtzenhaben so's we'll be able to spot him in a crowd. Any sign of him in town?"

"I peeked in at the Jardin des Choix and asked the grocer if she had seen a man that fit the professor's description, and she answered yes. She described a short fellow with a pointed beard and an Alsatian accent who asked if he could buy some Turkish cabbage."

"I'll bet he's shacked up with Gertyl somewhere," Bill said. "That old fox, the note he left was just something to throw us off his trail for a few days."

"I can't help it, Bill, but I'm afraid he might forget he has an appointment with us."

"Who's the nervous one now? Don't worry. I can handle it. In the old days on our ranch, we'd brand two hundred calves in a day, give 'em three different shots, dehorn 'em, cut the bull calves, and still have time for a game of pinochle. You know, Claudine, Andy Craik, our scrum half, claims that Flaubert isn't for ruggers. He looked at me funny when I said I was reading *Madame Bovary* to improve my French. He prefers Camus. Says he's modern, masculine, and direct in his prose. But he said that neither French author could stand up against the Scottish author, Lewis Grassic Gibbon."

"Reading novels is a waste of time," Claudine countered. "I'd much rather read the agriculture bulletins."

"I disagree. One thing I'm learning is that books like *Madame Bovary* and *L'Etranger* are a way to understand the world without having to go through the trouble of experiencing everything firsthand. Take *Madam Bovary* for example. While I never had sex in a taxicab or knew anyone who did, I used my cousin's pickup a few times. And like most guys, I been in my share of trouble but never went to the beach much like Meursault."

"The thing that angers me so much about all of this is the attitude of the Salers Association directors, all men who think that the idea of breeding cows to improve their intelligence as well as their milk production is stupid."

CHAPTER 21

Synching

It was already 10:30 PM when Bill and Claudine got to Garçelon's place in Murat. It was pitch-black at the farm: no lights in the house, gates locked, and cattle already in the barn. Claudine parked out of sight in the driveway behind a large linden tree. Both of them were dressed in dark clothes, and Bill pulled out a black ski mask from his jacket when they got out of the car.

"Don't put that thing on," Claudine whispered. "You will scare the dog for sure."

"Nobody said anything about a dog before."

"Albert has a giant Bernese Mountain dog called Lamarck who he lets out in the evening to guard the place."

Sure enough, just as Bill swung his first leg over the top of the gate, a large black dog, growling menace, ambled toward them. His low growling revving up until he recognized Claudine.

"Bon chien, bon chien, Lamarck," Claudine whispered as she dangled a pork chop in front of the dog's nose. "We are old friends. He remembers me well from the times I visited when I was the Salers breed representative. He probably would have torn you to fragments if you had worn that silly mask."

"I doubt it," Bill said. "I trained dogs ever since I was twelve years old, and none of them ever bit me. What'd you say this dog's name was?"

"Lamarck," Claudine whispered.

"Named after the French mathematician that discovered geometry," Bill whispered back.

"No," she whispered, "trigonometry."

Bill followed Claudine back toward the barn and watched as she slid the door open. Murielle was at the far end of the line of cows, mostly all champions, large boned, thick through the hips, perfect horns, and deep red in color. The animals sensed something was different and began shifting nervously. Lamarck found his usual spot in the corner and laid down.

Claudine cooed at the cows in French, something that seemed to calm them down. When they got to Murielle, Bill reached into his pocket and pulled out the syringe and the stubby bottle of Lutalyse, the drug that would start a new estrus cycle. He tipped the vial up-side-down in his left hand while he poked the needle through the rubber serum cap in the mouth of the vial. He tapped the side of the syringe with his index finger before he slowly drew back the plunger, taking care not to trap any air bubbles in the liquid. *So far so good*, he thought as he rubbed Murielle's neck, searching for a spot where he could poke the needle in just under the skin. When he found the spot and had just started pushing down on the plunger, Murielle jerked her neck back and pulled the needle away from the body of the syringe.

"Shit," he hissed. "I forgot to twist the needle onto the syringe."

"Stop pushing!" Claudine yelled. "You are squirting everywhere."

"Mon dieu, what amateurs," a voice from the shadows said. "It's a good thing I came, even though Gertyl was against it."

"Is that you, Professor?" Claudine asked.

"Yes, I've been waiting here since seven o'clock when that farmer left for the fireworks show in town. What took you so long?"

"I thought you had gone to Linz or Brünstatt or somewheres else," Bill said.

"Give me that syringe, you imbecile, before you lose the whole dose," Würtzenhaben said. The professor took the syringe and tipped it point up. "Only eight milliliters left. I hope you have another bottle," he said.

"Nope, Claudine only brought two doses."

"I didn't think you were going to spray it all on the ground," she said.

"There's probably twenty-five milliliters left in the vial plus what's still in the syringe," Würtzenhaben said. "Unless you want to come back tomorrow, I suggest you divide what you have in half and give equal shots to Murielle and that other cow in Pleaux."

"What's half of thirty-three?" Bill joked. "I was away workin' at my uncle's feed lot in Hanford when my class studied calculus."

Würtzenhaben stood on his toes to stare at Bill. "See if you can find the needle. If it's lost, so are we, unless you were smart enough to bring an extra."

Bill gently slid his hand along Murielle's neck until it bumped into a tiny protrusion the size of a pimple. He gently pulled the needle out and handed it to the professor.

"Würtzy," Bill said, "maybe it isn't so smart to divide what's left in half. Why don't we give a full dose to Murielle here and give whatever's left to Nosay's cow? That way, we'd be sure to have at least one cow in heat at the right time. Besides, I'm not sure I believe Nosay's ideas about cows with big mouths."

"I say we gamble on getting two or nothing," Würtzenhaben argued. "Most drugs are over prescribed anyway. Besides, you hired me to advise you. If you ignore my advice, I quit."

After Würtzenhaben had correctly given the shot, the three of them shook hands and sped off to Pierre Nosay's place at Pleaux to reprogram Bouche de Sancerre's reproductive functions. Pierre was waiting for them in the barn when they got there. Bouche de Sancerre was tied to a stanchion and completely occupied in eating a special tub of alfalfa pellets with fresh turnip greens that her owner had prepared. When Bill asked Würtzenhaben for the syringe and another try, the old man threatened a kick him in the shins if he got too close.

"You have eighteen days to choose a bull and collect his semen. If I were you, I'd be sure to have some extra doses in case you spill some," the professor added, his comment laden with sarcasm.

"Is it hard to inseminate a camel?" Bill asked the old man.

"I've never done it myself," Würtzenhaben said, "but I think it was tried in India in the fifties at the University of Hyderabad."

CHAPTER 22

The Camargue

Blondie Raimbaut was on the platform ready to meet Bill when he arrived at the train station in Hyeres.

"Bill, Bill, over here!" he shouted from a dozen meters up the track.

Bill cocked his left hand behind his ear to gather added oscillations so he could connect the sound with an image on the platform. He finally zoomed in on a flat wide-brimmed black hat, and even though he didn't recognize the hat, the body under underneath it had a familiar shape. When he waved, a hand attached to the body waved back.

"Blondie, didn't recognize you without your beret," Bill said as they closed the gap between each other. "Where'd you get that red neckerchief and fancy colored shirt? Looks like something a guy might see in New Mexico or Arizona."

"This is how we dress in the Camargue this time of year. Where is Claudine?" he asked.

"She drove back to Paris to take care of some paperwork. I'm supposed to meet her back in Aurillac in eighteen days."

Bill clamped a hand on Blondie's shoulder. "You better be careful somebody don't try to steal that chapeau you got on top your head. It'd probably fetch a couple of hundred euros in Abu Dhabi or Timbuktu, 'specially if you got it properly cleaned and blocked."

"Welcome to Provence, land of tomatoes, thyme, olives, white horses, and black bulls. My car is in the parking lot, and we shouldn't waste a minute getting out of this tourist trap and on to Arles, the Camargue, and the Bouche du Rhone."

"You bet. I'm really looking forward to breathing country air, seeing open spaces, and getting a horse under me. The Cantal ain't bad, but I had enough of hills, winding roads, and mediocre wine." Then he paused and got serious. "What kind of word is mediocre? Sounds French."

"Pure French," Blondie said as he motioned Bill toward a blue Peugeot in the parking lot. As soon as Bill got settled, Blondie revved up the little car and roared out of the train station parking lot. "The trip to Arles shouldn't take too long. I asked you to get off the train at Hyeres so that we could bypass the big traffic mess in Marseille. We'll take the scenic route up to Aix–en-Provence and then go straight west to Arles. When we get to Arles, we'll join an old friend of mine, Georges Bellatre. We'll have something to eat and then go out to his country house. Arles has some nice hotels, but I think you will be happier staying at the Bellatre estate."

"Might be better if I stayed in a hotel," Bill said. "My French isn't all that good. I might get mixed up, say something rude or crude, and get your friends all mad at me. I'm kinda nervous around folks until I get to know them some."

"Don't worry. Georges speaks excellent English, and his estate is comfortable and private. He is also a gracious host. I am sure you'll be happier at his place than in any hotel in Arles. Everyone will recognize you there, including the scores of Dutch, German, and English tourists that ride the river boats and clog the town this time of year. Don't forget, your picture was viewed worldwide: *France Soir, Deutsche Vela,* and *BBC TV.*"

"I guess you're right. I always thought I might like being famous, but I'm not so sure anymore."

"I'm not surprised by your fame," Blondie said. "Not only did millions of us French people see you on television the night of the Vital Nordhoff burglary, but we French have always been fascinated with the American West. And be assured, you do stand out in a crowd, especially when you are wearing that big Stetson hat and ostrich-skin boots."

Bill looked down at his feet. "Look, Blondie, I'm not wearing them anymore. They hurt my feet so bad that I went out and bought me some French loafers in Clermont-Ferrand. Anyways, I shouldn't really be complaining about being famous. I've been stacking up euros in my French bank account, something that Ariane Dercanges helped me do."

"*Tres bien.* So you've found yourself a girlfriend already."

"Sort of, but it ain't Ariane. You remember Ariane, she was the head cop on the scene when I roped the hat thief. She's been helping me gather and keep all my new moolah, and she handles my bookings and public appearances. She's already got me some TV commercials, I'm in line for an appearance on the Arnaut Maratz reality show, and we're also working on a cameo role for me on *Le Bateaux d'Vie*, the daytime soap opera. I'm gonna play a rich Texan who owns a grand prix racing team."

"You just said your French wasn't very good. How are you going to speak your lines for television?" Blondie asked.

"Pa day toot, mon ami. At first, they'll put captions on the screen when I talk, but with Ariane's help, I'm hopin' to be able to do my own talkin' by September."

"Good luck. I'll make sure you get plenty of practice while you're here. I've got you booked to give a two-day seminar on stress-free cattle handling in the Vaucluse, a demonstration of rope tricks for children at the Ecole Normal d'Belle Epoch in les Baux, and a reading of Jean Giono's *Trial by Jury* in English to the patients at the Maison d'Ancienne Professeurs d'Anglais in Nîmes."

"When do I get on a horse?"

"In between engagements. We're going to drive a herd of *toureaux* to the bullfight arena in Aigues-Mortes and go to a Camargue branding. I'll ride with you when I can, and Georges Bellatre will join you when I can't. We'll teach you the rules of the bull run, bull fights, and the branding."

"Sounds like fun, or tres amusant, ne c'est pas."

"Especially the manade, since the spectators will try to distract you and help the bulls escape. It's an ancient ritual. Sometimes it calls for some fancy riding to block the bull's escape. If they break, you must keep up with the leading bull by racing with him while keeping in a close formation."

"Before I do any of that kind of fancy stuff, I got to collect a few straws of semen from one of your black bulls.

"What for, if you don't mind me asking?"

"I want to take home some of that Camargue cow intelligence you were telling me about on the train ride to Clermont-Ferrand."

"I was mostly joking," Blondie said.

"I'm not. I've been thinking about how much time and money we waste by trying to breed cattle for length and rib eye when we'd be a lot better off breeding them for intelligence and dexterity. Smarter, daintier cattle could save us a bunch of money by doing some of the ranch work themselves. We kinda do that with rodeo stock, but I'm thinking we could do lots more with commercial cattle. With smarter animals, we wouldn't have to spend so much money building strong corrals and tight fences. And we wouldn't spend so much time chasing stock around, tryin' to get them to go into this field or that pen. Why, if we could teach them to remember their names, we could just tell them where to go and make sure they understood. Dogs do it, don't they? Why not cattle? Down the road we might even be able to teach them to read a few signs, nothin' too complicated, but maybe stuff like Keep Out or No Left Turn.

"OK, Bill, I get it," Blondie said. "I won't ask again."

"Can we go look at some bulls and collect a few straws of semen before we start on all the fun stuff?" Bill asked. "First, though, I got to rent a semen collector and find a freezer where I can store the stuff. Shouldn't take all that long, and then I got a couple of weeks before I have to hightail it back to Aurillac."

"I hate to put a damper on your plans," Blondie said. "But I don't think there's any way for you to collect semen from a Camargue bull. The animals are half wild to begin with, and we raise them completely naturally. As far as I know, no one has ever collected semen from a Camargue bull."

Bill dropped his head for a second. "You got to be kiddin', Blondie. I been thinkin' about nothing else."

"I'm sorry, I should have said something. Maybe Georges will have an idea. He's a pretty smart guy."

"I hope he's not gonna ask me a lot of questions."

"Don't worry, Bill. Georges is cool. He's a retired drug company executive, so he is used to dealing with government regulations. He is also an accomplished horseman and has a stable of horses, including a Choctaw pony he bought on a trip to Oklahoma. Believe me, he will be very happy to have the pleasure of your company."

"You think he'll have a horse that's big enough for me? I'm getting close to three hundred pounds. Murtry, my horse back home, is sixteen-and-a-half hands high and still struggles under my weight sometimes."

"Our Camargue horses aren't too tall, thirteen or fourteen hands, but they are stout. Legend has it that they descended from horses that Celtic warriors left to graze in the Bouches du Rhone. Over the years, these warriors would bring boats up the Rhone and collect the white horses for their military campaigns. This region also provided the mounts for the first crusade. I would guess that a medieval warrior in armor would weigh close to a hundred and fifty kilos." Blondie paused to search for the correct words in English and ended up patting his derriere. "Finding a saddle for you might be our biggest problem."

When they hit the outskirts of Arles, Blondie gave Bill a nudge. "Georges should be waiting for us at the Hotel Calendal, which has a good restaurant. Are you hungry, or shall we just have a drink?"

"I'm pretty dang hungry. I been missin' meals ever since I left Pylewood. Do you think we could get some grenoolies in Arles?"

"I think so, though I'm not sure if they are on the menu at Le Calendal. An excellent idea, however: frog legs, lots of garlic and olive oil, and a bottle of Bandol Cote de Provence to wash them down. Georges will approve. He is a connoisseur of Provençal cuisine."

Georges Bellatre was waiting for them at a table in front of the hotel, nursing a pastis. Small and trim, he looked to be in his early fifties. He had graying curly hair and log sideburns that went well with his slightly uptilted chin and wry aristocratic smile.

"I am very pleased that you have come to the Camargue, Monsieur Robeiro," he said when they shook hands. "Some years ago, I lived in Ann Arbor and worked at the University of Michigan. I loved America and relish the opportunity to repay the kindness that was shown me and my family during that time."

"Pleased to meet you," Bill said. "Never been to Michigan myself, but I think my first pickup truck might have been built there."

Bill noticed that the Frenchman was already dressed up for something: gray breeches tucked into high black leather riding boots, a matching, magnificently braided gray tunic, and a tall cylindrical hat with a visor, a chin strap, and topped with a bright plume.

"What kind of hat is that?" Bill asked.

"Second hussars, 1807."

"Careful, someone don't try to steal it."

Georges Bellatre snapped to mock attention. "I belong to a group that reenacts famous battles of the Napoleonic wars. This uniform is authentic down to the buttons. After we eat, I will ride into mock battle against the Prussians. Tomorrow, if I survive, we'll get you a mount and take a practice ride around the salt flats."

"Bill wants to collect some semen from one of our Camargue black bulls for a breeding project he has back home in America," Blondie interjected, "but I told him I didn't think it would be possible."

Georges assumed a thinking pose but said nothing.

"Why can't we make history, Georges?" Bill asked. "Cows are cows. If you can collect semen from Salers, Aubrac, and Charolais, you oughta be able to do it with your Camargos."

"We don't have the equipment," Blondie said. "Besides not having stanchions, squeeze chutes, corrals, or pens, we don't have modern collection gear: electric stimulator, electronic test equipment, and liquid nitrogen refrigeration."

"What if we just tie up a cute heifer to a gate and let the bull come to her," Bill said. "When he mounts her, we just clamp the collector on his pecker, or whatever you call it in French, and collect the semen. I saw one at the Ceemensee booth at the Sommet de l'Elevage at Clermont-Ferrand."

"That might work on one of your old dairy bulls, but never on one of our bred-for-fighting Camargue taureaux," Blondie protested. "He'll never let you get close enough, especially if the heifer is cute. Even if you trick him into using the collector, you'll never trick him into letting you take it off."

"If these cattle are as smart as you say, my guess is that he'll sure want to get that the little glass jar off his dong. Besides, he'll be open to a bribe: alfalfa nuggets, clover cookies, or éclairs if they come from Paris or Lyon? What do you think, Georges? Won't they catch on pretty quick?"

"Give me a chance to think about it for a while. I'm on your side when it comes to innovation. Just because it hasn't been done before doesn't mean it's impossible. Whoever thought that we would have a painless cure for rabies or be able to watch television in airplanes?"

"We could shoot one with a hypnotic dart and slip the semen collector on him while he was dreaming about lush clover or heads of rye grass," Bill said.

"Getting the collector on is only half the job," Blondie piped up. "You still have to arouse the bull so he drops a couple of francs in the tin cup."

"Maybe that's where the shouting comes in," Bill answered.

"I think we've exhausted the topic for now," Blondie said. "Let's move to the garden and order lunch."

Blondie opened the menu and read. "The prix fix plates are Cabillaud Minceur and Duo de Boeuf Gourmand."

"I have to watch my cholesterol," Georges said, "so I'll just have the Salade Nicoise."

"I haven't had a good chunk of beef since I got to France," Bill said. "I'll have the gourmet beef, but can I have steak sauce and ice cream for dessert instead of the tartar sauce and duck liver custard? What are you having, Blondie?"

"The cabillaud. It's cod baked in a small crock and served with a creamy sauce." When the waitress, a youngish girl who spoke good English, came, Bellatre ordered a Salade Mediterranean, Blondie the fish, and Bill the beef extravaganza.

"They forgot to cook my hamburger," Bill said when the waitress brought him a large purple plate almost buried under a mountain of ground red meat.

"No, no, Bill. You must eat the tartare raw. Mix it with the tapenade, which is made up of chopped capers, cornichon, and shallots in olive oil. The meat is already flavored with egg yolk and salt.

"You guys sure it's safe to eat all this raw meat? I didn't have time to get any special shots when I left Pylewood. Nobody told me French people ate raw meat."

"Just tartare," Bellatre answered. "I'm surprised you find it odd. In some places, this dish is called filet américain. Tartare is a specialty of this region, and it's meant to show off the high quality of our beef. Don't worry. The meat isn't chopped up until it's been ordered. Sometimes we even put a raw egg on top. That's what tartare is."

In the end, Bellatre devoured his salad, Blondie made short work of the cod, and Bill exclaimed that his chopped-up raw steak was delicious and easy to chew.

"Back home, even though I usually order my steak cooked medium-rare, the chef, usually overcooks it, and it comes out tough. From now on, I'm gonna ask him to skip the cooking and just grind up my steak and put it on a plate with a raw egg on top."

"Can you teach me to rope from horseback?" Bellatre asked Bill.

"Sure, but first, we gotta find a decent lariat. Back home, I use a stiff nylon rope."

"I'd be surprised if we can even find one out here in the Camargue. The *gardians* use a horsehair rope they twist themselves," Blondie offered. "Then there's the saddle problem. You'll need a saddle horn to dally off the rope."

"The saddle horn shouldn't be too big of a problem. We'll make that too," Bellatre said. "My Australian saddle has one. I'll get one of the gardians to carve a likeness out of wood, and we'll screw it into the tree of one of my older saddles. Someone had to make the first ones by hand, right."

After a round of calvados and a toast to homemade saddles, the three men sat around the table surveying the carnage of lunch: pastis vessels on their sides, a pile of empty white plates, two empty bottles drained of the pink bounty of Bandol's vineyards, and half a small tree's worth of crumpled paper napkins.

"I'm off to battle," Bellatre said as he got up, placed his tall hussar's hat on his head, and marched in a slightly crooked line toward the restaurant gate. When he arrived at the gate, he did a smart about-face and addressed Blondie, "Blondie, mon bon homme, please drop Bill off at my place. Gerrard will be there to greet him and show him his room. Tomorrow Bill and I will ride the famous white horses of the Camargue and prepare for the Course de Toureaux.

Blondie drove the blue Peugeot down the Boulevard Clemenceau and then took the road south past the sign that marked the turnoff for the bridge at Arles until he came to a small opening in a brick wall where he turned and followed a lane until they reached an imposing old house. A formally clad gent with an imposing moustache was waiting in front of the door and walked toward them, arriving at the passenger-side door at the same instant that the car stopped. He announced that he was Gerrard, the butler and a family friend and would be pleased to show Bill his room and, when he was ready, prepare him a light super. It only took Bill a few minutes to be ready, and as soon as he had a napkin on his lap, Gerrard arrived with a fine omelet he had whipped up from six fresh eggs, a handful of sautéed trompet de morte mushrooms, and a little bit of garlic. He fed it to Bill with some crusty French bread, a bowl of tiny artichokes, and a bottle of 2008 Drouhin Chablis.

"Sleep well, my friend," the butler said when Bill excused himself. "Monsieur Bellatre is an enthusiastic rider and will ride until you drop."

"I doubt it, Gerrard. I've been in the saddle for three days straight on cattle drives in Idaho and Montana. I've ridden in flurries of sleet, dust storms, and blistering heat." *Shit, the whole Camargue is no more than a drop in the bucket of Montana*, he thought to himself. *A little jaunt through a swamp ain't nothing.* Bill found sleep in minutes.

CHAPTER 23

Riding the White Horses

At 7:00 AM, Gerrard knocked softly. "Monsieur Robeiro, breakfast is ready, and the *patron* is in his riding boots and in the stable ready to go."

Huge cups, pitchers of hot milk and steaming coffee, bread, butter, jam, were spread out on the dining room table.

"Would you like some bacon and eggs with your petit dejeuner?" Gerrard asked. "I remember that our last American visitor, a chemistry professor from Canada, was fond of huge breakfasts: waffles, bacon, sausages, and eggs."

"No, thanks, Gerrard. This breakfast looks real good the way it is. A lot of times on roundups and brandings, when I'm in a real hurry, I just grab a couple of Snickers bars and a Coke before I hit the saddle. This is way better than I'm used to." Gerrard made a bad face for an instant before he realized it was rude.

When Bill got out to the barn, Bellatre was leading a medium-sized white mare out of the barn. The horse was already saddled up, and Bill couldn't stifle a broad smile when he saw the rig. The saddle looked brand new: all clean, tan leather, high and straight cantle, with a tuck-and-roll upholstery job that looked like it came out of a Mexican low rider, a pommel to match, leather arm rests like his La-Z-Boy, a big pillow of padding on the seat, and long closed stirrups folded up in front. A fancy rope was coiled up on the saddle and fastened to a strap on the bridle.

"Let me go change into some nicer pants. Don't want the grommets on my Levis scratchin' up your easy chair," Bill said to Bellatre.

"Don't worry," Bellatre answered. "This saddle has been used many times. It's made from the finest English leather and handcrafted in a famous saddlery in Cadiz. It has survived many bull runs. A bigger worry is whether or not it is long enough for you. The seat is seventy-five centimeters long, the largest saddle they make."

"Sounds like trouble. My waist is about forty inches, but the problem is my derriere might be even bigger."

"Well, there are 2.54 centimeters in an inch, so it certainly will be a tight fit."

"I never seen a saddle with so much padding. It must be real comfortable."

"It will take some time getting used to," Bellatre said. "If you're not accustomed to a seat so soft, it will seem to you like you have a barrel between your legs after a few miles. Novice riders worry that their legs will never straighten out." Bellatre took a step backward and stared at Bill's legs in mock seriousness. "You shouldn't have that trouble. Put on a pair of spurs. This pony is used to them."

"How do you call her?"

"Cubry," Bellatre answered.

The spurs looked handmade and were short with small rowels. Bill stuck his left foot in the stirrup while his hand searched in vain for the horn. Even though his behind was bigger than the space between the cantle and the pommel, his body started adjusting, and he slowly oozed down between the sides like an oversized peach being forced into a glass jar.

"How is it?" Bellatre asked.

"No chance of me fallin' out, that's for sure. But how you gonna get me out of this seat when we're finished? Might take a crowbar or a crane."

"I have an Australian saddle in the shed that might fit you better. It is quite all right to change, if you wish."

"Hell no. I didn't come all the way to France to ride around in an Australian saddle. Let's go."

"Do you want to carry a trident with you?"

"What the heck's that?"

"A long pole with a three pointed tip. We call it a *ficheiroun*, and the gardians use it in their work."

"Hell yes," he said. "Never rode with a spear before, but I'll give it a try."

When he saw the trident, he thought maybe he had agreed a little too quickly. The trident was a good seven-feet long and tipped with a crescent-shaped piece of steel with a short triangular point in the center.

"How do you guys use this thing?"

"We can use it to trip a calf to get it down for branding or treatment or, with a jab, stop a stampede or move a bull."

"Like a long HotShot, I reckon."

"A gardian may also use it to help maneuver through the many bogs we have in the Bouches."

"What else do I have to carry?"

"Gardians usually carry a seden, a horse hair rope, about thirty-five-feet long. We couldn't come up with a nylon lasso, but the seden that you see tied on your saddle is the finest of our kind, produced close-by in Aigues-Mortes.

Bill unloosed the rope, hefted it, and spooled out a couple of yards.

"This rope's real pretty, but a little on the light side for me. Wouldn't hold a loop too good."

"Yes, we use our ropes from the ground. We don't throw them from a horse."

"Yeah, but a loop this light won't carry very far."

Bill gave his pony a tiny tap with the spur, and the white horse moved out a ways and stopped when he sat back. "Good horse. This ain't gonna be too hard, if I can figure out how to balance this long stick you gave me."

"Point it straight up," Bellatre said. "There's a place on the stirrup where you can rest it. Or if you prefer, you can lean it back and rest it on your shoulder. Handling the ficheiroun will be the hardest thing for you if you decide to ride with the gardians in the manade."

"What else do I need to know?"

"There's also the branding, which we call the ferrade and the abrivado when we drive the taureaux through the streets of the towns to the bull ring."

"How come nobody ever talks about cows here? What do you do with 'em?"

"It's confusing, I know, but we call all of them—bulls and cows—taureaux. Yes, we have a number of strange customs here in the Camargue. Another, one you may find interesting is that the Camargue women are not only known for their beauty but also for their riding and animal work. It's customary here for the rausatires, the guys that wrestle the yearlings to the ground to hand the branding iron to one of the women spectators. They say that Camargue women burn some of the cleanest brands. Some years ago, branding with hot irons went out of vogue, but lately, it's come back, mostly done to show and preserve the tradition."

"I'm used to brandin', especially on a large scale," Bill said. "We used to do a hundred in a day on our ranch in Pittsburg. We'd gather calves, rope 'em, drag 'em into the branding area where we'd have as many as three fires, half a dozen irons in each pit, and three teams of branders."

"It's pretty much the same for us," Blondie said, "But we don't rope our taureaux, we walk into the herd and chase one of the calves out. Then two gardians, on horseback, close the escape path to keep the calf from returning to its mother. Others are waiting in the branding area to wrestle the animals down. Some of the fellows are good enough to put the calves on the ground by themselves."

"How do they do that without a horse? Where I come from, the horse plays an important part: keeps the rope taught and helps the wrangler pull the calf down."

"With us, one fellow grabs the taureau by both horns first, and then he lets loose of one horn and reaches around and grabs the tail. Once he's got a hold of the tail, he kicks the back legs out from under the animal. Then a bunch of fellows pounce on the animal to keep it still while they brand it."

"Sounds like somethin' I'd like to try, but I'll save it for the next time around."

"Well, you could be one of the two horsemen that make sure the calf doesn't escape back into the herd. You'd have to block the path back while you were holding the trident. It can be tricky if you have not done it before. Why don't you see if you can do some fast stops and quick starts this morning? When you feel comfortable with your mount, I'll hand you the trident, and we'll see how you do with one hand. I would guess it's a lot like roping where you hold the lariat in one hand and rein with the other. Your mare, Cubry, is experienced and knows instinctively what to do, so you shouldn't have a problem."

"Hope you're right," Bill said. "Over time, I've had a couple of really good cutting horses that I used in competition, but I haven't done much of that the last few years."

Bill and Bellatre headed out the stable toward the road, crossed it, and trotted their horses out into a small field of tight scrub grass. Bill clucked Cubry into a tight canter. He liked her gait but still hadn't got comfortable in the soft saddle. Besides, he felt kind of naked going to work cattle without a decent rope. True enough, he had a trident in his right hand, but he felt like it wasn't going to be much use to him. Bellatre followed him out, sitting loose and comfortable on his horse, a smaller but obviously spirited mount. The Frenchman shook his body into the shape of an experienced rider: back straight, legs and shoulders loose.

"What do you think, Bill?" Bellatre asked. "Are you getting along with Cubry?"

"She's as good a horse as I ever rode, but the saddle ain't. I guess I shoulda took you up on the offer of that Aussie one."

"I think you should get smaller. Why expect the saddle to shrink?" Bellatre said, rising up on his stirrups. "I'm telling Gerrard to serve you no more than one buttered croissant for breakfast. Instead of pastries, he'll fill you up with stewed pears and yogurt."

After a few quick stops and short turns, Bill signaled that he felt pretty good on Cubry. Bellatre rode over to the wooden gate in the corner, swung it open, and let in a young bull that he had picked out earlier, knowing that the animal wasn't too high strung.

"See if you can put this bête in a corner and keep him there for a few seconds," Bellatre shouted to Bill.

Piece of cake Bill, thought. He had done it a thousand times. He worked Cubry toward the left hip of the bull, a spot where the bull couldn't see him. No big deal, cattle and horses, they were the same everywhere: Pylewood, Australia, the Camargue. Bellatre worked his horse closer to the bull and got him to take a few tentative steps. When Bill turned toward Bellatre to get his signal, he shifted awkwardly in the tight saddle and dropped his trident, which startled the bull and sent him into a run toward the far corner of the field. When he got there, he skidded to halt and abruptly turned to face the riders. Instinctively, the two riders headed for opposite sides of the corner, while the young bull stood stone-cold still.

"Let's get him out in the center of the field. If I know him, he'll stay in the corner. He thinks it's a game now. See the way his head is tilted."

When the two riders got almost close enough to touch him, the bull bolted between the two of them and headed straight for the spot where Bill had dropped his trident and stood right over it. Bill walked Cubry over to the young bull and let her take over. She dipped and dashed a couple of times until she had the bull against the fence and then trotted him along into the corner. After a few seconds, Bellatre rode out from where he was watching and leaned way down to pick up Bill's trident.

"Don't worry, amigu," he said, passing the trident over to Bill. "You'll get the feel of it with a little practice."

Bellatre was right. With another couple of tries, Bill had it.

"This is a lot of fun, Georges. I think I'm ready to do it in front of an audience."

"Tomorrow we will go over to the Bonfort place near Saint Martin de Crau and help brand some cattle. Arnaut Bonfort is an old-timer, a blacksmith, long past his riding and branding days. He still keeps busy though raising champion fighting bulls and making exquisite trident tips at his forge."

"Don't forget, Georges, I still got to collect a couple of straws of semen for the project in Aurillac."

"Check out Bonfort's bulls tomorrow. He has some nice ones, not too large and very clever. I think you might find the right one over there."

"Georges, ten minutes ago, you called me amigu. That ain't French, is it?"

"No. It's Provençal, the language of the troubadours."

CHAPTER 24

The Ferrade

Early the next morning, Bill and Georges Bellatre arrived with their mounts at the edge of the broad, flat plain the people of the Camargue call the Crau. Bill finally relaxed when Bellatre's rig slid to a hypo-pneumatic stop in front of Arnaut Bonfort's smithy, a low, whitewashed building with a red tile roof, and swinging barn doors. Bill was finding that Bellatre, like most upper-class Frenchmen, was only truly at ease behind the wheel of a vehicle when the accelerator pedal was flat against the floorboard, and the pins on the dashboard gauges were in their red zones. Once out of the car, the two men headed for the wide-open front door of the mas. Peering in, they spied Blondie Raimbaut propped up on a rough wooden bench, shoulder against a white plastered wall, and head pushed forward, intent on hearing every word of the old blacksmith's discourse on the bygone days. Days when Roumanille and Mistral had resurrected the old Provençal language and Ricard and Baroncelli had brought rice and cowboys to the area.

"You know in the end it was pastis that saved the Camargue," Bonfort said, turning toward the two recent arrivals. "Ricard made wagonloads of money promoting and selling the drink in France and used this wealth to restore the economy of the Camargue. He even brought Buffalo Bill Cody out here to help reestablish cattle ranching. I remember old Jacob White Eyes, chief of the Dakota

Sioux nation, standing right here in front of the church in St. Martin de Crau."

"Heard you had some nice bulls," Bill interrupted, more interested in locking down a good source of semen than in stories of cowboys and Indians.

Bonfort looked up, eyes fixed on the big man standing in front of him.

"Monsieur Bonfort has the smartest arena bulls in the area," Blondie interjected. "Before you got here, I mentioned to him that you were looking for semen. He said he might be willing to let you have some of his, mostly because of his lingering memories of the Americans that came here in the early days and the high regard he has for the American West. You may choose one of the three bulls grazing in the field behind the foundry. Go get a look at them before we join the branding.

Bill touched his hat and nodded in the direction of the old man.

"But of course, there are certain conditions."

"What are the conditions?" Bill asked.

"First and most important is that you never use any of his semen to breed bulls for the ring. Second, you must never divulge the lineage of progeny you get from using his genetics."

"No problem. I promise. Cross my heart."

"But third, you cannot use any artificial restraining means like a hydraulic or mechanical squeeze chute or tranquilizer darts, injections, or pills when you collect the semen."

"That's a tough one. We might be talkin' about me facing off against a ton and half of muscle and sinew with nothin' more than a small bottle in my hand."

"Camargue bulls are rarely that big, but they are very fast and strong for their size," Blondie added.

"Well, what are we waitin' for? Let's just ride out and have a look," Bill said, smiling at his two friends.

Blondie declined, saying that he preferred to stay in the workshop and chat with Bonfort a while longer. "I'll meet you out at the ferrade."

Bill and Bellatre found the bulls out in the field, in separate paddocks, all three of them black, with sharp horns, and in perfect condition.

"The biggest one is the youngest," Bellatre said. "The middle-sized one is called Bernart after the Provençal poet Bernart de Ventadorn."

"What about the small one over there?" Bill asked, pointing to the far pen. "What do you call him?"

"He's called Bertran, after another Provençal poet."

"You guys sure got a lot of poets for such a small state. Bertran and Bernart, how do you keep them straight?"

"We manage. The big bull's name is Peire."

When they moved closer, Peire started scratching up the ground with a horn, while the smallest bull, Bertran, trotted off to the water trough at the east fence. Bernart, the middle-sized bull, turned his rear end toward them and stuck his tail straight up in the air.

"I think I like Bernart the best," Bill said. "His progeny won't have any trouble adjusting to life in Pylewood."

"He'd be a good choice for you. Bonfort told me last year at the bullfights in Mouries that he has the sweetest disposition of any bull he's ever had. And even more important for you, he is highly intelligent."

"How does he know that? I thought they killed the bull in bullfighting."

"Not in our bullfights. We put a ribbon called a cocarde between the bull's horns and give a prize to the bull fighter who can pluck the ribbon from the bull's head. And we bet heavily on the bulls, not on the bull fighter. The crowds will cheer for the bull if he thwarts the bull fighters. Bonfort will tell you that Bernart has the uncanny ability to size up a bull fighter and exploit his weaknesses. Last year at Nîmes, Bernart won Bonfort fifteen thousand euros. Remember, if you chose him, you will have to promise Monsieur Bonfort that the semen you get will never be used to breed any bulls for the ring."

"That'll be easy. The only bullfights we have in the Pylewood area are over in Gustine. No bull with any brains would go over there for the kind of prize money they offer."

"And extracting semen from such a smart beast will be no easy job without stanchions, a squeeze chute, and tranquilizers. To be successful, you will have to gain Bernart's trust and permission, which requires that you make a good first impression. If he forms a bad opinion of you, your chances of ever obtaining any of his little swimmers are miniscule. You might want to go easy on your first date, so to speak. A little treat of alfalfa and a compliment or two at your first meeting will go a long way in getting him to cooperate. It will also be important to avoid making jerky movements or hollering or swearing at him. I'm sure no one has ever tried to hook him up to any mechanical gadgets before, so he will be inclined to object strenuously on principle, or if your hands are cold, your gloves itchy or scratchy, and your voice harsh. He will think the practice unnatural, a violation of God's law, if you will."

"You know, Georges," Bill said, "I ain't got time for a long courtship. Even if Bernart is sensitive and intelligent, I already got cows cycling in Aurillac and a rugby match in two days. I never thought I'd end up having to seduce a bull when I joined this project. Maybe a woman would be better at it than me? I could ask Claudine to take charge."

"It's your airplane to fly, amigu."

***

"How did it go? Did you settle on one of Bonfort's bulls?" Blondie Raimbaut asked as he rode up alongside Georges.

"Good, Bill likes Bernart, the medium-sized bull. Let's ride over to the ferrade. Bill wants to try his hand and horse by taking a stab at being a gardian."

"You two gonna join the crew that wrestles down the *toros* and holds them still for branding?" Bill asked when they joined up.

"Not me," Blondie answered. "I'm way too old for that stuff. I think I'll join in with the branding crew. I'm still pretty good with a hot iron."

"What about you, Georges, you gonna ride with me?"

"I think I'll try my hand at finding a pretty girl to sit next to. I've been studying the troubadours lately, and I can recite a poem by Peire Cardenal by heart. I think it's about the pain of unrequited love written by a man taken away from the woman he loves by the Crusades. Who knows what might happen. My divorce has been bittersweet. I longed to be free for so long I forgot how hard it is to attract beautiful young women when you are over sixty-five years old and short in stature."

After Blondie had burned a few hides, Bellatre had recited a few troubadour poems to some elderly matrons—the younger ones didn't speak Provençal or had never heard of Peire Cardenal, and Bill had successfully turned back a few yearlings, mounted and trident in hand, the three of them rode over to a grove of linden trees where tables and benches and a refreshment stand had been set up.

"How about a pastis?" Bellatre offered. It's the beverage that saved the Camargue."

"Sure, but I don't need anything special. A glass of single-malt scotch with a beer chaser would be good enough. Blondie told me the other day that you used to be a scientist, a bionic chemist I think he said."

"Biochemist. I study nutrition, really the chemistry of what happens to food in the digestive system."

"So what happens when a cow eats a bunch of grass? How does it get to be milk, meat, and bones? Why do some stay skinny and others grow fast?"

"When we get to the house, I'll show you a couple of diagrams that will simplify things," Bellatre answered.

"It's probably a pretty dumb question."

"Not at all," Bellatre said. "Thank God it's complicated. If it were simple, people like me wouldn't have jobs. What are your plans?"

"I'm leavin' for Aurillac tomorrow, guys. I been workin' out with the local rugby club, and they have a game in a few days against Nîmes. I might even get on the field for a minute or two if the score gets lopsided, er, I mean one-sided."

CHAPTER 25

The Winning Try

Bill dropped his chin to his chest and let the hot water pound on him. The ironic thing was that everything hurt except his knee. Even his hair and teeth hurt. Under the showers pounding, the caked blood on his left ear softened and broke up until it ran down his neck in pink rivulets. He felt around for the goose egg that he knew was rising somewhere on his forehead, and instead of one, he found two. And he had only been in the game for fifteen minutes.

In the beginning, suiting him up for the Nîmes match had mostly been an attendance-boosting ploy by the Aurillacois Club officers who thought that if he did nothing more than sit on the bench with the other substitutes, a bunch more people would come out and buy tickets for the game. They were sure everyone in the area would want a look at the yank who had busted up the Black Hat gang and was featured in all the Michelin TV advertisements. The club's public relations guys had embarrassed him when they started inflating his exploits. They made him out to be taller, thinner, and younger than he really was. They had even published an old photograph of him celebrating his no-hitter in high school. But he went along with it, figuring it was unlikely that he would get in the game. Three of the eight forwards in the pack would have to get injured before he'd see any action. And after the game, he was hoping to entice a few of his teammates to come back with him to the Camargue to help with the semen collecting.

He pushed his face right into the center of the cascading water, wondering if all of it had really happened. The proof was the lumps on his head, the mashed ear, and the soprano singing in his hypothalamus. His team had come into the game as a big underdog. Nobody had given them much of a chance against the bigger, faster Nîmes side. In the first half, Nîmes had pushed the Aurillacois around, scoring two tries and making both conversions. If he had had a wristwatch, he would have been watching it, counting the minutes until the game ended. But when Bertrand Melanger, their big prop forward, was tossed from the game for throwing a punch at Jonathan Tomo, the Nîmes hooker, the game got more interesting. Next, for no apparent reason, Coach Themling substituted for Gilles Gillon. With Gillon's substitution, Bill's security system started flashing and sent a loud toot on a quick trip from his heart to his brain. First stop, a review of the rules of rugby: no forward passes, tackling had to be below the shoulders, and you couldn't use your hands in a scrum. Just as he got to the rules of the lineout, Wilson Nairobi, their husky Kenyan prop, trotted to the sidelines, blood oozing from a deep gash on his chin.

The bar of soap he was holding slid through his numb fingers, off the top of his head, and onto the floor, choking off the game replay and bringing him back to the present. When he tried to bend over to pick up the slippery white block, nothing moved. Besides the dizziness, something in his lower back was telling him a hinge or two was bent.

His thoughts went back to Coach Themling shouting at him, "Bill, get into the bloody game and make yourself useful." When he finally did trundle onto the field, a grinning Andy Craik was there to point him toward the assembling scrum. He remembered digging in, putting his arms around the guy next to him and starting to push when the ball rolled into the center of the scrum. He hadn't really been ready; neither fully warmed up physically, nor sufficiently charged up mentally. Without his big push, the guys from Nîmes had been able to swing the scrum around, giving them the advantage and the ball. From there, the Nîmes side moved relentlessly toward the goal with a series of runs, short kicks, and lineouts. He remembered finally catching up to the action and pouncing on a loose ball, only to be pushed and dragged off while another scrum built up around him. Being trampled in the ruck finally warmed him up and got him into the spirit of things.

As Nîmes drove close to the goal line and threatened to score, he remembered popping the Nîmes scrum half hard enough to knock the ball out of his hands. Manu had scooped up the ball and run east, giving his teammates a chance to gather behind him. When they got there, he gave the ball a good boot toward the sidelines or what they called touch in rugby. Andy Craik had come along and given him a big slap on the back and hollered at him to "get his fat arse into the game." While they lined up for the lineout throw-in, he had snuck a look at the scoreboard, Nîmes 24–Aurillac 15. It was closer than he thought, but Nîmes, who were definitely the stronger side, won the throw-in and started another menacing charge toward the Aurillac goal. In the next scrum, Aurillac won the ball.

Bill turned the shower off and grabbed a couple of towels from the stack on the table. He threw one on the bench and used the other one to start drying off. He smiled, even though it hurt, with the memory of Jules Bisoni pushing the Nîmes lads straight back and giving the Aurillacois a clean shot at the ball.

"Good show!" one of the Aurillac players shouted at him as he limped by, looking for his locker. When Bill touched the towel to his elbow, it stung and a red blotch appeared. *Must have scraped it in the lineout*, he thought.

He remembered keeping the Nîmes prop in view and dumping him when he tried to sneak out and smash Craik. "Yeah!" he had yelled when he saw the prop stagger out of the melee, trying to get his headband off from over his eyes and back onto his head. His hit had seemed to energize the flagging Aurillacois, and they began a promising move toward the Nîmes goal: Craik to Manu to the speedy Kevin Smith out on the wing. He had struggled to keep up with the surge, gasping for air, thinking he was almost empty when the ball squirted out of Manu's grasp and bounced his way. Almost by instinct, he had scooped up the ball, took three steps forward, and kicked the oblong bladder with everything he had in the direction of the Nîmes goal. It was a strong kick, but he hadn't seen where it had gone because a Nîmes player had leveled him as soon as the ball got into the air.

Even though his ear was damp with blood, and he had been flat on his back, he still remembered hearing the crowd screaming his name and his teammates pulling him back up on his feet. When he looked at the scoreboard the score was now 24 to 18. The Aurillacois gathered before the kickoff for a pep talk and a little strategy. When Coach Themling had pulled him aside, he had shouted in his ear, "Bill, the Nîmes players won't be expecting you to run with the ball! If we get the ball to you, run like hell! Head for the goal with everything you got! There's still five minutes left! Surprise will be on your side!"

He reached for another towel. The first was already soaking wet and streaked with blood. The game had seesawed back and forth with neither side scoring again. Nîmes had come close when their kicker missed on a penalty kick, the ball traveling just wide of the uprights, and Aurillac had come close to scoring a try when Doolittle, the fly half, was pushed into touch five yards from the Nîmes goal. Slowly, it was all coming back to him. When the Aurillacois won the scrum deep in Nîmes territory, Craik had pitched the ball out to Barry Harkins, the stubby Geordie, who tossed a perfect pitch to Smith as he headed toward touch. But when Smith suddenly cut back toward the center of the field where Bill was running, he remembered that he was in perfect position to throw a crack back block on a Nîmes player but refrained when he couldn't remember whether it was legal. Instead, he cut back around behind Smith and got into position for a backward pass. Smith saw him go by and flipped the ball in his direction. As soon as the ball was in his hands, he flashed back to the time he had caught a pass in the flat in a game against Clayton and run sixty yards for a touchdown. Then he had concentrated on holding the ball tight against his body, stretching his stride, and imagining that Marilyn Monroe was waiting naked for him in the end zone.

He had blinked hard when he saw there was no one in front him and the Nîmes goal looming only thirty yards ahead. He was sure there were faster guys already taking an angle on him so he had pumped his arms, fixed his eyes on the goal, and lengthened his stride until it hurt. Jonathon Tomo, the fastest Nîmes player, caught up with him at the goal line and belted him so hard that he felt the shock wave in his toenails before they went airborne. But he had held on to the ball and fallen over the goal line dazed but conscious. Five points for the try made the score twenty-five to twenty-four and the conversion added another two points. Tomo attempted to win the game with a kick from midfield with only seconds left but narrowly missed wide right.

Bill turned off the shower and plopped down on the wooden bench in front of his locker. Practicing with the team had been fun, and coming off the bench to help win the contest was also exciting, but the game had been way too hard on his already dissipated, dilapidated, and discombobulated body. At least, as far as he could tell, no bones had been broken, and he had earned his three thousand euros. But he really needed to get back to Arles and figure out a way to collect the semen he and Claudine needed. Time was racing by; it was down to ten days before Bouche de Sancerre and Murielle would be in heat.

"Will ye be about for the next dustup?" Andy Craik asked Bill when he passed by his locker.

"I think one dustup was enough for me, Andy. I'm lucky to be sittin' here breathin' with my head still attached to my body. I done some bulldoggin' in my day, but I ain't never been busted as hard as Tomo hit me. I expect my teeth to start fallin' out when the shock wave finally gets to my head."

"Auch, the bugger is something of an animal, isn't he? But ye could get used tae it with time. What are ye gonny do now. Become a trapeze artist or an arctic explorer?"

"Nope. Can't really say, but first, I got to go back to Arles and figure out how to get a couple of straws of semen out of a wild bull."

CHAPTER 26

Postgame

Bill walked out of the clubhouse to the parking lot and pulled open the door to the rental car he had driven up from Arles. It was no midget car, but when he hunched over to get in the driver's seat, everything hurt: back, neck, thighs, calves, and shoulders; bones, muscles, nerves, and tendons. He turned around and hobbled back to the Stade Aurillacois locker room to look for Andy Craik.

"I hate to bother you, Andy, but could you give me a lift to the train station and buy me a first-class ticket to Nîmes? See if they'll give me an empty compartment so's I can stretch out and grab a couple of hours of sleep."

"You must be daft? Why do ye want tae go tae Nîmes? You just scored the winning fuckin' try against their team. You'll no be too popular there. Don't forget they're French, and they still probably have the odd guillotine lyin' roon."

"I'll risk it, Andy. If I tell 'em me and Jonathon Tomo have been very close lately, maybe they'll even buy me a drink. I've never been in the town, so I might take a walk around and see sights: the arena and cathedral. Trains run almost every hour from Nîmes to Arles, so I can get one any time I want. Gerrard will pick me up at the train station if he's around. Besides, I need some veterinary supplies, and Würtzenhaben told me there was a store in Nîmes next door to the animal hospital and not too far from the train station."

"He's the old German professor that's helpin' ye with yer other monkey business, right."

"Alsatian. The name just sounds German. I'm hoping I'll get lucky and find a semen collector there."

"You'll be quite sight: a black and blue rugger walkin' roon town carryin' a semen collector. But fer God's sake, don't wear your Aurillac colors."

"I hate to be acting like some big shot, but I'm asking you for the lift because I'll never make it to Arles if I try driving back alone."

"What about the rental car?"

"Just take it back to the EuropCar office in Aurillac. I've got an account there. They'll know what to do."

***

Bill was lucky to find an empty compartment in a train waiting in the Aurillac station and another one when he changed to the Intercités train at 'Arvant. He slept well on both legs of the journey and woke up fresh in Nîmes. The bottle of Calvados that Andy had slipped into his pocket hadn't hurt either. He hailed a taxi just outside the train station and asked for the animal hospital. The hospital was only a mile away and right next to the tracks on the Route d'Avignon just like Würtzenhaben had said. Right next door was a store something like Sortino's in Oakley but without the tires. Through the window he could see bags of feed, a few tin troughs, some fence posts and wire, dog collars, and some used veterinary stuff scattered around on the shelves and counter.

He sucked up all the air he could, pulled open the door, and walked in. He looked the thin guy behind the counter square in the face and asked in French if he could buy or rent a bovine semen collector. The store went dead silent. Bill feared that maybe all of Nîmes had gone silent. Maybe all of France. Could they have recognized him as the guy that scored the try that beat their team in Aurillac? Finally, the owner summoned up his courage and timidly asked, "Comment?"

It probably was the result of his recent rugby beating, but all the French he had ever known fled his brain, barns, and fields until he too was silent. Another customer and a couple of old guys who had been sitting in the corner, smoking and pretending they were reading a newspaper, joined him at the counter but said nothing. They all stood around dead silent, poker faced, but intent, while Bill tried to describe in English his idea of what a semen collector might look like or be used for: kinda long and soft with a funnel on the end. Something that captures sperm from a bull or horse.

"Sperme," one of the newspaper readers finally sung out. "Apareil," his friend followed. "Taureaux," the salesman added at an octave higher. When they all finished clapping politely and patting one another on the back, the salesman marched toward the back of the shop. What he came back with was nothing like what Bill had seen at the Sommet de l'Elevage in Clermont-Ferrand. The thing in front of him was obviously homemade, more like an old boot sock with the glass tip of a basting bulb protruding through a hole in the big toe. He fully expected that Bernart would fall to the ground laughing when he saw it.

When he asked the salesman about the hole in the end of the tube, the guy rolled his eyes and told him that most users just stuck a wad of chewing gum on the end. He said the saliva on the gum helped preserve the contents. It was enzymes or hormones or some such thing. No warm fuzzy lining, Velcro straps, or graduated glass receiver for Bernart. Bill wished he had bought one when he had the chance at the Sommet. He signed all the papers for a five-day rental without reading the contract, thinking that he'd never understand the words anyway. Then the salesman asked him for a one-hundred-euro deposit. A hundred-euro deposit for a piece of junk like that, he thought: he could make one in an hour or two if he was back home, but he wasn't home, of course, so he peeled off a one-hundred-euro note from his cash roll.

"Could you put this thing in a dark paper bag?" he asked the salesman. "I got to carry it to Arles on public transportation. What if I have to sit next to a young lady or something?"

After conferring with the second newspaper reader, the salesman pointed to a sign behind him that said when roughly translated, "Paper bags one euro, no plastic."

As he walked back to the train station, Bill began to think that it would take more than a bunch of the local teenagers to put Bernart down on the ground and hold him still long enough to get the receiver on his dong and stimulate him enough to get him to discharge a few thimblefuls of semen into the sock. Then one of those inexplicable events happened. In spite of the two lumps on his head and various groups of ganglia in the wrong places, a bunch of electrons hopped onto the train that ran around the inside surface of his skull and got off at his smart station. Rugby players Stade Aurillac, Jules Bisoni, Andrew Craik, and Manu Sulapanni, with some help from the rest of the team, could probably do it. Bernart couldn't be too much tougher than Jonathon Lomo, and he was sure that if the ruggers could get him down, they could hold him still for a couple of minutes.

Anyway, the best thing to do would be to invite the whole team and make the trip to the Camargue a morale-building outing. Coach Themling couldn't refuse the offer. The Aurillac players were a quiet, well-mannered group when you got down to it. Sure, they'd drink their beers and pat the rears of their prettiest fans, but that was the extent of their rowdiness. A bunch of them were musicians and artists, and Okram Turgulu, the Turkish Center Forward, was even known to write poetry in ancient Persian.

When Bill finally got back to Arles, it was already too late to call Gerrard, so he walked over to the Regence Hotel, which was right by the train station on the river near the Place Lamartine and booked a room for the night. He'd telephone Gerrard and ask for a ride to the Bellatre estate in the morning.

CHAPTER 27

Man against Beast

"What's the problem?" Andy Craik asked when Bill got him on the phone the next evening. "Yer no in the hospital, are ye?"

"No. I'm fine, Andy. I got the semen collector, but to actually collect the stuff I got to have a way to restrain the bull, put the semen collector over his dong, and stimulate him enough to convince him to put a donation in the collection box."

"You mean put something on his tadger?"

"Yeah, yeah, whatever you guys call it. The problem is they don't do anything artificial to bulls in the Camargue, so there are no stanchions, alleys, or suitable pens anywhere around. When I was in Arles, just before I came up for the Nîmes game, I watched a ferrade. That's what they call a branding down here. Gangs of guys wrestle yearlings to the ground and hold them still while other guys and sometimes girls put the iron on him."

"Are these the same bulls they use in the fighting in the south of France: Nîmes, Tarascon, and Arles?"

"Yep," Bill answered.

"The ones where they put a ribbon on the bull's forehead and a bunch of guys in white suits try to pull the ribbon off the bull's head."

"They call it a cocarde," Bill said.

"You gotta be kiddin'. Those bulls are monsters."

"They only look like that from far off. Ten ruggers the size of Jules would outweigh the bull by twice. And I bet we're even meaner, even though we might be a bit dumber."

"Yer askin' if a bunch of the lads from the team might hold this bull down for you. Without even askin' them, I think we can try it for ye. You just helped the team move up a notch in the standings and earn us bonuses. Now we can do something to help you. Instead of the normal training for the next match against Toulon, we'll train to wrestle yer bull down and make him squirt into a test tube. We'll pretend he's Elias Toucas, the ox that anchors the scrum for Toulon."

"It's never been done before, Andy," Bill cautioned. "That bull is solid muscle and clever to boot."

"Our eight forwards weigh close to a ton. And the bull can't be that much smarter than us. A couple of us have university degrees. Doolittle's is from Cambridge."

"When you guys get him down, I still have to make him squirt?" Bill, now smiling broadly, said into the telephone.

"We can even help you with that," Andy said. "We'll get Manu to kiss him and Tookie, who's from Paris, to tickle him. If that fails, Diego, our new center half from Argentina, can moon him."

"Aren't there some kind of laws against that?" Bill asked. "I know there are in the USA."

"You said we'd be out in the Camargue, not Paris."

"I'll see if we can get Coach Themling to let us use the team bus," Andy said before he hung up.

***

Two days later, seventeen volunteers from the Stade Aurillacois rugby club, some of whom had started drinking when they stopped to pay their respects to Monsieur Bonfort in St. Martin de Crau, lined up at one end of the small field where Bernart was pastured. Their plan of attack was for Bill and Jules Bisoni to ease Bernart into a corner and catch him by the horns, one on each horn. As soon as they had a good hold of the bull, two teams of eight Aurillac ruggers would run to the bull and form up a scrum around him. That way, they'd have a human fence around him and wouldn't have to wrestle him to the ground. The scrum would be flexible and could move with the bull, which Bill hoped would minimize the stress on the animal. Bill cautioned them not push too hard, be careful not to hurt the animal, and to keep their voices down. He reminded them that Bernart was only on loan, and old Monsieur Bonfort depended on the bull to earn him enough money to supplement the income he earned making branding irons and trident points.

Santana Biswas, a fly half who had just joined the team from the Uganda Leopards and was only five feet one, was assigned the job of crawling into the center of the scrum and slipping the retriever onto Bernart's dong, oixseau, tadger, or whatever ever each rugger called it in his own country. Biswas was the perfect rugger for the job not only because of his size but also because of experience with semi-wild African cattle. He also had a whistle, which he intended to blow once the receiver was full.

When they gathered around for their pregame huddle, Biswas suggested that they dispense with the usual pep talk and have a prayer instead; but the captain, Andy Craik, nixed the idea, saying that it wouldn't be appropriate what with the guys being all different religions, and there also being a couple of atheists on the team. Instead, they asked Bernart to forgive them and understand that there was a bale of special alfalfa waiting for him if he cooperated.

At the signal, Bill and Jules left their teammates along the corral and started walking toward Bernart, who had assumed a pose of great nonchalance. He might have recognized Bill, or maybe he was sizing up the pair of them. He thought their costumes were more interesting than the all-white shirt and trousers Camargue bull fighters usually wore. Still, he thought the wide orange and gray striped jerseys (rust and dust), high socks, and short white pants looked ridiculous on such fat men. Vertical stripes would have made a more stylish statement, and the calf-length socks, well, they were a joke. When the two heavyset men got close, Bernart casually walked a few steps away. When the two ruggers started trotting after him, he put a little more distance between them, calculating how much space he would have when he decided to charge. When the older man, the one with the heavy knee brace, stumbled and fell, he stopped and waited for him to get up. Now he was curious. What were these fat tastelessly dressed old men up to? In a way, it was kind of insulting. No funny little hats and garishly embroidered vests like the Spanish and Portuguese bull fighters. And why the funny shoes with little cleats on the soles? So he stopped and let them catch up.

When they grabbed his horns, he didn't resist. He could have easily driven the two of them into the wooden fence and broken most of their bones, but he didn't. Then the rest of the tastelessly clad men raced out into the middle of the corral and snuggled up against him. It wasn't at all uncomfortable. It reminded him of his childhood in the herd. The warmth of bodily contact and the feeling of family was something that had been missing in his life since he had been cruelly weaned. When a tiny man crawled under him and attached a sock to his penis, he began to get nervous. He had heard that such things happened when animals had contact with humans, but most of their activities remained incomprehensible to him. The sock was soft, cashmere like his favorite meadow. One of the fellows, a beat-up looking guy with a Scottish accent stuck an iPod in front of his face and ran a video of a Salers cow with an incredibly wide mouth and voluptuous lips. Not bad looking if red hair was your thing, but black hooves and large udders, not his type. Then before he knew what had happened, he felt the strange happy sensation of release, and the guys all let go and walked away. However, he couldn't resist the temptation of tossing at least one of them over the fence. Since he didn't really know any of them, he picked the nearest one, a medium-sized guy with dark skin and curly hair. He didn't get enough horn under him to get him over the fence but knocked him a good distance. They were tough, those ruggers. The guy popped right up and made an obscene gesture at him with his hands. Then the fat American with the bad teeth, whom he seen around the place at least a couple of times, poured half a sack of alfalfa pellets in his trough. Not such a bad deal after all. From his pen, he could see all the guys get back on their bus. He hoped they'd have a safe trip home.

When the ruggers got back to St. Marie de Crau, they drank a couple of cases of beer, showered at the municipal stadium, and changed back into their street clothes. All of them got a tricolor ribbon with an iron medallion in the three-pronged shape of a gardian's ficheiroun. Diego del Fuego, the new Argentine player, got a new shirt and a couple of bandages from Bonfort's daughter, who promised him to keep in touch on FaceBack, the new social medium site for people who been injured by bulls. Claudine was waiting for Bill at Bonfort's with a thermos of liquid nitrogen and a rack for semen straws. They figured it would take at least four hours to get to Limoges, where Ceemensee had its nearest collection center. They'd spend the night there and wait for the results of the semen analysis in the morning.

Two days later, the Aurillacois played the powerful team from Toulon and beat them with tactics they had practiced for the Bull Cup, which was the name they had given to their exploits in the Camargue. But it didn't last, and when a weak team from Tarascon went up twenty-five to nothing on them midway through the second half, Jules Bisoni suggested that Santana Biswas crawl into the scrum and perform the same operation they had performed on Bernart on

Jordan Piot the Tarascon Lock. The trick was voted down twelve to eleven with seven abstentions, and they lost the game thirty-five to eleven.

On the way back to Arles, Bill returned the semen extractor to the odd little shop in Nîmes. A different salesman was behind the counter and refused to give him back his hundred-euro deposit, claiming there was a small hole in the sock part of the device. The Ceemensee semen report confirmed that Bernart's semen was excellent: twenty thousand little buggers in a milliliter of fluid, perfect oval shape, nice curly tails, and superb mobility.

CHAPTER 28

Dear Karen

Karen Clements pushed the door of her Heavy Duty pickup open and slid down the seat until her feet hit the ground. The tin mailbox with the red flag was at the end of the driveway almost to the street. Hers was the only one in the neighborhood that hadn't been gussied up with brick or wrought iron. It was a vestige of the time when everybody out in Oakley lived on five or ten acres and had animals and orchards. She sifted through the mail before she climbed back into the truck. It was mostly the usual stuff: hearing-aid advertisements, an alumni magazine from Montana State, and a few bills; but today there was a letter with a French stamp on it addressed to her but with no return address. She didn't recognize the handwriting and didn't think she knew anyone that was in France. Jose Herrera, who worked with her at the stable, was out of the country, but she was pretty sure he was on a Caribbean cruise.

She carried the mail into the house, dropped it on the dining room table, and turned on the fire under the kettle so she could make herself a cup of tea. She grabbed a chocolate chip cookie from the pantry, sat down, and nibbled around the edges of the cookie for a while before she opened the mysterious letter.

Dear Karen,

I bet you never expected to get a letter from me in France. I started learning French, and it helped me a lot with my English grammar and spelling. Blondie (In France, it's a nickname for a guy) said I should right down all the stuff that's happening so I can have something to look at and show people when I get old.

I'm in a funny kind of place in the South of France called the Camargue. How I got here is a long story. I'll tell you all about it when I get back to California. Anyway, after I roped and hogtied some burglars in Clermont-Ferrand, I came down here to ride some white horses that they use to work their cattle, which they call taureaux, no matter whether they're bulls, heifers, or cows. The horses are kind of small, especially for somebody as big as me, but they are sturdy and sure-footed. The saddles are also way too small, and my crotch hurt for a week after riding for a couple of hours. The saddle back is straight up and upholstered like the inside of a low-rider, and there's no horn on the pommel. Georges Bellatre, a Frenchman that's my host down here, is looking for a bigger saddle for me, but he's also trying to get me to lose some weight. Meantime, if I wanted, I could ride a quarter horse he got in Oklahoma and use an Australian saddle, but I'd rather do it their way. I can always ride a quarter horse on a Western saddle when I get home. Besides, their horses are way better suited for work in the Camargue, which is what they call this place. It's a big swamp full of creeks and bogs and at the end of a river called the Rhone. In a lot of ways it's like our Sacramento River delta.

These little horses love the water, and they can live on the marsh grass that grows right up to the edge of the ocean. They also have real big hooves that give them good traction in the sand and mud. I think I'd like to bring one home someday and see how they do in our country. Maybe I could even breed them up with a good quarter horse stallion and start a new breed. The horses are plenty smart and easy to train and ride. The vaqueros around here are called gardians, and they do things a lot different than us. Their cattle are small and black with big sharp horns. They work their cattle with long poles with sharp tips like spears, and they don't rope from horses even though they brand them just like we do. They chase calves around and grab them by the horns. Then they wrestle them down and brand them. Sometimes they trip them with their spears to get them down.

They eat some of them same like we do, but they have a special taste from the marsh grass they eat. Mostly, though, they raise them for sport. Some bulls get sent to Spain for bullfighting, and others they keep here for the abrivado, which is a French kind of bullfighting where they don't kill the bull but try to remove a ribbon called a cocarde from between the bull's horns. There's lots of betting on the bulls and the bullfighters and prize money too. Tomorrow me and Georges are going to St. Martin de Crau to practice for a ferrade, which is what they call their branding. Later on, when we get a bigger saddle for me or my butt gets smaller, we're going to ride our horses with a bunch of other riders in an abrivado and take some bulls to the bull ring in Mouries, which is close to Arles, the biggest town in the area. We got to keep the bulls bunched up and on the road to the bull ring while the people try to distract us so that

*they can escape. Georges says it's an old tradition here, and
they do it so's we have to chase them all over town, trying
to get them back together. It's the same sort of stuff we do,
but they made it into a game. I'll send you some pictures
on the internet.*

Hope everything is good.
Bill

She put the letter down and filled the cup with hot water. She
shook her head while she pulled the tea bag up and down through
the hot water.

"Bill in France, speaking French, and cowboyin' around. Who
would have ever thought it in a million years?"

CHAPTER 29

The Charge

"Could you drop me off at the rugby grounds?" Bill asked Claudine. "The guys should be there practicing. It'll give me a chance to say a quick hello and goodbye."

"Sure," Claudine answered before he had a chance to inhale. "It will give me a chance to grab a croissant and a noisette while you gossip with your friends. I can also stop by the hotel to see if Würtzy has checked in yet. If he hasn't, I'll check at the Salers office to see if anyone has seen him meandering about. I'll be back here to pick you up in a couple of hours."

"I sure hope you can find him. We don't want to lose track of him like last time. I'm pretty sure I could do the insemination myself, but it'd still be good to have him around." Claudine made the French hand signal for "my eye."

The two of them had driven down from Limoges with the semen straws earlier that morning, hoping that they might find Professor Würtzenhaben strolling in the town square, perusing cabbages at the morning market, or asleep at his hotel. The old geezer had promised he'd be there. Claudine figured that all parties involved in the insemination would benefit from a short powwow or rehearsal before they actually started pumping their dearly won semen into real cows.

This time around, the professor had asked Bill and Claudine to book a room for him and a friend at the Ibis Hotel on the outskirts of town: a big step up for a guy who had stayed at a youth hostel the last time he was in town.

"Probably trying to show off for one of them Austrian girls," Bill had guessed.

"No," Claudine countered, "I don't think so. I just bet he has picked up a sponsor for his choucroute research. Probably some big Swiss sandwich company."

Bill was surprised to see the Aurillacois players on the practice field lackadaisical and glum. They were hitting the tackling dummies in slow motion and kicking balls like they were watermelons. Bill, still in civilian clothes, trotted over to where Andy Craik was doing some stretching and asked, "Andy, what's wrong with the guys? They look like they just been relegated to the Third Division."

"Aye, they do, don't they. We lost a match the day before yesterday, artlessly, to a Tarascon side we shouldae blistered. We miss ye, Bill," the captain said to him. "It's the God's truth. Could ye no come back again, even if it's only for a game or two? Get in yer kit and just sit on the bench for the next game, even if ye don't feel like playin'. I truly think that we'd play harder just seein' yer fat arse on the boards."

"Wish I could, Andy, but the answer's got to be no. That game against Nîmes really took a lot out of me. I ached all over for a week, had a headache, and couldn't shit without an enema. Besides, I don't think I'd enjoy watching you all play from the bench."

"So it's gonny be a one game career and an off ye go, is it? What a pity. Ye got a talent for the game, Bill, and we could really use ye."

"I'm honored that yer askin' Andy, but I'm way too old to start a rugby career. It does bother me some when I think of what might have been. Twenty years ago, I would have loved the tackling, hard hitting, and rough stuff. And to tell you the truth, while I loved American football too, I could never get used to playing with all the padding, a helmet on my head, and a steel cage in front of my face."

"If yer no gonny join us, have you got an idea or two about what I can do to get these big lummoxes ready for a game, like we did for Nîmes."

"In the Nîmes game, their ugly center forward bit me on the elbow. That got me pretty fired up."

"Seriously, Bill, as Captain, I got tae think of somethin' quick to raise our team's spirits." Andy waved his hand from one side of the field to the other. "These lads haven't shown any fire since that Toulon game, just after we wrestled that bull of yours for his semen. It's like they've been sleep walkin' ever since."

"You just gave me an idea, Andy. I think you guys need a mascot. Something to break the tension."

"And what kind of mascot would ye suggest for Aurillac?"

"An animal. I'd definitely steer clear of ethnic or religious groups. You wouldn't want to call your team the Mongols or the Albigensians. The Detroit Lions used to have a real lion for their mascot, but that's probably too extreme for Aurillac. What about Bernart? He'd be the perfect mascot for the Aurillac team."

"You don't mean that bull we wrestled over in St. Martin d'Crau, do ye?"

"I sure do," Bill said. "My friend Blondie Raimbaut could haul him up here for your home games. Change your name from Stade, whatever that means, to Bulls, the Aurillac Bulls, or, even better, Taureaux. I'll bet old Bernart would stamp and snort for you guys when you ran onto the field, tear up the turf with one of them sharp horns of his when you scored, turn over a bench or two when you lost, and chase the other team's cheer leaders around whatever happened. If that doesn't get the team fired up, nothing will."

Andy laughed. "I already feel better. But Bernart is a Camargue bull, and we're not even in the Camargue. We got our own bulls here in the Cantal."

"I seen plenty of them Salers bulls you got here. Good for making beef and cheese, but they're way too big and serious. Besides, they got no sense of humor or audience savvy. Bernart, on the other hand, well, you seen him. He knows how to get a laugh out of a crowd. He'll probably have his nose under the skirts of the cheer leaders before you know it."

"We don't have cheer leaders in rugby."

"Well, get some then. Call 'em the Aurillac Heiferettes. They'll probably boost attendance. How long's it been since you filled your stadium?"

"Not since I been here. Some of the seats behind the goals look like they never been sat on."

A bunch of the players had gathered around Bill and Andy and were milling about nodding or shaking their heads in agreement or confusion.

"What the hell is Bill talking about?" Jules Bisoni asked Manu Sulapanni. "I don't know," Manu answered, "but I think they're talking about bringing girls and bulls to our games."

"What's an Albigensian?" Guy Floridan the hooker asked Pedro Gigret the Spanish lock.

"Got to go guys," Bill said. "Claudine's probably waiting for me in the parking lot. I don't reckon I'll be back here soon, but I'll always remember the Nîmes game and the Aurillac Taureaux. Remember, fellas, the door's always open at my place, whether it's Paris or Pylewood.

***

Claudine tossed her white lab coat into the corner and stumbled over to the edge of the bed. She sat down and pulled off her boots. Then she stood up and peeled down her pants, which she drop-kicked into the corner where the empty beer bottles were piled. She did the same with her socks and watch cap before collapsing back on the bed. She lay there for a while and started a long stare at the ceiling. It was almost midnight, and even though she was exhausted, she couldn't calm down. Her heart was tangoing, her hands were rumbaing, and her brain was break dancing. She looked over at Bill sprawled out on the other bed, already happily snoring away. *Didn't even bother to take off his shoes, the lourdaud*, she noted with a scowl. With that gripe off her chest, her brain dropped some rpms and started to cycle her through the events of the last few days.

First up was Professor Würtzenhaben. The old jailbird had failed to stay in touch as he had promised. She had tried to contact him several times without success. Then there was the estrus monitor, which Bill had rented from Ceemensee. The damn thing hadn't as much as peeped in the almost eighteen days that Murielle had been carrying it around. The gadget, basically a modified cell phone with a motion sensor, hadn't buzzed until Murielle was well into estrus, leaving them little time to gather their stuff and get to her.

In the mildly annoying category, Bill hadn't been much help. She looked over at him coiled up on the bed like a giant cinnamon roll on a warm baking sheet. She couldn't squelch a backward smile. In a way, she envied him. He was the kind of person who never looked ahead, deigning only to consider a problem when it was on top of him. He wouldn't start worrying about whether or not Murielle was ready until they were standing next to her, and if Würtzy never materialized, he was sure to come up with some screwball alternate plan on the spot.

When Würtzy still hadn't appeared, she had pestered Bill on the drive back from Limoges. He had just laughed, saying, "We shoulda put the estrus sensor on him instead of on Murielle." By then, she had been almost sure that they would have to put the penny in the collection plate by themselves. She had worried that if they missed the estrus, they would have to start all over again. In the end, they just drove to Albert Garçelon's place. While Bill drove, she had reread *Animal Husbandry for Dummies*. The first reading hadn't given her any confidence that they would be able to inseminate Murielle and Bouche de Sancerre themselves. Now that the hour of reckoning was upon them, rereading the manual only made her less confident. The insemination process wasn't that mysterious, but there was a lot of feeling, poking, and probing that seemed impossible to learn from a book. Bill had already proved that he lacked small-muscle motor skills when he dropped the Lutalyse syringe in the mud weeks before. All they needed now was for him to drop the precious semen straws in the mud or push the injector plunger too hard.

When they pulled up in front of Garçelon's place, it was completely dark, a good sign. Albert and Sophie were probably still at Mauriac, enjoying the Pentecost holiday.

"Let me take care of Lamarck," Bill had said. "I got a thick beef steak in my carryall for him."

When they climbed over the fence, however, Lamarck was nowhere to be seen or heard. Claudine could tell something was wrong when she felt her pulse pounding in her g8 incisor. She would have to change dentists as soon as she got back to Paris or maybe get the tooth recapped in Costa Rica. Bill pulled out his mini-flash, narrow-pocket flashlight, while they had tiptoed to the barn. He had scanned the ground in front of them with the flashlight until they heard the totally unexpected sounds of eating, a sort of slurping and puckering, with an undertone of whiny canine growl.

When they had reached the origin of the noise, they were startled to find three mammals, one four-legged, two two-legged, sitting on a large tablecloth spread neatly on the hay. One of the two-legged ones was a short recently paroled biology professor; the other a chubby Austrian girl in a dirndl. The third picnicker was a large black Bernese mountain dog, tail wagging, who was pulling out pieces of ham and sausage from a large crock of choucroute garni. Gertyl and Würtzenhaben had offered them a plastic bowl of choucroute and sausage. She had declined, but Bill accepted and asked if they had eating utensils other than plastic spoons.

While they had been shocked to find Würtzenhaben and Gertyl picnicking in the dark at Garçelon's place, they were even more amazed when they found Murielle tied up behind the barn, ready to receive her history-making insemination. Gertyl informed them that after fully servicing Murielle, she and the professor intended to proceed on to Pierre Nosay's place and perform the same operation on Bouche de Sancerre. Furthermore, they planned to stay in the area for another week to flush and collect the embryos, which they would drop off and register in Limoges. While she and Bill stood there speechless, shocked at the turn of events, Würtzenhaben had announced that Gertyl was much more than just a pretty face, amply endowed, and a top-notch kisser; she was also a talented, fully qualified veterinary technician. She had, he said, grown up in the Austrian Tyrol among mountain cattle and worked throughout high school for her uncle who was a veterinarian of distinction.

Bill had insisted that he didn't care if Gertyl was Madam Curie. He and only he would take the embryos to Limoges for registration, and that even if he didn't actually participate in the flush, he would be there to watch. For emphasis, he balled up one of his oversized fists.

Würtzenhaben recoiled by pushing Gertyl behind him and rolling up a sleeve to reveal a prison tattoo that said "University of Mulhouse, 1970" in old-style French script. He then made his own fist and announced that he and Gertyl were to be married as soon as he could prove that he had sufficient funds for her dowry. Therefore, Würtzenhaben had said, he was going to have to charge Bill more than what they had agreed upon back in Brünstatt because the two of them were now incorporated, and he was one thousand euros shy of being able to establish a household. Bill had rocked himself into a fighting stance, but Claudine was pretty sure he wouldn't hit an elderly academic or a young veterinarian.

Gertyl then had demanded that they quit arguing and turn over the semen straws so she could finish the job and get on to the next client. And there was to be no arguing about who was to take the embryos to Limoges. Theirs was a full-service insemination business, and she wouldn't permit an unqualified nonprofessional, especially a blockhead like Bill, to botch up one of her jobs. He wouldn't so much as touch an embryo until they had been legally transferred to him in Limoges. At that time, he would get a certificate of potency for each embryo and sign papers that acknowledged the embryos were now his responsibility. With that, she had grabbed her fiancé by the hand, dragged him over to the stanchion, and set to work. Claudine and Bill had watched speechless from where they stood while the two partners in the new veterinary practice of Gertyl & Würtzenhaben donned gowns and gloves, popped out their tools from hermetically sealed bags, produced a liquid nitrogen canister, loaded syringes, pushed plungers, deposited used materials in a hazmat sack, and, without a wave of the hand or a single goodbye, marched out of Garçelon's barn and most likely headed for their next appointment, Nosay's place in Pleaux.

At that point, Claudine's nervous rerun of the evenings faded out, and she collapsed into sleep and dreams.

CHAPTER 30

Finding Ivor

When she kicked off the quilt the next morning, Claudine felt a sense of relief. She had wanted to wish the Gertyl and Würtzenhaben couple the best of luck and express her hope that there would soon be little Würtzenhabens to celebrate and help carry on the choucroute research. She also had wanted to assure them that Bill would pay any reasonable new charges for the additional services. She was sure that she would have the chance to straighten out things later. At the same time, she relished the idea that she was free of all her embryo responsibilities. What a month it had been, starting with the burglary, planning the embryo breeding, learning about rugby, and finally putting the project in the hands of Würtzenhaben and Gertyl. Being with Bill had been an adventure of sorts, but she did have a career and a boyfriend in Gabon. She was also starting to miss Paris: the steak and frites, the baguettes, and the late nights. And she had her own troubled state of mind to mend. Although she had kept it to herself, she had been plagued by recurring nightmares of the burglary at the Hotel Gergovie. Frightening memories of the blow to her face, images of the blood, her rescue by Bill and Blondie, and the terrified look on the face of Ivor Gryyffwwdd had dominated her dreams.

The place to start was Clermont-Ferrand. She had to establish if Ivor Gryyffwwdd was still missing. If he was, was he being held for ransom? And had either the French or Welsh governments done anything to find him and free him? She had been so engrossed in the details of artificial insemination and embryo capture that she hadn't even thought about poor Ivor until now. She had not seen, heard, or read anything about his abduction or his rescue. As far as she could tell, he might just as well have been kidnapped by aliens.

She felt it her duty to make sure his case was brought to some conclusion. After all, she had been the last person to see him alive. She thought of his poor mother in Abrystwyth wondering why he hadn't returned home. Was she even aware that he had been kidnapped by Canadian separatists? When he had left Wales for the *Sommet*, his mum had most likely packed him a lunch and some snacks and hadn't given it a second thought except to remind him to beware of the loose women he was sure to encounter in France. She probably hadn't questioned him too much, assuming that he would be back in a week or two. Meanwhile, his cousins Gareth and David would take care of his herd. Claudine envisioned Ivor imprisoned in Canada, chained to an ice-hockey net, flurries of rock-hard hockey pucks whizzing past his terrified face, and Montreal techno music blaring at him from woofers and tweeters from behind the goal. It was time for someone to rescue the ill-fated Welshman.

As soon as she finished breakfast, Claudine would call the police office in Clermont-Ferrand and make an appointment with that Inspector Dercanges, who had been the ranking police officer at the time of the Chapeau Noir burglary. She'd find out the status of Ivor's case. If he hadn't been rescued, she would find out why. Then she would devote herself completely to gaining his return or retrieving his body, or at least until her boyfriend returned from Gabon.

CHAPTER 31

The Flush

The next time Bill saw Murielle, she was tethered to a post in the field behind Albert Garçelon's house. The old farmer had partaken of an extra glass or two of *eau d'vie* before bedtime to help him sleep. Bill could hear him snoring when he tiptoed past the house. Earlier in the week, Garçelon had alerted Bill that the swashbuckling veterinary team of Würtzenhaben & Gertyl was planning to flush the cows that evening, so Bill had shown up, uninvited, at sundown. Buoyed by his TV success, new denture, and French language progress, his self-confidence was sky high. He was convinced that having Claudine looking over his shoulder had made him nervous in his previous attempts at artificial fertilization. Now that she was gone to rescue Ivor Gryyffwwdd, all obstacles to him having a successful flush had been removed. He looked down at the new Phillipe Castifiore wristwatch he had bought in Paris. He shook his head in disbelief. He had paid more for the damn time piece than he had earned in 2009, a year when cattle prices and grass were both high. He didn't need his new watch to tell him that the embryo-flushing duo of Würtzenhaben & Gertyl was already late.

Screw it. He'd just do the flush himself. Why not? He had all the equipment he needed in a new black satchel he had bought the day before. He went over the embryo capture procedure in his mind. *Make a slit just between the upper leg and stomach. Squeeze the contents of the sack into a test tube. Pipette the embryos from the test tube into several ampoules. Fill them with amniotic fluid (he had a jar in his satchel), and hermetically seal the tubes.* He looked at his watch again. He was just finishing sharpening his knife when he heard a car-door slam and the sound of muffled German speech.

"Shhh," he hissed when Würtzenhaben and Gertyl got within earshot. "Garçelon isn't supposed to know we're doing this. With all the noise you two are making, you'll wake him for sure."

"What are you doing here?" Gertyl hissed back. "And what do you think you're doing with that knife? We don't do it that way anymore. It's barbaric. Who told you we were flushing tonight?"

"You want to get paid, don't you?" Bill answered.

"The surgical procedure hasn't been used in years," Würtzenhaben chimed in.

The flush went fast; Murielle stayed calm as if she suspected she might be on the verge of becoming the matriarch of a new line of thin supersmart cattle soon to be established in the New World. She did twitch and moo softly when Gertyl inserted the pipette in her cervix. Würtzenhaben had given her a local painkiller, but she still felt a twinge of pain. When they finished, Gertyl smeared Murielle's backside with Neosporin, and let the old girl amble off to the bunker where Garçelon had dumped a generous load of the sweetest local hay he could find.

"You and your boyfriend are sure getting a lot of money for a few minutes work," Bill scoffed.

"Good thing we got here before you started cutting her up," Gertyl shot back. "You owe us six thousand dollars. We prefer you pay us in cash."

"I'm going with you to the next stop. Me and Nosay are partners in this gig. I'll meet you over there."

Next stop was Nosay's place at Pleaux, where they found Bouche de Sancerre tethered and a nervous Pierre Nosay pacing back and forth.

"Calm down, old bean," Bill said. "There isn't anything to it. I just watched these two goofballs perform at Garçelon's place. More like changing the oil in your tractor than rocket science," he whispered in Nosay's ear. "Next time, old chap, we'll do it ourselves and save a bundle of money. We'll also be spared dealing with the likes of Gertyl, the prima donna of embryo capture, and her boyfriend, the jailbird professor of cabbage."

"How many embryos did you get at Garçelon's?" Nosay asked Würtzenhaben.

"Five," the professor answered.

"Is that average?" Nosay asked, still nervous.

"Four is average, five is better," Würtzenhaben answered.

Bill was adding up the cost in his head. He couldn't remember whether they had settled on five hundred dollars for each good embryo or three-fifty. At any rate, Würtzenhaben had wanted to double the fee because Gertyl, a professional, was now assisting him, and he was in a hurry to acquire some serious money for the dowry he would need if he was going marry her.

"Looks like only three good ones for you Pierre," Würtzenhaben stammered when Gertyl emptied the contents of the pipette. "We got seven total, but four don't look right."

"Must be the big-mouth gene expressing itself," Bill said with a laugh. "You can have the ones that don't look right, Pierre, for half price, right, Würtzy."

"Nope, I'm keeping the odd-looking ones for closer inspection and then destruction. It's a question of professional ethics. I may be a jailbird, but I still have my principles."

"So I guess you get one of yours and one of mine," Bill said to Nosay.

"Nope, you get one of mine and three of yours. I get two of mine and two of yours. That was the deal."

"I can't go back to Pylewood with just four embryos. My partners will kill me."

"Well then, keep all of yours, and I'll keep all of mine."

"Suits me," Bill said. "I don't believe your theory of big mouths anyway."

With that, Bill stuck his hand into his pocket, pulled out a wad of hundred euro notes, and tossed it at the dish that held the pipettes and syringes. Gertyl, snagged the wad of bills in midflight, popped off the rubber band, and started counting. While she counted, Bill stuck both hands into the cold chest, which held the eight good ampoules and the four bad ones, grabbed all he could hold in his cold hand, and gently loaded them into his liquid nitrogen thermos.

"Forty-five!" Gertyl shouted triumphantly. "And the bugger even left us a wedding present." Bill was out of Nosay's barn and into his car before any of the others realized he had eight ampoules. He drove straight for the Ceemensee storage facility in Limoges, where he logged in the eight embryos, four from Murielle, two good ones from Bouche de Sancerre, and two from Bouche de Sancerre that Würtzenhaben had rejected. Once he had his receipt for the eight embryos, he jumped back into the car and sped off for Paris. Ariane had booked him an appearance on the Wine Wrangler TV show at 3:00 PM the next day.

When Gertyl finished counting the money and Pierre Nosay got around to counting the remaining ampoules, he found there were only four left: two good ones, one from Murielle, another from his cow Bouche de Sancerre and two of the so-called bad ones. As soon as they realized that Bill had made off with two substandard embryos, team Würtzenhaben & Gertyl packed up and pointed their vehicle toward Zurich, where Pierre Nosay was certain that Bill would bank the embryos.

CHAPTER 32

Hrubel Kwasnik

Hrubel Kwasnik paused to shake his head and stare at the mess that lay in front of him before he started picking up the wet towels and dirty jerseys that were strewn about the locker room. He pitched them into the can in the center of the room and asked himself why the SkodaCats players couldn't just drop their towels in the cans themselves. Guys on teams he had played on had no problem picking up towels. What was the deal with the girls? He didn't mind sweeping up or taking their gear to the laundry, but the least they could do was to throw their wet towels in the can. He walked over and looked at the typed schedule on the bulletin board.

> **Prague, May 13.** That was in a couple of days, and the Cats had a decent chance to win.

> **Home, May 17.** The semipro team from Darmstadt was coming up for a nonleague friendly. Lerca would probably play the subs.

> **Dusseldorf, May 21.** The Giraffes had Hannah Tower, the All-League spiker and German Olympian. The SkodaCats would have to be on their game to prevent a rout.

Wienstampfen May 23. A newcomer to the league from the Liebfraumilch region along the Rhine. Pretty much an unknown except for their center, Myrah Balch.

Home, May 27. Most important game of the season with the Wolfsburg Wagons, who had beat the SkodaCats at their place earlier in the season.

Hamburg, June 1. Hamburg: big port city, cosmopolitan, transportation hub. Outcome would depend on the blocking capability of the front line. Maybe, in Hamburg, he could find a way to ship his special Czech bees back to Pylewood.

He already knew that he was going to get his bees in Melnik. He also knew he was going to package them in wooden logs, but he still hadn't figured out how he was going to get them across the border and into the United States. It was bizarre, but he kept thinking that the easiest way to get them into the country would be to let them fly in. Customs officers had no way of turning back or confiscating a swarm of airborne bees. Release them on the Canadian or Mexican side of the border and have them land in hives on the American side. He, Bill, and Delahunt were scheduled to meet on the Fourth of July in Hawaii. He'd suggest the ploy to his partners and hope one of them would be willing to go to Laredo, El Paso, San Diego, Bellingham, or even Niagara Falls to receive the bees.

Until then, though, he still had to get the team ready for their trip to Prague in the morning. He could only hope that the girls would be in bed early and be on time for the bus. It seemed like they were always late. If they didn't oversleep, they were missing shoelaces or socks. If they had all their gear, they were out of money. If they had money, they had borrowed it from their boyfriends and needed a loan to pay it back. The good side of it was that it was Prague, a good place to walk around and sample the sausages and schnickel pickles in Haradny Square. And if they were lucky, he and Lerca might get a chance to sneak off to the Atomic Café on Hersova Street near the trolley station, where they could get a pot of tea and a decanter of slivovitz.

CHAPTER 33

The Wine Wrangler

Bill tipped back in his ergonomic Norwegian chair, tilted his wine glass slightly toward the television camera, and spoke.

"I'd say this 2003 Burgundy was a little past its prime, more like a cow than a heifer, mostly fresh, but with a hint of old saddle blanket that lingers on the tongue. It would have been a lot better last year. Still, I think it will pair up nicely with a platter of Rocky Mountain oysters or a braised oxtail."

The show's director, Orgon Visuvini, motioned for the cameraman to slide back a few feet while a second camera panned around the studio audience.

"What's your pick of the week, Bill?" Marcel LeBland, the co-host of *The Wine Wrangler*, asked.

"It's a Vouvray from the Loire Valley. Kinda sweet and grapy with a refreshing bouquet that reminds me of the time we were tracking a bunch of rustlers and picked some wild berries near the Deschutes River in Oregon."

"Seems like this vintage would go well with King Oscar sardines that had been left out of the tin overnight," Marcel LeBland chimed in.

"You're absolutely right, Marcel," Bill agreed. "In the days when me and the boys was pushing steers up the Snaggle Tooth Valley in Idaho, we'd always toss a couple of tins of King Oscar sardines in our saddlebags. It was best done in the winter, cause the heat from the horse's body would warm them fishees up somethin' awful."

Orgon Visuvini motioned for Bill to go easy on the ham-bone theme. Orgon was always worried about the French translation for some of the over–the-top ham-bone. The show was being delivered to both France and Great Britain but was far more popular in France.

"In them days, it wasn't easy to get Vouvray in the McCall area, but my old man would ship us up a few bottles whenever he was in Berkeley or Boise."

Bill was thinking he shouldn't be lying about things, but the show was something of a hit and bringing in good money. The sponsors, the Association of Norwegian Fisheries, had been reporting an upsurge in sales, and their tracking algorithm had attributed the increase to their sponsorship of the Wine Wrangler.

"Anything for our watchers around the world to watch for wine-wise in the next fortnight?" Marcel LeBland asked.

"I'd be looking to Sicily," Bill read off the teleprompter. "Primitivo: it's inky red, and it almost leaps right out of the bottle and clubs you. It reminds me of the time Rico Campanelli, whose father had immigrated from Sicily, or maybe it was Puglia, got bucked off a buckskin pony called Mesquite at the Salinas Rodeo. He went up so high that he looked like a champagne cork launched from a bad bottle of Cold Duck."

"Don't forget to tune in for the next edition of the Wine Wrangler on Tuesday at 10:30 AM," LeBland interrupted. "This segment of the Wine Wrangler was brought to you by Norway, a country where fussy craftsmen build the most expensive ergonomic seating fixtures and the fishermen catch King Oscar sardines."

As soon as the camera light snapped off, Bill tossed his pearl-buttoned Panhandle Slim cowboy shirt in Marcel LeBland's lap, hung his iconic gray Stetson on a hook on the prop cart, and pulled a sweater over his head. He was already looking ahead to next week when he'd talk about Pays d'Oc reds and collect another five thousand euros.

CHAPTER 34

Delahunt in China

When Bill's partner, Jim Delahunt, got to Beijing, he went straight to the Chrysanthemum Lounge in the airport. His old friend Carmel Dias was waiting for him, perched on a thin stool in the center of the bar, looking like a mint Popsicle topped with raspberry drizzle and dark chocolate.

"Can I buy you a drink, sailor?" she purred.

"How about two?" Delahunt answered as he hopped up onto a bar stool next to hers.

"How long are you going to be here?" she asked.

"In Beijing, a week."

"Then what?"

"Going to Hawaii for a conference with my Pylewood partners."

"Ah, those mysterious men from the West you're always talking about."

"Yep."

"What are you going to do while you're here? You missed the Kick-Boxing Olympics."

"Have dinner with a beautiful lady, talk to Na Li about having the Chinese Bank of Dar as Salam and Beijing finance our TrunkWax startup company, and check on my suppliers in Hohhot."

"What's a TrunkWax?"

"Sorry, I can't tell you. It's a trade secret."

"Give me a hint. Who knows? I might be able to help you out of a jam someday." He leaned over toward her, one elbow on the bar, and slid a hand on top of hers. Of course, she already had done it, once at least. She had got General Chan to rein in his nephew, Jong Ma, who had been bent on killing or at least maiming him.

"Thanks for saving my life. Did I tell you Jong attacked me in the San Francisco Airport? If it hadn't been for the intercession of a bunch of scuba divers returning from Belize, we probably wouldn't be here having this conversation."

"An important part of the agreement was that I had to accompany General Chan, his uncle, on a weeklong fishing trip to Cancun."

"Did you catch any fish?"

"One big pompano, if you know what I mean."

"I fared a little better. I only had to grant the nephew an exclusive contract to supply all the loess for the TrunkWax venture. It's a critical ingredient in our paste. That's actually the main reason I'm here. While I'm here, I'm going to test his product and packaging before he ships a big batch to California."

"Now that I've earned the right to know, tell me what TrunkWax is."

"It's a topical paste that makes orchard trees healthier and more productive," Delahunt whispered quickly.

"Now I remember. General Chan was talking about something like that when we were fishing in Cancun."

Carmel gave Delahunt the old you're-one-in-a-million look and stood up to straighten her skirt, a Sap Green creation with loose raspberry-red knitted stitching that seemed to be barely holding her ensemble together.

"Careful you don't pull too hard, your skirt looks like it might fall apart," he said.

"In your dreams, laddie," she said. "Who's the *beautiful lady* you're having dinner with?"

"You, of course."

"I'm flattered, but sorry, I can't stick around. I have to be on a plane for Nairobi tomorrow. Na Li wants me to check out some Kenyan mining property. Next time you plan a trip here, give me a week or two's warning."

"Before you ship out, beautiful, do you know whatever happened to TT Gao?" The last I heard was that he had camped out in Taiwan or South Korea and was trying to get started manufacturing his DollyCart or whatever he decided to call the mobile ladder."

"Actually, he's back in China, Hefei. General Chan smoothed things out for his return, and our bank, the Chinese Bank of Dar as Salam and Beijing, raised the money to finance the development and commercial launch of the mobile ladder. A few months ago, Dieter bumped into him at a home products trade show in Singapore where he unveiled the first production models of the DollieLad. According to Dieter, he has completely recovered from his injuries except for a reddish crinkle on his nose and has stopped smoking. He attributes the change in his fortunes to his embracing Buddhism."

"Dieter or TT?"

"TT. Dieter's an atheist. He says he converted while he was employed in Rhodesia."

"I'm glad to hear TT's all right. You know we've been friends for years, and the mobile ladder was pretty much my idea."

"I seem to recall that we sent you some money before you left for home last time."

"Yeah, I sold him the rights to the invention."

"I hope you got a lot of money. Dieter's trip report emphasized the bright future of mobile ladders in the home- and hotel-maintenance sectors."

"I probably didn't get enough. The mobile ladder concept was sort of a joke, a trick to keep TT from discovering what I was really doing."

"What if you don't get the financing for your wax?" Carmel asked. "Ag products normally aren't part of our bank's investing strategy."

"I'll go back to Hohhot and write a book about Mongolia while I wait for my partners to get back to Pylewood. You remember Mandhuhai, don't you? She says I can stay in her flat if I cook and do the dishes every now and then. She promises to rub my back and head when business is slow."

"Does that mean you'll stay in China for good?"

"Nope. I'll probably stay for six months in Hohhot. Terciley's going to send me a thousand dollars American every month while I'm there if I come home in the spring to change the oil in the vehicles, put water in the solar batteries, and spray the star thistle."

"What's the book going to be about?"

"Genghis Khan's horses."

Carmel Dias drained her drink and slid off the bar stool like a Ginkgo leaf swept up in a clear, cascading stream. She waved and blew Delahunt a kiss as she rounded the corner leading to gate 15, looking like a long bag of pistachio's sliding down a loading chute.

CHAPTER 35

Dog Ears

Lamanon stretched out in front of the big black woodstove in Kwasnik's living room and groaned with relief. Thank God Hrubel Kwasnik was gone, off to the Czech Republic or Slovakia or whatever they called it now. Karen Clements was in charge. It was really nice to have a female master for a change, someone a canine bitch could relate to instead of the goofball that was usually running the show. She and Karen were instantly compatible. Karen washed her bowl every night, fed her with Teutonic regularity, and added a sausage or a few French fries to her bowl every now and then. Kwasnik was a typical man: he only scrubbed her food bowl when he knew company was coming or it got really grubby and if he wasn't preoccupied with business or sports. He was doctrinaire, brusque, and quick to lose his temper and raise his voice. To him, a dog treat was leftovers, usually things he couldn't or didn't want to eat himself. Often the treats he dished up were delectable tidbits, such as overripe figs, sprigs of arugula, or a cup of flat beer. Other dogs might be grateful for such leftovers, but not her. She had been told that her great aunt Hilda of Hannover and West Thuringia had been fed nothing but freshly cooked venison served on a special commemorative issue of silver canine bowls by her master, the Count of Saxony and Westphalia. And unlike Kwasnik, Karen didn't assume she had the right to warm her cold, bare feet on her tummy whenever they sat together in front of the fireplace on chilly nights.

According to Tigger, Bill Robeiro's herd dog, who she bumped into one rainy afternoon at the car wash, Kwasnik had gone off to Central Europe to procure special bees that would produce honey and wax for his latest dumbass invention, the poop squirter for trees. Working dogs always seemed to be up on the latest gossip. But then they prided themselves on their close, subservient relationships with their owners: a ridiculous, degrading concept if there ever had been one. As far as she was concerned, a dog's role was to be a companion, an equal of sorts, not an indentured worker like some common peasant.

Lamanon was proud of her lineage, having directly descended from dogs of whose owners had built the world's finest civilization: Mozart, Beethoven, Brahms, and Wagner in music; Behring, Schrödinger, and Molar in science; and Goethe, Heine, and Mann in literature. As far as she knew, none of them had ever pulled carts, dug for rodents, or herded livestock. Rather, they had been guards, companions, or dog-show champions.

If Kwasnik never returned, it was fine with her. On the other hand, she missed him in a way. She was sure Karen would take good care of her, but she was a single woman after all. What if she fell in love with a mailman or garbage collector? At least Kwasnik never beat or kicked her. Still she dreamt of being part of a family named von-something or other. She curled up by the fire, soaked up its warmth, and dreamt of embossed silver platters of venison and lamb.

CHAPTER 36

Hawaiian Rendezvous

"Zut," Bill said to Blondie as they sat rattling ice chunks in their cloudy anise-flavored drinks in a café on the Boulevard Clemenceau. "It's already the third week of June, and I'm supposed to be in Hawaii for the Fourth of July, which I plumb forgot about until just now when that tourist with the pineapple T-shirt walked by. July kind of snuck up on me while I was trying to learn French, memorize rugby rules, and search for supersmart cattle."

"Your French is improving fast."

"I'm still not there yet, especially when it comes to speaking my lines in *Le Bateaux d'Vie.*"

"That's the soap opera, right?"

"In next year's package, I fall in love with a Senegalese Peugeot mechanic who doesn't speak any English. So I really have to be up to speed. Up until now, I've been talking in English with French subtitles. The producer keeps telling me that our audience won't grow until I start speaking my lines in French. Then I also have a couple of Wine Wrangler programs to do, an interview for *Hot Flashes*, and I'm also in line for an appearance on the Pierre Lustig show, *Name That Tune.*"

"Sounds like a full schedule."

"Reminds me of the year when I put too many cows on hilly ground. I think that's what wrecked my knees. I got a bad habit of biting off more than I can chew. At least that's what most folks tell me."

"Yes, July fourth, American independence day, I remember it well," Blondie mused. "When I was a student in Stillwater, there was a big parade and fireworks every year. But why are you going to Hawaii? If I'm correct, Hawaii wasn't even a state in 1776. In fact, it was the last state to join the union, or was that Alaska?"

"Don't ask me anything about American history, Blondie. I was probably putting out salt blocks when they covered that period in school. Anyways, it all happened before I was born, and the Fourth of July doesn't have anything to do with individual states. That's why we call America the USA. All the states celebrate the Fourth of July at the same time, regardless of when they joined. Besides, Hawaii is the perfect place for a Fourth of July celebration because the weather's great, and they still permit outdoor barbecuing."

Blondie drained his glass and pushed back his chair.

"I must go, my friend. Enjoy your trip. I'm helping to plan the Alpilles leg of the Transhumance, a parade of animals across Morocco, Italy, and the south of France, so I probably won't see you until you return."

"Sounds like a long time in the saddle. By the way, you don't know of a good travel agent, do you?" Bill asked."

"There's a travel agency just up from the Boulevard Clemenceau, on the Rue de President Wilson called Cool Travel. If your French is not good enough to get the correct tickets, you can probably fall back on English. After all, the store is called Cool Travel, and it's on a street named after an American president."

"Bon jour, monsieur" had barely fled Bill's lips, when the travel agent, a short fellow with long moustaches, aimed a rapid volley of heavily accented French at him. Even after they switched to English, it took Bill nearly twenty minutes of frantic questioning to figure out that he couldn't get from Arles to Honolulu in less than a day, twenty-four freakin' hours. According to the mustached Pierre of Cool Flights, the fastest flights from Europe to Hawaii started in London with single stops in Los Angeles, San Francisco, Seattle, or Minneapolis. Faced with the facts, Bill reckoned the only option that wouldn't cripple him would be to divide his flight time into manageable chunks: spend a night in London, maybe take in a movie or a play in the Strand and then catch the eleven-hour Virgin Airlines flight to SFO. Once he got to San Francisco, he would be on familiar ground. He could relax with a nice dinner at the State Byrd, a place that Terciley O'Malley liked, and maybe see a couple of quarters of a Warrior's game before grabbing the morning flight to Honolulu. With layovers in London and San Francisco, he would need at least three days to get to Hilo, but it was still better than sitting for long hours in undersized airplane seats.

***

In spite of his clever planning, he was exhausted when he finally got to Hilo. *The Frog's Voice*, the play at the New Framblinghill Theatre in London, had opened the night before to deservedly lukewarm reviews, and his theatre seat wasn't much more comfortable than the one on the plane from Montpellier. *The Frog's Voice*, set in Croatia during the third Adriatic war, started with the accidental shelling of Grzecka by the Montenegrin navy. Confused by the postmodern sets and the overuse of artificial fog, he fled the theatre at the first intermission and walked back to his hotel on Russell Square. Then in the morning, he almost missed his flight to San Francisco when the airport shuttle was stranded in the middle of a throng of drunk soccer hooligans returning from the Maidenhead-Bournemouth match at Downspout Yards.

He hadn't fared much better in San Francisco: the line at the State Byrd stretched all the way down Haight Street to Ellis and wasn't moving much. He slipped out of the queue in front of Yoshi's and settled for a session with the Mag Pye Quintet and a couple of whiskey sours. The next morning, he had toyed with the idea of renting a car and taking a jaunt out to Pylewood to surprise Karen but gave up that idea in favor of Dim Sum at the Hashimoto Inn in Japantown. The chicken feet were not nearly as good as the frog legs he had got used to eating in France. He couldn't understand why the Japanese, once famous as emulators, were strangely unable to master chicken feet.

When he finally staggered up to the desk at Captain Manny's in Hilo, he only wanted to sleep. When he realized he had just taken a vacation, he hoped it would be his last. He left a note at the desk for either Delahunt or Kwasnik that read:

I'm sleepin'. Don't bother me for a couple days. Bill

***

Bill didn't know it, but his TrunkWax partner Jim Delahunt was already in Hilo. Unlike Bill, Delahunt hadn't had far to travel, catching the AirChina direct flight from Beijing to Honolulu and the Hawaiian Airlines shuttle to Hilo. The elderly former seaman and machinist had been busy in Beijing testing random sacks of the Bator loess, the soil that he was starting to import, which was a critical ingredient in Kwasnik's TrunkWax formula. While in Beijing, Delahunt had also managed to squeeze in a pizza with Na Li, his former exchange student and current president of the Bank of Dar as Salam in China, down a few beers with Dieter Kolb, the bank's helicopter pilot, and sail around on Lake Kunming with Mandhuhai Samuin, his former masseuse who had come down from Hohhot to rub his temples. A lot had happened in the six months since he had last seen his Chinese friends and American business partners. Among other things, he had returned to California, set up shop to manufacture TrunkWax applicators, hired technicians, and carried out a series of phase 1 tests. Now, in Hawaii, he was refreshed, eager to reconnect with his TrunkWax partners, and tell them of his series of successes.

***

While Bill slept and Delahunt bathed himself in satisfaction, Hrubel Kwasnik was at the Hilo airport, struggling to find a taxi and remember where he had put his passport and credit cards. He had left the SkodaCats in the middle of their goodwill tour of Brazilian car factories at a time when they were slumping. Smashes were going out of bounds, sets weren't going high enough, and serves weren't clearing nets. The only game the girls had won when he left was a squeaker at the Audi plant in Rio Grasso. In Belem, his best server and one of the subs had stayed out late to samba and had been arrested for assaulting the band's marimba player. Even worse, Nona Klobchek, the Slovak setter, his best player, had decided to defect the night before, which left the Cats down three players. Hard as he tried, Kwasnik couldn't recruit a Brazilian setter to join the team. Then back in Rio, no one wanted to sell him a plane ticket to Honolulu. Everyone assumed he was a madman because no sane person would fly all the way to Honolulu when the best beaches in the world were right there in Rio.

Tired as he was, Kwasnik was eager to see his TrunkWax partners. After all, he was the brains of the project. He had gathered them together, inspired them with his vision of a better world, and sent them off to gather the raw materials for TrunkWax II. How did they look after almost a year abroad? How much progress had they made? Did Delahunt have a workable prototype applicator? Was Bill ready to provide them with super poop? Did they have any news of how things were back home in Pylewood?

Kwasnik knew that Bill had become something of a celebrity in France from watching the international news when the SkodaCats were on the road. The story of the purple rope had gone viral in Europe while he was still in Pylewood but for some reason had never crossed the Atlantic. The first time he saw the video was in Bratislava, where the Cats were playing Slovan for the Moldau Cup. He couldn't believe his eyes when he saw Bill standing in his shorts, one stockinged foot, surrounded by an applauding crowd, holding up the coiled purple rope, all the while aw shucksing to a gorgeous female French cop. Quite an accomplishment, he figured, for a broke, dinged-up old cowboy. What Kwasnik was really dying to know was whether or not Bill had secured the makings for creating a reliable source of microorganisms for the excrement part of TrunkWax II. While he was somewhat happy to know that his partner was famous and was having a fine time in France, he was also irked that he had wandered off task.

And to be honest, he was also getting homesick. He longed to be back in Pylewood walking barefoot through his freshly plowed fields, watching the figs ripen, warming his feet on Lamanon, his German Sheppard bitch, and chilling out in front of his woodstove. When he finally stumbled out of his taxicab in front of Uncle Manny's Hotel, he lurched up to the front desk and announced himself as the team manager of the Pilsen SkodaCats. The clerk, a lanky woman in a flowery moomoo, hardly looked up. She stared right past him when she pushed a couple of keys and Bill's do-not-disturb message in his direction.

"What room's he in?" Kwasnik demanded.

"I don't think he wants to be disturbed."

"You want me to start at room 1 and knock on every door till I find him?" Kwasnik said, thinking that his year of being the general manager of a Central European lady's volleyball team had made him uncharacteristically aggressive. The receptionist, a master of Kapu Kuialua, thought about what to do for a minute and decided it wouldn't do much good to break the rude haole's wrist or ribs, so she answered with a shrug, "Third floor, room 543."

"How can room 543 be on the third floor?"

"Don't ask me, bub. I'm just working here to pay off my college loan."

"You look too old to still be paying for college. What did you major in?"

"Horticulture. I got back here from Cal Poly, Pomona, just in time for all the pineapple plantations to leave for the Philippines."

"You know anything about trees?"

"Mangos and papayas. We grow a lot of them in the Puna area on this island. They're not native to the Big Island. We have them here because the ring-spot virus destroyed the crops on the other islands. Then it followed us here and ruined our crop in one year."

Kwasnik revived as quickly as if somebody had dumped a bucket of figs on his head. "Back home, most of the yellow papayas still come from Hawaii. How'd you fix the problem?"

"Transgenics. Introduced a gene that did in the virus," the desk clerk answered.

"You want a job?" Kwasnik asked. "I could use a knowledgeable horticulturist like you on my farm in California."

"Maybe. I'm already forty-five years old."

Kwasnik waggled his head back and forth and said, "I don't care if you're a hundred if you're a good horticulturist. I'm here for a meeting with some friends. Can you show me some papaya orchards in the next few days?"

"I work from 10:00 AM to 7:00 PM Mondays, Wednesdays, Fridays, and Sundays."

"What's your name?"

"Edwina Wilson."

"I'm Hrubel Kwasnik. You can call me Rudy or Dr. Kwasnik, never Hrubel or Kwasnik. See you in a couple of days."

***

When he got tired of waiting for the elevator, Kwasnik climbed the stairs up to the third floor and banged on the door that had 543 scribbled on it.

"Go away," a sleep-groggy voice answered. "All's I got is an old Panther's baseball cap."

"It's Rudy. Get up, you old buzzard. I came all the way from the Czech Republic to see you."

When Bill opened the door, Kwasnik had to blink half a dozen times before he could believe his eyes.

"What happened to you? I wouldn't have recognized you unless you were wearing a name tag. You must have lost fifty pounds, and your hair's starting to grow back, and you got a mouthful of new teeth."

"Damn fucking nice of you to notice," Bill said, grabbing his friend's hand. I been eating good, playing some rugby, and hanging out with some smart, good-looking girls."

"And your diction has improved too. If I didn't see you standing right here in front of me, I'd think I was talking to Alastair Cooke."

"I been reading a lot and studying French. I seem to have a knack for the language, and it's helped my English speaking and writing a lot. I guess I always had the aptitude but never had the chance to use it. Aptitude. It's the same word in French, *aptitude*."

"How's the poop search going?" Kwasnik asked. "After all, that's what why you went to France. Or have you forgot already?"

"No, I haven't forgot. We got six good embryos and two questionable ones on ice in France, and all's we need to do is figure out how to get them back to Pylewood."

"That's great, but tell me I didn't hear you say we. I thought the three of us all agreed that the TrunkWax stuff was going to stay secret, just the three of us. Who's the we?"

"Well, there's no way I could have done it all myself. Too much science, too much French, and too much traveling. My two colleagues are Professor Marcel Würtzenhaben, a noted, recently paroled biologist, and Claudine Fortet, an agronomist who works for the French Beef Association. Actually, there's someone else too. Würtzenhaben has an Austrian girlfriend named Gertyl. All of them are topnotch, totally reliable, and only familiar with one part of the project. Gertyl keeps the tools clean and does the parts that require manual dexterity, if you know what I mean. Würtzenhaben does the scientific thinking, and Claudine knows all the farmers. And they only know about TrunkWax at the most superficial level. Same word in French, only spelled differently, *superficiel*."

"Can you trust these people, especially the guy that has just been paroled? What was he in for?"

Bill didn't feel like explaining the sheep-cheese issue, so he ad-libbed a bit. "Illegal genetic experiments. He had this idea that if everything on earth was smaller, life could be sustained for another ten or fifteen thousand years. If people were half the size they are now, there would be twice as much food, water, and air. Cars could be half the size they are now. That would go for everything: shot glasses, condoms, and even toenail clippers. The problem was that if it was done naturally, like natural selection or forced breeding, it would take forever, and the human race would likely die out before it got small enough."

"How did this Wortzendruber fellow end up in jail? You can't lock up somebody for being crazy, especially in France."

"He tried a gene transplant on an actual human being, which is against the law. Even worse, it partly worked. But only certain parts of the subject got smaller, like the ears, fingers, and the opposable thumb, which is the basis of our species' evolution."

Kwasnik had a terrified look on his face when he asked Bill what the take-home message was.

"Everything is on track except the travel arrangements, if you know what I mean. How do we get the product back to Pylewood, the good old United States of America?"

"Let me think about it," Kwasnik said. "Maybe we could use the resources of the SkodaCats volleyball team."

"That reminds me, how are you doing with your part of the plan, Rudy? Have you forgot why you left home? And what's all this palaver about volleyball, almost the same word in French, *palabre*."

"Tell you later. Get out of bed and let's track down Delahunt."

***

They found Delahunt across the street at the Volcanoes bar, sipping a mai tai and talking to a short buxom Filipina whose tight flowered dress and chef's hat left a lot to the imagination. "Yes," he was saying, "When I was in the merchant marines, Manila was my favorite port—"

"Grab your drink and say goodbye to your girlfriend," Bill said. "Time for a business meeting, sailor."

"How'd you guys find me? I was just reliving some old times with this young lady when you guys barged in. Never thought I'd be happy to see you characters, but am I ever." He grabbed Bill's hand and shook it hard and then gave him a big hug.

"Shit, you musta lost a hundred pounds."

"And when did you start hugging guys? I guess that's what too much foreign travel can do to a man."

Hrubel Kwasnik reached over and gave Delahunt a strong hug. "Good to see you Jim," he said. "How's the prototype waxer coming?"

"I got some pictures in my briefcase, but it's up in my room."

"You sure are exuberant, Jim. It's the same word in French, *exuberant*," Bill said.

"We got a lot to talk about," Kwasnik said. "That booth over in the corner looks like a good place to start."

"I'm starving,'" Delahunt said. "Let's walk down the road to Ken's Pancake House and get somethin' to eat. The coconut pancakes were great when I was here in '78."

"Eighteen or nineteen?" Bill asked.

"Seventeen," Delahunt answered. "Glad to see you haven't completely changed into an effete Frenchman."

"Effete is a French word, dumbbell."

When they had ordered, Kwasnik asked Delahunt and Bill to bring the group up to date on their TrunkWax progress. Delahunt started because he had been the first to leave the country. He went through the whole story, beginning almost a year earlier with his arrival in China. He described his meeting with Na Li Wang, Carmel Dias, and Dieter Kolb and then moved on to Hohhot and his reunion with TT Gao, his work at the Buffalo Precision Machine Works, his friendship with Mandhuhai Samuin, the test of the prototype waxer, his kidnapping in the Inner Mongolian grasslands, and his return to California.

"What were you doing in the Grasslands?" Kwasnik asked. "From what I remember, that wasn't part of our plan."

Delahunt recounted the tale of how TT had offered to show him the nomad life firsthand in a place where very few Westerners had ever been. He didn't say much more than that he had been in a car accident on the way home and was injured and discovered by nomads who took him to a hospital in Erenhot, where he was rescued by Na Li Wang's polo club.

"I swear, Delahunt, you make up the weirdest stories," Bill said. "Once you got us to believing you were trapped in a pickle barrel, you just kept piling it on higher and deeper, deeper and higher. Didn't you ever hear about the boy that cried wolf until no one believed anything he said anymore?"

"Your turn, Bill," Kwasnik said as his vegetarian burrito arrived.

"That thing is enormous," Bill said. *"Enorme,* in French. You see what I'm getting at?"

"Not really, but whatever it is, please stop. I think I liked you better as a barely literate English-speaking cowhand."

"I think I like me lots better as a rich French celebrity."

Bill recounted briefly how he had destroyed the Black Hat Gang and killed Vital Nordhoff. He told them he had collected a sizable reward but wouldn't say exactly how much, fearing that if they knew how much he was worth, it might damage their friendships. And he didn't say anything about his Michelin and Caisse d'Epargne endorsements either. But he did tell them he was going to start producing a television series on cattle ranching around the world.

"What about the cow shit?" Kwasnik asked in a way that betrayed his annoyance.

"Like I told you the first time you asked me, the embryos are flushed and on ice in France. These embryos could revolutionize beef production in a bunch of ways, but for us, they should make great TrunkWax. But they're still in Europe, and getting them home is gonna be tricky. The EEC will never permit their exportation, which means we'll have to sneak them out. You got any ideas, Dr. Kwasnik?" he asked. "This part of the scheme was all your idea. We probably could have done good enough with what we already had in Pylewood."

"Strong organizations don't waste time indulging in second-guessing," Kwasnik panted, putting his forehead in his hands. "I learned that when I was in boot camp. Besides, I'm going to have the same problem with my Melnik bees. I'm thinking that we might smuggle the bees out of the Czech Republic in a Skoda muffler. All of my players are associated with the Skoda works in some way: family members, ex-employees, or present employees."

"You haven't told them anything about TrunkWax, have you?" Bill said with a smirk, which Delahunt obliged with a deep laugh.

"The fly in the ointment is that Skoda doesn't export cars to the United States, probably because Volkswagen owns the company now and doesn't want Skoda competing in the VW market."

"That doesn't help us solve the embryo transportation problem," Bill said. "Embryos need to be frozen until they're ready to be used. You're the genius. Maybe you can figure out a way to preserve them at room temperature. Maybe hide a mini-freezer in a muffler or another part in one of your Skodattle cars."

"I could build a tiny battery-powered thermistor that would keep the embryos frozen for weeks," Delahunt piped up. "You could have your friends at the Skoda works stick a couple of them in the mufflers or even in a battery box or radiator," Delahunt suggested.

"We'd need to enlist helpers in the Pilsen plant to get them into the United States. More people means less security," Kwasnik cautioned.

"I know a stewardess on FlyUwhere? Airlines," Bill said. "I'm sure she'd keep them on ice for me, if I asked her."

"How reliable is she?"

"She's nice as can be. Got me a big seat on my flight to Paris and hinted she'd like to hook up with me again sometime."

"I think that's too risky," Delahunt cautioned. "My experience with stewardesses is that their schedules get changed all the time, and sometimes they mix up the vegetarian and kosher meals. What if she made a mistake and served the embryos instead of the little plastic cups of salad dressing?"

"Where do you stand with the prototype now?" Kwasnik asked Delahunt pointedly. "And have you lined up a supply of Bator loess?"

"One of the reasons I was already in China is that I have a supplier lined up, and I was there to inspect the packaging and make sure the particle-size distribution was correct."

Delahunt went on to tell his partners that he had rented factory space in the warehouse district in Berkeley and had found a technician who was setting up for fabrication. He added he had successfully sprayed some trees in Byron with a phase II applicator and a TrunkWax II formulation made up of Salers cattle dung from Terciley's place in Pylewood, some leftover beeswax that Decbie Dantzler had given him, and some clay he had dug up around one his stock ponds. What's more, he had added a slew of refinements to the design he had tested in China, including a remote on-off switch and a vibrating nozzle to prevent clogging. As far as he could tell, the applicator had performed well, but they would still need to do extensive field tests.

"Sounds like you and Terciley made up."

"Yeah, we kinda decided our rift was mostly due to poor communication."

"What about your disguise and your revenge plan?" Bill asked.

"She saw right through my disguise as a biker dude, and I didn't have the stomach for the revenge part."

"Shucks, I wanted to hear how the transplant worked," Bill said.

"How would you summarize your activities to date?" Kwasnik asked.

"The machine will spray and move around the tree trunk, and the test mixture we used sprayed good but didn't adhere well to the tree trunks. So I hafta say we don't have the optimum TrunkWax formula yet."

"I'll write down a list of compositions for you to try before you head back to Pylewood," Kwasnik said. "How are you doing moneywise?"

"I used up what was left of the first ten thousand a long time ago, so I'm spending my own money now. I pay my assistant a hundred dollars a day two or three days a week, so that's about twenty-four hundred dollars a month, which is about right for a guy who scored a perfect 800 on his SATs and has a PhD in organic chemistry. The rent on the shop is two thousand a month, not counting utilities. I inherited a chunk of money from a bachelor uncle back in Newton, enough to keep us working for a year or two more. When we hit the manufacturing stage, we'll need a capital infusion. I'll need to buy fittings, sheet metal, valves, brushes, and tubing. That will start running into big bucks."

"Don't worry, guys," Bill said. "I made a few lucky investments this quarter, so I can throw in a few thousand a month to keep the venture going. Remind me to write you guys a check before I go."

"I'm afraid to ask what kind of investments you made," Kwasnik stated in an accusatory tone.

"How about you, boss, you got a report?"

"I've got the honey and bees. The bees come from a relatively pure strain that has flourished for several hundred years in the Melnik area of the Czech Republic. When we're ready to leave for home, we'll probably send them in the mufflers of some Skodas bound for Costa Rica."

"Costa Rica isn't the USA, Rudy. How you gonna get them bees to Pylewood?"

"I wasn't going to say anything, but since you asked, I'm thinking of letting them fly in themselves. If one of you can get down to the Mexican border with a bunch of hives loaded with sugar water and some pheromones that I'll send you, I'll release them on the other side of the fence and just let them fly over the border."

"Brilliant," Delahunt said. "I bet Decbie and Terciley will help. I'll tell them that the bees have been rescued from a Mexican nuclear power plant."

"You sure they got nuclear power in Mexico?"

"Does it even matter?"

"Let me summarize," Kwasnik said. "Delahunt is already in phase II testing prototype waxers and TrunkWax II formulations. He will need extra financing for rent, supplies, and salaries of at least twenty thousand dollars, which Bill Robeiro will contribute in two thousand dollar increments when asked."

"I expect to get paid back eventually."

"Bill has seven good embryos from an exceptional bull and two Salers cows. He hasn't decided on how he is going to transport them to Pylewood. One idea is to smuggle them in mini-freezers in imported cars or with the complicity of an airline flight attendant he knows."

When it came his turn, Kwasnik confessed that he was the farthest behind. "But I started last and have more administrative responsibilities than the rest of you," he moaned.

"And you also gave yourself the easiest job," Bill said.

Kwasnik wobbled his head and rolled his eyes. "I have determined that the best bees are in Melnik in the Czech Republic, and we will ship them, probably by boat, to either Canada or Costa Rica, take them by truck to a US border, and allow the bees to fly over the border to hives that we have set up on American soil. Instead of a prayer, I'd like to wrap up the meeting with some inspirational words from the Poet Lariat of Byron, Fess Dempster:

When the creeks dry up and the weather gets hot
When your ears get scorched and you curse your lot
Just search the hills for a shady old oak
Give thanks for the breeze and the rain that'll come
And thank the Lord you ain't totally broke

Bill made loud gagging sounds. "I thought ole Fess was in a correctional institution in Nevada."

CHAPTER 37

Spiritual Help for Smugglers

Even though Bill was bunked in a high-priced SuperSleeper for the trip back to France and tired as a first-time heifer with a nervous calf, real sleep eluded him. His cerebral tour guide eventually led him onto one of those half-dream, half-drowsy trails where distant memories persist. He wandered through some early days and some later days before he stumbled plumb into the middle of a spring roundup in the late '80s. There he was, straight and lean, a young buck looking forward to the fun and camaraderie of the roundup: calf roping, branding, old friends, good food, beer on ice in a galvanized tub, seldom-seen cousins, and pretty girls in tight jeans and pearl-buttoned shirts. A branding was an event that could raise all kind of hopes. Then the old man popped his bubble by putting him in charge of the barbecue food. Why him? He had brothers and uncles that could have done it.

The barbecue menu at the roundup was never too complicated: steaks, calf fries, beans, tortillas, and a green salad, but like everything the old man had a hand in, the standards were high. Beans had to be soaked overnight but not too long: tender when cooked but not too soft. The steaks had to hit the hot grill at room temperature, sizzle for a couple a minutes on each side, and end up crusty on the outside and medium rare inside. If he screwed up, he knew the old man would take it as a reason to make him do it again next year.

He rolled over in the SuperSleeper, trying to find a little more room to stretch out, and banged his elbow against the rock-hard drink holder. The SuperSleeper upgrade had cost him a bundle: three times what the normal tourist-class seat cost. It sure as hell wasn't three times more comfortable. But along with the jolt of pain he usually got when he banged his elbow, he got tortillas instead of stars flying through his headspace. Flour or corn? There was no way to tell for sure. It was the little things like tortillas that could mess up a barbecue. Robeiro roundup tradition demanded that tortillas be handmade from fresh, never-refrigerated, yellow-corn masa. And they had to be ten inches in diameter give or take a half inch. It was also traditional that Manual Fargas, the Cadillac salesman who lived close to Sylvia's Grocery and Deli, brought the tortillas to the roundup. Sylvia's tortillas were mandatory for any decent barbecue, endorsed by the Catholic Church for all the local fiestas, and guaranteed to meet the requirements of fresh, handmade, and organic.

In Bill's dream, Manual was big as life: dark, skinny, big nose, and drooping mustache. He was banging the door of Sylvia's without getting any kind of response. In the next scene, he was in the Robeiro ranch kitchen, tossing a big brown paper bag on the table. The paper bag hit the table with a clang instead of the normal soft thud. Then Manual dashed out of the kitchen so's he could saddle up his horse and join the action in the corral. Bill knew something was wrong. Normally, Manual would have stayed a few minutes to shoot the breeze, try to talk him into buying a used Cadillac, or complain about the weather. When Bill stuck his hand in the big paper bag, he felt extreme cold instead of the soft warmth of fresh tortillas. They were frozen. The tortillas were fuckin' frozen. His dad would raise hell when he found out. Of course, he'd get the blame, not Manual, because he was in charge.

"How do you cook a frozen tortilla?" Bill asked a young version of Romaldo Cruz, who had come floating through the kitchen door carrying a festive platter of nopalitos garnished with onions purple and tomatoes brilliant red. The Mexican thought it was another one of Bill's crazy American riddles.

"I don't know," he said in mock seriousness. "Ask an Eskimo."

The memory, purple and red and cold hands, was almost thirty years old but a vivid rerun just the same. Even the writing on the front of one of the tortilla packages was clear, "Organic Tortillas-made from non-genetically altered corn, grown from seeds found in ancient Mayan burial sites." Then the vision unexpectedly morphed into a tiny smiling pear-shaped embryo sitting on a block of blue ice. He sat up straight in the SuperSleeper and cracked his head on the overhanging light dousing the lights in the Sleepy Flier cabin and ending his dream.

Luckily, there were still a couple of ice cubes in his complimentary cocktail, and he used them along with a napkin to fashion a cold compress, which he applied to the top of his throbbing head. Could it be, he wondered, that the dream was a supernatural suggestion? Did it mean that he should abandon the TrunkWax project in favor of starting an organic tortilla business in France? No, that was ridiculous. The French would never give up their baguettes for tortillas. It had to be something more subtle. What was the meaning of the smiling embryo? Was it a clue to smuggle his embryos into the United States in frozen tortillas? But how could you hide an embryo in a tortilla: rolled up in a taco, hidden under the cheese in an enchilada, or maybe in the garnish of a chimichanga? The more he thought about it, the less sense it made. Mexican food and embryo smuggling just didn't seem like a good match. Besides, Mexico was already a long way from France. Could it be that all dream-induced, supernatural ideas weren't great? Maybe the Mexico and frozen-organic-corn tortilla thing was just an extraterrestrial hint, not a down-to-earth suggestion. He thought a while longer. Maybe it didn't have to be Mexico. There was always Canada or Puerto Rico. Why not Europe? That was where the embryos were. Maybe stuffing them in frozen raviolis or piroshkies would work.

What if there was an upscale grocery store in Pylewood that imported frozen foodstuffs from France, Belgium, or Switzerland? Chocolate bars and cheese were the first comestibles that flashed through his mind. As soon as he got back to France, he'd have to get in touch with someone in Pylewood who could search the frozen food bins at grocery stores for frozen products that came from France, Switzerland, or Belgium, someone he could trust, someone relatively sophisticated who could tell a *bonbon* from a *haricot verte*. That left out most people he knew in Pylewood, except for Headley Richards, the ex-Pylewood cop who had been a US Navy SEAL.

With that, he dozed off and, against all odds, returned to his dream. He heard Manual Fargas' voice in one ear, telling him that the frozen tortilla fiasco hadn't been his fault. When he had got to Sylvia's, he lamented, the place had been locked up tight, padlock on the door handle, and sign taped to the door saying that Sylvia was gone to Monterey Park to see her mother. The only recourse he had had was to stop at Gordon's Fine Groceries, which was famous for gourmet foods and wasn't too far out of his way. So he had stopped there and grabbed the first couple of dozen packages of organic handmade tortillas that he found. That was it, the last clue in the dream: Gordon's Fine Groceries.

CHAPTER 38

Execution

When Bill got back to Paris, the first thing he did was telephone Inspector Ariane Dercanges in Clermont-Ferrand.

"Ariane, this is Bill. I got a big favor to ask you."

"Bill who?" she answered.

"You know, the one with the cute American accent," he answered.

"Not another favor? Let me guess. You want me to buy you an airplane ticket to Ouagadougou."

"No. But could you call the Pylewood Feed Store for me and ask them if they can locate a guy named Headley Richards. If they can, call him and have him phone me immediately. You have my phone number. Tell him it's Harrah's Casino, and he's just won five-hundred dollars in the Nevada State Lottery, and he has to call to collect his money."

"Why don't you call him yourself? This is a French police station, not the Nevada missing person's bureau. Use that new Sniper Phone I bought you for Bastille Day."

"First, Ariane, I don't remember his phone number. Second, I can't figure out how to use that damn phone, and third, if he knows it's me, he won't ever call back. Tell him to call collect."

"What makes you think I know his telephone number?

"Use Interpol, the KGB, or some Mediterranean country's most wanted list. Headley was in the US Navy for a long time, so I'm sure he's wanted in a bunch of European port cities: try Naples,

Marseilles, and Rotterdam. While you're at it, transfer a few thousand more euros from my account to a charity of your choice, as long as it doesn't have anything to with birth control or vegetablism."

***

Three days later, Bill's phone rang. When he picked it up, the party on the other end said he was the international operator and asked Bill if he would accept a toll call from a place in California called Planesworld.

As soon as he said yes, the voice on the other end hollered, "How do I collect my five-hundred dollars?"

"Go over to Gordon's Fine Groceries in Pylewood and dig around in the frozen food section until you find something that's imported from France, Switzerland, or the Republic of Belgium. Then report back immediately to this telephone number."

"Oh yeah. Who's this, and where are you calling from?" Ex-Officer Headley Richards chirped.

"You called me, you bonehead."

"If this is who I think it is, the answer is no until I see my five hundred smackers plus the fifty dollars you owe me for those Dodge spark plugs I gave you."

"I'll wire you half now and the other half when I get my answer, and I never owned a Dodge pickup. Buy your own spark plugs."

"What answer?"

"Imported frozen food. You know: raspberries, cumquats, endives, stuff they make better in French-speaking countries. Do they sell any of this stuff at Gordon's? Don't try to telephone me again. Write down the information in a letter and send it to Inspector Dercanges. That is if you still remember how to write."

***

Bill had his answer in five days. Inspector Dercanges called to tell him she had received an airmail letter from Pylewood with postage due. She read the letter over the phone:

"Dear who I think you are, the Pylewood Gordon's has frozen Brussels sprouts from Belgium, frozen Russian caviar and pilsudskis from Prague, frozen cumquats from Spain, and frozen string beans and macarons from France, whatever a macaron is. I'll tell you the names of the farms that packaged the Brussels sprouts, cumquats and string beans, the delicatessen that preserves the caviar and stuffs the pilsudskis, and the bakery that bakes the macarons when I get my two-fifty plus another seventy-five for gas, spark plugs, and postage."

"What do you think?" Bill asked Inspector Dercanges after she finished reading him the letter.

"I think he means piroshkies, not pilsudskis."

"No, I mean about packaging embryos in frozen food for direct shipment to the United States. Headley's note says that there are five frozen foods that are shipped from Europe to Pylewood: Brussels sprouts, cumquats, green beans, caviar, pilsudskis, and macarons."

"I have no idea what you're talking about," she answered.

Bill gasped when he realized he had inadvertently violated TrunkWax security by mentioning embryos over an unsecured telephone line.

"Eh, er, I mean, hummingbird eggs," he stammered. "You know, tiny eggs, salty, blue shells, sweet, but not too sweet, a new delicacy from Slovakia, ready for American gourmets."

"It's a crazy idea. I've never heard of anyone eating hummingbird eggs. I think they sauté the birds whole in Italy, and the nests are used for soup in Burma, but I never heard of anyone eating the eggs. It must take a lot of them to make an omelet."

"They say the taste kinda explodes on your tongue like sesame seeds," Bill said. "Our problem is how to get them into America."

"Why don't you just mail them? You've heard of Occam's razor. The simplest explanation is usually the best."

"They'll never make it through inspection in any European country, and even if they do, American customs will find them and flag them. I'm sure there are all kinds of regulations about importing hummingbird eggs: protected species, bird mites, and warning and content labels. All that stuff has to be preapproved. I think the only timely way to get hummingbird eggs into America is to hide them in some other kind of food. According to Headley Richard's letter, Brussels sprouts, green beans, caviar, cumquats, pilsudskis, or macarons are good candidates."

"I'd be against caviar. It might impart a fishy taste to the eggs," Inspector Dercanges said. "And how would you ever get a tiny egg inside of a string bean or a Brussels sprout, and cumquats are prefrozen in the Canary Islands. Piroshkies are too fragile. That leaves macarons," Inspector Dercanges said.

"What's a macaron, anyway?" Bill asked, "Some kind of tropical fruit."

"It's a European confection. You'd probably call it a cookie in America. The best ones are made in France, but they also try to make them in Switzerland, Italy, and Germany. Basically, they are a sweet meringue-based confection made from egg whites and sugar with some almond flavoring."

"What do they look like? Round, square, triangular, donut shaped?"

"They're usually round, about three or four centimeters in diameter. The cookie is full of air holes like a sponge and has a tough baked outer layer. Most bakers put a filling between the two rounds, kind of like an egg-salad sandwich on a holeless bagel."

"Sounds perfect to me," Bill said. "We can put the hummingbird egg between the cookie halves instead of the egg salad. The way you described it, a macaron is potentially a virtual tiny egg carton. Now all we'll need to do is to work out the details on how we get the eggs into the macarons and the macarons into America."

"Smells like smuggling to me," Inspector Dercanges said. "Remember, I'm a law enforcement officer. I can't participate in any kind of smuggling operation. I've sworn an oath to enforce all the laws of the republic."

A hundred billiard balls started rolling around in Bill's head. "You have to trust me, Ariane. It's for a good cause, but I can't tell you about it over the telephone. I'm driving up to Clermont-Ferrand next week for a photo shoot at the Michelin plant. Why don't we get together for a couple of hours so we can talk more about our macaron problem? Let's meet in the lobby of the Hotel Gergovie for old time's sake."

"Just one minute," Inspector Dercanges said. "I only signed up to be your financial advisor, not your travel agent, secretary, and partner in crime. You've roped me into all sorts of schemes lately: a movie on cattle ranching filmed in Hawaii, TV appearances, and tire commercials, and now you're trying to get me to help you smuggle hummingbird eggs into the United States. All I can see is trouble ahead."

"Don't worry, Ariane. I'll make sure you stay in the clear. All I want to do now is bounce some ideas off your head." A long silence ensued while the high-ranking French cop tried to visualize what ideas bouncing off her head might look like.

"You won't have to do anything except listen. I promise."

"OK, I'll come to the Gergovie," Inspector Dercanges said, "but don't expect me to help you do anything illegal."

Bill made sure he got to the Gergovie fifteen minutes earlier than the scheduled appointment time. It gave him a chance to order a pot of tea, a plate of Madeleines, and a couple of yellow roses for the table.

"Ariane," he called when he saw her stroll into the lobby. It was the first time he had seen her out of uniform. She was smartly decked out in a creamy white skirt and a blouse of Prussian Blue topped with a printed silk scarf of Fools Gold and Winter Rust. "Over here, come sit over here. You don't mind if I call you by your first name do you? Inspector Dercanges is so formal, and we've been working together for months now."

She surveyed the table with its flowers and teapot before nodding her approval and sitting down.

Bill led off. "All we'll need to do this afternoon is work out the details of how we come up with the macarons, get our eggs between the macaron halves, make a box that looks like a normal macaron carton, pack the box, get the box to Pylewood, and mark our box so I'll be able to find it in a jumble of boxes piled up together in the frozen food case."

"Is that all?" she said. "Baking the macarons shouldn't be that difficult. Most French people can do it. The rest will be more simple if you get your contact, this Monsieur Headley, to buy a box of macarons at that shop you mentioned and ship it to you in France. If the box arrives in good condition, you can just reuse it. If not, you'll be able to mock up a facsimile. Once your hummingbird-egg salad macarons have been placed in the box, slip the box into the baker's next shipment to your town. You can mark the box with some tiny emblem."

"You're a genius, Ariane. God, was I ever lucky to bump into you."

Bump into was probably like *bounce off*, she guessed. "Flattery," she said. "I don't believe a word of it. But you have been more than generous in your donations to charity and your countrymen did help liberate France, so I am obliged to help."

"Just think, if it wasn't for old Vital Nordhoff and his Black Hat Gang, our trails might never have crossed. As soon as we get finished here, I'll telephone Headley Richards back in Pylewood and tell him to get down to Gordon's and buy us a box of macarons and send it to us tout de suite. But we still have to figure how to sneak our macarons into a shipment from France to the US."

"Have you identified the bakery that produces macarons for your Gordon's Groceries?" Ariane asked.

"Yeah, it's a fairly small family-run business in Aix en Provence called Marquise Macarons. They make nothing but macarons, and nine flavors at that: champagne peche, vanille, chocolat, litchi rose, pomme, speculos, caramel, and myrtyle-violette."

"Can you get one of your agents into this bakery?" Inspector Dercanges asked.

"What do you mean my agents? I'm a former cowpoke, not Jay Edward Hooper."

"All right, an undercover operative, perhaps a baker's assistant, someone who could substitute your box of macarons into one of their normal shipments or add hummingbird macarons into one of their regular boxes. Whatever you want to call it, an undercover operative will be the best way. Bribing the baker or trying to intercept the shipment somewhere between Aix and Pillsworth will be too dangerous."

"I don't have a clue about how to find an undercover agent," Bill said. "You and Claudine Fortet are the only two beautiful French girls that I know," Bill said. "And neither of you could pass for a baker's helper."

"Who said the baker's helper had to be a gorgeous girl? You men have so many female stereotypes. It makes me furious. Look at me, a female chief inspector who, by any measure, should have been promoted to chief years ago."

"Sorry, honey," Bill said. "I didn't mean to get you all riled up."

"I forgive you," Inspector Dercanges said. "I have an extensive list of informants in my office in Clermont-Ferrand, but no one in the field of pastry."

"How about that Officière DePluson you had drive me around Clermont-Ferrand? She seemed like a clever girl."

"No. She isn't even from a macaron-baking region."

"You just gave me an idea, Ariane. I have a friend in Arles, Georges Bellatre, a scientist, an ex-biochemist, which is almost like a baker. He's retired and has lots of hobbies but seems bored. I bet a little excitement as an undercover operative would do him some good: something really dangerous that has a small but real chance of landing him in the slammer."

"I don't know this word slammer," Ariane said with an unhappy pout.

"I have to go back down to the Camargue to give a busload of Italian tourists a roping demonstration next week, so maybe I can ask him if he can do a little undercover work for us."

"Please quit talking about us, Bill. Nothing could hurt my chances to become chief more than a hint of impropriety, especially something like an association with a smuggler of hummingbird eggs."

***

Two weeks later, back in his Paris hotel, Bill found a heavy brown envelop waiting for him at the front desk. When he cut open the envelope, a flattened brown box and a piece of yellow legal paper tumbled out. The box was about six inches by eight inches, brown and tan, and had the title *12 Macarons a la parisienne* printed on it and a little warning in the bottom left hand for the buyer to keep the box's contents frozen. The typed message on the yellow paper read:

"Here's what you asked for. You still owe me seventy-five bucks plus eight for the macarons and five for shipping. Me and your cousin Frank ate all the macarons to keep the postage down. There were twelve all together, so we each ate six, three vanilla and three chocolate a piece. They sure as hell weren't worth the eight bucks we paid for them, mostly just air. They were pretty small and stuck in our teeth (Frank's got dentures) when you tried to chew them normally. We both like the chocolate better than the vanilla ones. Have you thought of just using fig newtons or Oreo cookies instead? Here's some extra intelligence that I'm not gonna even charge you for, but if you were honest, you'd pay me a couple a hundred more for. Frozen macarons bound for Northern California travel by refrigerated truck from the bakery in Aix to the Marseille airport and then directly to San Francisco International Airport, where they are logged in and loaded onto refrigerated trucks that carry frozen products to Gordon's stores from Modesto to Redding. Vince, the guy that manages the Pylewood store on weekends, told me that he could track the Pylewood order from Marseille to SFO and from SFO to the Pylewood store online and even get the license plate number of the delivery truck that was going from SFO to Pylewood in case you wanted to highjack it.

CHAPTER 39

French Radio

MFB: *Bon jour* and Welcome to *Hot Flashes*. I'm Marcy-France Belast, and I'm sitting in for Pierre Lustig, who is scuba diving in Honduras. I'll be your host this afternoon. Our guest today here in our Paris studio is cowboy writer and French television personality, William Robeiro, whose book *L'histoire de Roger Jones* was released just two weeks ago and has already become a best seller.

MFB: So first of all, William, tell us about yourself.

WR: First off, Marcy, there ain't too much to tell, and you can just call me Bill. I was born in California, went to Antioch High School, started cowboyin' around the West, and eventually came to France, where I'm livin' temporarily until I can earn enough money to buy a new truck and get back together with my girlfriend.

MFB: So what brought you to France?

WR: Didn't I just tell you?

MFB: Yes, but I'm sure our listeners would like to know how you intend to earn money here and why you picked France instead of Luxembourg or Latvia.

WR: I been around cattle all my life, and I just wanted to see some French breeds. I already knew about Charolais and Limousin and a little about Salers but nothing about Aubracs and the black cattle of the Camargue. The idea was to maybe introduce some French blood into my herd.

MFB: So your visit to France has nothing to do with foreign relations, gay marriage, national security, cultural exchange, or promoting tourism in the American west?

WR: Nope, Marcy, just livestock.

MFB: So, William, I'm curious as to why you wrote *Roger Jones* in French. Obviously, English is your first language. You grew up in California and have spent most of your life there, right.

WR: You're right about that. But I never learned proper English. Starting in junior high school, English classes were always at the end of the day. Mostly, just about the time my dad needed me to help out with the ranch work. He thought nothin' of walking right into the classroom and draggin' me out of class right there in front of the teacher. In the end, it didn't work out too good for me, kept me from getting a baseball scholarship because of my low SAT scores and a bad written essay.

MFB: So then, how did you learn to write in French?

WR: When I decided to take this trip to France, there wasn't enough time for me to buy a beginners book like *French for Dummies*, but my girlfriend back home did give me a little yellow French-English dictionary as a goin'-away present. When the stewardess passed out the newspapers, I asked for Le Figaro because we once had a big old Hereford bull named Figaro. But before I even had a chance to start reading it, I had an altercation with the passenger in the seat in front of me. When they finally moved me to a larger seat, I started translating with my dictionary. I took right to it. I always thought I was a poor student, but learning French seemed to bring out the latent scholar in me.

MFB: *Encroyable*. So what happened next?

WR: Before long, I was reading French and speaking a little bit. I think it's more logical than English, and I love the sound of it, even if my accent isn't all that good. My best friend in France, Claude Raimbaut, we call him Blondie, got me a French book called *Madame*

Bovary in the train station in Lyon on our way to Clermont-Ferrand, and I started reading it to improve my vocabulary.

MFB: It's a French classic but somewhat outdated.

WR: Right. Halfway through, I switched to Albert Camus. I'm more suited for simple, direct realism. Later on, when I had some free time, I took a couple of weeks off so I could take a crash course in French at the Académie Francaise in Paris. Vernon Waynbright, my principal at Antioch High, probably wouldn't believe it, but I got a book of Verlaine poems for being the best student in my class.

MFB: So that's so fascinating. Can you tell us about *Roger Jones*? It's already been a best seller in France and half of Belgium and is sure to be a hit in England and Australia.

WR: It started out as a kid's story about a cow dog I used to have. Blondie got me a literary agent who told me it was a cute story but had a better chance of being financially successful if I added a bit of sex and violence to the story and aimed it at young professionals who were still dating and had dogs. To tell you the truth, I didn't really know what he was talking about, but I did add some nasty bits because I was tired of being broke all the time.

MFB: So did you make Roger gay or straight? I can visualize the story now. A herding dog that couldn't do his job until he came out of the closet. Always chasing the sheep out the wrong door, so to speak.

WR: No, Marcy, we never kept Roger in no closet. He always had a doghouse of his own. He did sleep in the back of the pickup sometimes and every now and then in my bed when he was really upset but never in a closet. And we haven't had sheep on our place since 1937.

MFB: So what was so interesting about Roger that made the book a best seller?

WR: The reviewers said that the fact that Roger was named after a boyhood friend of mine that had cerebral palsy and had himself overcome the adversity of losing an eye in a freak accident had all the elements of great literature: pathos, loss, triumph, resurrection, unqualified love, and a good retirement package in old age. Personally, I think people liked the descriptions of cattle roundups and fishing on the Delta and didn't even notice the sex, violence, and adversity stuff. And I think French is the perfect language for writing Westerns. It's more expressive and alliterative than English.

MFB: So any plans for future books?

WR: My agent wants me to write a cowboy cookbook. She thinks our target audience is bored with tiny leaves, duck fat, small portions, charcuterie, and yeasty bread. I was telling her about some of things we used to cook out on the ranch, and she got me to start writing up some of the recipes.

MFB: So what are some the dishes you describe in the book?

WR: My favorite one is doves and polenta. We always have a good dove season in the fall. The birds get real fat on mullen seeds and have an extraordinary delicate taste. Rocky Mountain Oysters ranchero is another one. We usually have these at a roundup when we cut calves. Rolled in corn meal and sautéed, they make a wonderful accompaniment to steaks and beans, especially when washed down with a 2001 Chablis or a cold BulgeWidener. The trick to getting delicious Rocky Mountain fries is the preparation. The outer membrane has to be removed completely and gently. I tell you what, Marcy-France, just talkin about this stuff makes my eyes water. Fresh peach pie, deer stew, and Pylewood beans, they'll all be in the cookbook.

MFB: So what will the title be, and will it be available in French and English?

WR: Definitely. And maybe even in Italian and German. I think we'll call it *la Cuisine Especial de la Region Contra Costa*.

MFB. When can we expect to see it in bookstores?

WR: If all goes well, it should be in bookstores by fall.

MFB: One last question: you said you lived in Arles. Why there and not Paris or Mulhouse?

WR: After all the excitement of breaking up the Vital Nordhoff international hat gang, my friend Blondie Raimbaut asked me to come out to the Camargue and teach his ranch hands some of the tricks I know with horses and cattle. I don't know if your listeners are aware of it, but out there in the Camargue, where they're close to the ocean and the land is poor, they have small cattle that they breed mostly for games. These cattle are unusually smart and can be taught to play tag, four square, and jai alai, probably because they're close to the Basque region. They also possess a sense of humor that's remarkable in the animal world. When you're around them, you can expect lots of practical jokes like wedgies and things with poop. But to answer your question, why the Camargue, I feel at home out there in a way I wouldn't in Paris because of the crowding or Mulhouse because of the heavily accented French they speak.

MFB: So, William, it's been a pleasure talking with you, and good luck with your books.

WR: My pleasure, Marcy.

CHAPTER 40

The Phony Baker

Bill was sitting with Blondie Raimbaut under a tree on the hill just below the old Roman amphitheater in Arles, eating paella out of a paper carton, when Georges Bellatre came trudging into their picnic. The diminutive Frenchman stopped to catch his breath before he unstrapped his metal breastplate and dropped it on the grass.

"Even though this piece of armor weighs twenty kilograms," he announced, "it probably wouldn't stop a bronze-age arrowhead."

"Didn't recognize you in your costume," Bill said.

"Costume, indeed. For your information, my friend, I've spent the morning sweating out the Battle of Marengo in the peaks and valleys around Les Baux. This costume, as you so flippantly called it, is an exact replica of the uniform worn by an early-nineteenth-century officer of the horse grenadiers. Look at this helmet," he said as he pulled the plumed bowl of shiny metal from his head and propped it up against the tree trunk.

"I'd say that helmet is chrome-plated steel," Blondie conjectured. "You sure they had those materials back in the eighteen hundreds?"

"My neck isn't strong enough to support the kind of heavy steel actually used in the battle. Either is yours. Look at the gold-colored chin strap and the ridge running through the center. The ridge supports the red plume and the horn-shaped brass fixture," Bellatre said. This helmet is a regular piece of artwork

"You're right, Georges. Forgive my impudence."

"How come it's not in a museum?" Bill said, reaching for the helmet and almost toppling over Blondie's bottle of Orangina. "Why all the feathers and fur in your uniform? Just makes you a better target. I'm surprised that one of them Spaniards didn't just shoot you out of the saddle."

"All the cavalries of that time wore fancy uniforms," Bellatre explained, "maybe so they could distinguish one and another. I don't think there were any Spaniards involved. According to the history books, we vanquished the Austrians, or should I say their Lichtenstein mercenaries. We finished them off early, so I came here directly to see what you two lazy rustics were up to. Took me a while to find you fellows. I thought for sure you'd be in some cafe along the boulevard not camped out here on the damp grass."

"Time for me to go," Blondie said. "I think Bill has something up his sleeve, some secret mission, which fortunately doesn't include me."

Blondie drained his drink, shook hands with his friends, and disappeared into the market-day crowd.

***

Bill passed his carton of paella over to Bellatre, who declined the offer, but couldn't quite stifle a quick look of disgust.

"I had a snack on the battlefield," he said, mopping his head with a fancy handkerchief. "OK, Bill, what's on your mind?"

"Macarons," Bill answered. "Do you eat them? Can you make them? And are you willing to smuggle them?"

"No, yes, and maybe. Except for the occasional fruit tart, I don't bake much anymore. Macarons are simple to make, and I used to help my mother prepare them when she invited friends over for afternoon tea. Smuggle them, maybe, if it's for a good cause like the Girl Scouts or Doctors without Patience."

"Perfect, Georges. You meet all the qualifications. Can we use your kitchen to bake up a batch some Saturday when Gerrard is visiting his *maman* in Chateaurenard?"

"Sure, just give me a week's notice."

"Before we get too deep in this, Georges, you should know that there's more to this project than baking cookies. After we bake them, but before we slap the halves together, we drop in a bovine embryo. Then we freeze the little sandwiches so we can ship them to America."

Bellatre made a face. "Yuck, you Americans will eat anything. No wonder you have to smuggle them."

"The next thing you gotta know is that the embryos aren't to eat. They're to transplant in my cows."

"Wow," Bellatre gasped after a long silence. "Isn't that illegal?"

"That's where the smuggle part comes in. I'm telling you it was a big surprise, but I found out from a friend back home that every week boxes of frozen macarons baked at the Marquise Bakery in Aix en Provence are flown to California, and then delivered to a store in Pylewood, my hometown. Someone, maybe you, will have to go undercover to gain access to the Marquise Macarons. Whoever it is will have to get into the bakery and slip our eight embryo-filled macarons into a box of the unadulterated cookies headed for Pylewood."

"Why eight? Wouldn't it be simpler to just slip in a complete box of twelve?"

"We only have eight embryos. I wish we had a dozen, but we don't."

"We'll, why don't we just add four normal macarons to the box we prepare. That way, we won't have to handle individual macarons and risk getting caught hanging around the shipping room."

"Good idea. I knew you were the right guy for the job."

"I can see some big problems though. How are you going to keep them cold enough on the trip to America? You know you just can't put them in a regular kitchen freezer like a can of orange juice and hope they don't spoil. I think the normal air-transport frozen food shipping containers rely on dry ice and don't get any colder than -78 Celsius."

"The way I figured was that the embryos, which we have stored at Ceemensee in Limoges, would stay frozen enough for a few days inside the macarons, which I thought would be good insulators."

Bellatre made some noises by forcing air through his lips, nose, and teeth before he spoke. "Laboratory embryos are usually shipped in liquid nitrogen containers, close to -200 degrees Celsius, 321 degrees below zero Fahrenheit for you Americans, and 77 Kelvin for scientists like me. This is much colder than the standard dry-ice shipping temperature of -78.5 Celsius. But I must also say that as far as I know, no one has ever tried to ship embryos inside of macarons or any kind of cookie for that matter."

"Does that mean we're screwed?" Bill asked. "Will we have to figure out a better way to get our embryos to Pylewood? What if we get a dogsled and take the northern route through Alaska or hire a submarine to go under the polar ice cap?"

"Maybe with a little ingenuity, we can keep them cold enough. You know, throughout my scientific career, I never really understand why tissue samples had to be kept so cold. My friends in Minnesota always claimed that the chilling procedure was just as important as the storage temperature. Most of the damage comes from ice crystals rupturing cell walls."

Bill's disappointment in the technical details was mitigated by his surprise at Bellatre's enthusiasm for the project. Deep down, he was sure the French scientist would figure something out. He had expected a lot of questions from Bellatre: like why were they even bothering to smuggle French embryos to California, but instead of provoking scepticism, the plan had piqued Bellatre's scientific interest.

"And you know, now that I think of it, they have done some research in California on synthetic foams that capture neutrons. Most of their work is secret, but I think some of this material has actually found practical use in the preservation of foods for the space program. I'm not sure of the details, but I think that one of their foam products just became commercially available as foam for egg cartons. It all has something to do with spiral annihilation of bacteria."

"You know, a guy from Polonitza, the Polish embryo transfer company, told me at the Sommet that they had just introduced some new space-age low temperature shipping containers. Maybe it's the same stuff."

"Can you get someone in to California to airmail us a couple of the new egg cartons? I can slice them into very thin sheets on my mandolin kitchen slicer and wrap a test sample in one of the sheets. Then we can measure the temperature drop of a fully loaded embryo-macaron as a function of time before we do any real shipping. Meanwhile, I'll ask an old colleague at the Pasteur Institute if he knows anything about the Polonitza containers."

It was already 3:00 AM in Pylewood when Bill called Headley Richards and asked him to airmail a Forever Fresh egg carton to an address in Arles, France.

***

On a Saturday when Gerrard had the day off, Bill donned an apron and white chef's hat and joined Bellatre in his kitchen. A small army's worth of kitchen weapons were arrayed on a rolling maple table in the center of the kitchen: stainless-steel whisks and spoons shiny as chrome, wooden spoons, glistening with the oily sheen of a potentate's thumbnail, mixing bowls as yellow as a Provençal mustard field, and a baking sheet as smooth as a poppy's petal. Four big brown hen's eggs rested in the shade of the cabinets where Bellatre had placed them so they could slowly warm up to room temperature. With Bill at his side, Bellatre took the first egg, gently cracked the shell, broke it in two, and rocked the contents back and forth until he had completely separated yolk from white. He slid the egg white out of the half shell into the smallest yellow bowl, tossed the shells and yolk into a small plastic tub, grabbed a second egg, and repeated the procedure. On the third try, though, he got a speck of yolk in the egg white.

"Merde," he hissed, "It doesn't take but a speck of yolk in the white to ruin the meringue."

He separated the next egg perfectly and pushed the bowl of egg whites aside. "I'll let these sit for a few minutes while I prepare the solid ingredients."

"Do know anything about the battle of Marengo?" he asked Bill.

"Only that it has something to do with a French author who called himself Stendhal."

"Bravo. In fact, it made a hero out of a general who later lost a lot of battles. Planning a battle is a lot like baking a perfect macaron, which has to be lacy on the flat side and puffy on top. Everything has to happen at the correct temperature and time. And just because your last batch was perfect doesn't guarantee that your next will also be perfect. It's like starting another battle. Just because you won the previous one doesn't mean you'll win the next or the one after that." With that bit of wisdom released, Bellatre walked over to his electronic balance, tared a beaker, and set the scale for 210 grams. He poured some confectioner's sugar into the beaker to get the digital display close to 210 and then used a spoon to sprinkle in a few more grains of the fine powder until he was right on the mark. He transferred the sugar into the medium-sized yellow mixing bowl. He put another beaker on the balance and used the same technique to measure out 125 grams of almond powder, which he mixed with the sugar. He sifted the almond/sugar mixture onto a sheet of parchment paper, making sure the particles of the mixture were as fine as dust. Next, he quickly beat the egg whites frothy.

"Bill, we call this the bec d'oiseau," Bellatre said, touching the froth with the tip of the whisk and pulling some egg-white into a stiff point.

"A bird's beak," Bill said.

Bellatre stared at the mixture for a few seconds and then added some confectioner's sugar, about a tablespoon, Bill guessed, and whisked the egg whites for about five more minutes.

"Chocolate and vanilla, you said? Why don't we make eight chocolates and four vanillas? That way, you'll know which ones have the embryos in them. The white ones will be normal." Bellatre divided the almond/sugar mixture in half and dumped a spoonful of chocolate in one of the piles. Little by little, he folded the tan mixture of sugar, almond, and cocoa powder into the egg whites.

While he folded carefully, Bellatre made a point of emphasizing the importance of using a silicone spatula. "This is an important tool. The silicone spatula slides easily through the egg whites without bending or tearing the protein strands. Now, my friend, we are ready to bake. Check the oven please," he asked. "It should be around 150 Celsius."

"Here," Bellatre said, handing Bill a pastry bag and the bowl of meringue. "Fill the pastry bag with meringue and squeeze out enough to form inch-and-a-half disks on the baking sheet. Make sure they're not touching each other, and then place the tray carefully in the oven. I'm going to whip the chocolate and vanilla fillings." When the cookies had come out of the oven and cooled, Bellatre halved each and delicately carved out little half vaults in them with a platinum spoon. Next, he placed the tray of macarons in the freezer.

"We don't want temperature excursions at any point in the preparation of your embryo-macarons, so it's best to get the cookies cold, but not so cold as to crack them."

***

With the cookies in the freezer, Bellatre offered Bill lunch, a simple affair of onion soup, a small lamb chop, and a plate of cheese and fruit. When they finished, he fetched the cold macarons from the freezer, retrieved the embryos from the liquid nitrogen thermos, and deftly pipetted the eight frozen embryos into thin tough ampoules that he had fashioned from a ganache laced with gelatin microspheres and marzipan. He wrapped each ampoule in a thin sheet of Forever Fresh egg carton foam that he had sliced from the egg carton Headley Richards had air mailed form Pylewood. He spread chocolate filling on two cookies, placed the embryo ampoules in their tiny vaults, and pressed the cookies together to make a sandwich of sorts. When he had the eight chocolate macarons loaded, he finished the job by punching two tiny holes in each cookie, flushing out the volatile impurities with ultrapure argon, and plugging up the holes with a microdrop of gelatin mixture. He placed the eight chocolate macarons back in the liquid nitrogen thermos and prepared the four vanilla cookies. Half an hour later, the two of them were drinking glasses of Bandol rosé and admiring their work: twelve perfect macarons cooling in a liquid-nitrogen-cooled thermos.

"Looks like the real thing, doesn't it?" Bill said.

Bellatre raised his glass and clinked it against Bill's.

"Now," Bill toasted, "let's sneak them little cookies into the Marquise Bakery's next shipment to the Pylewood Gordon's Fine Groceries."

"Remember what my tests showed," Bellatre cautioned. "We have three days, including the plane flight, to get those cookies chilled back to liquid nitrogen temperatures, and after that, no more than a week or two to get them planted."

"Maybe we should ask Gerrard to help us with the bakery part. He's from the Aix area, isn't he?"

"Brilliant, old man. I'll bet he has a cousin or two in the trade or at least a friend that works at the Marquise bakery."

***

The idea was a good one. It turned out that the head baker at Marquise was an old school chum of Gerrard's, and Gerrard had even worked in the bakery one summer when one of the bakers fell ill with a gluten allergy.

"The Marquise family are old friends," Gerrard protested when Bellatre asked him to do the macaron switch. "The last thing I want to do is make trouble for them. Messing with food is a serious matter in France. Tell me again why you want me to substitute your macarons for the genuine Marquise macarons in a box headed for the United States."

Bill took a deep breath. "It's part of a big television charity fund raiser. A chain of stores back home, Gordon's Fine Groceries, is having a big sale of European food: raviolis, scones, bonbons, piroshkies, sausages, and wontons that contain letters of the alphabet hidden in them. If a customer can collect the right letters to spell out GORDONS, they'll win a year's supply of frozen cheese cake."

Gerrard started blinking in three-two time. "What does the charity get?" he asked.

Bill and Georges Bellatre looked at each other, each hoping the other had the answer. "A thousand dollars," Bill said.

"A scholarship to the University of Dayton," Bellatre said at the same time.

"Don't worry, Gerrard," Bill said. "It's hard to explain in French."

"Isn't Dayton the place where they signed the Vietnam Treaty?" Bellatre stammered.

Although he had plenty of doubts, the next day Gerrard inveigled his way into the shipping room at the Marquise Bakery on the pretext he was helping his niece with a term paper on the exportation of French bakery goods to Northern California. In his brief case, he had the fake box that held the twelve fake frozen macarons, eight with embryos and four plain. The box was identical to the one that Headley Richards had sent from Pylewood except for a tiny red bull's-head sticker in the top right-hand corner.

Gerrard let himself into the walk-in freezer and searched until he found a shipping container with a manifest that indicated that the shipment was bound for Gordon's Fine Groceries, Pylewood, CA, 94513, United States of America. He made a mental note that the temperature was only -70 Celsius. Gerrard pulled out a box of genuine Marquise macarons, replaced it with the box of bogus macarons, and slipped the genuine box into his briefcase. He'd put them in the freezer when he got home and give them to his mother in Chateaurenard on her birthday.

The macaron shipment was due at the San Francisco Airport the next day, which didn't give Bill much time to get to the Pylewood Gordon's and intercept the package. Luckily, he was already in Paris, packed and ready to go.

CHAPTER 41

Macarons in America

As soon as Bill got Gerrard's fax telling him that the macarons were in transit, he grabbed his coat and suitcase and charged out the door to hail a taxi for Charles De Gaulle Airport. From then on, it was full speed back to Pylewood. He was only in the air for a little over ten hours, but the simultaneous arrival of three monster planeloads of travelers at the International Terminal at the San Francisco Airport seemed to catch the customs and immigration people by surprise. By the time he had extricated himself from the airplane and advanced to a stall in the men's room, the line from the customs and immigration stretched from the main terminal all the way out to the ramps and doors of the arriving aircraft. He had the funny idea that if one more monster international flight tried to land at San Francisco, the plane would have to be redirected to Oakland and the passengers made to queue up at the Bay Bridge. He prayed that his cargo of macarons was faring better than he was and that they had already been unloaded and safely put to bed in their frozen hostel in South San Francisco.

His next setback was at the UHurts car rental agency where he found out that the Ford Explorer he had reserved had been given away to a family of tourists from Bombay when he hadn't shown up on time. After pacing the floor for another hour, the UHurts agent informed him that the only car they could find for him was a Nissota Vesar, a car smaller than one of his Uncle Gino's sweatshirts. He took the car anyway, initialed all the waivers, and made a less-than-thorough inspection of the scratches and dings, all the time worrying about the awful consequences of another Gordon's customer beating him to Gordon's and snagging his TrunkWax macarons.

When he finally did get to Pylewood, the only parking place he could find was almost a block away from Gordon's in front of the BigFish sushi parlor. After a long walk across the hot parking lot, he finally staggered into Gordon's panting and sweating. He was so tired he had to stop and hold on to the wooden banana tree at the head of the first aisle while he caught his breath. He was sort of sure that not too long ago he had been in good enough shape to play professional rugby, but there he was clinging to a fake yellow tree draped with bananas, trying to recuperate from a brisk walk across a parking lot. Maybe he wasn't who he thought he was, or maybe his rugby exploits had occurred in some alternate reality.

He was also hungry. Without thinking, he grabbed a banana off the banana pole and started walking toward the free-sample cart at the rear of the store. He hoped the lady with the apron who was dishing up tiny samples of corn chutney could tell him where they hid the frozen macarons. By the time he reached her cart, all that was left of the banana was the peel. He looked around for a trash can but didn't see one.

"How come you don't even have a garbage can in this place?" he asked.

"This is a high-end grocery store, not some burger joint," she informed him while she ladled a little blob of chutney topped with bluefin tuna foam onto a Sriracha-coated multigrain cracker. "By the way, don't you know you're supposed to buy the banana and take it home to eat?"

"Sorry, I've been abroad for almost a year, and I'm also suffering from jet lag, exhaustion, and arthritis. What do I owe you?"

"Bananas are forty-seven cents apiece, but you have to pay at the cashier. Hang on to your banana peel. It has a barcode embedded in it."

"Can I have a little of that stuff you're putting on the crackers, but I'd like mine on a Cheezit, please."

When the free-sample lady ignored his request, Bill walked gingerly down the aisle that separated the two rows of frozen foods trying to figure out where the frozen macarons might be hidden. Would they be with the ice cream, fish, and cookies or on the other side of the aisle with the frozen vegetables, waffles, and chocolate bars? He paused for a moment to let his mind clear and drop the banana peel before resuming his search, musing that here he was, a rehabilitated local cowboy searching for frozen French macarons, stuffed with fertilized bovine embryos cobbled up from the semen of intelligent black bulls and the oocytes of skinny red cows in an upscale food market formerly devoted to yogurt and fancy crackers. He had never been a regular patron of Gordon's. In fact, he had only been in store a couple of times before and had never paid much attention to how the food was organized. In the past, he had mostly gone to Gordon's to buy bottles of cheap wine to share with his friends like Jim Delahunt and Hrubel Kwasnik, who boasted they could distinguish a Beaune Burgundy from a Bakersfield Merlot while blindfolded and with clothespins on their noses. One thing he did remember about Gordon's, though, was that they packaged everything in plastic, except for the bananas, which they sold by the piece, one of which he had just eaten and disposed of before paying.

Then he laughed so hard other shoppers turned to gawk. Wasn't life just one kick in the ass? You never knew how or where you were going to end up or what you'd be having for lunch. And to make it all the more doodleflapping, he was looking for one particular box of macarons: a box with a red, bull sticker pasted in the upper left corner just under the picture of a brown chocolate macaron. Inside that box were eight special cookies, each one with a tiny imprint of the red bull on its puffed-up top.

Failing to find any macarons on three round-trips up and down the frozen food aisle, his fatigue returned, and his good humor flagged, turning to worry and from worry to doubt.

"Where do I find the frozen macarons?" he asked a clerk at the end of the aisle after spinning him around roughly. The clerk, a lean, youngish-looking fellow with tattoos up his arms and a spiky hairdo, smiled and apologized for not noticing Bill, saying he was totally concentrating on pitching sacks of frozen artichokes into a bin between the green beans and okra.

"They're usually right over there with the frozen brownies," the clerk said, pointing his tally gun at a spot midway between the blueberries and waffles, "but they're all sold out."

"What?" Bill gasped, doubt turning to panic.

"They've been sold out for almost a week. They're selling like hotcakes for some reason, maybe because of weddings or some Asian moon festival. Who knows? But have no fear, sir, a shipment is due in today."

"What time?" Bill whispered, not wanting to let others in on the secret of the next delivery. "Usually around midnight when the store is closed. We do it at night because of the traffic. It's murderous across the bridge. In the summer, most of our frozen food deliveries come after dark. Last year, we had a truck sit in traffic so long it ran out of gas, and a whole shipment of Cuban sandwiches thawed out and spoiled. Hey, it's June after all. If you leave your name and phone number with Glenn up there at the desk, he'll reach out to you when we start stocking macarons again."

Bill cursed quietly under his breath, but it was loud enough for the clerk to hear. "Sorry, sir, but if you really need them right now, I can call over to our Concord store and see if they have any."

Bill just muttered and walked off. Now what was he going to do? From the start, they had tried to plan for every contingency, but they had never anticipated a run on imported frozen macarons in a backwater like Pylewood. They just assumed that the macarons would arrive on schedule and be waiting in the frozen food case. Now the whole plan was in jeopardy. First, they had already been out of liquid nitrogen for almost two days, and he'd have to wait until tomorrow for them. And then who could tell what might happen? A thousand macaron enthusiasts might suddenly descend on Gordon's door in the morning. He had a vision of a howling mob of macaron enthusiasts racing to Gordon's frozen food case like suburban shoppers to a sale of oven cleaners. Without a doubt, he'd have to be there in front of the frozen food case when they started stocking or risk some macaron snatcher already halfway home with his cookies. And if he did strike out, hell, he'd have to go back to France and start all over from the beginning.

***

The next morning, Bill was at Gordon's five minutes before the door opened. Even so, half a dozen shoppers were ahead of him. He asked all of them what they had on their shopping lists. Ginger granola, peanut-free trail mix, and fair-trade Ethiopian coffee beans were all high on their lists, and his hopes rose when not a single shopper mentioned macarons. All the same, his heart was racing.

Win or lose, though, he had to be proud of his international team of macaron smugglers. It hadn't been an easy trot; time had been short and there had been much to do. Inspector Ariane Dercanges, her expertise gained from her many years of investigating criminal activities, had provided the strategy. Georges Bellatre, scientist, raconteur, and equestrian, had added the necessary artistry, baking the phony macarons from an airy meringue created from ingredients measured out to the milligram. Gerrard Delpeche, Bellatre's daring orderly, had been just as important. He had snuck into the Marquise Bakery in Aix en Provence and exchanged their box of altered macarons for one he found in a frozen food shipping container bound for the Gordon's Fine Groceries store in Pylewood, California, Etats-Unis. And ex-cop Headley Richards had been instrumental in providing intelligence in California. Now it was all up to him to retrieve the embryos and get them implanted in healthy Pylewood cows. He hated it when things were left *up to him.*

"No," he had answered brusquely to a perky woman of indeterminate age who, noticing his nervous pacing, had come over to suggest that he might like to use the frozen artichokes in a torta.

"I defrost them in lukewarm water, mix in some beaten eggs, put them in a Pyrex baking dish, and cover the mixture with goat cheese," she said. "Then I bake the whole thing in a medium oven for forty minutes. It goes really well with pasta."

Bill stared at her without seeing, frightened by the return of the realization that a thousand things could still go wrong with his macaron scenario: a freeway wreck, an earthquake, or even a damaged shipping container.

The helpful woman wasn't finished. She tapped him on the shoulder. "The roasted corn, on the other hand, goes well with any kind of sausage: chorizo, Italian, linguisa, or Polish. In fact, it would even go well with artichoke hearts."

Just then, a youth in black-and-orange Gordon's livery came bursting through the swinging door in the back, pushing his loaded cart right past Bill. He slammed on the brakes in front of the vacant slot usually reserved for boxes of macarons and, in a single furious movement, grabbed an armload of boxes from his cart and started tossing them into the empty space like a Vegas blackjack dealer sliding cards at a busy table. Bill's brow beaded up with sweat, and his knees started to buckle at the thought that he might soon have that special box of macarons in his mitts. It was the same funny feeling he got when a roping partner dropped his loop over a calf's head in the first few seconds of a roping competition. This time, though, there was more at stake than a few hundred dollars and a silver buckle. His macaron box held eight embryos that could grow into a new breed of clever cattle worth millions of dollars.

The next few seconds were fateful. It was as if everyone in the store had been waiting for his macaron delivery. People who hadn't mentioned macarons earlier when he had quizzed them about their frozen food intentions were now grabbing for boxes of the airy treat. Luckily, he had a good position and the widest body. He shuffled through the boxes wildly, looking for the one that had the red bull sticker on it. When he saw it, he grabbed for it. Two hands hit the box simultaneously, but only one of them was his. He and another person each had a hand on an opposite corner of the same macaron box. He noted that the other hand was definitely male, pudgy, and hairy around the knuckles. Bill didn't even look up to see who the foreign hand belonged to for fear of losing his grip on the box, but he also realized that he dare not squeeze or pull too hard lest the box break open and send his priceless macarons flying.

"Say, pal," he said to the hand next to his. "Mind if I take this box, there's more in there for you to choose from. They're all the same, you know."

"I was first," the hand said back. "Why don't you find another box? Like you said, they're all the same."

"I got a special reason for wanting this particular box," Bill said, looking up at the face now.

"How's come? This one got a special coupon or prize inside? What's that little red bull sticker mean, anyways? Maybe a coupon for a free box of macarons. So let go. I had it first."

Bill had raised his fist, his face flushed with anger, when the Gordon's free-sample lady, who had been watching from her booth, threw herself between the two men and flashed a shiny badge that said Pylewood Police, Community Service Branch.

"Stop it youse guys," she said, "I'm an off-duty social worker, trained in conflict resolution in New Jersey. You guys knock it off, or I'll have the both of youse locked up. This kind of conflict happens a lot in New Jersey. Here in Gordon's, it's less frequent, but us community service officers are mucho experienced in resolving disputes of this kind without bloodshed. So I propose that we cut the macaroon box in two, so both of youse can have half of it. What do you say?"

"Can't do it fairly, ma'am," the other guy said. "There's fifteen macarons per box."

Bill thought quickly, *What's this guy up to? He must know that there are only twelve macarons per box. Besides, no kind of compromise will work for the TrunkWax project. If he takes the whole box home, at least they'll be intact somewhere.*

"OK, miss, let him have the box," Bill said. "I'll just take another one." He turned to face the other man. "Sorry for the uproar, amigo. What's your name?" he said, sticking out his hand.

"Clyde Townsend. No hard feelings?"

"Naw. You look familiar. Live around here?"

"Over in the ShadyAcres development."

"You sure we haven't met before? Maybe I've seen you at the bowling alley."

"I used to bowl, but not no more. Golf's my game now. Better for an older fella like me. Gets you out walking around in the fresh air."

"You married?"

"Used to be. Lost my wife to cancer a few years ago. Sorry, what didya say your name was? But I got to go quick and get these macarons in the freezer. Don't want them thawin' out before the wedding."

"Sorry, I mean about your wife. It's a shame. When's the wedding?"

"Next Saturday. I'd invite you, but I don't want to upset the schedule. All the favors and food are already bought."

"See you around, Carl. Maybe at the golf course. And if you don't mind me sayin', I'd be sure that you get those cookies in the freezer and turn the temperature down to maxim cold."

"Clyde," the man said as he walked over to the checkout stand.

***

An hour later, Bill walked through the door of a small house on Pioneer Street in Antioch without bothering to knock.

"Whatchew doin' here?" the thin guy who was sucking on a water pipe in the front room asked Bill. "I thought you were in Paris or Barcelona or some other socialist country fermenting a revolution. Want a puff?"

"Nope. I don't smoke anything anymore. And I haven't had a Dorito or a Dr. Pepper in six months. All I eat now is organic vegetables and locally sourced meats and fish."

"Yeah, and my name is Harvey Weissmuller."

Bill and Headley Richards had been friends since the second grade, when the Richards family arrived from Arkansas. He and Bill had played on baseball teams from Little League to semipro and only stopped when they graduated from Antioch High School. After that, Bill got married, divorced, and went up to Idaho to work as a cowhand. Headley joined the navy after a year of semipro baseball.

"What's on your mind?" Headley asked Bill. "I'm sure you didn't come all the way from Europe just to shoot the breeze with an old buddy."

"I need some help getting back a box of frozen macarons some bozo stole from me at Gordon's."

"Serves you right. Don't you know that Gordon's is nonunion except for the state of Hawaii?"

"No. And I don't really care. I got to get them macarons back pronto before they get served at a wedding. Shit's gonna hit the fan if somebody eats one of them."

"May I ask why?" Headley queried, grin forming.

"Nope, just help me get 'em back."

"How much you payin' me? This job ain't dangerous, is it? How's about fifty bucks an hour?"

"How's about nine-fifty an hour? That ain't too much below the minimum wage."

"Yer not gonna ask me to risk my life for nine-fifty an hour, are you?"

"No, all you have to do is get the guy who stole my macarons out of his house in ShadyAcres for a few minutes."

"Where the fucks that?"

"Between Feudeer Valley Road and the bypass. You know, you've been there a thousand times. It's the place where we pastured that monster bull, Bock's Carr, years ago."

"You mean the one that was a cross between a Brown Swiss and a Simmental. Your old man bought it because he liked the color, chocolate milkshake. They got houses over there now?"

"Of course. Where do you think this guy lives? In a tent?

***

After an hour of banter, they had a plan: Bill would make friends with Clyde Townsend, the guy who had his macarons, and get himself invited to Clyde's house to have a drink, buy a golf club, or help him move some boxes. Once he was in the house, Headley would come to the door dressed up like a cop and get Clyde to step outside for a while for a phony smog check, or write him a ticket for a loose side-view mirror, or remind him that putting Styrofoam in a recycling can was now a misdemeanor. While Headley was occupying Clyde Townsend's attention, Bill would snatch the box of embryo macarons from Clyde's freezer and substitute the unadulterated box of macaroons, which he'd have in his golf bag or a satchel. They had to do it soon, preferably in the next day or two, and definitely before Clyde's niece's wedding.

CHAPTER 42

Macarons Rescued

The next day, Bill was at the ShadyAcres golf course, decked out in a new set of plus fours and a yellow knit Byron Palmer golf shirt. He couldn't help stopping and looking at himself in the giant mirror just inside the ShadyAcres clubhouse door. He had to admit, he looked pretty damn good. He was leaner and straighter than he had been in years from all the rugby training and knee exercises he had been doing in France. He asked around the clubhouse, a mammoth structure of wood and polished metal that reminded him of the Great Northern Lodge in Montana, until he found three other golfers looking to form a foursome. One guy was a bowlegged retired cattleman from Nebraska, another one was a real estate broker, and the third guy was a former baseball player in the insurance business. Turned out they all hit it off like they had been friends for years. That's what he liked about the game.

Same as the last time he played, his drives were long and straight, but his putting stunk. Anyway, he was only there to accidentally run into Clyde Townsend, who had had his macarons. After having a drink with his new friends, he hung around the clubhouse bar for a while, but no Clyde. He was on the verge of going to plan B (hiring a home security salesperson to drug Clyde) when he spotted Clyde in the parking lot unloading his gear into a golf cart lot. He pulled his classic Gatsby cap down close to his eyes and slid along the lacquered walls until he got to the huge double doors. Once in the parking lot, he hunched over and crab walked between cars until he maneuvered himself into a position where he could accidently bump into Clyde, who was still in the parking lot trying to get his golf bag strap untangled from his trunk latch.

"Excuse me, friend," Bill said when he accidently bumped into Clyde. "I was looking the other way and didn't see you. Hey, aren't you Clyde Townsend? What a coincidence me meetin' you here at my favorite golf course. How's it going?"

Clyde blinked a few times, ran through his mental rolodex, and finally came up with a hit. "You're the guy that put the solar panels on my house in Hayward, right?"

"Nope, I'm the guy that tussled with you over that box of macarons at Gordon's."

"Oh yeah, sorry, but my short-term memory is shot."

"Ate those macarons yet?"

"No. Didn't I tell you when we were at Gordon's that I'm saving them for my niece's wedding party next week? You got a tee time?"

"No. Sorry. I just finished up a round with three guys I met in the clubhouse. Too bad I missed you. Maybe another time."

Clyde Townsend looked Bill up and down. "Say, could I ask you a big favor? You look pretty strong, and I'd like to move my BuzzMaster out of the house and into the garage. Most of my neighbors are older retired fellas with bad backs, so they can't help. It wouldn't take more than a few minutes."

Bill took a long deep breath and exhaled slowly. He couldn't believe his good luck.

"Right now?"

"Yeah," Clyde answered. "I live close by, and it shouldn't take more than a couple of minutes, I was looking for a pickup game anyways."

"Happy to help, Clyde, but let me make a quick pit stop. Shouldn't have had that second cup of coffee. Which way's the men's room?"

Clyde Townsend pointed toward the big doors at the entrance
and said, "First right after the entrance and just down the hall after
you pass the pro shop."

Bill lumbered off. He went in the first stall and pulled out his
cell phone.

"Headley, get your ass over to ShadyAcres and get this guy out
of his house like we discussed."

"I'd like to, Bill, but I'm on top of a roof over in Byron right now
fixing a leaky vent pipe, and this guy's payin' me thirteen-seventy-
five an hour."

"Get over here, you scoundrel. I'll give you fifty, if you're there
in fifteen minutes."

"Where's there?"

"Fourteen twenty-two Gorgeous Drive, just off of Spectacular
Lane."

***

"What took you so long?" Clyde Townsend said when Bill
rejoined him in the parking lot. "You're not sick are you? We could
do it some other time."

"It's these plus fours. Just bought them and the dang zipper got
stuck already. "Can you beat that? Paid more than three hundred
bucks for 'em and the dang zipper jams the first time I try and take
a leak."

"Follow me over to the house," Clyde said pointing to the road.
"It's only a couple of blocks."

***

"What is this thing?" Bill said when Clyde showed him the BuzzMaster.

"It's an exerciser. Bought it on the internet. It's got four cuffs and an electronic icon generator. You put the cuffs on your ankles, wrists, and around your neck. Then you program it to put electric pulses through your muscles. You can get twenty minutes of exercise without getting up from the chair. You don't sweat, so you can go straight back to work or do a crossword puzzle or Sudoku while the BuzzMaster exercises your muscles. The cuff around the neck keeps you from getting Alzheimer's and vaporizes dental plaque."

"Well, let's get this fuzz buster into your living room. I'll take the heavy end and you take the foot rest."

The BuzzMaster must have weighed three hundred pounds, and Bill was thinking he could have used the help of someone the size of Jules Bisoni. Clyde offered Bill a glass of water when he sat down.

Where in the hell was Headley? he asked himself. *You'd think an ex-cop could at least get to the scene of a crime on time.* Bill stalled. He went to the bathroom again. He questioned Clyde about what he had done before he had retired and then asked about his niece's wedding. When he had run out of small talk and Clyde had started to twitch, saying he needed to get back to the club and get in his round of golf, the doorbell rang. When Clyde opened the door a little, Bill snuck a look out. He had to stick his fist in his mouth to keep from laughing. Then he got angry. *That fuckin' Headley Richards always has to overdo everything.*

The man at door was wearing what looked to be a UPS uniform: Dark brown shirt, Bermuda shorts, and a surplus Russian Army hat.

"Please step outside, sir," the voice under the visor said to Clyde Townsend. "And remember, keep both your hands in plain view and don't make no jerky movements."

"What's this about, Officer," Clyde, now trembling, asked.

"Please step outside," Headley repeated, his voice rising.

As soon as both of them were outside, Bill dashed for his golf bag, pulled out his frozen macaroons, wheeled about, raced to the kitchen, flung open the top door on the refrigerator, and started rummaging through the packages. Most of the stuff looked old and much of the meat had freezer burn. Boxes of frozen waffles, French fries, and artichoke hearts were all thrown about higgledy-piggledy. There were bags of blueberries, peas, and lima beans, but no macarons. He could hear Headley and Clyde talking in the doorway.

"Underinflated tires, sir," Headley was saying. "It's a new public safety program. You only have twenty-three pounds of pressure in your left rear. Do you realize thousands of accidents are caused every year by underinflated tires?"

There probably was another freezer, maybe in the garage, Bill guessed. But when he looked, he couldn't find one. *Maybe in the laundry room,* he thought.

"I'm sure I just had the car serviced," Clyde whined. "They always check the tires. Hold on a second while I look for my QuicklyLubed receipt."

Laundry room. Where in the fuck is the laundry room in one of these places. Bill went back into the kitchen and pulled open another door that he assumed had been a broom closet, and there it was.

"Sir, it don't matter if you had Kale Yardberg service your vehicle. In this moment of time, your tire is underinflated. Please walk over to your vehicle with me so's you can sign this here ticket."

"No, I want to look for my receipt," Clyde Townsend complained.

"If you don't start walkin', Carl, I'm gonna hafta handcuff you and take you to the station," Headley said, reaching into his pocket and pulling out a rusty old set of magician's handcuffs.

Bill, working quickly, exchanged the macarons, his, the authentic ones, for the bogus box in Clyde Townsend's freezer (the ones in the box with the tiny red bull sticker in the right corner). He gently placed them in his golf bag and headed for the door just in time to hear the conversation between Clyde and ex-Officer Richards.

"This isn't going to cause a rise in my insurance, is it?" an agitated Clyde Townsend pleaded. "I already had to drop towing when it got too expensive."

"I feel your pain, Carl, but I don't make the law. I'm just sworn to enforce it. Besides, you should have checked your tire pressure this morning, and then we could have avoided all this drama."

When Headley caught a glimpse of Bill, coming out the door, he softened is voice and said to Clyde. "OK, I'm not going to write you up since you apologized, but promise me that you'll check your tire pressure, all four tires, at least once a day."

"Why does your shirt say UPS on it?" Bill couldn't resist asking when he walked up to the two men.

Headley paused for a moment, tilted his head, wrinkled his lips and said, "Stands for Uniformed Police Services, and who in the fuck are you, fatso? For your information, we're a contract police company based in Cold Stream, Illinois, hired by the county to save money. You oughta be happy. We don't get no benefits, no health care, no retirement, and low wages. You boys drive careful now."

***

Next stop for Bill was Allota Motors out on Highway 4. He found Manual Fargas out in the lot, trying to convince an elderly lady that she really needed a long old Cadillac car. Bill couldn't identify the actual vintage, but he put it somewhere between 1907 and 2002. It wasn't one of the real super longs that had been popular in the '80s, but it still took up two parking spaces. Manual was trying to sell her on the rubber pads on the back bumper, assuring her that they would save a bunch of money if someone ran into her from behind.

Bill sort of recognized the old lady. She sure looked like Nobetta Santucci, the daughter of Joe Schwartz, who used to run cattle at the end of the road in Pittsburg. She had been Nobetta Schwartz in high school, frizzy black hair and perpetually puffy eyes. When guys teased her in school, he usually told them to shut up. Picking on people because of their looks was just something he couldn't tolerate. She had married Gene Santucci, a small-time real estate developer with a couple of strip malls in Antioch. Bill probably hadn't seen her since high school.

"Ms. Santucci," Manual crooned, "you won't find no greenhorns drivin' a El Dorado like this one around town. It's the kind of car your late husband would have wanted you to have. Not so expensive as to be a showoff but nice enough to drive to church on Sunday."

"I don't know," she said. "We never had a car that was more than five years old. Gene wouldn't think of it. A new vehicle every few years put us in the group of successful people. Older cars were for the grocery clerks and waiters."

"With all due respect to your late husband, Ms. Santucci, he never had no Cadillacs. Oldsmobiles and an occasional Buick but never a Caddie. Excuse me a second, Ms. Santucci, but I see an old friend coming my way."

The widow Santucci blinked at the image of Bill Robeiro coming her way and mumbled to herself at the sight of him. She recognized him immediately, although it had been at least ten years since she had seen him and fifty since she had actually spoken to him.

"Bill Robeiro. Somebody told me you got killed robbing a bank in Walnut Creek they said."

"If it isn't old Nobby Santucci" he said. "You look great. I didn't recognize you at first. My cousin Donnie told me about your husband. I'm real sorry. Hey, Manual, can you do me a quick favor?"

"Can't you see I'm busy with a client? I'm in the middle of closing a big deal with a valued customer."

"You're not trying to sell that old monster to a poor old widow are you? I got an honest job offer for you: a couple of embryo plants. Remember what that is?"

Manual turned back to his customer. "Ms. Santucci, why don't you sit in that Coupe Deville for a few minutes while I take care of this hobo who wants to cash in a few pop bottles?"

Manual walked Bill over to a shady spot under an awning that had the words "Allota Motors, the Best Reels on the Woad."

"You know you got a couple of words misspelled on your awning."

"Of course. Since when did you learn to spell? I remember you always got an F in English except for when the words were about sports. You'd be surprised how many people stop in to tell us about the sign. Once they're in the office, we usually can sell them a car. The last guy was an editor from the government lab over in Liveryville. Knew how to spell but didn't know anything about cars. Bought a seventy-nine Dodge Valiant with 112,000 miles on it and a new paint job. Told him to recommend us to friends over there."

"What about the embryo transplants?"

"These your cows or some you borrowed from the neighbors?"

"They're mine, you old clown. And you better watch out how you talk to me. I ain't the same guy you used to ride with. I'm rich now."

"You rich? I don't believe it. D'you inherit a marijuana plantation or something?"

"Better than that. I'm a movie star."

"I thought they gave up jackass movies when Rin Tin Tin died."

"I've had good run of luck lately, and, Manual, if you make me mad, I'll buy General Motors and have you picking pubic hairs out of public urinals."

"You don't sound like a stockbroker."

Bill laughed hard, and Manual threw his arm around him.

"Sure I'll do your embryos. I might be a bit rusty, but I'm still the best in the East County and probably everywhere else. Cows haven't changed that much over the last few years. And I'll make Nobby a good deal since she's a friend of yours."

CHAPTER 43

Bee Logs

When he got back from the Fourth of July TrunkWax II confab in Hawaii, Hrubel Kwasnik still felt like he needed a vacation. The plane ride had been easy, and he had gained a few hours of sleep on the night flight, but he couldn't stop his brain from tumble drying Bill's embryos, Delahunt's loess, and his bees. And when his dryer finally stopped on TrunkWax, it started in on SkodaCats: dirty uniforms and towels, reserving hotel rooms and buses, large gnarly feet, and knotted necks. Then there was babysitting: getting his players to practice and games on time, bed checks, and post-curfew beers and sausages. All this had left him little time to spend with Lerca Nemecek, his girlfriend and the SkodaCats coach. Traveling with fifteen tall athletic, beautiful women, not even counting Lerca should have been a blast for him, but all they ever did was complain about their feet and fingers. He had had enough of calluses, bunions, athlete's foot, and broken fingernails, hangnails, and sprained wrists. And they all had boyfriends, some of the biggest losers on the planet. He had never imagined in all his life that girls could also have fungus growing between their toes.

He even had to play in a couple of games when the team was shorthanded. The thing that bothered him most was when the girls all screamed at him for court mistakes as if he were just another professional volleyball player. What did they expect? He had never played professionally. He was putting himself out on the court for them, to keep from having to forfeit games. The only volleyball he had ever played before was pickup games on the beach in San Clemente and half-drunken games when he was in Vietnam. Even Lerca criticized his play. While he was in Hawaii, the Cats were in Manaus to play a three-game series against the team from the Caloi bicycle works. How well had they got along without him? Who had taped up their ankles, washed their uniforms, and rubbed their bunions. Besides, at six feet two, he was getting tired of being the shortest person in the organization, even if he was only the team's business manager, the boyfriend of the coach, and the only man on the team.

During the preceding months, the Beeswax Team had been hard at work. He and Lerca had traveled to Melnik in Western Bohemia, where they had located a source for the kind of bees that Kwasnik was banking on to produce the high-quality beeswax necessary for his TrunkWax II formulation. They brought an entire hive back to Pilsen, bedded down the occupants in hollowed-out logs (just like the earliest European emigrants) and prepared them for a trip to a Hamburg and a long sea voyage to America. Their plan was to sneak the beelogs into Hamburg in the baggage compartment of the SkodaCats team bus, which was bound for a game against Hamburg Aurubis, and, while in Hamburg, get the beelogs onto a freighter departing for North America.

On the morning of the day of the Hamburg game, Lerca dropped Kwasnik and the team off at the food courtyard in Hamburg's Wandsbek District, explaining that team needed an outing and she had to get the bus's tires rotated. With Kwasnik's hand-drawn map spread out on the seat beside her, she drove the "empty" bus across the Elbe River to the South Hamburg dock area, drove along a seldom-used road until she came to a group of dilapidated warehouses on the east side of the Fahrkanal, and carefully loaded the seven sacks of beelogs in number 27 warehouse. When the beelogs had been safely stashed, she wearily pulled herself back into the driver's seat and pointed the bus east, back toward Tonndorf, to the hotel where the team was staying. She too would be happy when this bee business was over, and she could concentrate on volleyball again.

On paper, the game that night against Hamburg Aurubis figured to be an easy win. The Aurubis team hadn't won a game in over a year, but instead of relaxing at the prospect of a one-sided game, Lerca became evermore more wary of them. As she was forever telling the team, winning the easy games was what made a team a contender. Another worry for her was that Aurubis had recently acquired Julie Jasova, an old teammate of hers when they both had earned caps on the Czech national team. Jasova was no spring chicken, but she could still deliver a left-handed smash from almost anywhere on the court and doubtless would consistently serve aces.

Kwasnik, far from being weary, turned frisky as a cheerleader with two new pompoms. In Wandsbek, on the site of the old concentration camp, he had gobbled down a couple of matjes herring filets at the fish market, joked around with the SkodaCats players he had been feuding with, granted them the rest of the day off, and cheerfully admonished them to be back at the hotel in Tonndorf by five. Then he hoofed it over to the train station and boarded the U-Bahn to Landingsbrücken. When he got off the U-Bahn, he walked over to the entrance to the St. Pauli Elbe tunnel, rode down the elevator, and walked the half mile under the Elbe to Pier D on the Fahrkanal where he had arranged to meet Detlef Bockwinkel, a ferry captain well known on the river. According to Jiri Mlejenek, the bartender at the Schweik Restaurant in Pilsen, Bockwinkel was someone who might be convinced to transport a little contraband down the river if the price was right.

Over cups of steaming coffee, which they snagged at the snack wagon on the wharf, Bockwinkel assured Kwasnik that he could move the beelogs over to the Hapag Lloyd dock when it was dark without being noticed. The customs officers would be watching the clock for the end of their shift. When Bockwinkel questioned Kwasnik about the nature of the cargo, he would only say that it was a half-dozen sacks of logs of exotic Bohemian wood that were bound for Mexican dollhouse furniture makers. He said nothing about the honeybee passengers. Bockwinkel, for his part, discounted that information with a shrug and assured Kwasnik that he had done small jobs for friends over the years without ever being caught: a few tins of Russian caviar, the odd elephant tusk, and small boxes of Cuban cigars. They agreed to meet later that evening, around 2:00 AM, for the transfer of the beelogs.

That evening, the SkodaCats squad hardly worked up a sweat against a disorganized Hamburg Aurubis side. Jasova, who had lost an inch or two in her leap and had a jammed thumb, hit a bunch of serves long but was still a force at the net. The rest of the Aurubis squad seemed more interested in the after-the-game buffet than the game itself. Even so, Lerca had paced the edge of the volleyball court frenetically substituting as if the team was playing for an Olympic gold medal. As soon as the victorious SkodaCats had loaded up and left for the hotel in Tonndorf, Kwasnik hailed a taxi for the ride back to the warehouse at Fahrkanal, where Bockwinkel was waiting for him.

By 2:00 AM, most of the mist that had blanketed the riverbank had blown away, unmasking a deep ultramarine blue sky dotted with dabs of mauve and pink clouds, misty remnants of the earlier fog. The lights of St. Michaelis Cathedral and the Landingsbrücken Tower Clock twinkled on the other side of the bank, while the black silhouettes of the dock cranes lined the river like giant mantes praying. Off to the east, the construction lights on the Elbe Philharmonic Hall signaled that much work still remained to be done. While Kwasnik found the scene transcendental, his practical worry was that the moon might be too bright, and that once on the water, Bockwinkel's boat would sparkle like a herring at the Hamburg Fish Market and alert the Zoll officers at the Finkshaben observation tower that an unauthorized boat was on the river. He considered calling the whole thing off and waiting a couple of weeks for the next Vera-Cruz-bound ship but concluded that it wasn't a real option. Besides, Bockwinkel assured him that his logs would reach their destination without as much as a *schluken*. If they didn't move the beelogs that night, they'd have to take them back to Pilsen and wait for another game in Hamburg. Besides, Kwasnik was homesick and longed for his arugula, figs, and dog and escape from the SkodaCats.

CHAPTER 44

Saving Ivor Gryyffwwdd

Bill slept in that morning. And why not? He was back in his trailer in Briones Valley, where the only sound was the slow, syncopated whisper of the nearby creek. It was good to be home. The TrunkWax II embryos were safely stashed in Decbie Dantzler's liquid nitrogen thermos in Knightsen, tucked in between straws of goat and sheep semen, and some other stuff that he dared not ask about. Manuel Fargas, the moonlighting Cadillac salesman, had signed up to transplant the embryos, and Ariane Dercanges had e-mailed him to say that *Cattle Ranching around the World* was attracting interest among avant-garde French moviemakers.

Top of his list, meantime, was to ask Karen for a date: a quiet dinner at the Three Panchos out on Highway 4. Maybe if things went well, the two of them might even attempt a climb to the top of the silo after dessert. He had reason to be optimistic. He was fifty pounds lighter than what he was when she had dropped him off at the Pittsburg BART station nearly a year ago, his rugby knee brace allowed him to do nearly anything he wanted climbing-wise, his teeth were new and shiny, he was well off financially, and he even almost spoke a foreign language. He just had to be more attractive than the broke-down, penniless, cowboy he had been when he left Pylewood. He got up and put a kettle on the stove. He'd call Karen as soon as he had some breakfast.

Around noon, his phone chirped him away from of his bowl of Cheerios. He had considered not even answering but instead picked up the phone to see who was calling. *Someone calling from France. Mon dieu.* He hadn't been gone that long, less than a week. *Who could be calling?* Not his fan club, Michelin, the *Wine Wrangler,* or Ariane. They all knew he was in California and didn't want to be disturbed. Then SmartyPants, his new telephone app, took over and flashed a picture of the caller. Took him a second or two of squinting at the fuzzy image before he recognized the agitated face of Claudine Fortet.

What could she want? As far as he knew, she was still in Paris trying to catch up on her paperwork and boyfriend.

"Yeah," he said. "What's the matter?"

"Ivor Gryyffwwdd," she said.

"Say it in English, sweetheart, please. I'm already startin' to lose my French."

"Ivor Gryyffwwdd. The Welsh cattleman the Black Hat Gang kidnapped at the Sommet de l'Elevage. He was in my room when they broke in. Remember, you found me with that horrible welt across my face?"

"Oh yeah, him. You mean he's still missing. I thought he would have turned up by now. Did he get lost: amnesia, old-timers disease?"

"He was kidnapped! They've finally sent a ransom note."

"Just pay' 'em. I'll kick in a couple of thousand euros if it helps."

"They don't just want money. They also want a prisoner exchange."

"So send them a hundred Canadian terrorists. Israeli's do it all the time."

"They don't want a hundred prisoners. They want you!"

"Why me, and who's they?" he asked after a silence long enough to make Claudine worry that he had hung up on her. "I thought the Black Hat Gang was out of business. Didn't they collapse after Vital

Nordhoff popped his noggin on the steps at the Gergovie Hotel and never woke up?"

"That's what everyone hoped, but they have resurfaced, this time as an Esperanto terrorist group. One of Nordhoff's ex-girlfriends, Vilma Valli from Vaasa, Finland, was with him during the burglary but escaped from the Gergovie Hotel with Ivor as her prisoner. I'm pretty sure she was the one that hit me in the face with the little stick. A few months later, she took over leadership of what was left of the old Chapeau Noir gang. She now goes by the *nom de guerre*, V3, and is demanding a million euros in ransom money for the return of Ivor, a guarantee that Esperanto I be a required course for graduation from all secondary schools in countries that belong to the United Nations, and that you be put on trial for murder."

"Why me? There's plenty of guys lots richer and worse than me. Did she try Ronald Druck, the steamship magnet?"

"She wants you tried for the murder of Vital Nordhoff with extenuating circumstances. She claims that the EEU has always had a special law against the use of ropes in the interdiction of burglary suspects."

"Tell her I'm not interested. I'm stayin' right here in Briones Valley. Besides, I read somewhere that there ain't no extradition agreement between Switzerland and East Contra Costa County."

"Bill, you have no idea how evil she is. She says she will cut off one of Ivor's toes every month until she gets the ransom money and has proof that you are locked up in a small Swiss jail cell."

"That's less than a year. If you keep busy, that amount of time will fly by."

"Have you no compassion for a fellow human being, a stockman like yourself?"

"Why do I have to be the one to clear up this mess?"

"You're the one that might end up in a Swiss dungeon. Besides, it wouldn't be right if an innocent Welsh farmer lost some toes because of you, even if you hardly know the man."

"How much time do we have? I was planning to stick around Pylewood until Manual preg-checked the cows that are carrying our embryos."

"V3 warns that she'll cut off the first toe on May 1. That only gives us three weeks."

"Did she say which toe she's thinking of chopping off first? If she starts with the little ones, at least that'll give me a couple of months to finish up my business here before she does any real damage. Did she say how she was goin' to do it: tin snips, pocket knife, hatchet?"

"Can't you ever be serious?" Claudine sputtered.

"Well, what do you think I should do?"

"Rescue Ivor. Start getting ready right now. It shouldn't be too difficult. You are already close by."

"Close by what?"

"Canada, the Canadian Special Forces base in British Columbia. According to the Crime Laboratory in Clermont-Ferrand, the ransom note was mailed from Kleena Kleene, British Columbia. I think it's a small community just north of Vancouver. The French police got a couple of DNA samples off the stamp on the ransom letter and confirmed that Vilma Valli was indeed the person that had licked the stamp. An aerial photograph of the area taken by the Royal Canadian Mounted Police shows a rusty Eagle Premier sedan registered to a Hans Geschwinder, V3's second husband, abandoned in field owned by a Danish cowboy named Tex Hamsen. Everything points to the V3 gang being holed up at the Hamsen Ranch in the Cariboo Region of British Columbia. She is probably well-armed, has accomplices, and has imprisoned Ivor and the Hamsen's in the nearby outbuildings."

"Doggone. Come to think of it, Claudine, I used to know a Danish cowboy up there by the name of Tex Hansen, not Hamsen. It's probably the same guy. We rode together on a long cattle drive from Williams Lake to Bonner's Ferry one year when I was running cattle in Montana. I remember his wife was one helluva cook. She cooked us wild blueberry pancakes with home-cured bacon and put out genuine Quebec maple syrup. That changes everything. Sure I'll do it."

"The Canadian reconnaissance photos do show continuous smoke from a kitchen fire."

"I'll bet old Ivor ain't losin' any weight even if he is being tortured. Can't even remember her name. Musta been at least twenty years ago. What am I supposed to do once I get to Kleena Kleene?"

"Spring Ivor, bring back the kidnappers, and see that the Hamsen's are safe. Interpol wants V3 to stand trial for a string of crimes. The Canadian government will put all its resources at your disposal as long as no one knows about it. I'll bet there's another big reward in it for you if the rescue is successful."

"You know, now that I think about it, I wouldn't mind going back up there to the Cariboo. It's beautiful country, and now it seems to me that Ivor, whatever his name is, is a piece of unfinished business. The old man told me to never leave a job unfinished. If you did, he said, it would only come back to haunt you some day. Let me see if I can round up a rescue crew. Four or five might be enough, if they got the moxy and training."

"If you need me for anything, we can be in Canada in less than ten hours."

***

When he thought more about it, Bill figured it wouldn't be too hard to collar V3 up there in the Canada wilds and bring Ivor home to his mom. Shoot, he already knew the area and would sure like to see V3, the burglar that had messed up Claudine, do a long time in prison. The Canadians already had a picture of the Hansen place and would probably give them a ride out to Williams Lake. From there, they could saddle up some horses and be in Kleena Kleene in another couple of days. He didn't think they'd need much in the way of heavy weaponry either: ficheirouns like the ones they had in the Camargue and a couple of shotguns just in case old Vilma was looking for a firefight. Of course, he'd have to clear that part with the Canadian police. He was thinking it might be cold up there too, so he'd hafta dig out the wool clothes he had worn up in Montana years ago. As for human muscle, he reckoned a four-man—two Frenchmen, two Americans—commando team would probably be enough.

Bill would have liked to have Blondie Raimbaut on the team, but he was pretty sure Blondie was still tied up with the Transhumance. Claudine Fortet had already volunteered to help, but he knew first hand that she got dizzy at the sight of blood. Ariane Dercanges, the Clermont-Ferrand cop, on the other hand, would be a huge asset, to any rescue team. She was trained in demolition, crowd control, and international law. He had seen her certificates for markswomanship and martial arts on the wall behind her desk in Clermont-Ferrand along with campaign ribbons from the French intervention in Djibouti. An added benefit was that she was already part of the French security system and most likely would be able to assume direct custody of prisoners. It didn't take him long to choose Georges Bellatre as the second member of the French team. Bellatre could ride, shoot, and was a veteran of countless mock battles dating all the way back to the siege of Orleans. Bellatre knew firsthand about the noise and confusion of battle. He had tasted the acrid sting of gunpowder, and smelt the sour odor of equine sweat at many a reenactment, and he probably already had the proper uniform. He would be eager for adventure and available as the second member of the French unit.

On the American side, there weren't very many pomegranates left on the bush. His cousin Donnie was in Oklahoma with Barbara, selling saddles at rodeos and fairs, Jim Delahunt, besides being a little too old for combat, was back in China; and as far as he knew, Hrubel Kwasnik was somewhere between Pilsen and Patagonia doin' god knows what. Karen Clements would have been a good addition to the team, but he worried that he was too emotionally involved with her to put her in harm's way. That kinda left Headley Richards, the ex-Pylewood cop. Seems like it always came back to Headley, who had just helped him out with the macaron smuggling. He'd be hard to find now that he had a couple of thousand bucks in his pocket, so, he'd have to set out immediately to find the old goat.

After trying all of Headley's old haunts, Bill finally found him sleeping in an old trailer over in the trailer park on Marsh Creek Road. He only had to shake Headley for a minute or two to get him to open an eye.

"Wake up, you old otter," Bill hollered in his ear. "I got a job for you."

"Not another one. I ain't impersonating no more cops. You know I coulda got incarcerated for a damn long time if I'da got caught impersonating a law officer like on your last dumbass job. I'm not pushing my luck. Go away. Can't you see I'm resting? I been pounding expensive nails all week in a mansion in Hillsborough."

"I'll give you five thousand bucks if you come up to Canada with me and rescue a kidnapped Welshman."

Headley Richards sat up straight. "Where you gonna get five-thousand bucks, you old rattlesnake?"

"Like I told you before the last job, I been away in France where I made a ton of money helpin' the police, doing cookie commercials, playing rugby, and performing rodeo tricks."

"Yeah, sure, and I'm Norman Einstein."

"You mean Albert, don't you?"

"Whatever? Show me the money first."

***

The next morning, Bill drove over to Kwasnik's farm to see Karen Clements, who was looking after the place for Hrubel while he was in the Czech Republic.

"Whatchew doin' around here stranger?" she said when she saw him. "I thought you were in France checkin' out cattle."

"Done that. Now I'm back for a while. Remember, before I left, I promised to take you up top of the old silo when I got back. Sorry, but I'm gonna have to take a rain check for a couple of weeks. I got to do a little job first. But I promise we'll get back together soon as I get back."

"What kind of job?"

"Gotta rescue a Welshman from some kidnappers up in Canada."

"Glad to see that being in France all that time didn't change you," she said. "Still the same old bullshitter." She grabbed for his ears and gave him a glancing little kiss on the lips. "Guess I can wait a few more days. How long's it been already?" she said in a hoarse voice that was unusual for her.

Bill pulled out a package from his back pocket and handed it to her. "Here's a little somethin' for you from Paris, France. Don't open the box just yet. Let me get out the door first. If you don't like them, I don't want to see the disappointment in your eyes. See you in a couple of weeks."

Karen waited until he was out the door before she opened the package. The box was pretty enough, said Cartier on it. When she finally got the box open, she found a couple of gold hoops with a bunch of sparklers attached to them. The light danced around in the gems in a way she had never seen before. *Almost as good as diamonds. Don't matter, though. It's the sentiment that counts."*

CHAPTER 45

Canadian Raiders

The Franco-American rescue team of Robeiro, Richards, Bellatre, and Dercanges quickly found out from Mayor Godard that they wouldn't be doing any rescuing without the guidance and approval of the Canadian Special Operations Regiment (CSOR). Claudine's protest that Ivor wouldn't have any toes left by the time the Franco-American rescue team had been fully vetted fell on deaf ears in Ottawa. Not even the pleas of Mayor Godard could move the Canadians, even though Lyon and Montreal had been sister cities since 1947. Ariane Dercanges guessed it would take at least two weeks for the Franco-American team to prove their mettle and maybe two more to prepare for their rescue mission. She looked upon it as kind of a trade union thing: no bona fide special forces organization wanted poorly trained amateurs horning in on their business. Bill did his best to calm Claudine. He assured her that they could all pass the CSOR requirements without too much fuss. After all, he was a rugby player who had won an important contest with a game-ending three-point try, Headley Richards was an ex-US Navy SEAL who had been decorated by President Reagan for valor in the war against Grenada, Chief Inspector Ariane Dercanges was a high-ranking French cop with a black belt in judo and an advanced degree in psychology, and Georges Bellatre was an expert horseman, gymnast, and reenactor.

Nevertheless, their spirits fell when they saw the list of minimum requirements for participating with the Canadian Special Forces in any covert operation: forty continuous pushups, forty continuous situps in one minute, five pull-ups, and a twenty-five-meter swim in full uniform including rifle. And that was just the start. If they qualified, the next hurdle was carrying a soldier of equal weight a hundred meters in less than a minute.

Bill, who was first up in the preliminary test, could only manage ten pushups, three situps, and no pull-ups, but did the full-uniform swim in under the allotted time. Headley Richards did twenty-five quick pushups and asked the drill instructor if he could bum a smoke. When the instructor obliged, he finished his pushups and ripped off the required number of situps. He failed his pull-ups but did the full-uniform swim easily. Inspector Dercanges did all exercises but failed the swimming test, claiming that there weren't any beaches to storm where they were going in Western Canada. Georges Bellatre did his pushups quickly but refused to do more than ten situps, arguing that the hinge-like motion of the exercise was known to cause enzyme excretion problems. It was, he protested, old science and berated the sergeant who was testing them for being so out-of-touch with research that was already ten-years old. The officer in charge, Sgt. Preston King, put in a call to Ottawa to inform the defense minister that not one of the Franco-American team had passed the minimum requirements for the CSOR.

After a hurried confab with the prime minister, the defense minister called back to say that they should call the intended raid an Euro-American venture and find a country in the EEC that had less stringent requirements for their special forces and use those requirements for the Franco-American group. Switzerland was an early favorite because as a landlocked country, they had no swimming requirement, and the exercise number was low because of the high altitude. But when a Canadian colonel reminded them that Switzerland had never joined the EEC, they were forced to look for another country. Finally, Inspector Dercanges remembered from a security convention in Luxembourg City that Luxembourg had no swimming requirement and only asked that candidates have a clean driving record and be able to carry a case of wine across the border into Belgium without being noticed. The rest was easy. The Franco-American Four (FAF), as they were known to the Canadians, took shortened courses in geography, high explosives, Canadian culture, marksmanship, helicopter manners, and fingerprinting. They were issued gear and did a single practice drop in a field on the outskirts of Petawawa. Standard gear included black Kevlar jumpsuits, machine pistols, Kevlar caps, stun grenades, flashlights, shaped-charge explosives, plastic handcuffs, and cell phones. Georges Bellatre was granted a special request that allowed him to wear an outfit identical to the one Jean Moulin wore when he parachuted into France in 1942 to lead the French resistance against the Nazis. Bellatre's clothing was authentic up to the cotton tunic and cashmere scarf the hero wore to hide the well-known scar on his throat.

A week later, the Franco-American four gathered on the tarmac at the Petawawa Aerodrome for a final check of their gear before they loaded it onto the Westland Cormorant helicopter, which would ferry them over to Kleena Kleene for the drop. The Cormorant was perfectly equipped for the rescue: ropes, cables, and winches, a mini bar/hospital, and an onboard waiter/medic. It was all spit and polish from the pistols, caps, and ski masks to the ropes and clips they would use in their descent from the chopper. Bill was thinking that as the leader, he should lead them in a nondenominational short prayer before they boarded the helicopter like Coach Binyon always did before the homecoming game against Pittsburg, but he couldn't remember the words, so he just wished everybody good luck. Their pilots, Alain and Dugan, reminded the Franco-American Four that should they have to puke, to make sure it all ended up in the paper sacks they had been issued and that they didn't want to find any gum wrappers or paper coffee cups in their chopper when the raid was over. Dugan told a story about having giant ants in their chopper when they got back from Afghanistan after having given a lift to two American congressmen.

Bill slept while Inspector Dercanges fiddled with her pistol, Georges Bellatre scribbled furiously in his notebook, and Headley Richards rambled about in his brain trying to remember how a Navy SEAL was supposed to disarm a Cuban with a machete. Dugan came back and checked their gear for the final time as the Royal Canadian Air Force helicopter slowed down. When everything looked right, the team banged their fists together and pulled their ski masks over their heads. Bill fingered the coil of purple rope he had over his shoulder that he had been carrying ever since the burglary at the Gergovie Hotel in Clermont-Ferrand.

The plan was for each of them to make a quick rope-assisted exit from the chopper's bay when they got to the hostage site. Bill, Headley, and Bellatre would each race to a building, secure it, and bring out everybody they found. Chief Inspector Dercanges would stay in the yard to coordinate their activities and maintain radio contact with Alain and Dugan. Their goal was to free the hostages and capture the terrorists as quickly and with as little bloodshed as possible. When they had secured the area and the hostages were safe, Ariane would launch a flare that would signal the copter crew that they were ready to be picked up. It was clear to all that if anything went seriously wrong, the chopper would ditch the rescuers, and they would be on their own. The leaders of the four countries involved in the rescue were well aware that the rescue of a Welsh hostage, kidnapped on French soil by a Canadian terrorist group and freed by a joint Canadian, American, French group, which included a female French cop, a retired French biochemist, an American cowboy turned French television personality, and a former US Navy SEAL, with the help of Canadian Special Forces, was a potage way too rich in international intrigue to ever be dished up to the public.

CHAPTER 46

Vilma Valli

Curly golden hair tumbling over her shoulders, cigarette dangling from her lips, Vilma Valli was uneasy. She pushed the fingers of her right hand through the curls from her forehead to the top and then did it again. The two men in the house, each shackled to the edges of their beds, had their eyes focused on her waiting for the outburst they knew was coming.

"When do we get to go home VeeVee?" the shorter man asked. "We been here for six months. Way more than the contract we signed."

She looked up at the two men, anger flashing in her eyes. "When justice is served. When we get the compensation we're entitled to. When the killer is in our custody. And if I find you've been disloyal, I'll start taking back your privileges. You'll be back sleeping in the barn and eating your bread in the tool shed."

The second man said nothing, keeping his eyes glued to the door. He was sure he had heard a faint hum, maybe the sound of an airplane, or maybe it was just the wind.

Vilma let her hand drop down to the holster on her hip, double checking that the pistol was really there. She'd use it if she had to. She had waited too long and suffered too much to fail. She thought of the old family house in Vasa, or Vaasa as the damn Finns had renamed it. Images of the fields of barley and the orchard, the cellar, and the sweet smell of cherries and apples surged into her consciousness.

Fate had cast her far away, she lamented. British Columbia, she hated the name, was an ocean and an eternity away from Finland, where she had been born and where her roots were. Rather than returning to the place she loved, she seemed to be getting farther away with every passing year.

Her exile had started when Swedish speakers lost their bid for an autonomous region in Finland. During the War, her father had moved the entire family across the Gulf of Bothnia to neutral Sweden for their safety and kept them there when the War ended, hoping the children would at least have proper schooling. But she lamented, the family never returned home to what they called Swedish Finland.

She was no more comfortable in Sweden then she had been in Finland. The family moved from Umea to Sundsvall and then inland to Ostersund, but she never adjusted and never lost her yearning for the western shore of Swedish Finland. *Yes, it was a long time ago already.* Her parents were long deceased, and she knew well from the way her body felt that she would soon join them.

"Why are you staring at the door?" she snapped at Lew. He said nothing and shrugged his shoulders. "You should have stayed in Cambodia."

She put her hands together and looked at the thick blue veins on her wrist and her just-starting-to-get-gnarly fingers. She felt the sagging skin under her chin and knew her jowls were next.

Lew, the taller of the two shackled Cambodians, leaned toward his partner on the next bed and asked in whispered Khmer if he had heard anything.

"I thought I heard voices," he said.

V3 pointed a menacing finger and reminded them of her threat before she lapsed back into melancholy. She had knocked around Europe after a couple of years at the University of Umea and met Vital Nordhoff in a youth hostel in Spain. He was on his way to Portugal to see the Algarve, and the two of them decided to make the trip together. He was a dashing companion for a girl from a Scandinavian backwater: shaved head, when long hair was the sign of rebellion, and loose dungarees and skin-tight T-shirts that showed off his muscular physique. They did the usual things for the time: hitchhiked, lived on day-old food, drank cheap wine, and bummed money when they ran short. They also found they were kindred spirits, felt the same pain, and nursed feelings of resentment over their cultural displacement and loss of language. French Canada and Swedish Finland were so much alike. He had been a brilliant chemistry student, but his real passion was in seeking independence for Quebec.

She didn't know what she wanted to do but had fallen for the whole French-Canadian package. She pawned her graduation watch to buy a ticket on a Polish freighter so she could follow Vital back to Canada and join his crusade for an independent Quebec. They went to rallies together, attended clandestine meetings with other radicals, smoked, snorted, and toasted all the worldwide liberation movements until they decided they had to take some action. At first, they tried organizing strikes, posting manifestos on telephone poles, and writing protest songs but got nowhere until she came up with the idea of symbolically burning non-Gallic hats—almost every kind of head cover that wasn't a beret. The Burning Hat rallies were huge, and some people said that they finally drove the politicians to grant the Province of Quebec a certain degree of autonomy.

She was smiling at the memory, when there was a stupendous boom and a huge man came crashing through the front door. The intruder stumbled, regained his balance, and pointed a huge funny-shaped spear in her direction. The two men chained to their beds froze in surprise and then laughed when they realized that they were being rescued.

CHAPTER 47

The Rescue

As the Canadian Air Force helicopter swooped down on the Hansen Ranch in Kleena Kleene, Dugan Elkins, the first officer, gathered the Franco-American rescue team close to him and shouted at them to double-check their flashlights. It was midnight, he cautioned, a narrow moon, and pretty damn dark down below. Then he slid the side door of the Cormorant open, wished them good luck, and told them they were as bloody prepared as they'd ever be.

Ariane Dercanges was the first one out. She slid down the rope, released at the right time, and hit the ground running. She trotted silently to the water tower in the center of the compound where she dumped her pack and quickly deployed her communications equipment. She surveyed the scene and found everything to be as she expected: three main buildings, a water pump and trough, corrals, a hitching post, and a hay barn. To the west of her was the ranch house, biggest building, lights still on. Twenty meters east of it was the tool shed, dark, with windows barred. The bunkhouse, still further east, was set back to the edge of the woods with the door chained.

Ariane flashed her light at the chopper three times to signal that the coast was clear for the next rescuer. Bill exited the chopper gracefully enough, but his landing was something that would never appear in any special forces highlight films. He hung on to the rope too long, hit the ground awkwardly, dropped his ficheiroun, and fell backward on his fanny. But like the old cowboy he was, he popped back up in an instant, purple rope slung over his shoulder, and ficheiroun pointed straight up at the sky. He spotted Ariane in the shadow of the water tower, right where she was supposed to be. When she put her beam on the farmhouse door and flashed it twice, the signal for him to charge and break down the door, he sprinted, balls out, toward the house. He collided with the door at full throttle, producing a shock wave that caused conifers to drop their needles and cones and shook the water tower so hard that Ariane feared she might be drenched or, even worse, buried.

Headley Richards was the next one due out. From the chopper's exit port he gazed approvingly at the three buildings, arranged exactly as they had appeared in the reconnaissance photos he had studied. *At least they're in the right place, not like the frickin Grenada invasion.*

"Go, go, go, *allez, allez.*" Dugan and Alain hollered at him. "We don't have all day, Sergeant. This ain't no movie picture."

"Chief, to you, bub!" Headley yelled above the din, "I'm navy, and don't you jokers forget it."

Headley slid down the rope and hit the ground lightly, just like the Navy SEAL he had once been. When he reached the water tower, Inspector Dercanges clamped a hand on his shoulder, pointed her flashlight at the bunk house, and ordered him to take it. "Be careful, going in, Sergeant," Ariane said. "The police report says that the ranch owners, an elderly couple in their eighties, may be frail, so don't knock anybody over or start any fires. It looks like the door is chained shut, and the windows are barred. According to the report, the kidnappers only allowed the Hamsens to come outside on odd-numbered days of the month."

"That's so cruel," Headley moaned. "I'll be happy when I see that V3 bitch behind bars."

Headley pulled out a tiny shaped-charge explosive that he had borrowed from the Millway Police Department a few years earlier when he was on a regional SWAT team and showed it to Ariane. "This little baby will blow that chain plumb to Williams Lake, and you won't hear more than a pop."

Georges Bellatre hit the ground last and quickly found Ariane hunched down under the water tower.

"Go to the building in the center," Ariane whispered, pointing her flashlight at the tool shed. "I'll bet anything that's where they're holding Monsieur Gryyffwwdd."

***

The clatter of the helicopter and the sound of Bill crashing through the door of the ranch house hadn't registered on Ivor Gryyffwwdd's applause meter, even though he was semi-awake. As usual, he was having trouble getting to sleep. He had been tossing and turning since his captors had doused the lights. Most nights it was the rattling of squirrels on the tin roof, the lumpy straw mattress, or thoughts of his mother back in Abrystwyth worrying that kept him awake. How long had it been since his kidnapping? A year, maybe. He hadn't kept track in the beginning, certain that he would be rescued quickly. *Blimey*, he thought, *if I was English, they would have rescued me weeks ago: called out the Coldstream Guards, the Royal Navy, and the Special Air Force.* Then he backtracked some. *Maybe, there's a jurisdictional dispute. A British citizen kidnapped on French soil. Perhaps, the two countries are fighting over who gets the honor of rescuing me.* Whatever the reason for the delay, he did miss Wales, his mum, and his animals terribly.

Georges Bellatre, last man out, bolted toward the tool shed, virtually invisible in his Jean Moulin outfit. When he got to the door, he pulled a ring of keys from his pocket and began trying them in the padlock on the door. On the fourth try, the key moved, and the lock sprung open. An astonished Ivor Gryyffwwdd, sat straight up in his bed looking irritated and stared at Bellatre.

"What do you mean by breaking into my bedroom at this hour?"

After several hand gestures, Bellatre announced, "I've come all the way from France to rescue you. Can't you at least be civil?"

"I don't believe you," the Welshman announced. "Why are you dressed like some character out of a World War II spy film?"

"I would have worn a morning coat and top hat, old chap, but I just jumped out of a helicopter," Bellatre answered back. "For god's sake, get dressed and pack your things. You're leaving."

***

When Bill had come crashing through her door, the concussion had thrown Vilma Valli (V3) from her chair and sent her sprawling. As soon as she got herself up, she went fumbling for her gun but found it had fallen out of her holster and skidded across the floor. Bill, who saw the gun, reckoned she couldn't reach it before he collared her but still wasn't taking any chances. He leveled his ficheiroun and swung it in a wide arc, whacking her ankles and sweeping her feet out from under her.

"Not you!" she screamed when he approached her and started to uncoil the purple rope in his hand. "Not you again. You could have broken my shins with that pole." Then she began to sob.

"Yep, it's me, lady, your worst nightmare. You should have retired from crime when you had the chance."

V3 regained her composure quickly and went on the offensive. "Did you bring the ransom money?" she asked sternly.

Bill had to laugh. "Your terrorist days are over, Fraulein," he said. "There's a nice little cell waiting for you in Vancouver. What did you do with that poor Welshman? He better be here and have all his teeth and toes. His mother's been worried sick. If you killed him, you're looking at thirty to forty years if you stand trial in England. If the French get you, it's probably the guillotine."

Quick as a Camargue *gardian*, Bill had V3 bound up in the purple rope and tied to a chair.

"Why have you put that hideous rope around me? Do you wish to further humiliate me? Untie me immediately. You have no warrant, no badge, and nothing on you that identifies you as anyone with the authority to tie me up and threaten me."

"I'm just part of the International Franco-American Rescue Force, lady, the IFAR. We all been deputized by Queen Elizabeth and Pierre Trudeau, your prime minister. There's a high-ranking French cop just outside, along with a former US Navy SEAL, and a retired pharmaceutical executive. You're in one heap of trouble."

"Not as much as you are. I'm a Swedish citizen, a representative of a neutral country and the home of Ingmar Johansen, the famous movie director. Untie me immediately so that I can contact the Swedish embassy."

Ariane interrupted their conversation with two short toots on her whistle, the signal that she was leaving her station at the water tower and would visit all three buildings to make sure their mission had been accomplished before she fired the flare that would bring the chopper back to pick them up.

***

Ariane paused to admire the sound of the whistle and smiled. It was a souvenir from the early days of her career in law enforcement.

First stop was the ranch house where Bill's mission had been to capture V3 and her accomplices. She shook her head when she saw the devastation. He hadn't just gone through the door, he taken the jams, threshold, and half a wall with it.

When V3 saw the *tricolore* patch on Ariane's jumpsuit, she was quick to shout "Vive Quebec Libre!"

"I am a French citizen," she announced. "I am so happy to see another French citizen. I hope you can deliver me from the hands of this American lout with his terrible purple rope."

"You just said you were Swedish," Bill interrupted.

"Who are these guys sitting on the beds?" Ariane asked.

"United Nations Peacekeepers," V3 answered quickly. "Assigned to guard me in my search for justice."

"No, no, miss," the shorter Cambodian interrupted. "We are from Vancouver. We answered an ad on the internet for electricians and were taken up here against our will. We haven't seen our families in months. When we asked to go home, she," he said, pointing at Vilma Valli, "locked us up and forced us to cook for her and repair the clutch on that old car in front of the house."

"That's a lie," V3 said. "I put them under arrest because they were stealing from me."

Ariane nodded toward Bill who untied V3 from the chair, pulled up tight on the purple rope, and dragged the gang leader out onto the grass in front of the house. Ariane followed and slapped handcuffs on her.

"Go find Headley," Ariane said to bill. "See if he has any more of those tiny shaped charges. We'll use them to free these poor electricians. If Headley doesn't have any more, bring Georges over here. He has a set of skeleton keys for every lock known to man, and if it's a combination lock, he can crack most of them in minutes. I'll stay here and interrogate the prisoners."

When Bill got to the bunkhouse, there was already a fire in the stove and a kettle whistling. Headley Richards was sitting at the table in the center of the cottage, slurping very hot tea and rubbing a biscuit against a small island of blueberry jam.

"Can't say as I've ever had a biscuit and jam this scrumptious," Headley was raving when Bill came through the door. "There used to be a place on A Street in Antioch that was pretty good, but their biscuits and jam were never this tasty."

Bill recognized Tex and Irmgard Hansen immediately. "Well, I'll be kicked, kneed, and swallowed whole, if it ain't Tex and Irma. I thought this place looked kinda familiar, but it was real dark. How long's it been?"

"Near on to twenty years I'd guess," Tex said. "I never expected to see you or Headley again in this life. A million thanks. That lady, Vilma Valli, V3 they call her, has to be one of the cruelest folks I ever met. She says she's Swedish, but she has a Spanish sounding name. Came busting in here a year or so ago and wouldn't leave. At first, she said her car broke down. When I finally told her she had to leave, she locked us up in our own bunk house. Then she came back with that poor English kid and the two Cambodian boys. She locked them up too."

"What about Ivor?" Bill asked. "Inspector Dercanges thought he was in the tool shed out yonder."

"He's probably sittin' in bed pinchin' himself," Headley Richards said. "Ole Georges is over there visiting with him. I brought them a couple of biscuits and a pot of hot tea as soon as we had secured the area. Poor guy. He had about given up all hope."

"Ariane thinks you might have a couple more of them tiny shaped-charges for blowing up small chains and handcuffs. Them two electricians are still chained to their beds, and V3 won't tell us where the keys are."

"Nope. You told us to pack light, so I just took one of everything. No margin for mistakes. That's the way the SEALs do it."

"OK, I'm going next door to see if Georges can unlock them."

***

When Bill pulled open the door to the tool shed, Georges and Ivor were still arguing about the timing of the rescue. Ivor still couldn't understand why they had planned the rescue for the middle of the night. Dawn would have been the proper time. He would have been dressed, fresh from a good night's sleep, and it would have been bright enough for everyone to see. Bloody flashlights were never any use. The light in the tool shed was too faint for him to pack, and how was he supposed to find a missing sock and his pajama bottoms? And the tea that Headley had brought over a minute ago was too hot, the biscuits too cold, and a splash of milk would have been jolly. Georges was sitting in the corner reduced to making facial and hand gestures.

"Georges, grab your keys and lock breaking stuff and come with me to the ranch house," Bill said. "We got a couple of Chinese electricians chained to their beds, and we can't go anywhere without 'em."

"With pleasure," George whispered. "Anything to get away from this confounded Englishman. Had I known what he was like, I would never have come all this way to rescue him."

"You get yourself dressed and go next door, Ivor," Bill ordered. "As soon as we get them electricians loose, we're leavin'."

The chain that held the Cambodian electricians was joined with a single key-operated padlock.

"This will be a snap," Georges said when he saw the lock. "I could open this lock with a paper clip or hairpin. I never could understand why people join a stout chain to a cheap lock." Two clicks later, the Cambodian electricians were rubbing their sore wrists and laughing and jabbering.

"Come on, everybody. Get your things together," Bill hollered at the two electricians. We'll have you home in a couple of hours. I'm going to tell Ariane to signal the helicopter to pick us up."

Ariane was about to fire off her flare when Irmgard walked out and beckoned them all to come to the bunkhouse.

"What's the hurry, folks?" Irmgard said. "Stay and have a cup of tea and a biscuit. I was just taking them out of the oven when that old Headley Richards blew the chain off the door."

"Sorry, Irmgard," Bill said. "We can't stay long. We got a Canadian helicopter waiting for us, and we got to move. Grab your things and let's get out of here."

Tex and Irmgard shook their heads. "Haven't seen you in twenty years, and you can't even stay for another fifteen minutes," Irmgard said. "Don't see any reason for us to go with you. You got your hostage, and we got our ranch back. That crazy woman that you got tied up over in the grass didn't do much around here except play old Buffy St. Marie tapes, so there's a hell of a lot of straightening up to do."

"I'm not going either," Headley said. "Tex needs someone to help round up his strays and put his corrals back to order, and I'm his man." Then he looked straight at Bill. "If you mail me my wages for this fiasco, two thousand George Washington's sticks in my mind, plus expenses and hazard pay, I'll use it to buy me an airline ticket home, if and when I get tired of this place."

"What are we forgetting?" Inspector Dercanges asked.

"Shouldn't we interrogate the kidnapper and the victims before we put them on the plane?" Bill asked.

"Already did that while you were freeing the electricians," Ariane said.

"We forgot all about Ivor Gryyffwwdd," Bill remembered. "After all, he's the dude we came for, after all."

"He must still be in his cabin," Headley said.

"Can we just leave him here and say we couldn't find him," Georges said in heavily accented English."

***

The Cormorant was there in minutes, and loading was quick because there was plenty of room. Headley and the Hansens weren't going back to Vancouver with them, and V3 didn't take up more than a square meter when she was bound and gagged and stuffed in a duffle bag. Bellatre and Ariane, the French contingent, fell asleep as soon as the chopper leveled off, which left Bill, Ivor Gryyffwwdd, and the two Cambodian electricians to make small talk. Turned out the guards were really not electricians but school crossing guards on loan from RentUGuards, a small Vancouver security contractor. They had been sent to RentUGuards by the British Columbia Unemployment Office for jobs. Ivor brightened up as soon as they were in the air. He insisted that his guards not be arrested or deported. They had treated him kindly, he said, smuggling in books and extra food for him whenever they could. After a quick conference, Bill and the pilots decided to let down the ropes on the outskirts of Vancouver and let the guards go home, no questions, no red tape, and no regional police.

"If you boys are ever in California, drop in and see me," Bill said as the former bodyguards exited the chopper. "We always got work on the ranch for hard workers that can fix fences, tend animals, and build a decent gate."

"What are you going to do when you get back to America?" Ivor asked Bill.

"Get back in the cattle business. I have some very special embryos planted in eight of my best cows back home."

"How 'bout you?" Bill asked.

"Same as you, but maybe a little different. I had a lot of time to think while I was locked up in that shed. I'm going to make some changes in my operation. I had the idea that I'd like to start breeding cattle for other things besides meat."

"Why? That's pretty much all they're good for. Hides used to be worth somethin', but not anymore."

"Chemicals," Ivor answered. "You ever thought about harvesting chemicals from the manure?"

"Uh, no," Bill said. "What kind of chemicals?"

"Amines, phosphates, amides, and sulfates."

"You must be crazy," Bill said.

CHAPTER 48

Rabbit Eggs

Bill looked out the window of the second-story Mazet he had rented in Paradou. Karen was away at the market in Maussane, buying groceries for the afternoon meal. It hadn't been easy to get her to come to France. She had tired of Bill's cancellations and procrastination and got used to the idea that they never would get back together, not even if it was only for a few minutes on top the silo.

His return hadn't turned out the way he wanted. When he got home from Canada, the first thing he did was rent the top floor of the new Pylewood Hilt Inn so he'd have all the modern communication facilities he had got used to in France. He had a movie company on location in Hawaii, a TV series on French television, and friends in Aurillac, Arles, and Claremont-Ferrand. It only took him a couple of days to realize it had been a big mistake. From the moment he checked in, he was accessible to anyone who wanted to reach out to him.

Everybody wanted to get into the act: the bunch at Don Gusto's wanted to have a welcome home night, KTVX in Oakland wanted him on board to do color for Cal rugby games, and Michelin wanted him to push their tires in the East County. And that was just in California. Ariane Dercanges was on the telephone every hour, asking for advice on what to do with Vilma Valli. The Canadians wanted to jail her in Canada for Ranch Invasion, Imprisonment,

Trespassing, and Tax Evasion; the French Government wanted to try her in Claremont-Ferrand for Aggravated Assault, the British Lord High Commissioner wanted her for Unlawful Confinement of a British National; and the Swedes wanted the whole mess transferred to the World Court in the Hague. The rescue of the kidnapped Cambodian electricians first reported only in the Khmer-language press of Vancouver had been picked up by media and became hot news all over Southeastern Asia. All over the world, it seemed, people wanted more information about him. Then there was the financial aftermath to deal with. Besides the substantial reward that the Franco-American team got to divide up, articles associated with any aspect of the rescue began to fetch colossal prices at auctions, flea markets, and jumble sales. Counterfeiting became rampant overnight. A Vietnamese company started selling Canadian Rescue Flashlights online for $19.99. Millionaires kept telephoning offering Bill huge sums of money for the purple rope. A promoter from Talladega even pitched the idea of selling segments of the rope at stock-car races. On the other side of the Atlantic, collectors hounded Georges Bellatre for keys from his collection of skeleton keys, and Ariane Dercanges was finally promoted to deputy superintendent of police in Clermont-Ferrand.

Amid the commotion, he had to finish reviewing the contracts for filming the first episode of *World Cattle Ranching: The Big Island*: a couple of million euros for cameras, salaries, sets, travel, livestock, and living expenses. It seemed way too expensive, but the financial backing seemed to be there. He also had to start rounding up Hawaiian cowboys and get them camera-ready for the roping and cattle-swimming scenes for the filming. According to the pictures his people in Hawaii were sending back, they had already tethered a couple of cows to a whaling boat and swum them out to a buoy in the bay. But it was obvious to him that they still needed more work. When they were ready to shoot, he'd probably have to hop a plane and rent an old steamer and make sure his crew could actually lift a cow or two up onto the big boat in front of the cameras.

When it all became too much, he fled to his trailer in Briones Valley, where the locked gate was a mile away, the WiFi signal was too weak most of the time, the telephone company repeater was blocked out by the hills, and the only noise was the burble of Briones Creek. One night, he snuck over to Marsha Misch's place to pick up Tigger, his dog. Even Tigger wasn't happy with him. It took a couple of packages of grass-fed hamburger to mollify his old friend. And even then, Tigger pissed on his boots, hid his socks, and tore up his underwear. It was even harder for him to get Karen to forgive him. He had run out on her at least three times in the last few months, and he had been in Pylewood for weeks without even calling. It took almost a month before she'd talk to him.

"Why don't you call Alexis Duplex for a date? I'm just a twice-divorced, middle-aged, broke-down, barrel racer, and you're rich and famous now," she had protested.

He had never heard of Alexis Duplex but guessed she was a French fashion model from the name. Ever since Bob the barber had retired, there was no place in Pylewood to look at *Vague* or *Victorico Secreti* magazines. Truth was that he'd take Karen over any of them. Skinny fashion models, shit, they never had appealed to him. Anyway, he had invited her to sneak over to the silo like they had talked about before he went off to France and got famous. He reminded her it wasn't all that long ago that she had said she wouldn't mind climbing to the top just for old time's sake, and she had finally agreed.

On a clear night, he had picked her up at Kwasnik's place and drove across town to the old dirt road that led to where the old feedlot used to be. They had both dressed for the climb: tennis shoes, gloves, dark caps, and safety harnesses. When they got close, they found the old silos were surrounded with a "keep out" fence and the gate tied shut with a huge lock and chain assembly. The sign said Keep Out by order of the Pylewood School District.

"Too bad Headley's still in Canada. I'd like to blow this chain to kingdom come with one of his shaped-charge police bombs."

Bill had cursed and suggested that they tie a chain to the fence and pull the dang thing over. Unlike the old Bill, he thought for a minute and said it probably wasn't worth the trouble.

"Let's you and me go to France instead," he had protested. "Ariane says there's a big reward waiting for me in France for freeing Ivor Gryyffwwdd, but they want to present it to me in person at a ceremony in Clermont-Ferrand."

Of course, she had protested; she had her animals to care for, house to clean, and oil to change. But he prevailed. That was another new thing about him; he could get people to do things without hurting them physically. The flight to France had been grueling for her, but she fell in love with Provence and the Alpilles area immediately. She had even started taking pictures again. In the old days, she had mastered the medium with a Leica reflex camera and a load of lenses, filters, and light meters. Now she was relearning her craft on a new digital camera. Her photos of the lavender fields and rocky olive orchards were exquisite.

Bill walked over to the table, poured himself a glass of wine, and took a slow swallow of the red nectar from the Mas de Gourgonnier and reckoned he was finally OK. He had escaped the paparazzi, had his girl back with him, had more money than he'd ever need, was about to make a movie, and with the introduction of TrunkWax II, would soon be famous in his hometown and the agricultural world. He had his teeth back in French literature, and since he was in Provence, he was reading Marcel Pagnol. So it was with a sense of accomplishment and well-being that he collected his morning mail. He was even more excited when he found a letter from Manuel Fargas. He was sure it was a report on the maternal progress of the eight cows that had received the smuggled embryos. The message was short and to the point.

Sorry Bill. Fetuses all aborted! Doc Menzies thinks embryos were bad.

He stared at the letter. He couldn't believe his eyes. Aborted. How could it be? He had delivered the embryos to the Ceemensee laboratory himself, they had been given the highest rating by the technician that received them, and he had seen them go into the freezer. Several months later, he had retrieved them from the Ceemensee laboratory, hidden them himself in macarons he and Georges Bellatre had prepared, did the research to guarantee that they would stay frozen, was assured by Gerrard the butler that they had been smuggled into a shipment bound for Pylewood from the bakery in Aix en Provence, and collected them at Gordon's Fine Groceries, albeit with some difficulty, and delivered them to Manuel Fargas, who had guaranteed him that the transplant had been flawless.

He thought for a minute and came up with Pierre Nosay, who had ended up with four embryos, one of them from his donor cow, Murielle, and three from Bouche de Sancerre, his own donor cow. He had to get in touch with Nosay and find out if his transplants had taken. There was no telling when Karen would return with the groceries, so he scribbled her a note saying there was an emergency and that he'd be back in a day or two. He grabbed a jacket and jumped in his car and typed in his destination: the Théière, Cantal, Pleaux, Pierre Nosay.

***

"I'm surprised you had the nerve to come back here after your sudden departure last month," Nosay said when he met Bill at the door. "Gertyl and old Würtzenhaben were far from pleased with you. They claim you owe them ten thousand dollars."

"A lie. I won't take too much of your time, Pierre. Just one question, in fact. Did your embryos take?"

"So far so good, as you Yanks say. All four of my cows are pregnant. How are yours doing?"

"Even Murielle's?"

"Yes. Why are you asking?"

"Mine all aborted. My guy at home said the vet told him the embryos were bad."

"If I were you, I'd go back to the Ceemensee Lab in Limoges and complain."

Bill had found out all he needed to know and did an abrupt about-face and left without as much as a thank-you.

"Sure you won't have a cup of tea?" Pierre Nosay hollered behind him.

At Ceemensee headquarters in Limoges, Bill, obviously angry, was refused entry until one of the guards recognized him as the guy in the Michelin commercials.

"Mind if I take your picture?" he asked. "My kids won't believe I met you unless I show them your picture. Sign this piece of paper, and I'll Photoshop it on the photo. If you write something like 'My good friend, Maurice,' that will be even better."

Maurice took Bill straight up to the office of the superintendent of quality assurance.

"Well, monsieur," the superintendent said, "our records show that you withdrew your property in July and replaced it with eight new ampoules."

"Impossible," Bill said, his voice rising in anger. "I was in Hawaii at the time."

After looking deeper into the records, the superintendent produced a couple of pictures and a written description of the transaction.

"It says here an authorized agent of yours, Christian Bouvedre, and his wife, exchanged the original biological property for a similar property on July 6."

Bill got all red in the face like in the old days and screamed at the superintendent, "I ain't got no fuckin' agent, knucklehead!"

"It says here that there were two of them, an old German gentleman with a French accent and a chubby girl dressed in a Germanic folk costume."

"Let me see them pictures," Bill hissed.

Bill sucked in enough air to make the curtains rustle before he said, "Würtzenhaben and Gertyl. I'll be hogtied, crucified, and vilified. That cagey old jailbird and his slice of strudel stole my embryos. When I find him, I'll cut off his cojones and feed 'em to the squirrels."

"I wouldn't do that, sir," the superintendent said. "At least not in any country in the European Union."

Bill stood up and was about to push back his chair when the Ceemensee supervisor asked him if he would mind filling out an evaluation form. "We're always trying to improve our service."

"Sure, but first, can I use your phone for an important call? I got to get in touch with someone in Maussane des Alpilles."

"Sorry, sir, but the phone can only be used by Ceemensee employees. It's a liability insurance thing. But there is a pay phone in the next town."

Glossary

A

abrivado — The collection and transport of the bulls from the salt flats of the Bouche de Rhone to the fighting arenas of Provence and Languedoc. The bulls are driven through the villages, and it is a tradition for the spectators to disrupt the passage of the bulls through their towns.

Auvergne — Rural, mountainous region in central France.

AV (artificial vagina) — A rubber torus with a warm-water reservoir, a state-of-the art plastic cover, soft inside lining, and a graduated conical glass receiver that is used to collect semen.

B

biodynamic — A form of agriculture similar to organic farming pioneered by Austrian Theosophist Rudolph Steiner.

black baldy — A nickname for cattle crossbred from the Hereford and Black Angus breeds.

BART — Acronym for Bay Area Rapid Transit. A rail network that joins communities in the San Francisco Bay Area. Known for its confusing system of fares.

Bovary, Madame — Romantic novel written by Gustave Flaubert originally published in 1856. Once considered avant-garde, the work is now considered old-fashioned and overly romantic sentimentalist.

C

Camargue — Rhone River Delta famous for its gardians, black cattle, and white horses.

Camus, Albert — French author, winner of Nobel Prize for literature in 1957. Often called an existentialist, he eschewed categorization. Died at the age of forty-six in a car accident.

Cariboo — Region in the center of British Columbia encompassing the Fraser River Valley.

Carlos, the Jackal — Illich Ramirez Sanchez, Venezuelan terrorist serving a life sentence for murder in Clairvaux prison.

cocarde — Ribbon placed between the bull's horns in some bullfighting events. Contestants must remove the ribbon and are judged on the stylishness of their effort. The bull is also awarded points and can earn money for his owner.

Cooke, Alastair — British author and television host, known for his perfect elocution.

D

dirndl — Austrian pinafore typical of clothing worn in the mountainous Tyrol region.

E

Ejactomatic — A veterinary supply house that used to manufacture spermometers but now imports them from Bangladesh.

EPD — Experimental Progeny Data. A calculation based on several parameters including sizes and weights used to evaluate cattle.

estrus — A reoccurring period of sexual receptivity in cows. Sometimes called heat. Spelled "oestrus" outside the United States.

Expedia — An old Internet browser, displaced by Grooble.

F

ferrade — The cattle branding event in the Camargue.

ficheiroun — A seven-foot-long pole fitted with three-pointed iron tip used to work cattle in the Camargue.

fruit cocktail — A mixture of leftover canned fruit popular in the United States, especially in the twentieth century.

Flaubert, Gustave — The author of *Madame Bovary*.

G

Geordie — Nickname for an Englishman from the north, often Newcastle.

Grenada Invasion — 1983 invasion by United States Special Forces that toppled the government of the small pro-Cuban Caribbean country of ninety-one thousand.

H

HotShot — A portable charged prod used to move cattle.

hoosegow — Slang for jail. Derived from the Spanish word *juzgar*, "to judge."

I

Intercités — Classic French rail system linking major towns and cities.

J

jewel box — Cowboy slang for a bull's scrotum.

K

kapu kuialua — An ancient Hawaiian form of martial arts based on bone breaking.

L

Lutalyse — Progesterone-based drug used to cause abortion in animals. Used in the cattle industry to ensure that a group of cows comes into estrus at the same time.

M

macarons — A popular confection consisting of a filling between two pieces of baked meringue. Sometimes spelled macaroons in the United States. The best ones are baked in France despite the claims of Germans and Swiss.

manade — A Provencal word for a group of at least four white mares of reproductive age living in the open on at least twenty hectares.

Marengo, Battle of — Battle fought in 1800 between the forces of Napoleon Bonaparte's First Republic and the Austrian Hapsburg Empire that resulted in the expulsion of the Austrians from most of Italy.

mas — A farmhouse in Provence; sometimes available for tourists to rent.

Mistral — Strong, cold northwesterly wind that blows from Southern France into the Mediterranean. Also the last name of Occitan writer and lexicographer Federic Mistral who won the Nobel Prize for Literature in 1904.

MonoPrix — Major French retail chain with over three hundred stores in 85 percent of French towns with populations greater than fifty thousand.

Moulin, Jean — WWII resistance hero who parachuted into Provence to organize the French Resistance. Eventually captured and tortured to death by the Nazis.

N

O

Old Bulldarnach, The — A venerable slightly aged whiskey distilled at the old gasworks on the Garscube Road in Glasgow.

Orangina — A carbonated, citrus beverage popular in much of the world. Developed in French Algeria in 1935.

P

palpation — Method used to check the pregnancy of cows and heifers in the livestock industry by forcing a hand up the animals rectum, reaching for the cervix, and feeling for the fetus.

Panhard — French automobile manufacturer established in 1887 and responsible for pioneering many vehicle innovations such as the front-mounted engine with rear-wheel drive.

Parker, Tony — Popular professional basketball player on the San Antonio Spurs who grew up in France and has played for French national teams.

pastis — Licorice (anise)-flavored liqueur commercialized by Paul Ricard, usually mixed with water and ice. Ricard is considered by some to have been the financial savior of the Camargue.

Petawawa —Canadian town in Southern Ontario: home base of the Canadian Special Forces.

R

Rocky Mountain Oysters — Calf testicles removed at branding time. Usually enjoyed with beans and cold beer. Also called fries. Not to be confused with the French variety.

S

sapristy — A French word meaning "goodness gracious."

schluken— The German word for hiccup, called *nikottaa* in Finnish.

semen — Thick fluid containing spermatozoa. Sometimes stored frozen in a straw.

straw — A long thin plastic tube that contains semen. Called *olki* in Finnish.

St. Marie, Buffy — Canadian singer-songwriter. Made many appearances on Sesame Street in the 1970s.

superovulate — Controlled ovarian hyperstimulation, which in the cattle industry, is meant to cause a cow to release more than one egg.

Super Sleeper — A type of airplane seat touted by FlyUwhere? Airlines as being particularly comfortable and sleepable. Seating in the Super Sleeper cabin is arranged in a reverse herringbone pattern, which allows all-aisle access to each seat.

T

Taylor, Elizabeth —Beautiful turn-of-the century Hollywood movie star distinguished by her black hair, perfect skin, and remarkable jugs.

Taylor, Robert — Handsome Hollywood movie star distinguished by his black hair, perfect skin, and remarkable moustache. No relation to Elizabeth.

TGV — *Tout gran vitesse.* A rail system linking the major cities of France.

Transhumance — A French roundup that starts in Morocco and ends up in Marseille. It usually includes horses, sheep, and cows but can also include donkeys and yaks.

transgenics — Methodology whereby a foreign gene is transferred into a genome using recombinant DNA methodology (see definition of genome in *Biology for Dummies* (Krats and Sigfriend).

U

uterus — Sometimes called "the womb" is the female anatomical region where calves are conceived and gestated.

utilitarianism — The idea that that action that promotes the greatest happiness of the greatest number human beings is the most ethical.

V

W

Walget — Pylewood's newest big box store formed by the merger of two other big box stores and run entirely by ex-oil field roustabouts.

X

Y

Z

zut — French word that is used to replace almost any swearword, especially "dammit."

Lightning Source UK Ltd.
Milton Keynes UK
UKOW01n0050070318

318986UK00002B/38/P